THE
CIVIL WARS
OF
JONAH MORAN

A NOVEL

Marjorie Reynolds

Marjorie Reynolds

BERKLEY BOOKS, NEW YORK

B

A Berkley Book
Published by The Berkley Publishing Group
A division of Penguin Putnam Inc.
375 Hudson Street
New York, New York 10014

PRINTING HISTORY
William Morrow & Company hardcover edition published in 1999
Berkley trade paperback edition / April 2001

The Penguin Putnam Inc. World Wide Web site address is
http://www.penguinputnam.com

Library of Congress Cataloging-in-Publication Data
Reynolds, Marjorie, 1944–
The civil wars of Jonah Moran : a novel / Marjorie Reynolds.
p.   cm.
ISBN 0-425-17834-X (trade pbk.)
1. Olympic Peninsula (Wash.)—Fiction.   2. Arson investigation—Fiction.
3. Autism—Patients—Fiction.   4. Quinault Indians—Fiction.
5. Divorced women—Fiction.   I. Title.

PS3568.E8954 C58   2001
813'.54—dc21   00-051942

Printed in the United States of America

10   9   8   7   6   5   4   3   2   1

For my son, Matthew Shoemaker,
who searches for truth and knowledge.
He is loved more than he can imagine.

Acknowledgments

I owe a great deal of gratitude to the Quinault Indian Nation for graciously welcoming me and helping with this novel. I would especially like to thank Lelani Jones, cultural director; Kathy Law; Natalie Charley; Marjorie Valdillez; Larry Workman (of the Hoosier tribe), and T. Conrad Williams, who told me about meeting Bigfoot. The QIN's book, *Land of the Quinault,* was an invaluable resource on Quinault history and culture.

I also received a great deal of technical help from the Mercer Island (Washington) Fire Department's arson team and from Dean Lum, Tom Adams, and Gary Boynton. Marilyn Dean and Mickey LeClair of Washington Adoption Reunion Movement, an organization that reunites families, provided information on adoption. Any errors regarding arson, the law, or adoption are mine, not theirs.

I want to thank my excellent and patient agent, Angela Rinaldi, and my equally excellent and patient editor, Claire Wachtel. I cannot possibly express enough appreciation to my writing friends: Cindy O'Brien, Judy Law, Jane Sutherland, Karen MacLeod, Nancy Jordan, and Kay Morison, as well as the members of the Oregon Writers Colony and the Pacific Northwest Writers Association. Thanks also to Joy Glaze, Eric Witchey, Steve Roskamp, Stella Preissler, and Carol Ross for their assistance.

For those relatives and friends who believe you've found yourself among these characters, I must emphasize they are *all* strictly fictional.

Lastly, but by no means lightly, I want to thank my husband, Michael Shoemaker. I made him read this novel in one day.

Prologue

Mom's prematurely white hair gleamed like sugar in the angled sunlight. She leveled her stern gaze at Jonah. "One way or another, son, you will learn to swim this summer."

He'll drown, Jessica thought, all because she couldn't tolerate any weakness in him.

Dad ruffled his fingers through his thick red hair in restrained exasperation. "He doesn't have to learn to swim, Lila. A lot of people don't know how."

They were standing in the sprawling yard behind their house. After a winter of unrelenting rain and a late, damp spring, the sky opened that morning to a sun so dazzlingly bright they all seemed momentarily blinded.

Mom jerked her hand toward a ragged patch of blue, barely visible through a stand of old-growth red cedars. "We live near a lake, for God's sake. He should at least be able to dog-paddle."

The tension between Jessica's parents these last few days felt thick as a swarm of bees, but until now it had been confined to the two of them. She didn't know why Mom's gray-blue eyes glinted like ice or why that little muscle in Dad's jaw twitched repeatedly, but at sixteen she had enough sense to stay out of their way. Her brother, Jonah, who was only nine, didn't.

Despite the unseasonable eighty-degree temperature, Jonah shivered in his bathing suit.

Dad thrust his callused hands into the pockets of his dirt-stained brown work pants, stretching his frayed suspenders taut. Big Mike Moran, the other loggers called him. He was six-four and weighed two hundred and sixty-five pounds, and when Jessica grabbed him around his waist she couldn't clasp her hands together. "He's still the best cutter around," said the men who worked for him. He liked to eat, drink, and laugh, and when he wasn't in trouble with Mom, he often did all three.

There went that little twitch in his jaw again.

The previous summer Mom had hired a muscled young instructor to give Jonah lessons in the lake. Jessica could still see her brother sinking and surfacing, gulping and sputtering, grabbing at the dock or anything else he could get his hands on. The teacher quit after three sessions, saying he'd never before had a kid who wouldn't at least try to learn. He claimed Jonah had "serious problems." Jessica had always known he was different, but at that moment she'd wanted to punch the instructor.

Dad cleared his throat. "Come on, Lila, you know this isn't going to work."

"It won't hurt him to get in the water and flap his arms. Jessica can talk him into it."

"She's tried before."

"So, she tries again."

Jessica tugged on her new shiny black Speedo. She knew the lake would be cold. She had braved its frigid depths every summer since she could remember, until she could swim back and forth between the dock and the wooden float thirty times without even breathing hard. But with the tightness in her chest now she could barely breathe at all.

Jonah stood hugging himself. He followed Mom and Dad's conversation with a confused, apprehensive look, his head swiveling between them. The enlarged pupils of his pale blue eyes reflected the sun like polished beads.

Mom glanced at him. "Where's your towel?"

"In . . . in the house."

"Well, go get it."

After he went inside, Dad took a few steps forward, his heavy boots sinking into the sodden grass. "This is enough, Lila. Don't take your feelings toward me out on him."

Her lips tightened. "This has nothing to do with you."

"Like hell it doesn't. Just tell me what you want, and I promise I'll—"

"I've had enough of your promises. They aren't worth the time it takes for you to say them." She swung away from him.

Jessica stepped between them. "I'll look after Jonah. He can hang out with me. I promise I'll never complain about him again."

Mom shook her head. "You're both too easy on him."

Jonah came walking back, his towel slung over his shoulder, its edge dragging along the mossy bricks of the terrace. It bothered Jessica that his thin little chest caved in like a bowl, but she'd heard Dad tell him he'd fill out someday, no question about that.

Once he had joined them, Mom pointed him toward the lake.

As they hiked along the dirt path, Dad flung his arm around Jonah's shoulders. "How about I just build you a boat, pal?" His voice sounded jovial, as if he thought he could humor Mom out of her edgy persistence. "You'd like that, wouldn't you?"

Mom gave a sniff of disgust.

Dad patted Jonah on the back and carried his towel for him. They all trudged along in silence. A quarter mile farther, the trail opened onto the crescent-shaped lake that Jessica's grandfather, Jonah Hartman, had created a half century before by damming Thunder River. Until the railroads came to Misp, the lumber mill used it as a holding site for logs. She glanced at the mill across the lake. It was normally humming with men and machines working in a haze of fragrant wood dust, but today was Sunday and the sorting yard and the squat cedar buildings were silent.

Jessica didn't know exactly how much property her family owned, but she'd heard people say that when Grandpa Jonah died, he passed the mill and several hundred acres of the Olympic Peninsula's richest timberland to Mom, who was his only child.

A thin strip of land separated Thunder Lake's southern shore from the heavily wooded Quinault Indian reservation. Mom made it clear she and Jonah had no business straying over there.

As they stepped onto the twenty-foot dock, Jessica could see the shadows of massive trees on the water's surface, although she was never sure whether they came from the dozen or so toppled giants on the lake bottom or from the living ones that rimmed the shore. She thought the water had an odd green hue this summer, as if the cedars, hemlocks, and Douglas firs had leaked some of their color into it during the winter rains.

Dad's heavy boots clunked on the wooden planks. "Lila, I swear I'll do anything you want."

Turning away from him, Mom gripped Jonah's shoulders and fixed her gaze directly on him. "What I want is for Jonah to swim. Tell your dad that's what you're going to do today."

Jonah's eyes widened. He drew in a long breath and murmured, "I'm going to swim today."

Jessica saw the thin cord in Dad's jaw jerk like a fish line. He grabbed Mom's wrist. "Leave him alone."

"All right, then, he can do it alone." She pulled away and with one hand pushed Jonah off the dock so quickly he didn't have time to register surprise.

Dad took two quick steps toward the edge. "Aw, Jesus Christ, why'd you do that?"

For a moment, she seemed as stunned as he was, but then she set her mouth in determination. "It's what my father did to me. He wouldn't have thrown away good money on swim lessons."

Jessica bent forward to dive in after him, but Mom lowered her arm like a bar. "You stay here. Give him a chance."

Jessica watched her brother's head go down, his blond curls briefly splaying out like seaweed. He wrapped his arms tight against his chest and tilted up the perfectly shaped face with its sculpted nose, slightly parted lips, and large, luminous eyes. So beautiful, he should be a girl, the old women in town said. He sank, not even fighting the water this time. He looked as though he belonged in it now, as though he had given himself to it. She watched him drift away.

"Christ, Lila, he's not even moving his arms," Dad growled.

"He will. Everyone's born with the instinct to save himself."

Jessica gave her a hard look. "Jonah isn't like other people."

Mom's eyes narrowed. "Yes, he is."

Jessica didn't say any more but she flopped onto the warm boards and curled her fingers over the edge, digging her nails into the soft, damp wood. Dad paced the dock, his jaw clamped so tight Jessica thought it might crack.

Silt rose in the lake and hovered like dust motes just beneath the surface. The warm sun beat down. Neither the air nor the water moved. Jessica thought there should be circles. If nothing else, there should be the bubbles and the circles that even a fish will make.

Dad threw the beach towel onto the dock. "That's it, I'm going in."

"No, he's there." Mom pointed toward the water. "See him?"

But Jessica saw nothing more than a dead leaf floating on top.

She rose to her feet and, without so much as another glance at her mother, dived off the dock. She entered the lake like a knife blade, the cold surrounding her. Gasping, she tasted slimy water. Its texture surprised her.

The lake had changed over the winter. There had been weeds in it for years but nothing like these. Returning to the surface, she spit out the foul water and gulped a breath. She thought she heard her mother's voice, but she plunged again, not stopping to listen.

Spotted brown fish glided past her. She fluttered her feet, twisted and spun, trying to catch a glimpse of Jonah.

Diving deeper into the eerie stillness, she spotted him in a tangle of weeds that wound around the roots of an immense half-buried tree. She knew it was simple luck that she had found him so quickly in this bitter green soup. His body was curled and slack.

She swam to him, reached for his thin wrist and tugged. The spiny runners clung to him.

Her lungs demanded air, but she knew if she rose to the top, she would lose him. She grabbed his limp head with her hands and pulled him through a hole in the snag. A spike of wood from the sunken tree dug into her palm, but she felt no pain, only the fear she might be too late. Looping her arm around his chest, she scissor-kicked her feet hard and thrashed the water with her free hand. Her journey to the surface was much longer and harder than it had ever been during practice sessions in the Red Cross lifesaving course. Above water, she swallowed a quick breath, then struggled toward shore, Jonah in tow.

The trip to the dock seemed endless. When she reached it, she clawed at the ladder with her fingers, then pushed Jonah up, toward the two broad hands looming just above the lake's surface. They lifted him as if he had no more substance than a spray of milkweed, and she thought they must be her father's powerful hands. As she bobbed in the water, she caught sight of Mom's ashen face. Her lips moved, but Jessica heard only a pulsing roar in her ears.

Her foot found the bottom rung of the ladder, and she pulled herself up step by step. She collapsed onto the dock and lay there coughing and choking, still tasting the lake water in her mouth.

The wooden planks warmed her skin through her wet bathing suit, and she felt as if she could stay right where she was for the rest of the day. She lifted her head just enough to see Jonah. He flopped limply over Mom's arm, like the stuffed teddy bear he still carried to bed at night. Mom was frantically clearing his throat with her fingers. As she laid him facedown on the dock, water spewed from his mouth. She glanced at Jessica, her face moon-white with panic. "Did you see him?"

Jessica struggled to sit. "See who?"

"Your father. Did . . . did you see him under there?"

Jessica scrambled to her feet. One of Dad's scarred leather work boots lay tipped over on the dock, its frayed rawhide lace dangling loose, its sole caked with dirt and sawdust. She looked around. Unless his other boot had fallen into the water, he hadn't even taken the time to remove it. Her heart ratcheted up a notch, and her breath came hard and fast.

She swung back toward her mother, who was kneeling over Jonah, pressing rhythmically on his back. Mom's shoulder muscles strained under her short-sleeved blue cotton blouse. Her strong hands pushed and withdrew, pushed and withdrew. Jonah's glistening limbs remained slack.

"Can you look for your dad?" Her voice quavered. "I can't leave Jonah."

She turned him over. As she reached down to put her mouth over his blue lips, her single white braid fell to the side of her neck.

Jessica began to shake. She couldn't go back into the water. She wasn't breathing evenly yet, and her muscles ached with fatigue.

And, yet, her bare feet seemed to cross the warm dock of their own will. Reaching the edge, she bent forward and slipped cleanly into the olive-green murkiness.

This time she ventured deeper into the frigid water, until she could hardly feel her fingers and toes. She felt as though she were entering a forbidding underworld, a place far less predictable than the lake of her childhood. The stringy weeds twisted in and around the fallen trees, shrouding their roots. Backing out, she rose to the surface through a tunnel of relatively unclouded water and sucked in air with such eagerness that it burned her lungs.

It took every bit of her courage and remaining strength to dive again and search the maze. He had to be here somewhere. Of course, he was. Nothing could hurt Dad, not even the old-growth giants he felled in the woods. She would find him in these wavering shadows, swimming effortlessly, still looking for Jonah. She would find him safe.

She came upon him in a graveyard of massive sunken conifers. The water was clearer here, but his one remaining boot had caught in the V between two trees jammed together. Their peeled branches encircled him like arms. He looked soft and smaller somehow, his work pants bagging out and undulating in the water, his chin drooping onto his chest.

She lunged at his boot and yanked on it, slicing her hands on the wiry runners and jagged wood until a pink cloud formed in the water. Her breath gave out and she had to surface.

She dived below the water three more times, knowing by then he had been under much too long. Her lungs ached and her limbs lost all feeling. She realized that even if she could free him, she didn't have the strength to tow him to shore. With a sob of despair that bubbled toward the surface, she fought her way back to the ladder and pulled herself onto the dock.

Jonah was sitting up, with Mom squatting beside him. She looked up, asking a question without words.

Jessica lowered her head, tears searing the inside of her eyelids, her entire body trembling.

"He's there," she whispered, "but he's caught in the weeds and trees, and I can't get him loose."

She heard her mother's long, slow exhalation of breath.

Jonah coughed and gagged, then spit up another mouthful of water. He stared up at Mom, his eyes as glazed as any hooked fish Jessica had ever hauled onto the dock. "Did I swim, Mommy?"

MISP, WASHINGTON
March 28, 1998

Pearl Hobbs and her friend Charlotte Johnson stepped onto the front porch of Pearl's craftsman-style bungalow. Although the afternoon breeze was chilly, it also carried in the lusty ocean smell Pearl loved. She clutched her teacup poodle, Dixie, against her plump midriff to keep the dog warm. "I'll call you when I find that photograph, Charlotte. I know I've got it somewhere."

"Well, it would make a great cover for the auxiliary cookbook even if two of the ladies are dead now." Charlotte stopped on the top step and peered in the direction of the neighboring three-story, Victorian-style home. "Isn't that Jonah Moran cutting across the lawn by that halfway house?"

Pearl followed her gaze, then gave a little shudder that had nothing to do with the brisk air. "I should talk to him—tell him to stay away from there."

Charlotte folded her arms around her as if she too felt a chill. "I don't know how you can stand living next door to a bunch of criminals. I'd be scared to death."

"I am scared," Pearl admitted.

Ever since the state had turned the peeling gray, gabled behemoth into a residence for ex-convicts, she had been praying continually for the Lord to keep her safe. She'd protested the establishment of the halfway house along with nearly everyone else in Misp, but their objections made no difference. Some bigwigs came from Olympia, held a town meeting at the high school gym, and told everyone the four men who were moving into that place had served their time and deserved a chance to rebuild their lives.

Well, what about the lives of the people who were already here, who had built their homes and raised their families here? Guess they didn't matter, Pearl thought.

Charlotte was still watching Jonah, who was scuffing through the grass with that odd, clumsy gait he had. She pressed her lips together, the tiny lines around her mouth deepening. "You'd think Lila would do a better job of looking after that boy."

"But, Charlotte, he's a grown man."

"If he was really grown up and *normal*, he'd be working at a job. I suppose as long as his mother supports him he'll just wander all over town."

Having known Charlotte for more than forty years, Pearl was accustomed to her criticisms, but sometimes they seemed so unchristian. She realized it was easy to find fault with others. Charlotte herself wore too much powder over her wrinkles, but Pearl would never have mentioned that.

A mud-splattered blue van with the words A ROOM WITH A VIEW lettered prominently on the side zagged across the road and pulled up next to Jonah. The driver's window rolled down, and a woman with short, tight curls the color of flaming coals stuck out her head. Pearl could see her speaking to Jonah, although she couldn't hear what she was saying.

Charlotte gave a henlike snort. "And there's that sister of his." Shielding her mouth with her hand, she leaned close enough so that Pearl could smell her Wind Song. "Now she's a piece of work, isn't she? Disappearing the way she did for what—eighteen or nineteen years?—and then coming back last spring and acting like the town should just take her in, no questions asked."

"But I thought your son Pete was dating her."

Charlotte sighed. "I'm hoping he'll come to his senses. Like I told him, she may end up inheriting everything Lila owns, especially since it's obvious Jonah can't run that mill, but the man who marries her will pay with his sweat and tears. I mean, can you imagine having Lila Moran for a mother-in-law?"

But Pearl liked the Morans. Lila had done a lot of good for the community. Because of her sawmill, men had jobs. She kept her logging operation going when others couldn't. The Olympic Peninsula had been suffering hard economic times ever since those tree-huggers and government people discovered the spotted owl and shut down logging on half the area's timberland to protect it.

Pearl liked Lila's daughter too. Jessica had been the best newspaper carrier she'd ever had.

Pearl fidgeted, wishing Charlotte would hurry up and leave. She watched Jonah lope to the passenger side of the van, open the door, and climb in. As the van sped past Pearl's house, Jessica thrust her arm out the window and waved cheerily.

Charlotte smiled and returned the greeting with a quick flap of her hand. "She dotes on that brother of hers but avoids her mother like poison ivy, have you noticed?"

Pearl knew that if she didn't change the subject, Charlotte would bring up the nasty rumors about Jessica from years ago.

"I always liked her because she put the newspaper in those plastic bags," Pearl said, "not like today when the kids don't care if it gets wet."

Charlotte grabbed her wrist. "Did you see that?"

Pearl froze. "What? See what?"

Dixie's head snapped up, and she gave a low growl.

Charlotte, her faded green eyes narrowed to slits, nodded almost imperceptibly at the house next door and whispered, "Someone's watching us."

Pearl studied it but didn't see any movement. "Where?"

"Second floor, middle window—a man," she whispered ominously.

"What does he look like?"

Charlotte gripped her wrist tighter. "Shhh."

Pearl lowered her voice but complained, "They can't hear us."

"How do you know?"

"Because I can't hear them unless they're yelling."

"Yeah, but their ears are younger." She released Pearl's wrist and stepped back into the shadow of the porch column.

At that moment, the front door of the halfway house opened, and a tall, thin black man wearing dress slacks and a sport coat stepped onto the sprawling front porch. Charlotte jumped back, pressing herself against the wooden siding. Pearl reflexively grabbed Dixie's muzzle to prevent the dog from yipping. It struggled and whimpered, but she held on until the man crossed the yard and turned toward town.

Charlotte poked her head around the porch column, lowered her chin, and studied the departing figure through the top of her glasses. "Who's that?"

"One of the drug addicts."

"Does he always dress like that?"

Pearl shifted to get a better view. "Most of the time. Edith Meyer says he used to be a high school teacher."

Just watching him strut down the sidewalk sent a shiver of fear through Pearl, and her alone here in this house twenty-one years now since Frank had died and never even needing to lock the doors before. Her friends said she shouldn't have to barricade herself inside, but she had dead bolts put on her doors and carried the key on a pink grosgrain ribbon around her neck so she wouldn't lose it.

Once the man was out of sight, Charlotte stepped into the open and straightened indignantly. "Well, if he thinks he can get a job at one of our schools, he'd just better think again." She took a deep, determined breath, sending the patterned flock of geese on her hand-knit sweater into a flutter. "And, when I get home, I'm going to call the sheriff. Those men shouldn't be allowed to walk our streets."

Pearl nodded, glad that for once she could agree with Charlotte.

Two NIGHTS LATER, Dixie stirred around one A.M., persistently licking Pearl's eyelids until she opened them. Knowing this was her dog's urgent request for a piddle, Pearl reached for her lilac chenille robe. Poor old thing's just like me, she thought—can't make it through the night anymore.

She carried the poodle out the kitchen door, plopped it in a patch of grass, and stood between two rhododendrons to wait. While Dixie nosed around the base of a nearby dogwood, Pearl wrapped her plaid flannel scarf over her head, tied it under her chin, and tucked the ends into her robe. The night air smelled musty. Over the long winter, rainwater had fused the fallen leaves with the conifer needles and rotted them to mush. A person could slip and break a bone. Pearl sighed. Just one more reason to stay inside these days.

She glanced almost reflexively at the halfway house and saw a yellow flame the length of a man's arm leap behind the dining room window. She blinked several times, wondering how there could possibly be something burning in there. The fireplace was located in the living room.

She stared for several seconds at the shadowy house, but it was as dark as the inside of a root cellar. Well, of course, it would be. Or at least it should be at this time of night—if decent folks lived there.

Looking around, she glimpsed the sparkle of Dixie's rhinestone collar among the rhododendron leaves. When the poodle emerged from the bushes, Pearl leaned down and scooped it up. "Did you do your business?" Her voice rose to a whispery warble. "Did you do your business, sweetie?"

As she turned to go inside, she couldn't resist another glance at the neighboring house. A bright flame winked back at her. Her stomach seemed to leap right into her throat. *Good Lord,* what could be happening in there?

Maybe they were burning candles in some sort of satanic ritual. She knew that one of the four criminals was the worst kind of sinner—a sexual predator. Pearl had read once in *Reader's Digest* or some such magazine that sexual molesters couldn't be cured. They were imprinted for life. That's the word the article used—imprinted, something stamped into you like a cattle brand, so deep and permanent a person couldn't get rid of it.

Besides the drug addicts and the sex fiend, there was the mental case. Pearl ran into him at the post office, almost smacked right into him. A squat, sandy-haired man, he looked to be in his early fifties. He and Pearl were the only two people in that niche off to the side where all the metal postal boxes lined the wall. He was fitting a tiny key into the box lock and muttering something to himself. That wasn't so bad, Pearl thought. A few people in town talked to themselves and she'd been guilty of it herself more than once, but the guttural tones he produced chilled her right through her JCPenney raincoat and her thick wool sweater. They were unearthly—the utterances of a person whose voice box has been severely damaged. She ran from the post office.

"Drāno," said Cindy Croghan, her hairdresser, when Pearl went in for her blue rinse.

Pearl drew in a shaky breath. "Drāno?"

Cindy's reflection in the beauty salon mirror nodded. "He tried to kill himself by drinking it. Seared his vocal cords. Suzi Bates's sister Molly is a nurse at Western State Hospital, and she said he was in and out of there a dozen times. He claims people talk to him, telling him to do awful things. I'll bet he's had shock treatments."

The hair rose on Pearl's neck, tiny blue-gray filaments catching the warm breeze from the blow dryer. And now this crazy man lived next door to her, she thought.

She studied the halfway house windows again. There was no

flame. Only darkness. She poked her stubby fingers behind her bifocals and rubbed her puffy lids. Charlotte was right. Their ears *and* eyes had grown old. Sighing, she turned again toward her kitchen door.

A beat-up, putty-colored truck in the road caught her attention. It had stopped under the yellow cone of light from the streetlamp, or maybe it had been there all along and she had simply not noticed it. She couldn't understand how she could not have. Its headlights were aimed directly at the halfway house, its engine was still running, and a man with a heavy profile and a middle-aged paunch stood beside the open driver's door. His straight, ink-black hair fell to his shoulders. And what was that shiny thing on his wrist? Looked like one of those wide silver watchbands with the big turquoise stones. An Indian, Pearl thought. She lived close enough to the Quinault reservation to have seen plenty of *them*.

He was staring at the gabled house too. A pointed tongue of fire darted behind the dining room window. Oh, my goodness, there it was again. Did he see it? Or, she wondered with a shiver, did he have something to do with it? As if he'd heard her thoughts, he jumped into the truck.

She wanted to run inside but felt rooted to the damp earth. Dear God, *someone* was crawling out of the downstairs window of that halfway house, straddling the wooden frame, one foot still inside, the other on a covered whiskey barrel below. For one brief moment, Pearl had a clear view of the person's face. She gasped, clutched Dixie tighter, and retreated into the shadows of the rhododendrons. The dog whined and squirmed, its tiny name tag clinking against its collar.

She glanced at the truck. The Indian had switched off its headlights and was driving slowly down the street.

There was a low poof and a series of brilliant orange flashes. Events happened so quickly, Pearl couldn't breathe. Against the sky, the halfway house leered like a jack-o'-lantern. Jagged triangles of fire ripped the darkness behind the dining room window.

Pearl felt her legs buckle and Dixie slip from her arms. The dog yelped and streaked toward open space. Pearl lunged, caught the powder puff tail, and yanked it back. She gathered the trembling poodle to her breast, turned, and rushed into her kitchen.

She slammed the door, clicked the dead bolt into place, and drew the shade so quickly it snapped and shuddered against the wooden window frame. Shedding her scarf and chenille robe along the way, she ran toward her bedroom and scrambled into the old brass bed. She clasped the poodle against her sagging belly and dragged the down comforter over her head.

"Oh, dear God, this is terrible—just terrible." She gripped the dog so tight it yelped. They were both trembling all over.

Releasing the poodle, she pressed her arthritic knuckles against her mouth. "I'll say I didn't see a thing," she murmured fervently. "Not a single thing. I never left my bed. That's what I'll tell anyone who asks." She clasped her hands together. " 'Lord, relieve the troubles of my heart and bring me out of my distresses . . . and . . . and forgive all my sins.' "

She rose from her bed once, about ten minutes later, to peek out the window at the house next door. It was fully engulfed now, black smoke boiling from under the eaves. She heard the crackle of the blaze and the wail of the approaching fire trucks. Neighbors were already crowding the street. Dixie bounced along the edge of the bed, baring her sharp little teeth and yapping furiously.

Pearl returned to her bed, tunneled deep under the comforter, and pretended sleep.

2

Jessica Moran awoke that morning to the smell of charred wood. She sat up and sniffed the breeze drifting through her partly opened window. It was too wet outside, too early in the spring for a forest fire.

She stuck her feet into satin scuffs that were worn through to their foam padding and wrapped herself in her plaid flannel robe. Her ex-husband, Patrick, had given her the slippers their first Christmas together, and the fact that they were pale pink with rosette pom-poms symbolized everything that was wrong with their marriage. She was the least likely person she knew to wear pink satin or pom-poms. They had met at UCLA, where he was teaching an evening class in psychology and she was teaching a university extension class in literature. He apparently didn't notice she was sporting jeans, a black-and-beige-striped turtleneck shirt, and a black beret. The marriage lasted only two years. She kept the slippers and wore them daily as a reminder of what to avoid.

As she walked by her dresser mirror, she was careful not to glance in its direction. The shock was too much at eight in the morning, seeing her hair shoot out like rusted springs from a broken mattress.

From the porch steps, she scanned the horizon. No smoke rising from the treetops, but still there was that acrid odor. She shivered.

She couldn't smell smoke without remembering the fire she'd started when she was sixteen, a few months after Dad had drowned.

When she'd told Patrick about her recurring nightmares, he'd said with elaborate nonchalance, "Like most people with bad dreams, you'll keep having them until you've done enough penance."

She wondered where she'd acquired the peculiar notion that psychologists were sympathetic.

The *Misp Tribune* lay in a puddle of rainwater on the bottom step. Customer service had slipped. When she was a carrier, she'd routinely tucked the newspapers in plastic bags. It stuck in her mind that the *Trib* was late, and when she picked it up and pried it open, she saw why. No doubt the staff had been up all night working on the front-page story. A six-inch-deep banner read THREE MEN DIE IN HALFWAY HOUSE BLAZE.

She closed the front door and walked into her office, originally the dining room. Spreading the *Tribune* on her sprawling metal desk, she flattened its damp pages with her palms and read the account of the fire. Only the ex-felon who had served time for rape survived the smoke and flames. The live-in social worker had spent the night with his girlfriend in Forks. There were implications his absence would cost him his job. Jessica was still intent on the banner story when the phone jangled.

Grabbing it on the second ring, she automatically murmured, "A Room with a View, your visibly better window-cleaning service."

"Homer Nichol here, Jessica." The line buzzed with static. "Did I wake you?"

"No, I was just reading the *Trib*. Homer, did you know that the halfway house over on Sixteenth Street burned down last night? I thought I smelled smoke in the air this morning."

"You're too far away to smell it."

"I suppose it was my imagination then."

Outside, the neighbor's tan, slack-jawed mongrel Buster sauntered into Jessica's yard. He lifted his bowed leg against a rhodo-dendron's bright new growth and took aim. Wincing, she grabbed the newspaper and thumped it against the window. "Stop that!"

"Pardon me?"

"Sorry. It's the Tooberts' dog."

Buster turned to stare at her with an expression completely devoid of guilt or remorse. "He comes over here every morning to anoint my plants." Jessica stepped back to her desk and tidied a stack of invoices. "Excuse me for interrupting you, Homer. Need your windows washed? I'll trade my services for your legal time. Who knows when I might fall through a skylight and want to sue."

"That's not . . . calling." His sentences crackled and completely shorted out in the center. "Your brother . . . trouble . . . sheriff called me . . . knew I was your family lawyer and—"

"Your cell phone's cutting out, Homer. I must have misunderstood you. I thought you said Jonah's in trouble."

He cleared his throat. "He is, and I would call it a delicate situation."

Although she was standing near a register with heat pouring out of it, she felt a chill. "What kind of trouble?"

"The sheriff is saying that . . . fire . . . arson."

"Fire? He isn't hurt, is he?"

"No."

She laughed nervously. "You scared me for a moment."

"But he *is* upset. The sheriff just finished . . . couldn't reach your mother. I was hoping you'd drive down here to the sheriff's office and . . ."

She stopped dead still. "Could you repeat that, Homer?"

She heard two quick *thumps* and realized he must have smacked the phone.

"Darned technology," he said, his next words coming through with sound-bite clarity. "The sheriff and Bud Schultz questioned Jonah about that halfway house fire."

"Did he see who started it?"

"They have some concern he may have set it."

Jessica tried to absorb what he'd said. "Concern, Homer? Is that a legal term?"

His quiet voice skittered over the next sentence. "Battery's going out."

JESSICA MADE THE drive from Misp to Big River in fifty minutes, sloshing through a ten-minute downpour that abated only as she parked her blue van in a space opposite the historic brick municipal building. She walked across the street, the soles of her white athletic shoes squeaking on the wet pavement.

Although the county sheriff Milt Tarr worked out of Big River, he'd had enough contact with her family to know Jonah wasn't malicious or destructive. She was furious that the sheriff had questioned him, but it wouldn't do him any good for her to go in angry. She straightened her shoulders to steady herself.

She met Homer Nichol in the empty hall outside the frosted glass windows of the sheriff's office. He strode purposefully and gracefully toward her, reminding her of a giraffe in a television wildlife special. He was almost seven feet tall.

His blue suit was neatly pressed, but his bow tie perched crookedly below his Adam's apple as though he'd dressed in haste that morning. His face had the texture of muslin, stippled with bumps, pockmarks, brown spots, and unshaven whiskers. It also possessed a dignity and a kindness that Jessica respected.

"I don't like leaving your brother in there alone," he said, "but I want to talk with you first."

Jessica stepped to the side of the hall to allow a deputy and a man in a rumpled blue suit to pass. She kept her voice low. "Maybe the fire wasn't arson. Maybe it was an accident."

"Apparently not. It looks like someone crawled through the dining room window and lighted some sort of accelerant."

"Well, Jonah wouldn't do that. They hauled him in here because he's an easy target."

"Let's not rush to any conclusions just yet."

"Remember last spring when somebody vandalized those mail-boxes on Timberline Highway and a deputy picked up Jonah because he happened to be walking down the road that morning? The deputy told me that Jonah acted guilty so he figured he must have done something wrong. Now what does that tell you?"

Homer pinched the bridge of his nose between his thumb and forefinger. "It's different this time."

Her resolve to remain calm snapped. "I want Jonah out of here now. He can't handle something like this." She strode past Homer toward the door with the frosted-glass pane.

His footsteps echoed on the marble floor behind her. "Jessica."

"What?"

"The survivor of the fire identified him as having thrown rocks at the house the night before last. It seems he broke the dining room window."

Jessica stopped and swung around. "Well, I don't believe it. He must have seen someone who looked like him. Why would Jonah do that?"

"I don't know, but before I got here, he admitted he did."

She stared at him for a long moment, debating what could have been going through Jonah's mind. "He probably didn't know what he was agreeing to. Did you ask him?"

"He wouldn't answer me directly. He just talks about—well, you know, what he usually talks about—those soldiers. Of course, the important thing now is that he shouldn't say anything at all."

"Where did they pick him up this time?"

"Walking toward Tangletree Junction, away from your mother's house, around five this morning."

"There, you see. He probably *looked* suspicious."

"There's a bit more. The survivor saw him prowling their yard last night around seven o'clock."

"It's dark at seven o'clock."

"Not quite."

He opened the door for her, gestured her through, then ducked in after her. "Your mother's out somewhere with a logging crew. One of the secretaries at the mill is trying to reach her."

"Pity the sheriff when she finds out."

He nodded his head vigorously. "Oh, yes, I do. I certainly do."

Inside, someone had made an attempt to brighten the sheriff's office by painting it pumpkin orange with white trim. A deputy sat behind a scarred gray metal desk, his fingers hooked around the handle of a coffee cup that was decorated with a tired-looking lion. The inscription read IT'S A JUNGLE OUT THERE.

On the bulletin board behind the deputy, Wanted posters of shadowy men and women clustered around a photo of the sheriff's department Employee of the Month, a clean-cut deputy who, Jessica thought, didn't look old enough to drive a car.

Homer gestured toward the side hall with its string of doors. "Jonah's in that second room on the left." He lowered his voice. "I don't think the sheriff has enough evidence right now to arrest him, but he'll be looking for more."

"This is Mr. Moran's sister," Homer said to the deputy on duty. "We'd like to see my client."

A door down the hall opened and the sheriff emerged, hitching up the pants of his buff-colored uniform. Tall and lanky, Milt Tarr wore black-framed Buddy Holly glasses that made him look more like a math teacher than a sheriff. His gaze landed on Jessica, and he nodded in solemn greeting.

The last time she'd seen him, it was early morning on Willow Creek Road just about a year ago and he was leaning into her van window, smelling of Altoids and aftershave. "Got a driver's license?"

She fished it out and handed it to him. She had been back in Misp less than a month, and she hadn't yet dumped Patrick's last name from all her important documents. She was still listed on her license as Jessica Moran Stafford. Sheriff Tarr studied it, and she saw the recognition in his shrewd eyes.

He squinted at the rising sun. "Normally, I wouldn't have stopped you 'cause seventy-five ain't all that fast and I've got better things to do, like get to the office. But there are more deer crossing the road this time of year than you can count. You hit one of them, and you and it both are going to sail ass over teakettle into that ditch." He crunched his teeth, spraying a whiff of peppermint. "Maybe worse."

She had liked him, not because he'd let her off without a ticket but because he didn't mention her mother.

Now that she was in his office, she wondered if he'd remember her. "Apparently, there's been a mistake, Sheriff Tarr. Could you please release my brother?"

He nodded agreeably. "For the time being."

"Good." She breezed by him.

"Mrs. Stafford?"

She stopped, surprised that he remembered her married name. "It's Moran now, Sheriff."

He stroked his Adam's apple. "Your brother's not an easy man to converse with, Ms. Moran, but he did remind me that there's a history of fire-setting in your family."

"So, arrest me."

He smiled slightly. "Are you confessing?"

Homer's head shot up. "Absolutely not. She's not confessing."

Jessica raised her chin higher. "Well, I'm certainly a more likely suspect than my brother."

WHEN JESSICA STEPPED into the room, Jonah was sitting on a scarred wooden chair, hugging himself. He jumped to his feet, and she saw relief flood his face.

"It'll be okay now," she said, wrapping her arms around his narrow shoulders, noticing not for the first time that he had the same boyish face at twenty-eight that he'd had at ten. The golden hair on his chin was so faint and downy that she wondered with some familial discomfort if puberty had passed him by.

She reached up to push the blond curls off his forehead. "They didn't hit you or shove you around, did they?"

"They said they could put me in prison, Jessie."

"They were just trying to scare you."

He didn't answer but seemed to shrink into himself. Along with the stale cigarette stink imbedded in the room's walls, linoleum floor, and curtains, she could smell his anxiety on his plaid sport shirt, damp with sweat. The tight space contained three desk chairs—the clunky, blond wooden sort that might have come from a classroom or a library—and a small but heavy oak table marred by coffee cup rings.

Homer stood in the doorway of the interview room watching them.

Jonah glanced at him. "Can we leave now?"

He nodded, handing Jessica a set of keys. "Go out to my car. After I try contacting your mother again, I'll join you and we can talk some more."

While he stayed behind to use a pay phone, Jessica hustled Jonah out to the 1985 blue Buick. He stumbled alongside her, tripping on an untied leather lace in his scuffed black work shoe.

She grabbed his sleeve. "Stop right here, Jonah. If you keep walking around like that, you're going to fall."

He came to an obedient halt, and she squatted down beside him and tugged on the broken lace. "What did you do—step on it?"

He stared at it as if he hadn't noticed it before. "I don't know." He patiently waited for her to realign the leather strip and fashion a half bow.

The rain had stopped, but fat drops pearled on the Buick's heavy coat of wax. Jessica opened the rear passenger door, motioned Jonah in, then scooted onto the bench seat herself. The car's interior was immaculate, devoid of the Styrofoam cups, road maps, and ballpoint pens that littered her van. A green cardboard tree hanging from the rearview mirror infused the air with a fake pine scent.

Jonah sat with his elbows tight against his sides, his hands balled in front of him.

Jessica shifted sideways and rested her arm atop the cushioned rear seat. "What did they say to you in that room?"

"They said there are rats in prison."

His answer, thick with fear, didn't surprise her. She understood the way his mind tracked, the way he sometimes tossed out thoughts like they were the misshapen pieces in a puzzle, requiring someone with experience and patience to sort them out. If she stayed with it, the picture would eventually emerge.

"Who told you there are rats?"

"Bud Schultz. He said there were giant ones, man-sized ones that would jump on me at night and bite me in the ass. He said I'd be mighty tasty for some of those big black buggers."

Jessica felt the anger rise inside her. "What did Sheriff Tarr say?"

Jonah fixed his gaze on the windshield. "I don't know. I didn't listen anymore."

"Bud was trying to scare you into confessing you'd set the fire. Do you understand that?"

He nodded, but as usual she wasn't sure whether he did.

"Who called Homer?" she asked.

"I don't know."

She saw he was rubbing something with his fingertips. "What have you got there?"

He opened his fist and revealed a tiny metal soldier on horseback, gripping a musket the length of a matchstick in his right hand. "Lieutenant General Nathan Bedford Forrest."

"Confederate, huh?"

"Yup."

"Which battle are you doing?"

"Bowling Green." He stirred at her interest. When it came to his Civil War soldiers, he was always ready to talk. "That was Lieutenant General Forrest's first combat engagement. He didn't have any military training, but he was a hero. He came in the mail last week with General Braxton Bragg." A puzzled, anxious look crossed his face. "But I can't find General Bragg, Jessie. He's missing."

"Missing in action, huh?" she said, trying to keep her voice light, knowing how any disorder among his soldierly ranks bothered him. She held out her hand. "May I see Lieutenant General Forrest?"

He laid it on her palm. She studied the miniature, which was realistically detailed down to the pinpoint buttons on his uniform and the crease in his hat. She handed it back. "You did a nice job of painting him."

Jonah drew some white tissue paper from his pants pocket. "Nathan Bedford Forrest was the bravest man in the war. He fought in the Army of Tennessee right alongside his men and killed thirty-one Union soldiers himself."

She watched him neatly fold the paper several times around the general. "Jonah, did they ask you about the fire at that halfway house?"

He hesitated, then nodded tentatively.

She tried to keep her voice even, without accusation. "Homer said there was a survivor who claimed you threw rocks at their windows the night before last."

He laid the shrouded soldier on the velour upholstery between them, carefully lining up the bundle so that it rested along a seam. Reaching into the pocket of his shirt, he drew out two other miniature soldiers with muskets forged on their backs and held them out for her to see. "Union infantrymen. Got a bunch of these guys yesterday too, but I haven't had time to paint them yet."

"Jonah?"

He leveled flat, unflickering eyes at her. "What?"

"You're not listening to me."

"Yeah, I am." But his gaze turned back to his collection. He arranged the Union infantrymen on the bench seat, switching them to conform to some order that wasn't apparent to Jessica.

She suddenly felt adrift in deep water, and she had a horrible sinking feeling. "Jonah, you'd never do anything like that, would you? Set a fire, I mean?"

He waited a few seconds to answer. "I don't like fire, Jessie. Remember when you burned the dock? I hated that."

"I remember," she said. In that single moment, she had probably introduced him to the concept of arson.

There was a time when she believed his peculiarity, his eccentricity or whatever it was that made the kids in school call him "retard" and "weirdo," began the summer he was nine and she was sixteen—the summer their father died, the summer she'd burned the dock. But there had been problems before that. By the end of first grade Jonah could read, but his teacher, Mrs. Berman, said he seemed inattentive, lost in his own world.

Jessica remembered waiting with Jonah in the hall outside his classroom while her mother spoke with Mrs. Berman. At first, they kept their voices low, and she couldn't hear them.

But then her mother's voice suddenly boomed. "There's nothing wrong with him. Does he behave himself in class?"

"Yes," the soft-spoken Mrs. Berman said.

"Is he learning?"

"He excels in the subjects that interest him."

Her mother's voice dropped to a more normal level. "Well, then, just don't coddle him, and he'll be fine."

"But he has serious social problems. He won't participate in group activities, and if his classmates speak directly to him, he rarely answers or looks at them. I think you should have a psychologist evaluate him."

"That's the stupidest thing I ever heard." A chair scraped against the floor, and Lila marched out of the classroom.

Jessica wondered if Mrs. Berman knew Jonah couldn't fall asleep at night unless his head was positioned directly under an orange water stain on his bedroom ceiling.

Jonah spent most of grade school hunched over a desk at the back of the room. When something upset him, he hyperventilated and ran outside to hide in the woods. The school nurse then called Lila to go look for him. He made it through high school with fewer problems, because by then his teachers and his classmates were accustomed to his ways.

Through the open car window, Jessica heard Homer say, "Here she comes."

She watched Lila ignore the crosswalk and charge toward them, propelled by the anger so obvious in her expression. Jessica grudgingly had to admit that, at fifty-five, her mother was still attractive. She had classic, solid features and better skin than she deserved, having spent most of her life outside in wind and rain. Jessica knew men admired her. They respected her ability to heft a forty-pound chunk of wood from her pickup and pitch it as if it weighed no more than an empty box. They respected the way she stood with her loggers in a skin-chafing downpour and supervised the loading of trucks. And when she bounced down the rutted forest roads, her ribbon-tied braid snapping from side to side, they waved and whistled at her with the exuberance of teenage boys.

Even now, Homer eyed her with the loopy grin of a sixteen-year-old. Jessica figured he'd been in love with her for at least two decades, maybe even before his wife died, but, from what she'd heard, Lila had no interest in remarrying. Jessica's best friend from high school, Mary Grace Snow, had kept her up-to-date about Lila and the town through Christmas letters and phone conversations. There were rumors of the occasional boyfriend during the last eighteen years, but no one current.

No wonder, Jessica thought. Who could meet her standards? Not even Dad could do that.

There was a time when they all got along, when she actually liked her mother, but that was when Jonah was a baby. Her parents often took them to the ocean beaches in the summer. The waves churned a salty green foam high enough for her to stand in. Her mother and father usually lounged on one of the hundreds of logs that had washed in and anchored there. Sometimes they even held hands and looked directly into each other's eyes when they spoke.

She opened the rear door just as Lila reached Homer's car.

When Lila saw her, she straightened with a little twitch of surprise. "It wasn't necessary for you to show up."

"Someone had to make sure he was all right."

Her mother directed her gaze upward, to Homer. "Did you telephone her, you old coot?"

A dull red crawled up Homer's neck.

Jessica stepped out of the car, tugging her UCLA sweatshirt down over her hips. "He didn't have to call anyone. It's all over town." She wasn't certain the remark was true, but it couldn't be far off.

Her mother rested her hands on her hips, displaying knuckles that were red and raw from wrestling with tree branches and logging equipment. "Well, I'm not putting up with this nonsense anymore." She turned to Homer, her elbows jutting out in defiance. "Let's sue them."

He bent slightly, shading his eyes against the morning sun. "For what, Lila?"

"False arrest."

"They didn't arrest him. They questioned him, and they had probable cause."

As Homer told her about the rock throwing, the color flared in Lila's face.

"They're taking a drug addict's word that my son was outside that house?"

"Sexual offender. The two recovering drug addicts and the former mental patient died in the fire. The sex offender survived. He said they saw Jonah throw rocks at the windows. Broke one in the dining room."

"That window could have popped during the fire."

"That's what I said to Bud Schultz, but he said—"

"Bud Schultz is an idiot. A volunteer fire chief—what does he know?"

"He's paid to be chief. The other men are volunteers," said Homer, his watery blue eyes peering down at her. "Would you like to hear why the men didn't report the rock throwing at the time it happened, Lila?"

She gave a dismissive wave of her hand. "Easy enough to say anything after the fact."

"I would like to know," Jessica said.

Homer, not the sort of man to appear unshaven in public, rubbed his thumb across the short gray whiskers on his jaw. "According to the survivor, they were going to leave as soon as possible. Apparently, what with Edith Meyer and her gang picketing and handing out flyers, the newspaper printing editorials against them, and people dumping dog—well, dog feces—on their front porch, they figured they could persuade the state agency to move them to Seattle. Another week or so, and they would probably have been gone anyway."

Lila was silent for a moment.

"Well, I don't believe it was arson," she said finally. "We've always had drunks and misfits in this town, but nobody's ever burnt them out. If that's the way people handled things around here, there'd be charred bodies strewn across the landscape."

"Jesus, Lila," Jessica said through clenched teeth.

"It's the truth. Bet they'll find one of those cretins accidentally set that fire himself, and I'll be damned if I let them blame my son for it."

"Well, you can't blame the victims," Jessica said.

"But that sexual pervert wasn't the victim, was he? They're trying to pin this fire on my son. He's the victim."

Jessica glanced at Jonah, who was sitting quietly in the car, his head bowed. "Seems like a simple matter of telling them where he was last night."

Lila poked her head through the open passenger door. "Since this conversation's about you, son, you'd better get out here."

Reacting reflexively, he scooted out of the car, but he kept his eyes riveted to the ground. Jessica suspected he was furtively clutching his miniature soldiers in his hands.

Lila laid her hand on Jonah's arm. "I can tell you where my boy was last night. He was at home, playing until all hours of the night with those toy Civil War soldiers and all their little horses and tents and cannons, painting them and propping them up on that plywood board he's got in the basement. I went downstairs around one o'clock and told him to come to bed. And if the sheriff doesn't believe that, then he'd better be prepared to call Lila Moran a liar in front of this whole town."

"They're not toys," Jonah whispered, slowly rubbing the soldiers as if they were talismans.

3

Without another glance at Jessica, Lila directed Jonah toward her black Ford pickup. Thinking Lila's reaction had been just about what she'd expected, Jessica climbed into her van and drove back to Misp. She knew why Jonah's behavior made him a convenient target when someone needed one, but she doubted she would be able to convince Lila he even had a problem.

During the eighteen years she was away, her memories of her brother remained vivid, and she called him at least once a week. Her ex-husband, Patrick, had never met Jonah—neither he nor Lila came to the wedding—but, when she described him, Patrick nodded in a supercilious manner she had come to hate. "Asperger's syndrome," he said. "Of course, in a backwater place like your hometown, they wouldn't have even heard of it, much less know how to spell it."

Jessica stared at him. "*I've* never heard of it."

With good reason, she discovered later when she did the research. It didn't become an official mental disorder until 1994. Each clinical phrase felt like a body blow: "Normal or above normal intelligence but a touch of autism," "flatness of emotion," "socially inept," "inflexible adherence to rituals and routines," "excessive preoccupation with a single activity or interest," "victims of bullying or teasing."

Of all the words she read, the ones that stood out in chilling black print were "no specific treatment." He couldn't be cured.

She could still recall her initial disappointment—no, more than mere disappointment, a visceral feeling that left her hopeless, defeated. She hated the thought there was nothing she could do.

It was a difficult time. Her marriage, not yet two years old, was shriveling like a plant without water. She'd already filed for divorce when she came across some information on the Internet that said an Asperger's sufferer could *learn* better social and practical skills the way he might master a new language. It would be difficult, especially if he was older. He would require guidance and repetitive explanations to make sense of the world and other people, but mostly he would need endless patience and love.

Jessica felt her optimism rise like a bubble in water. The last two ingredients she could provide; the others she could work at.

She knew Lila would never allow Jonah to come live with her, so, after the divorce, she made the decision to return to Misp— despite her mother's occupation of it. That's the way she thought of Lila, as a hostile force, entrenched and unyielding, so dominant in her position as owner of one of the few lumber mills left in the area that she practically ran the town.

She tried once to talk to Lila about Jonah's disorder. She thought she owed her that attempt, and on her third day in Misp she visited her mother in her office at the mill.

Lila's mouth set in a hard line. "What are you doing here?"

Jessica shook her head in amazement. "After all these years, that's all you have to say to me?"

When she told Lila about Asperger's syndrome, she dismissed the diagnosis with a wave of her hand. "So your psychiatrist ex-husband says your brother's a nutcase—even though he's never met him."

"A psychologist," Jessica said lamely.

She didn't bother arguing. She went away angry, thinking some people never change. She wondered how much Lila knew about Patrick, but of course the grapevine traveled both ways. Her mother must have had her informants too. ·

At the edge of Misp, Jessica turned onto Sixteenth Street. She wanted to see the halfway house before it was boarded up, inaccessible. Although she knew Jonah occasionally walked by it, she hadn't paid much attention to it before. She had not been one of those who protested its establishment.

At the corner of Sixteenth and Clark, she passed St. Bavo's, the Gothic-style stone church where her father's funeral had been held. Even now, she couldn't go by the church without recalling every moment of that Saturday morning. From what Jessica could tell at the time, people assumed Big Mike's death was simply a tragic accident. It was well known that Jonah was clumsy and afraid of the water. Lila and Jessica didn't discuss the details, but it seemed understood neither would contradict prevailing opinion.

Jessica thought Jonah had acted confused, as if he were unaware of his part in the drowning. When Lila told him his father had gone to heaven, he cried a bit and said he didn't think Dad should have left.

Jessica remembered huddling in the front pew of St. Bavo's with her hands folded, watching as though she were at the opposite end of a long tunnel. It was the first time she'd seen grown men weep when they weren't drunk. Lila, in her plain navy blue dress, looked grim and depleted. Jonah clutched some tiny plastic Civil War soldiers Dad had given him, completely absorbed in moving them along the church pew. After the mass, her father's friends and employees told funny stories about him and read aloud some of the logger's poetry he'd written.

Jessica edged the van off the street in front of the halfway house, a few yards behind a shiny green Explorer that was noticeably new in this quiet neighborhood of well-used trucks and clunker sedans.

As she stepped from the van, she glanced at Pearl Hobbs's home next door and caught the ripple of blue gingham at the kitchen window. But when she looked again, the curtains were motionless. Judging by the tightly drawn shades and dark windows, Pearl was holed up in her house, probably still shaking with fear.

Jessica walked up the uneven brick path to the halfway house, stopping at a yellow tape that swayed between two cedar trees. She read the words FIRE LINE—DO NOT CROSS, then lifted the tape and stepped under it.

As she stood at the base of the porch, the light rain found its way down the back of her neck. She pulled her jacket collar tighter and stuffed her hair more securely under her baseball cap. Tucking her cold, wet hands into her jacket pocket, she stared up at the charred remains of the century-old house. She wondered exactly how much she had taught Jonah about arson.

At the time, setting the fire had seemed a perfectly reasonable response to her frustration.

A few days after the funeral, two men came to Thunder Lake in a truck and dumped an herbicide into it, killing the weeds. The herbicide didn't harm the fish or other wildlife, but there was no more swimming that summer. For several nights in a row, Jessica dreamed of diving into the water. She searched frantically, futilely, among the tentacled trees, but it wasn't her father's body she was looking for now. She'd seen the divers bring that up from the lake, stuff it in a black zippered bag, and carry it off. She'd been told to stay in the house, but she had watched from an upstairs window. No, it was his soul that was still trapped in its depths, his soul that needed to be liberated.

She went to Thunder Lake daily and stared into its shadows, desperate for a solution. Sometimes, she thought she heard her father's voice calling out to her, and then she felt more helpless than ever.

Whenever she looked at that long stretch of dock and thought of Mom pitching Jonah into the water the way she might have tossed a broken branch, her stomach churned with rage. One afternoon, she stomped on several of the weaker boards and snapped the ends right off. They fell into the lake with a plop and floated on the surface like toy boats. That small act alone gave her tremendous satisfaction.

But it wasn't enough. There was a night in mid-June when she stood on shore, unable to contain the fury boiling up in her. The next thing she knew she was squatting on the wooden planks, teasing a pyramid of twigs, brush, and leaves with a lighted match. It fluttered out.

When she couldn't revive it after several tries, she trudged to the garage, located a nearly full gallon container of kerosene, and lugged it back. She wasn't aware of spilling the kerosene, but suddenly it glazed the boards and reflected the moonlight, like black ice in winter. She felt cold, and her hands shook.

She had no memory of throwing the match or leaving the dock. But there was the *whoosh* and a roar, and seconds later she was standing safely on a grassy rise about forty feet away. In time, the flames shot as high as a house, and curling smoke blotted out the stars.

Soon, Jonah was beside her in his blue-and-red Superman pajamas, his open mouth as round as a choirboy's, his unearthly scream piercing the air.

Lacy white ashes floated skyward, like snowflakes returning to their source. The dock burned down to the waterline.

The following morning, one of the Quinault Indians, a broadly built man about fifty years of age, walked over from the reservation, stood in the front yard, and conferred with Mom. Over his T-shirt and jeans, he wore a dark green jacket with the silver outline of an eagle on the back. He secured his hair, which was the flat gray of river rock, into a ponytail. Jessica thought he might be the tribal chief, but she wasn't sure. She couldn't hear what they were saying, but she figured by the way Mom gestured and nodded her head that she was agreeing with him.

After he left, Mom came back into the house, her face tight with displeasure. "They saw the flames last night. He asked if I knew how the fire started."

Jessica didn't reply.

"I told him some evil spirits must have been creating mischief." She shook her head in disgust. "They believe stories like that, you know. They think most of the lakes around here have demons or monsters in them."

"What did he say?"

"Nothing. He just smiled in that secretive way those people have and clammed right up."

"He's not stupid. You insulted him."

"Oh, I insulted him, did I?" Her eyes went hot. "And what was I supposed to say, Miss Director of the United Nations? Should I have told him my daughter was out there last night burning down the dock like some loony?"

Jessica didn't answer. She was mentally drifting away, thinking how dark and bleak the kitchen looked. Not even a bright rug on the plank floor or a spindly green plant on the windowsill. Her mother had been cleaning the house for days—organizing, changing, moving things. From what Jessica could tell, she was giving Dad's clothes to the Misp Family Services Center and storing his other belongings in the basement.

Her mother's voice twisted tight as a knot. "If there had been a wind last night, young lady, any wind at all, you would have started a fire that would have raced through these forests. And I would have had more than just an Indian over here asking questions. I am doing my best to hold this family and the business together. Don't I have enough to worry about without wondering whether you're nuts?"

"Can't have any more kids with psychological problems in the family, can we?" Jessica murmured.

The slap across her face sounded distant to her, like a flyswatter landing. It came so fast she didn't have time to duck, and it set her ears ringing. Resisting the reflex to reach up and touch her cheek, she balled her hands and pressed them against her hips. She stepped forward and dared her mother to strike her again—in fact, wanted her to.

Mom's hands shook, but remained at her sides. "For God's sake, don't do this to me."

Jessica stared hard at her. "I'll bet *he* feels better because I burned it."

"Who?"

"Dad."

"Oh my God." Mom raised her hands, cupping them over her eyes, and Jessica wondered if she might be crying. Mom's voice dropped to a supplicating whisper. "Please, I *need* you to be strong."

"We have to release his soul."

Mom lowered her hands from her damp eyes. "What are you talking about?"

"It's still in the lake. Can't you feel it?"

Mom's expression turned to annoyance. "You've been hanging around those Indians, haven't you?"

Jessica looked over her mother's shoulder, through the window, toward the ragged patch of water that was visible between the trees—the very tip of Thunder Lake. Maybe she could blow up the splash dam so that all the water would drain out and Dad's soul could rise heavenward. Mom kept the dynamite at the mill locked up, but maybe she could steal the key. If she blew up the dam, some fish would die, of course. She would feel awful about them, but there wasn't much she could do. She didn't know how to save them either.

As JESSICA STOOD in front of the halfway house, her throat felt tight and sore. The urge to run swamped her and momentarily disoriented her, but she couldn't leave yet, not if she wanted to help Jonah. She forced herself to move toward the porch.

More of the structure remained than she expected, but what wasn't charred was cracked or blistered. Soot coated the windows

that were still intact. Although she had hardly noticed the old, or-
nate house when she was younger, she felt an unreasonable grief
now, as if a relative she'd never appreciated suddenly passed on. As
she took hold of the porch railing, a beam somewhere deep inside
creaked, shifted, and settled with a groan, and she quickly retreated
to the brick path.

She strode around the corner of the house, her tennis shoes
squishing in the spongy grass. Sidestepping a clothesline that
drooped with a pair of waterlogged, carbon-streaked jeans, she
stopped in front of a shattered first-story window. Homer had said
the fire started here in the dining room. Shreds of melted beige
nylon curtain dangled like flesh from the splintered wooden frame.
Glass shards littered the burnt grass. She could smell human death
in the air.

A covered oak barrel rested upright on the ground under the
window, a trail of muddy ridges leading from the backyard. She
couldn't imagine Jonah dragging the cask across the lawn, crawling
into the house, and setting the fire. It was too calculated, too cold,
not at all like him.

"Can't you read?" asked a voice behind her.

Jessica stiffened in irritation. Turning, she saw that the man, lean
and darkly complexioned, appeared to be about her age, somewhere in his mid-thirties. In his gray pin-striped suit and crisp white
shirt, he looked overdressed for tramping around a charred house
in the rain. He wore his black wavy hair short, neatly feathered at
the edges. His nose was crooked, his features too rough to be handsome. A scar curved across his left cheekbone like a pale pink string.

The image of a sixteen-year-old in high-water jeans and a faded
hand-me-down T-shirt rushed back. The shape of his face and the
texture of his skin had changed to a man's, but she saw the boy in
him, and she knew he was Callum Luke.

Her friend Mary Grace Snow had said he lived in Seattle and
rarely visited Misp or the reservation. Even so, when she moved
back, she realized he could turn up someday, perhaps in Jelly's

Diner, Rudy's Tavern, or at the Snows' minimart. But not in this place where memories were already flooding her.

Long ago, she had decided that if she saw him again, she would be cool, distant, poised. She would pretend she barely remembered him or what he'd done.

"This isn't a tourist attraction." He sounded officious.

Realizing he hadn't recognized her, she yanked her baseball cap lower over her eyes. "I haven't touched a thing."

He stepped closer to her. "You're disturbing the grass."

"And you aren't?"

"Yes, but that's two of us trampling the evidence, not one, and I have good reason to be here. How about you?"

His tone brought out the rebel in her. Her gaze flashed to the house, its soot-blackened windows staring back at her. "I'm the town window washer. I plan to bid on this job."

She saw him smile in tight-lipped appreciation of her answer. She remembered his scar as being redder, more jagged. Mary Grace had said he was an attorney, but she hadn't mentioned that he worked for a law enforcement agency. Jessica recalled her mother predicting he would never make anything of himself. Yet, ironically, she was the one who washed windows for a living.

Jessica turned to leave, then stopped. There was something at the base of the barrel—a twig, a dead night crawler, something curved, dark, and still. The remnant of a leather shoelace.

She didn't dare pick it up, not in front of him.

"You going or not?" His voice came low and husky, stirring more emotion in her than she cared to feel.

She had to restrain herself from looking at the leather strip again. Although it could have come from any one of a million work shoes, the coincidence was too great. She wanted to be away from Callum before he recognized her, but she couldn't leave the shoelace for him or someone else to find. The sheriff might recall that Jonah's was broken. She moved closer to the barrel, then shifted her gaze to the window. "Terrible thing that happened here, wasn't it?"

"I'm glad someone in this town feels that way." His eyes tracked the ruts the cask had left. He took several steps as if to follow them toward the back of the house.

She reached down and closed her fingers over the leather strip. When she lifted her head, he was walking back. He held out his hand, damp from the rain. She hesitated, then laid the shoelace on his palm. Their eyes met again, and this time the color drained from his face. "Jess?"

She swung around and strode in the direction of her van.

He was at her heels. "I didn't recognize you at first."

She kept moving. "That doesn't surprise me. I've changed."

"I couldn't see your hair under that cap."

"That's the same. Nothing else is."

"Could you slow down so we could talk?"

"No."

"I didn't know you lived here. When did you move back?"

She didn't answer.

"Jess!"

She stopped and leveled her gaze at him. He was looking more the way she remembered him, and she hated the queasy effect it had on her. The rain was coming down harder, splashing noisily on the pavement. Her soaked clothes were gluing themselves to her skin.

He pushed his rain-slickened hair back from his forehead. "Let's go somewhere and have a cup of coffee."

"I don't drink coffee." She turned and hurried across the soggy grass.

Callum followed her, not saying anything. She opened the door and scrambled into the driver's seat, struggling to dig out her keys from the pocket of her wet jeans. He stood a few yards away, his shoulders hunched against the downpour.

He stared at the lettering on her van, not even trying to conceal his surprise. "You really are a window washer."

She slammed her door shut and shoved the key in the ignition.

The engine complained and sputtered before it caught. She wrenched the transmission into drive and tore off. His parting remark annoyed her so much she would have run over his toes if she could have.

WITH THE RAIN still pelting him, Callum strode to the green Explorer, climbed in, and vigorously dried his face and hair with a towel from his gym bag.

She had filled out. The last time he saw her, she was willow thin. He could have encircled her wrist with his thumb and forefinger, and he tried to recall if he had ever done that.

He remembered the first time they had been alone—well, almost alone. Her brother, Jonah, was there, but he occupied some other cerebral plane. Callum was hiking along the boundary of an allottee, one of the Quinault Indian reservation's timber units that bordered Moran property. When he came to a section of Moran timber that had recently been cut and yarded, he saw Jessica sitting some thirty feet away on a chunk of broken log. Gouged earth, sawed-off stumps, and branches from the bucked trees stretched in front of her like the aftermath of a storm.

Where he stood, though, the forest had not yet been touched by loggers. The giant conifers rose like arrows and teemed with vegetation so thick there seemed no other color in this wooded vault but green. Although he could smell the rich musk of decaying trees and plants, the forest floor felt spongy and alive.

He liked watching Jessica while she was unaware of him. He had seen her at school but they had rarely spoken until their history teacher assigned them to the same research team for a paper on the New Deal.

Although the late afternoon sun was warm, especially under the open sky where Jessica sat, she wore all black—a T-shirt and baggy cotton pants cinched with a man's leather belt that could have wrapped around her waist twice. The end of it dangled from a loop on her pants. He knew her father had died six days before. Her eyes looked bruised, as if someone had punched them. The rest of her skin was milk-white and lightly freckled.

Her red hair frizzed around her face, and coils of it shot out here and there at odd angles. Callum, whose entire family had hair that was some variation of black, brown, or gray, thought he'd never seen anything as fascinating as her hair. It wasn't even one color but a hundred different shades of red and gold and bronze. Although he'd never touched it, he wanted to. He thought it must feel as soft and springy as the moss under his feet, but he had no way of knowing for sure. He wondered if he asked to touch it, whether she would scream and run off. He decided that she would but it would be worth the attempt.

Her brother was poking a stick at the exposed roots of a scrawny tree the loggers had spared.

"Come away from there, Jonah," she yelled. "That fir's a widow-maker."

When he didn't move, she rose from the log and placed her hands on her hips. "I said get away from there."

Callum stepped from the shadows. "Be careful, Jonah. There are demons in that tree."

The boy snapped back, tripped over a jagged stump, and sat down hard, the stick still in his hand. He blinked in bewilderment.

Jessica swung around and squinted at Callum. "Don't tell him that. He believes people when they say those things."

Callum shrugged. "Well, it's true." He'd even heard white loggers admit that spirits inside the trees cried and clamored as they crashed to the ground.

Jessica turned away. When the sunlight caught her hair, she looked as though she'd gone up in flames. "Whether it's true or not, he doesn't need to know it."

She said it with such finality that he didn't think to argue. Nor did he want to. He knew he should say something about her father, although he couldn't decide what that should be. He could say what his mother had said, that he was a fair man to deal with, but then he probably should add the rest of her remark—"for a white man." And, of course, there was that other business he'd heard his mother mention in hushed tones to his aunt. He thought if he said anything at all about her dad, he'd stumble over the words.

Jonah took his stick and moved away from the fir toward a giant stump that had been upended during the logging. It looked to Callum like a fiendish octopus he had seen pictured in an old book at the library. The roots became tentacles, thrusting out and wrapping themselves around clumps of dirt. A knot on the side protruded like the bulging eye of the creature on the yellowed pages. Callum was forever seeing familiar images in the splintered ends of toppled trees—or in leafy branches, rock outcroppings, and swirls of sand. Once, on a clear-cut hillside, he saw his father's face, leering and mean, the way he looked when he staggered in after a night of drinking.

When he was about ten years old, Callum was certain he saw Mickey Mouse on the side of a piece of driftwood the surf had carried in. There Mickey sat, as plain as if someone had etched the skillet-shaped ears and the bulbous nose into the sodden timber. Two white kids, about his own age, came along the beach just then, and in his eagerness to tell someone, he showed them his discovery. They said they couldn't see anything but a scummy old log. He heard one boy tell the other that Callum was just some weird Indian kid who'd been chewing mushrooms. He claimed his dad said Indians did that.

After that encounter, Callum was more careful about mentioning what he saw to whites, but he hoped Jessica would be different from the others. Indians understood there really were spirits in the rocks and trees and mountains. All things had living spirits inside them. Even so, Callum couldn't figure out how his dad could be on the side of a hill when he was sitting right there in the living room cussin' out Mom.

Jonah whacked the roots with his stick, and a ground squirrel skittered from under them. Jessica, who had settled onto the log again, rubbed her hands on the knees of her pants. Up close, Callum could see her clothes were splotchy and streaked. They must have started out a different color, and then been dyed black. She'd also painted her chewed-to-the-nub fingernails with slick maroon polish.

Callum could taste the dust that rose from the damaged ground. He squatted in the dirt beside Jessica and gazed up. A week before, the canopy of trees had been so thick the sun could barely filter through to the forest floor. Now, the sky was remarkable in its openness. Hearing a distinctive screech above, he scanned the treetops. A pair of bald eagles, their broad wings beating the air, their white heads and tail feathers catching the light, glided toward their nest in a craggy fir on reservation land. Jessica fixed her gaze on the birds too.

"If you could go anywhere," Callum asked, "any place at all, where would it be?"

She turned her raw eyes on him, her answer coming in one long breath. "I would go to the place where people go when they die."

Jonah was suddenly beside them, his voice high and excited. "You aren't leaving, are you, Jessie?"

"No, Jonah. Not right now." She nodded toward the stump. "See if you can find some beetles in the wood."

"You won't go anywhere without me, will you, Jessie?"

"No, Jonah, I won't."

He smiled and wandered off.

Callum eased himself onto the log. "What do you think it's like there—I mean, the place where people go after they die?"

She lowered her gaze, but not before he noticed her eyes had filled with tears. "It's lonely," she said, "because everyone's missing someone."

"And the people. How would they look?"

"They wouldn't have any eyes, but they could see. They wouldn't have ears either, but they could hear."

Callum nodded his head. "That's how I think it would be too."

She leaned toward him then. Her hands didn't touch him, but she rested her head just to the right of his chin. Callum didn't know what to do. He kept his hands by his sides, as reluctant to move as if a sparrow had landed on his shoulder. He'd kissed several of the girls on the reservation, and more than once he'd put his hand inside Ramona Shale's underpants, but he'd never touched a white girl like this before. Her springy curls tickled his face, and he took one of them into his mouth and ran his tongue over it. It tasted like new grass and smelled like soap.

He drew back just enough to speak. "I wouldn't want you to stay there."

"I don't want to stay. I only want to visit."

Her voice was low and quavery. He tried to think how he could make her feel better. "Jessica?"

Her reply was a small sound.

"There's a big stump close to where Jonah's standing that has an octopus trapped in it. If you want, I'll show it to you."

She nodded, her hair lightly brushing his cheek. He took her hand, and it felt warm and soft and thrilling.

In thinking back to that time when he and Jessica were sixteen, Callum wished for their innocence again, that purity of heart that had brought them together. But she had been wounded, and he had only made things worse.

It was no secret how her mother felt about Indians. After Jessica left Misp, leaving him to agonize over why she had gone, he tried to find a reason that didn't involve him.

Mary Grace Snow confided to his younger sister Bethany that Lila Moran shipped Jessica off because she was a firebug. Everyone knew she'd burned the dock. He would have preferred that explanation, but he didn't believe it. It was more likely her mother went crazy after she heard the gossip. The memory of the rumor that coursed through Misp with the momentum of an avalanche, and his own part in starting it, still filled him with shame.

One of the girls on the reservation said Jessica's mom sent her to live with an aunt because that's what white people did when they wanted to get rid of their kids. His sister said there was another rumor that he'd made Jessica pregnant and that she went away to have the baby. But he'd always believed the rumor had been just that, idle talk in a town where gossip ranked as prime entertainment.

Long ago, he decided that if he ever saw her again, he would ask her why she had left, no matter how disturbing her answer might be. That question and the effusive apology he'd intended to mumble were wedged so deep inside him that when she did appear before him, he couldn't manage to utter either one.

Callum sat watching the rain splash his windshield, thinking that through the years very little had worked out the way he'd planned.

He picked up the car phone and dialed the local fire department number. By leaving the halfway house without securing it and posting a guard, Fire Chief Bud Schultz had made his first mistake. He had effectively released the fire scene. Now, Callum would have to get a "consent to search" from the survivor and possibly a criminal search warrant. When it came to dealing with a possible arson and triple murder, Misp's fire chief was bush league.

4

Leaving the halfway house, Jessica drove her van along Reservation Road. She wasn't cold, but she had to grip the steering wheel tight to keep her hands from shaking, hardly the poised reaction to Callum she had planned.

While she had been debating the move back to Misp, she'd phoned Mary Grace from Los Angeles. She'd casually asked about Callum and learned he no longer lived there and rarely visited.

"According to his sister Bethany, he married some Indian woman who doesn't like the 'rez,' " Mary Grace said. "I haven't seen him in about ten years." Mary Grace paused. "Hey, come on home, honey. Nobody remembers what happened in high school."

Jessica wondered if Mary Grace crossed her fingers as she said that.

At the intersection of Highway 101 and Bitter Road, Jessica turned her van toward the Snows' minimart. She could call Jonah from the phone booth outside the store.

Just past the railroad tracks and the Totem Pole Motel with its row of white stucco tepees, Jessica slowed the van, flipped on her left-hand turn signal, and pulled into the Misp Mall. They'd installed the towering sign while she was living in Los Angeles. The first time she saw it, she laughed out loud. Only in Misp could a quick-stop grocery, two gas pumps, a Sani-Can for tourists, and a phone booth constitute a shopping mall. Below the permanent sign was a board with removable letters that currently read CONGRAT-ULATIONS TOM & ELAINE. It didn't say what Tom and Elaine had done to deserve recognition, but Mary Grace must have figured that anyone who cared already knew they'd just had twin boys.

Jessica parked near the phone booth, away from the view of the store windows, and punched in her mother's number. Jonah answered on the fourth ring.

She leaned against the glass door. "I just came from the halfway house, Jonah. I found the other half of your shoelace in the grass there."

He mumbled something.

"Jonah, did you hear me?"

"I said yes."

"Well, talk louder, will you? Remember a few days ago when I picked you up near the halfway house?"

Another mumble.

"Do you think you could have broken it walking across the yard there?"

She could have counted to five while she awaited his reply.

"I guess," he murmured.

She pressed the heel of her palm against her forehead. "Don't you remember? Pearl Hobbs and Charlotte Johnson waved at us from Pearl's front porch."

"Uh-huh. I think it was that day. I always cut through there on my way to town."

She released the pent-up air in her lungs. "Well, that makes sense. It's not any big deal to walk across someone's yard, but maybe you should throw away those laces. No reason to keep tripping over them."

"Okay."

After she hung up the receiver, she felt guilty. She hadn't told him that Callum had the strip of shoelace now, that she worried he would consider it evidence. So much for explaining things to Jonah so he could understand them—but no sense upsetting him unnecessarily either.

Jessica glanced at the minimart. Pink neon tubing in the store window flashed PEN. Mary Grace said her husband, Bob, promised to fix the burned-out O soon, but she grumbled about his procrastination at least once a month. Wooden signs tacked to the outside wall advertised movie rentals, smoked salmon, buffalo jerky, and espresso. The Snows had the best price in town on gasoline.

Through glass panes that dripped with condensation, Jessica could see Mary Grace's sleek black hair bobbing over the cash register. She would know why Callum was in town.

As Jessica pushed open the door, a bell jingled and the store imparted the buttery aroma of the popcorn that Mary Grace prepared by the bucket-load and gave away free. She claimed that by being liberal with the salt, she had tripled her soft drink and beer sales.

She was standing at the counter with two customers, the elderly Meckler sisters. Their conversation conspicuously stopped, and the three women stared at Jessica with expressions that said they were gossiping as clearly as if they'd announced it aloud.

"Maybe I should come back later," Jessica said.

Mary Grace grinned and waved her in with a licorice stick. "Don't be silly."

In her tight black stretch pants and short-sleeved pink T-shirt with a tiny toppled evergreen on the pocket, Mary Grace could have been a model for a Stihl chain saw calendar. They were a logging family. Her father, father-in-law, two brothers, and husband had all gone to work in the woods right out of high school.

Dottie and Della Meckler, nearly identical in their light blue polyester pants and sweatshirts with machine-stitched flowers, stood like skinny bookends alongside the magazine rack. Both had gray hair so sparse Jessica could see their Band-Aid-colored flesh shining through.

She nodded at them. "Hello, Miss Meckler—and Miss Meckler." She never could tell them apart.

One of the sisters leaned closer. Although they were the only customers in the store, she shielded her mouth with her hand. "We were just saying what a brave young man your brother is."

Jessica stared at her, puzzled. "Excuse me?"

The other sister patted Jessica's arm. "Della and I believe he did the right thing."

Della nodded in solemn agreement. "We weren't going to mention it to anyone, except Mary Grace, of course, but since you're here—"

The sisters exchanged meaningful glances, and Dottie cleared her throat. "We just want your family to know we're grateful."

An uneasy feeling came over Jessica. "For?" she prompted.

Della leaned forward. "We saw Jonah crawling through the grass at that . . . that house the evening of the fire."

Jessica felt the moment stop. She stared numbly at the women.

Dottie nodded vigorously. "It was already getting on toward dark. I told Della we shouldn't even walk anywhere near that place. One of those criminals could come out and conk us over the head."

Jessica would have smiled, but her sense of humor had dropped through a crack. "Why would he be sneaking around there?"

"To steal our money, of course." Della shuddered. "And to do who knows what else to us."

Jessica realized Della had misunderstood. "I mean why would Jonah crawl around their yard?"

The sisters looked at each other again.

"Well," Dottie said, "your brother was crouching against the foundation of that house. We said hello, but he scooted behind a shrub and hid. A few hours later, *poof*, the place goes up in smoke. In our opinion, he did the whole town a favor." She grabbed Jessica's hand and gave it a squeeze. "Don't worry. We won't tell a soul."

Jessica sagged against the wooden counter. "Thanks, that makes me feel better."

Mary Grace packed the sisters' purchases into a bag. Dottie's knobby fingers withdrew six dollars from her purse. Each bill was neatly folded into a two-inch square packet that the children in grade school used to call a cootie-catcher.

After they'd left, Mary Grace folded her arms across her middle and exploded with laughter. "Did you notice the dollar bills?"

Jessica didn't smile. "Cootie-catchers."

"They claim it keeps the bills from sticking together." She laughed again, then stopped abruptly and eyed Jessica. "You're upset."

"Wouldn't you be if they told you your brother is an arsonist?" In truth, she was feeling sick to her stomach.

"Oh, come on," Mary Grace said with a grin. "Everyone knows the Meckler sisters have the most vivid imaginations in town. They've read every Stephen King and Dean Koontz book in the library. They're always seeing men lurking in the shadows. Wishful thinking, Bob calls it."

"So you think they made up that part about Jonah?"

"Let's just say they saw what they wanted to see. I'll bet they walked past that halfway house every evening because it gave them a cheap thrill. Can't you just see them holding hands and giggling, 'Oh my goodness, this is so-o scary'?"

Mary Grace held out an open package of licorice sticks.

Jessica peeled one off and nibbled on it, thinking she'd read somewhere that licorice had a calming effect, like chamomile. "I can't see them imagining the part about Jonah."

"They probably heard someone mention the sheriff had questioned him about the fire, and that's all it took—the power of suggestion. Why, once, they came running in here to warn me that a rapist had escaped from the penitentiary in Monroe. Never mind that Monroe is a hundred and fifty miles from here."

"What did you say?"

"Bob was working that night. He told them that if they stood out on the highway and lifted their skirts, they might be able to catch him."

"Shame on Bob."

Mary Grace grinned.

Jessica glanced around to make sure the store was still empty. She turned back to Mary Grace and, without even feigning nonchalance, asked, "Why is Callum Luke in town?"

Mary Grace pulled a folded rag from a shelf and swabbed off the counter. "Probably visiting his relatives." But her expression told Jessica there was more.

"It has something to do with that fire, doesn't it? I drove by the halfway house. He was standing in the front yard." No need to mention she had talked with him.

Mary Grace appeared intent on her cleaning. "I wasn't going to tell you because I didn't want you to get upset, but he's in charge of investigating the halfway house arson for the Bureau of Alcohol, Firearms and Tobacco."

"Alcohol, Tobacco and Firearms."

Mary Grace shrugged. "I always get that turned around. Those ATF guys stop here for junk food and drinks on their way to the reservation. They're always telling me about their cigarette and firecracker busts. You know, if I called the reservation right after they left here and told them the ATF guys were coming, I'd be a hero."

"I thought you said Callum was a lawyer."

Mary Grace folded the cleaning rag like a burrito. "He is. In fact, until this morning, I thought he was still with a big law firm in Seattle. Apparently, I'm out of the reservation gossip loop, because now he's on this ATF team called Arson and Homicide Investigative Something Something, making sure people like Bud Schultz and Sheriff Tarr don't botch the case."

"He told you all that?"

She shook her head, her inky hair swaying and reflecting the overhead light. "His sister Bethany did. But Callum did stop by for take-out coffee this morning, and we talked, mostly about the town. He was complaining about everything here looking older and run-down. But I told him he should see the new high school football bleachers and the drive-through espresso stand near Jack Everett's hardware store. When I mentioned that Misp's biggest and toughest loggers and fishermen are slurping up double tall lattes with extra foam, he laughed." She tilted her head. "I always thought he was handsome, except for that scar. I don't remember how he got it, do you?"

"No," Jessica said, although she did.

He had turned up in seventh grade one day with the three-inch wound on his cheek, cross-stitched black surgical threads poking from it like unshaven whiskers. The other Indian kids said he'd been in a car accident, but a white girl whose mom volunteered as a nurse at the reservation clinic claimed his dad went after him with a broken beer bottle.

"Who did you say his wife is?" Jessica asked.

Mary Grace gave a lopsided grin. "Now, why would you care?"

"Just curious. Maybe she's someone I know."

"She's not from here. They met at Gonzaga Law School."

"What tribe is she from?"

"Muckleshoot, I think."

Jessica could see Callum's wife in a tailored gabardine suit, her black hair pulled straight back and coiled stylishly into a tidy knot at the back of her head, her demeanor professional and scholarly. Of course, as a Native American, she would have a lot more in common with him than Jessica did.

She looked down at her worn jeans with the knee patch. She'd caught the fabric on a bent carpenter's nail while cleaning T. J. Boynton's windows. Her stained Forrest Gump T-shirt proclaimed STUPID IS AS STUPID DOES. Her confidence evaporated in the aura of the woman attorney's perfect image.

It had been Mary Grace who suggested she clean windows for a living. In Los Angeles, she'd taught university extension classes and community college courses, but she found that a teacher with a master's degree in English literature was not in demand in Misp. It didn't take long to discover how limited career options were in a small town.

"Ben Stotter was complaining there's no professional window washer in this town," Mary Grace said. "You could do windows."

Jessica laughed. "There's a standard punch line for that."

"No, I'm serious. You wouldn't need much in the way of supplies—a bucket, a little ammonia, some rags. We'll loan you a ladder. Bob and the boys have enough old T-shirts to polish the windows on a twelve-story building. What more do you need?"

"A station wagon or a van."

"Trade in that Beemer of yours. Don't you think it's a bit much for Misp anyway? It's so . . . well, it's so foreign."

She sold the BMW, bought the van, and set up her small business. The first few months were rough, but her client list was growing.

At first, Jessica had strapped a Walkman to her jeans and listened to music—classical and jazz, nothing with words to it—while she swabbed the glass. Then the Walkman slipped from her belt and somersaulted to the pavement, cracking its plastic case and scrambling its circuitry. She didn't bother to replace it.

She began to listen to whatever sounds happened to be playing outside that day. It depended on where the job was. West of Misp, where the railroad tracks ran by a patch of houses, she knew when the train would clatter by and how many times the whistle would blow. Near the elementary school, she heard the kids shouting at recess. Close to the mill, the logging trucks shuddered and downshifted. Occasionally, the trees sang with the commotion of birds. Other times, they were strangely silent.

Some days, when the coast was enveloped in a misty fog, she saw no farther than the glass she was cleaning, and she heard nothing at all. Absolute stillness. That was when she discovered the satisfying, Zen-like nature of the job.

Now, as she stood before Mary Grace, she wondered what she had to show for the last year. A brother who, despite her best efforts, still seemed flustered and socially isolated most of the time and who might be in serious trouble. And—she looked down at her red hands—a bad case of detergent-chapped skin.

She sighed. "How long is Callum going to stay?"

Mary Grace stared at her in surprise. "I don't know. I don't pry. I just repeat what people tell me. Look, Jessica, he'll hang around a few days, act like an important bureaucrat, and then he'll leave. What's the big deal?"

"No big deal at all."

Mary Grace smiled. "Let it go, hon. Hardly anybody in town believed that rumor. You know how it is around here. Most people just figure Indian boys make up stories about sleeping with white girls."

"That's not what I'm concerned about," she murmured. She turned away. Now was not the time to tell her the rumor was true.

When Jessica looked back, Mary Grace was studying her reflection in the window and finger-combing her bangs so they fell sideways. Although they'd been in the same graduating class, she was thirty-six, a year older than Jessica. She had four children, two boys and two girls. Her oldest daughter, Monica, was already the mother of a fifteen-month-old son. Like Mary Grace, she had married at seventeen and given birth within the year.

"Why was it so much easier to see her mistakes than my own?" Mary Grace wrote in her annual Christmas card to Jessica, who was in Los Angeles at the time.

She complained that her son-in-law had wood chips for brains, her teenage boys ate up the store's profits, and her husband, Bob, should be known as "the father of unfinished projects." But, having spent the last twenty years spying on happy families, her nose pressed against the plate glass, Jessica envied her.

"Your hair looks terrific," she said softly.

"Thanks. I keep finding little bits that stick out." Mary Grace wet her finger and plastered down the edges, seeing wayward strands where Jessica saw none. As if she'd been reading Jessica's mind, she said, "You know what you need, kiddo? You need a husband."

Jessica laughed. "Is Bob going to become available?"

Mary Grace eyed her from under lowered lashes. "How about Pete Johnson?"

Jessica shrugged. She had known Pete since first grade, and now they socialized with many of the same people, including Bob and Mary Grace. When the four of them drank beer and shot pool at Rudy's Tavern on Friday nights, Pete made her laugh.

"He's an incredible father," Mary Grace said.

"Ye-es," she agreed. She knew he shared custody of ten-year-old Emily with his ex-wife, Darla, and she admired his devotion to his daughter.

"What's wrong with him?"

"Nothing."

She tried to think what *was* wrong with Pete. He began pursuing her a few months after she'd moved back, and although she'd tried not to string him along, he was amazingly persistent. Tall and bear-shouldered, he was handsome by most women's standards. He was good-natured, kind to old folks and animals, and a hard worker. He was even halfway decent to Darla, a benefit in a town where former spouses might fight for the same parking spot at the Thrifty Market.

Jessica sighed. "I'd like to be in love with him, but I'm not."

Mary Grace gave a little sniff. "Your problem with Pete is that he's too easy. You want a challenge. I know your type."

Jessica opened her mouth to point out that Pete was a little too handsome, a bit too flirtatious—he should have BAD RISK stamped on his forehead—but then, he *was* one of Bob's friends. "Since when do I have to marry any nice guy who comes along just because he likes me?"

"Not good enough for you, huh?"

"Give me a break. Pete, the logger, not good enough for Jessica, the window washer?"

Mary Grace looked at her sideways. "He's not a college grad. He didn't come from a family with several hundred acres of prime timberland and a sawmill."

"My mother's property," Jessica said stiffly, "not mine."

"Yeah, but it will be someday. Besides, everybody's influenced by their families, don't you think? We pick up ideas about who we should date or marry through our skin, like . . . what was that word we learned in biology?"

"Osmosis."

"Yeah, that's it."

Jessica wondered when she had become a snob. If she had never left Misp, she might have thought Pete was the hottest catch in town. By L.A. standards, he was provincial. It had been a trade-off coming back to a place where basketball games and fly-fishing were high culture.

Mary Grace walked to a nearby display and patted a stack of I LOVE OPRAH T-shirts into place. "Now, you and Callum Luke . . ."

"He's nice, but we didn't connect."

Mary Grace blinked. "Who? You and Callum?"

"No, Pete and I."

"He said you connected for twelve dates before you suddenly lost interest."

"Not that many."

"He counted."

5

By the time Jessica returned home, the sun had slid well below the horizon. At the door, she kicked off her tennis shoes and peeled off her grimy socks, then padded into the dark kitchen. The signal on the answering machine flashed crimson. She had hooked the device to the kitchen phone so she'd be more likely to see its winking light, but the endless messages made her want to shove it into a drawer.

She glanced out the window toward the squares of bright light next door. Morrie Toobert, wearing his sleeveless Farmer John T-shirt, stood hunched over the sink, scrubbing out a soup kettle with a long-handled brush. Morrie and Ada had raised five children, and as far as Jessica could tell, Morrie did most of the cooking and cleaning. His belly drooped into the soapsuds. His face glowed red from the steamy water. His hair was the color and texture of cigar ash, and the longer Jessica stared at him the more he began to look like his grizzled dog Buster.

Ada, a pinched, gray-haired woman who was an inch or so taller than her husband, strolled up behind him and leaned forward so that her lips touched his temple just north of his bristly sideburns. She smiled and said a few words in his ear, and Jessica could almost hear her high-pitched, girlish voice. Morrie turned and pressed a passionate kiss square on her mouth. When Ada withdrew, her cheeks were flushed pink with ardor.

Jessica backed a few guilty steps from the window. What she had witnessed was clearly pure, comfortable, wholehearted love, and for the second time that day she felt a spasm of envy.

She turned away and punched the play button on the recorder.

The first five messages were from Misp and Big River business owners who wanted to hire her services. Then came a long pause, followed by Jonah's hesitant voice. "Guess you're not home." Click.

He didn't say anything about the fire, the sheriff, or Lila. The call sounded like the usual sort, his need for reassurance—and that she could provide. She would call him back after she ate dinner.

She shuffled across the linoleum, enjoying its coolness on her tired feet, and opened the refrigerator door. Not much there, but she could turn out a basic salad with the remainder of week-old lettuce, a handful of baby carrots, and the inch of homemade red wine vinaigrette in the mason jar. At the sink, she rinsed the limp greens and shook the water from them.

The next message said, "I guess you're still not there."

She took a clean, white crockery bowl from the dish drainer, tore the lettuce into chunks, and dropped them in. His third, fourth, and fifth messages were identical, except that Jessica could hear the increasing panic in his voice.

She tried to remember if there had ever been a time when he wasn't afraid, and she wondered if it was his transparent fear that invited bullying. She'd seen dogs pursue him, smelling his terror. It was as though he wore a neon sign around his neck that flashed VICTIM.

She remembered one incident when he was in third grade. They were riding home on the school bus when skinny little Wendell Schultz swaggered down the aisle, his backpack banging against the metal seat frame.

Laughing, he nudged his buddies and pressed his fingertips to

Jonah's head. After they left the bus, Jessica noticed a fat wad of pink gum stuck to her brother's blond curls. With clenched teeth, she took him home and snipped it out.

"You shouldn't have let him get away with that," she grumbled. "You should have screamed or kicked him."

She realized now he didn't understand what had happened.

The next week, Wendell, wielding a plastic squirt gun filled with pee, shot Jonah in the eye. Jessica hadn't been there at the time, but the evidence drizzled onto Jonah's white shirt and dried in a long yellow streak. When he came home, he looked scared and flustered, but he didn't seem angry.

She had been furious. "You're as big as Wendell Schultz. Why don't you beat him up?"

When he didn't answer, she snapped, "I don't know how you can be such a coward."

Just last week, she saw Wendell leaving the Cock's Crow, a seedy bar with a chipped plaster rooster over the door. He was a volunteer fireman and a logger now. Flanked by two buddies sporting stubbled haircuts identical to his, he tripped over the uneven sidewalk, belching and laughing. She wondered how he could be so cheerful when he'd been fired recently from Thunder Lake Timber, her mother's mill. She heard he'd been late for work once too often.

When he saw Jessica, he bristled. She smiled and waved. He glared at her for a moment, turned, and strode away. She felt a small measure of satisfaction.

Jessica took a paring knife from the kitchen drawer, diced the carrots, and tossed them into the salad. She rinsed her hands and dried them on a blue, lint-free, window-washing cloth that doubled as a dish towel. She picked up the bowl to carry it to the table, then set it down again. Until she talked to Jonah, she wouldn't be able to eat.

As she reached for the phone, she heard a *clunk* outside, the sound of something hitting the foundation. If she had lived on a slope, she would have thought a rock had rolled downhill and smacked against the house, but her property was level. She walked to the back door and listened. When she heard another *clunk,* this one fainter, she flipped on the porch light and opened the door. The sky was dark and overcast. The air smelled of freshly cut wood.

She squinted into the shadows. "Hello?"

A burly form moved into the light. "Thought I'd be able to sneak in and out of here without your seeing me."

"Pete, what are you doing?" She stepped onto the porch, its damp concrete chilling her bare feet.

"Well, I intended to surprise you."

In the dim light, she could see he was still wearing his logger's uniform: rugged jeans with the leg hems crudely chopped off to avoid snagging them on branches, a heavy pin-striped "hickory" shirt, and wide red suspenders. She took a few steps toward him and realized he stood next to an orderly pile of split logs cut into fireplace lengths and stacked in crisscross fashion under the roof overhang.

Jessica stared at him in surprise. "Do I need to say you shouldn't have?"

He grinned and brushed some sawdust and wood chips off his shirt. A sheaf of blond hair fell onto his forehead. "Last time I was here I noticed you'd used up your winter stash. Can't wait until fall, you know. Green wood won't burn."

Jessica walked over and took a closer look at the logs.

"Maple," Pete said.

She smiled. "I see. I just can't believe you stacked a half cord before I heard you." She looked toward the rear of her property and realized he'd parked his huge red Dodge diesel truck in the alley. "I can't believe I didn't hear that thing rumbling a block away."

He laughed. "The Hulk and I drove up before you got home." He wiped his hands on his jeans. "What say I finish up and we go down to Rudy's for a beer?"

Jessica looked back toward the kitchen. "Oh, I don't know,

Pete. I'm really tired. I was just going to have a salad and fall into bed."

She had slept with him twice, and while the experiences were pleasant enough, she knew she would never marry him. Wondering what he saw in her, she decided she was probably the only single woman in town who had ever turned him down.

He glanced at his watch. "It's early. We can get a couple of burgers at Rudy's."

He was making it difficult for her to refuse, and she wondered why she should. "Just for a quick supper, nothing more."

He grinned. "Only a burger and a beer."

She thought of Callum, standing at the halfway house, looking competent and professional in his business suit—a man who had his life completely in order. She smiled at Pete. "Okay, but *I'm* buying."

He managed to frown and smile at the same time. "That's right. You're one of those feminists, aren't you?"

"Of course."

"Fine with me. We'll arm-wrestle for it."

Jessica heard the phone ringing. "Let me grab that first, and I'll come out to the truck in a minute."

His eyes glinted with amusement. "You might want to put something on your feet. You know Rudy—no shoes, no service."

Thinking of the sweat-rank loggers and brackish commercial fishermen who frequented the tavern, she laughed at the notion that Rudy would turn away a barefoot window washer.

By the time she reached the phone, the answering machine had kicked in, but she could hear Jonah's adrenaline-charged voice leaving another message. She picked up the receiver and said, "Just a second."

"Jessie?"

"Hold on, while I turn this off." She pushed the stop button on the recorder so that it wouldn't tape the conversation. "Okay now, what's wrong?"

"I still can't find General Bragg."

"Who?"

"General Braxton Bragg. I've looked everywhere."

Jessica gave a long sigh. "He'll turn up." She glanced at the back door, then lowered her voice. "Jonah, did you get rid of the shoelaces?"

"I don't know where he is."

With the phone cradled on her shoulder, she tore off a length of plastic wrap and stretched it over the salad bowl. "You probably left him in Homer's car. Did you get rid of the shoelaces?"

"I didn't have him in Homer's car."

"Did you check your pockets?" She rinsed off the paring knife and dried it. "He's probably nestled right alongside Lieutenant General Forrest."

There was a long silence. Then Jonah's shocked voice came across the phone line. "I wouldn't do that, Jessie. He doesn't get along with Lieutenant General Forrest. Bragg robbed Forrest of his command after the Battle of Shiloh. I'd never put them in the same pocket together."

Jessica held the paring knife poised above the cutlery drawer. Good God, what had he just said?

"Jonah?"

"Yeah?"

"Do you ever hear voices?" As far as she knew, that was not a symptom of Asperger's syndrome, but maybe she had misdiagnosed him.

"Voices?"

"You know, like General Bragg and Lieutenant General Forrest talking to each other, maybe discussing the Civil War?"

"No-o."

To her relief, he sounded offended.

She laid the knife in the drawer, reached for a paper towel, and wiped the perspiration from her upper lip. "Well, of course you wouldn't. I was only joking." She tossed the crumpled towel in the wastebasket. "I'll stop by the house tomorrow, and we can look for General Bragg."

"Will you come early tomorrow?"

"First thing. How about eight o'clock?"

"All right," he said, and she could hear the relief in his voice.

She hung up the phone, thinking that one of Rudy's juicy, quarter-pound burgers and a bottle of Pyramid wheaten ale were looking better all the time.

RUDY'S TAVERN WAS an old converted house just down the road from the Misp Mall. Pete was telling Jessica about the upcoming Orphan Car Show in Forks, but she could barely hear him over the song on the jukebox and the blare of the television behind the bar.

"Doesn't make any difference if the car runs or not," Pete said as they passed a pool table. Wendell Schultz and Dewey Tyrrell looked up from their game and gave Pete sly, knowing smiles. Grinning, he slid his arm around Jessica's shoulders.

He guided her toward the slightly quieter back room, and they eased into a booth under a lighted Heineken windmill that hung from a heavy wooden beam. A Rainier beer sign flashed on a nearby wall. Linda, the barmaid, didn't bother to ask what they wanted. She brought them their usual brands of beer—the Pyramid for Jessica and a Pabst Blue Ribbon for Pete. Linda had won the coveted Grizzled Loggers Association Award for her phenomenal memory as well as for exceptional service.

The hamburgers and fries came in webbed plastic baskets with paper liners and condiments on the side. Pete piled on the pickles, onion, and mustard, creating a sandwich the thickness of a brick. "One end of your house is six inches lower than the other," he shouted between munches. "Did you ever consider doing something about that?"

Jessica thought of the two-bedroom wood-frame bungalow she'd bought with money from her divorce settlement. The house had been built in 1926, and the moment she'd walked into it, she had immediately liked it. It had high, airy ceilings with crown molding and a sunny kitchen, oversized by modern standards. Later, when she painted the living room, she peeled off five layers of decorative paper on the walls, a testament to its history.

The home had been well maintained, but she knew it had its problems. If she laid a marble on the living room floor, it rolled into the kitchen. But she'd come to think of the slope as part of its charm—a settling into the earth from millions of footsteps softly pummeling the hardwood floors.

Pete slopped a little ketchup on his fries. "You know, I could get a couple of guys, and we could jack up those floor joists on the low end, slip in some six-by-sixes, and level that sucker out." He shoved a hefty, red-coated potato into his mouth. "Do it in a weekend, easy."

"But I like it, Pete," she yelled over the quick beat of "Brown-Eyed Girl."

He swabbed his mouth with a wad of paper napkins. "Good, I'll take care of it then."

"Oh, no," she said, realizing he'd misunderstood. "I like it the way it is—the sagging foundation, I mean. I appreciate the offer, though."

He looked disappointed. "You don't mind that your house leans like the Tower of Pizza?" he shouted back.

"Pisa," she said automatically, and then could have kicked herself for correcting him.

He pushed the ketchup bottle aside. "Yeah, whatever." He gave her a puzzled glance. "Why would you like it that way?"

"Because I think of all the feet tramping through that place in the last seventy-some years—little kids, old people, dogs and cats—and sometimes I feel as though they're still there, keeping me company and . . ." She looked at him and realized he didn't get it. She smiled. "Honest, Pete, I don't even mind that I have to shove folded cardboard under some of the table legs."

He shook his head in amazement. "Well, let me know if you change your mind."

The song on the jukebox stopped. Linda passed by, and Pete ordered another round of beers. A few minutes later, Jessica heard Wendell say, "Give me those, Linda. I'll take them over." She turned in time to see Linda shrug and hand him the bottles.

Wendell, a small, wiry man with a brown goatee to offset his stubbled head, strode toward them. He set the fresh beers on their table and nudged Pete's shoulder with his elbow. "Hiding out, huh?"

"Nah, grab a chair," Pete said.

Wendell ignored the suggestion and scooted into the U-shaped booth next to Jessica. Dewey, who had lagged behind, came with two more Pabst Blue Ribbons and a bowl of peanuts. He set them down, spun one of the nearby chrome diner chairs around, and straddled it. Jessica didn't know Dewey as well as she knew the others. Short and beefy, he had moved to the Olympic Peninsula a few years before with his girlfriend and their two-year-old son.

Wendell turned to Jessica with narrowed eyes. "How's your mother?"

She smiled coolly. "Fine, as far as I know."

Wendell took a swig of beer and set down the bottle with a thump. "So, what did you think of the fire, Pete?" His cheerful expression told Jessica what he thought.

Pete shrugged. "Took care of the problem for us, didn't it? What does your old man say?"

His grin broadened. "Said it couldn't have happened to a nicer bunch of guys." He snagged one of the peanuts, cracked open the shell, and popped it into his mouth.

She stared at Wendell, then shook her head in disbelief. "Aren't you interested in finding out who *set* the fire?"

"Heard it was your brother."

Jessica felt her face heat up. "Well, it's not true. Jonah doesn't have that kind of meanness in him. I would be careful if I were you, Wendell. Next thing, people will be saying you did it."

He gave her a cold look.

Pete pushed his empty plastic basket aside and, leaning against the back of the booth, belched softly. "The truth doesn't really matter here."

Jessica lifted her eyebrows. "Doesn't matter? Three men die in a fire, and you say the truth doesn't matter?"

"They were criminals," he said flatly.

"They had served their sentences."

"Even so, they shouldn't have been sent here in the first place. They were idiots to stay where they weren't wanted. So, they get burned out. Where's the surprise in that?"

"I doubt they were given a choice, Pete. Even if they were, it's not a crime to be stupid. But it *is* against the law to set fire to a house and kill three men who are minding their own business." She crumpled her paper napkin and dropped it on top of her half-eaten hamburger. "Look, I can understand why people don't want a halfway house in their neighborhood, but what are you supposed to do with these people coming out of prison, just throw them directly back into the community? That would be worse."

Pete frowned. "I don't care where they go as long as they don't come here. Maybe this fire will send losers like them a message."

"For God's sake, you can't murder people because you don't like them."

His blue eyes looked dark in the tavern's dim light. "So, you think we should wait until they do something to us first?"

"No, I didn't say that, but—"

"Someone did us a favor burning that place down."

Dewey was quietly chugging his beer and looking increasingly more uncomfortable.

The lopsided curl in Wendell's upper lip deepened. "I told the old man not to look too hard for the guy who set this one."

Jessica swiveled toward him. "How do you know it was one person?"

The smirk disappeared. "How do you know it wasn't your brother?"

She hoped her glare was answer enough. Inside though, she still felt uneasy.

During their awkward standoff, Dewey pushed himself back from the table and stretched lazily. "Think I'll head on home. Got to be up at four in the morning."

Jessica nudged Pete. "I have to get up early too. Let's go, okay?"

He nodded. Although it meant taking the long way out of the booth, she scooted in his direction, away from Wendell.

6

Driving toward her mother's house the next morning, Jessica thought about how Jonah had looked when she talked to him in Homer's car. His soft blue eyes were troubled and evasive, his boyish chin all atremble. Something was wrong.

But then, of course it was wrong. Bud Schultz had threatened to put him in a prison cell crawling with rats. That would unnerve anyone, especially somebody naive and innocent enough to believe him. And Jonah was. He'd never left Misp. Even now, he rarely left his Civil War world.

Winding her way along Thunder River Road, she passed some ramshackle rental houses, where itinerant workers paid too much for too little shelter, and a small shake-and-shingle mill with black smoke rising from its chimney. The brush along the shoulder was still slick with dew. The morning light broke through a crack in the clouds and aimed itself straight at her eyes. She would have missed the narrow private road that led to the mill and her mother's home if an unloaded logging truck hadn't been nosing its way onto the highway. She waited for it to pull out, then made the sharp turn.

The gravel road split, and Jessica took the left branch of the Y, threaded the van between a row of towering salal shrubs, and pulled into a parking area edged by cedar logs and unruly rhododendrons.

There was no sidewalk leading to the fifteen-room house her grandfather had built in 1922. The lack of one seemed to Jessica another example of Moran stubbornness and egoism. A visitor could either slog through the waterlogged grass like the family did or he could stay home. The house itself, constructed with hand-sawn massive timbers and split cedar logs, had settled through the years into a disorderly nest of red-leafed photinia, unpruned hydrangeas, and runaway ivy. A covered porch sprawled across the front, wound around a corner, and stretched halfway down one side. The exterior cedar was weathered to dusky gray. The gutters, window frames, and doors were painted pomegranate red. While her dad was alive, the trim was forest green.

To the west, a ridge of ramrod-straight conifers topped a gently sloping hillside laced with sword ferns and blackberry vines. A few miles beyond the ridge, the land dropped precipitously to the long, blue-gray swoop of the Pacific Ocean. To the east of the Moran home, on the other side of the narrow but dense stand of ancient western red cedars, was the sawmill. Jessica couldn't see it, but as she stepped from the van, she heard the grind and squeal of trucks and machinery and she breathed in the perfume of freshly cut wood.

The gaps in the clouds had closed, returning the sky to its familiar gray. Although there was no illumination behind any of the house's paneled, leaded-glass windows, a plume of smoke rose from the chimney. She tramped across the grass, her shoes sinking in a half inch.

She tried to time her visits when she thought her mother would be at the mill. Lila still worked six days a week, occasionally seven. Jonah would likely be alone, deep in the cellar recesses where he staged his Civil War battles. She knew the front door would be unlocked, but she knocked anyway. It was no longer her home. When no one answered, she walked in.

As she passed through the cedar-paneled foyer with its antique brass chandelier and photographs on the walls, memories revisited her like ghosts, some friendly, a few fairly disturbing. She stopped to look at a picture of her father standing on the stump of the first tree he'd felled. He couldn't have been older than nine or ten when it was taken.

She was nine when she started going with him into the woods. The other loggers teased her and said she looked like a pint-sized version of him in her dirt-stained jeans, frayed shirt, billed cap, and wide suspenders. She watched him fell tree after tree, studying each one carefully, looking for rot and unhealthy branches, gauging its twist and lean before bringing it down.

"Hey, little darling, see this old man here?" he'd said once, patting a western red cedar that was as tall as a fifteen-story building and as wide as the bumper on a Volkswagen Bug. Then, he strode away from it, set an upended empty coffee can on the ground about fifty feet from the base of the cedar. "I'm going to lay this big fella right on this spot."

He hoisted his buzzing chain saw to slice it twice, undercutting the side facing the direction he wanted it to fall and backcutting the opposite side, spraying out a cloud of sawdust. After several cuts, the cedar creaked, groaned, and leaned, releasing its rich, aromatic sap. It splintered and popped, then swayed and snapped off at the base, hitting the ground with a boom that reverberated through the forest. Bark, cones, lichen, and soil spewed into the air. He had brought it down so neatly it struck the coffee can dead-on, the can's sharp metal rim carving a thin circle in the dirt. The trunk mashed the can flat.

Jessica never failed to be impressed with her dad's skill—and saddened and awed by the fallen tree's grandeur. The cedar that had lived for centuries, that had taken all those years to grow, toppled within twenty minutes.

After watching her father for two summers, Jessica coaxed him to let her take down a tree. Her first was a Douglas fir with a diameter no bigger than that of a large pizza. He helped her steady the nineteen-pound chain saw while it bucked and chewed through the wood. It was a stubborn tree, gnarled a few inches in where lightning had struck it, but she managed to level it. After that the loggers' teasing held respect as well as affection.

Dad said if she kept it up, he was going to have to put her on the payroll. She grinned so hard her mouth hurt.

But after he drowned, she never went out with the loggers again.

Jessica wandered into the living room, which hadn't changed much through the years. The high beams retained their original deep bronze, a shade not all that dissimilar to her hair. The room had the same massive overstuffed sofa and chairs from her childhood. They were threadbare now, but like well-raised children they blended into her mother's spartan brand of interior design.

She wound through the dining room, past the maple table that could seat twenty-four people, remembering the times she and Dad had dragged the chairs into the living room on Sunday mornings and draped old blankets over them. The result was more a dark tunnel than a tent, requiring them to crawl into it on their hands and knees. Once inside, she ate her breakfast of Cheerios while Dad read the Sunday *Tribune* by flashlight.

She walked into the intensely silent kitchen, which still smelled of her mother's habitual breakfast of bacon, eggs, and boiled coffee. She could never step into this room without thinking of the bitter argument they'd had here the day Lila sent her away.

The basement door was open, with only a single bulb illuminating the steep stairs.

She poked her head into the stairwell. "Jonah?"

"Hi, Jessie." His voice echoed against the cellar's stone walls.

She found him in the furnace room, sharing the space with canning jars, bins of apples and potatoes, an old earthenware pickle crock, and a cracked porcelain laundry tub. He was huddled over his miniature battlefield, a four-by-eight-foot painted plywood board mounted on two sawhorses. Green clay lumps represented grassy hills. Lakes and ponds were smooth foil. Thin silver ribbons of water cut across a crumpled landscape where hundreds of tiny blue-and-gray-clad soldiers skirmished between stands of toothpick-sized trees. Cannons puffed wisps of cotton smoke.

He smiled eagerly. "Can we look for General Bragg now?"

"Sure." She sat on the edge of a three-legged stool and picked up one of the Lilliputian soldiers on the board. "Shiloh?"

He shook his head. "Bowling Green."

"Oh, yes, I'd forgotten." She returned the miniature to the display. "So, how is General Bragg different from the rest of these guys? And don't tell me he has a beard, because it looks like half of these fellows did."

Jonah scratched his forehead thoughtfully. "Well, he's in a Confederate uniform and he's on horseback."

She sighed, thinking that description wouldn't help much either. She glanced at the dozen or so carefully labeled plastic margarine containers that lined the metal shelf behind him. "Have you looked through everything here?"

He nodded.

She knew that he kept the objects of his obsession methodically and tidy, but two floors above them his bedroom looked as if it had been hit by a tsunami. "So what about upstairs?"

"I've searched the whole house."

"Jonah, are you saying it's outside somewhere?"

He avoided her gaze. "It's between here and town. I always walk the same way."

"When did you lose it?"

"Two days before the fire."

"Two days before the fire," she repeated slowly. Then she smacked the heel of her hand against her forehead. "Of course. That makes sense." Her shoulders went slack with relief. "That's why you were crawling in the grass near the halfway house, wasn't it?"

He gave her a blank look.

"The Meckler sisters said they saw you sneaking around the halfway house the evening of the fire. But you were just looking for General Bragg, weren't you?"

He nodded. "I thought maybe I dropped him there."

He picked up one of the cannons on the board and moved it over the silver river, still averting his eyes. "Gaze avoidance," the Asperger's material called this behavior. Nothing unusual about it. He'd always had trouble looking directly at people when they spoke to him.

Jessica considered his remark for a moment. His route to town was a good three miles. "But why the halfway house, Jonah? I mean, you could have dropped it anywhere along the way."

He bent closer to the board. "I wish I could have been General Nathan Bedford Forrest. He was a great military officer."

She eased herself onto a rickety wooden stool near him. "Did you ever talk with the men who lived in that house?"

He stared up at the single bare light bulb dangling from the rafters. "When the battle started, there were about twenty-five thousand Confederates in and around Bowling Green—and thousands more Federals."

"Jonah, answer me. Did you ever talk to those men?"

He shook his head emphatically, then ran his finger between two rivers on the board. "This is where Johnston made his mistake, first at Fort Henry and then at Fort Donelson. He lost fifteen thousand men."

Jessica picked up a Union soldier who looked to be either dead or sleeping. His hand clutched a musket that was nearly as long as he was. "Jonah, did you ever go into that house?"

"No," he said in a low voice.

"Did you throw rocks at their windows?"

He shook his head.

She blew out a long breath. "Then, for God's sake, why did you tell the sheriff you did?"

His eyes flickered in confusion. "Because Bud Schultz was going to put me in jail?"

She knew he was trying to guess the answer she wanted, and that thought only frightened her more.

Usually he was the one asking questions: Why was Mom mad at him? Why did the kids on the school playground stare at him when he walked by? Why did Donna Kittle, the clerk at the Thrifty Market, call him a nasty name when he dropped the jar of pickles? Jessica tried to answer his questions, explaining at length why other people reacted as they did—because she realized he had no clue.

Shortly after she'd moved back to Misp, she took him to Jelly's Diner for breakfast and spent three hours telling him about Asperger's syndrome. She slid the stack of information she'd photocopied across the booth's varnished tabletop.

He read the first two pages, then looked up.

"So what do you think, Jonah?"

His expression didn't show any emotion, but he laid his hands palms down on the table in what seemed to her a gesture of resignation. "I guess it's what I have."

She leaned forward. "But how does that make you feel?"

The pain filled his eyes. "Relieved. It makes me feel relieved because I didn't know before why people teased me or called me names or got mad at me."

"You had no idea?"

He shook his head.

"Does Lila still get angry with you?" she asked.

"Sometimes."

"Do you know why?"

He nodded. "She told me last week. She has a weak-kneed son and a bullheaded daughter."

Jessica briefly closed her eyes. "Oh, Jonah."

"She got mad at me yesterday too."

"What were you doing?"

"Slicing an apple on the kitchen counter."

"With a paring knife?"

He nodded.

"Did you put cuts in the Formica?"

"I don't know. I guess I did."

"Well, what did she say?"

"She said, 'Don't do that.' I thought I wasn't supposed to eat the apple," he said, looking embarrassed. "I threw it away because I didn't want her to yell at me. But then she really got mad."

Jessica slumped against the back of the booth. She realized he had misread Lila—and not for the first time. Wondering how she could possibly repair twenty-eight years of damage, she felt defeated almost before she had begun.

That morning at Jelly's Diner, she didn't talk to him about their father's death. She told herself he had enough to absorb for one day, that eventually they would discuss it.

She scooted off the three-legged stool in the cellar, bent down, and picked up a miniature supply wagon that had toppled onto the floor. As she set it back on the battlefield board, she thought of a scolding she'd given Jonah once when he wanted to talk about the drowning.

While Lila worked at the mill after their father's death, Jessica looked after Jonah. Lila said the business was a disorganized mess. Jessica didn't mind her absence but hated the implication that Dad had been a poor manager.

She and Jonah roamed the woods around Misp that summer, not going anywhere in particular but always moving to remind herself she was still alive. She talked Jonah into hiking the logging roads with her and, when the wild blackberries came into season, they picked plastic milk jugs full of them. Although he had trouble keeping his attention on the berries, he managed to stuff enough in his mouth to turn his tongue and lips purple.

When he complained he was thirsty, she would locate a fast-moving mountain stream that cascaded off a rock cliff. She told him to lean forward and catch the spray in his mouth, but he didn't like to drink water that way. As though he'd forgotten they'd had the same conversation the day before, he complained, "Mom says if we drink from the creek, we're going to get jarda."

"Giardia. It's a parasite."

"Yeah, Mom says it could kill us."

After a while, Jessica stopped answering, but on one occasion, tired of the repetition, she kicked a rock with her foot and snapped, "Mom doesn't know everything, Jonah. This water hasn't hurt us yet."

"Water killed Dad."

"That was different."

He eyed the rushing stream. "Looks the same to me. It's scary. Even Mom says so now."

She huffed in exasperation. "That's why you have to swim, Jonah. Water's okay if you know how to swim."

They made their way along the slope, loosening rocks and dirt that skittered downhill. She tripped on a root and, graceless as a broken branch, hit the ground sprawling. Grabbing hold of a leafless bush, she righted herself.

He staggered after her. "But Dad knew how to swim, Jessie."

She whirled around. "For Pete's sake, shut up. Don't say another word. It's over and done with, and there's nothing anybody can do about it now. So . . . just . . . forget . . . it!"

He cried then, and she had to comfort him, guiltily pulling him into a hug and telling him he could talk all he wanted, but not about their father's death.

He probably still didn't know why he'd drowned. That was just one more occasion when she had failed him. She realized they had all failed him, even their father. In his infinite patience and kindness, he had tried to protect Jonah, always excusing him and telling him he would outgrow his problems.

But he hadn't. Now, with this arson fire, he was acting more peculiar than usual, and she worried he was regressing. Or, worse yet, concealing.

She watched him push a cannon between two sections of a stone fence, accompanied by a quiet little *boom-boom* under his breath.

"Jonah?" she said.

"Yeah?" He didn't meet her gaze.

She rose from the stool, walked over to him, and cupped his face in her hands. "I know in my heart that you would never really do anything to hurt someone else, but I'd feel better—I'd feel so much better if you'd look right at me and say, 'I didn't set that fire.' Could you please do that? Just say those words."

He lifted his head and with a stubborn set to his jaw repeated, "I didn't set that fire."

She felt the welcome release in her chest. Smiling, she wrapped her arms around his narrow shoulders and gave him a quick, joyful hug. "Do you realize how happy that makes me?"

"No," he said.

She sighed. His answer would have been funny if he hadn't meant it.

As soon as she freed him, he turned back to his plywood board and intently studied the layout. "Next time I'm going to do the Battle at Brice's Crossroads."

JESSICA LEFT HIM in the cellar with his soldiers. When she stepped onto the wide, covered front porch, she saw Lila walking toward her across the mucky grass. Her mother stopped and gave her a hard, unsmiling look.

Jessica leaned against the rough cedar porch column. "I think I'm entitled to visit him once in a while."

Lila thrust her hands in her blue jeans pockets. "Never said you weren't. But I don't want you telling him things that get him all upset."

"Like what?"

"Like he's got a disease that makes him act crazy."

Jessica frowned. "I never told him that."

"You told him he's got that . . . what's it called?"

"Asperger's syndrome. It's a neurological disorder, not a disease. He was born with it." She wanted to add, "Like some children are born with Down's syndrome," but she was certain Lila would resist that comparison.

"Well, it's one thing to tell me about this syndrome business, but be careful what you tell him. You know he takes everything at face value."

"I'm careful."

"So, what's the cure for this thing?"

"There isn't one, but—"

"Well, that's just great." Lila gave a sniff of disgust. "You slap some label on him and make him feel bad about himself, but he can't do a thing about it. What good does that do?"

Jessica suppressed the urge to point out that if anyone made him feel bad about himself, she did. Instead, she said, "He can learn to change the way he thinks and acts."

Lila stared at some gray clouds scudding along the treetops. "He's fine the way he is."

"I never said he wasn't, but he could be happier. He could learn to work with people. He could have a decent job and friends. He could even get married. It's not that he isn't capable of all that. He just needs to be taught things that come naturally to most other people."

Lila gave her a quick, skeptical glance.

"Look," Jessica said, "whenever somebody bashes a row of mailboxes, breaks a window, or sets fire to a house, Jonah doesn't have to be the first person they go after. He can be taught to understand what's going on and react better."

"You think I haven't tried all these years to make a man of him?"

Jessica shook her head in resignation. She'd have a better chance of changing Jonah than her mother. Jessica walked down the porch steps toward the graveled area where her van was parked.

"Before you leave, there's something else—" Lila said.

Jessica stopped and looked at her.

Lila's mouth suddenly drew taut as a rubber band. "Callum Luke is in town."

Didn't take long for that news to make the circuit, Jessica thought.

"So I heard," she said.

"He's in charge of that fire investigation." Lila stared shrewdly at her. "But you already knew that, didn't you?"

Jessica nodded, wondering what it was about her face that so easily revealed her thoughts.

"Have you talked to him?"

"We exchanged a few words."

Lila studied the sky again. The incoming clouds resembled balls of crumpled black paper. "Do I need to remind you we had an agreement about . . . about the child?"

"She's not a child anymore, and I never agreed to anything."

Lila's gaze swung sharply back to Jessica. "It was understood we would forget it ever happened."

"That was a unilateral declaration on your part."

"You made the decision to give her up."

"I did what I thought was right at the time. Now I regret it."

"I didn't pressure you into it."

"I'm not saying you did." No sense pointing out that she hadn't given her any support either. She hesitated, knowing her next announcement would have the effect of a grenade. "You might as well know I'm trying to find her."

Lila's eyes went wide. For several seconds, she didn't say a word, but her anger was brightly apparent on her face. "You can't do that," she said finally, in disbelief.

The lack of a violent explosion gave Jessica courage. "Happens all the time."

"And you think her adoptive parents will allow it?"

"She's almost eighteen. When she reaches that age, she can search for me through the national adoption registries, with or without their permission. I've already signed up."

"Don't you even think about her coming here to visit." Lila's voice shook with anger.

"That would be up to her. Doesn't it bother you that almost eighteen years have passed and you've never seen her?"

Lila didn't answer.

"I have a daughter," Jessica whispered. "You have a granddaughter, and we've never had the chance to enjoy her."

"It's a little late now," Lila said crisply.

"Not for me." Jessica hunched her shoulders and walked past her toward the van.

allum Luke surveyed the men assembled in the fire station office: Sheriff Milt Tarr, Fire Chief Bud Schultz, Rob Villalobos from the state fire marshal's office, and eight volunteers from the Misp Fire Department. He knew Wendell Schultz and Pete Johnson from high school. They sat slouched in the second row of folding metal chairs, sipping coffee from paper cups and talking in low voices.

Callum leaned against the edge of a heavy wood table cluttered with bulging manila folders and a laptop computer. He flipped over a page on his notebook and cleared his throat. "Listen up. I want to talk about what we have so far."

The men ended their conversations and turned toward him. Wendell and Pete were the last to shift their attention. It seemed to Callum, not for the first time, they were sending the message they didn't have to defer to him. High school all over again, he thought.

He picked up a stack of firefighter observation reports. "Wendell, I don't have your report here. Did you turn it in to someone else?"

Clasping his hands behind his head, Wendell sat back in his chair. "Didn't do one."

Callum frowned. "Why not?"

"Nothing to tell. I got the call, drove to the station, and went out on the fire truck with the rest of the guys. That's it."

Callum circled Wendell's name in his notes and wrote "Missing" beside it. He had made clear the importance of the reports in their first meeting. But Wendell was classic passive-aggressive, Callum thought. No need to challenge the chief investigator outright. Just ignore his instructions.

"What color was the smoke when you got there, Wendell?"

Wendell casually turned to Pete. "What color was it?"

"No, I'm asking you," Callum said. "I already have his report."

"Didn't pay any attention to the smoke." Again, he glanced at Pete, who grinned back. Wendell laughed. "Too busy putting out the fire."

Callum didn't smile. "As I mentioned in our first meeting, the color of the smoke helps us identify the fuel source. What was the survivor wearing when he jumped from the porch roof to the ground?"

Wendell shrugged.

"Well, was he wearing street clothes or pajamas?"

Wendell shifted uncomfortably in his chair. "This guy isn't the pajama type, if you know what I mean. He had on a T-shirt and undershorts, but I can't see why that matters."

"It matters." He knew he was goading Wendell, and from the pink creeping up the volunteer fireman's neck he was getting the results he wanted. "We get suspicious if it's the middle of the night and the only survivor is fully dressed."

Callum thought of the information in the inch-thick folder on the survivor. Not your usual middle-class family man. No, Dennis Kretz wasn't the type to wear pajamas. Wendell was right about that.

"Don't know why we're going to all this trouble anyway," Wendell muttered. "Everyone knows Jonah Moran set the fire."

Pete nudged him. "Shut up."

"Look," Callum said, "I realize some of this work seems pointless, but a single detail can change the outcome of the investigation. Procedure is critical. We conduct the interviews, gather the evidence, and analyze all of it before we reach *any* conclusions." He knew he was sounding stern and didactic, trying to impress them with his expertise. He had let Wendell under his skin.

Bud Schultz rubbed a hairy-knuckled hand across the top of his bald head. "What's this about some ATF photographer who took pictures of our evidence? Hell, your people wouldn't even let us into the house."

Callum looked past Wendell to address the fire chief. "It wasn't anything personal, Bud. We wanted to preserve the scene as much as possible until she'd shot stills and videos."

Across the room, Sheriff Milt Tarr cleared his throat. "Have we got statements from all the neighbors?"

Callum nodded. "Larry Parks across the street called the fire department, but by then the house was fully involved. There was no explosion that the men might have heard, and the smoke detector didn't go off because someone had removed the battery. The survivor told us one of the other residents took the battery for his radio. He woke up because he heard the fire crackling. The others didn't."

"Did Parks see anyone running from the property or anything unusual?" the sheriff asked.

Callum shook his head. "The other neighbors didn't either. The next-door neighbor, Pearl Hobbs, said her hearing is so bad she slept through the whole thing."

"What about the call from the reservation?"

Callum looked at his notes. "That came ten minutes after Mr. Parks's call. It was placed at the public pay phone just outside the Queets Community Center."

"Seems strange, don't it, someone all the way over on the reservation reporting the fire?" Pete said.

Callum straightened. "I'm talking to tribal residents, seeing what I can find out."

Bud Schultz tugged at his earlobe. "Seems to me somebody else should be doing that—somebody who isn't so tied up with the tribe." He glanced at Callum. "No offense, of course."

Across the room, Milt took off his Buddy Holly specs and rubbed the bridge of his nose with his nicotine-stained fingers. His neck was a dull red. Rob Villalobos, a broad-shouldered man with graying black hair, rolled his eyes as if to say "There's one in every crowd." From what Callum could tell, there was more than one in this bunch.

A caustic reply popped into his head, but he silenced it. After all these years, Bud, Wendell, and Pete shouldn't be able to provoke him with a few jabs. He wasn't a sixteen-year-old reservation kid anymore. He knew humor worked better than anger with most people, so why was he responding exactly as they wanted?

Callum turned to the fire chief with an easy smile. "Tell you what, Bud. You confine all your investigating to the reservation, and I'll take the town and the surrounding area. That way you'll deal strictly with my people, and I'll deal strictly with yours."

A few chuckles erupted around the room.

"Didn't mean you had to go that far," Bud muttered.

Callum looked at his notes. "Tomorrow morning, we've got an arson dog coming in to sniff for accelerants. Then we can start collecting evidence. By Friday, we should be ready to sift through the ashes, so we'll need a full crew. If any of you can't make it, let me know."

There were a few questions, and then the men stood to leave. He watched Pete stride toward the door, pushing back the clump of blond hair that fell across his forehead—Pete, the high school jock who effortlessly collected girls and just as easily jilted them. When his sister Bethany told him Jessica was dating Pete, he'd felt an initial stab of jealousy. But then he decided it was only a nasty rumor. Jessica was smarter than that.

As Pete passed him, Callum said, "Can you be there on Friday?"

Without looking at him, Pete tossed his cup into the wastebasket. The remaining coffee in it splashed through the air, missing Callum's suit trousers by inches.

"Oh, I'll be there," he said, his tone heavy with meaning.

Callum scanned the wet floor. "Well, I don't think we'll be serving coffee."

8

Friday was overcast but dry, allowing Jessica to complete a window-cleaning job for Seacliff Savings and Loan in Big River. Evening brought the familiar drizzle, but by that time she was at home in her living room rereading *The Sun Also Rises* and reminding herself that she preferred Northwest green to southern California brown.

She heard heavy footsteps bounding onto the porch and saw the figure of a man through the filmy nylon curtain on the front door's small window. The knock came a few seconds later.

She opened the door to Pete Johnson straddling a puddle on the porch steps. Under the yellow light, his hair glittered with raindrops. He wore a green-and-white laminated button on his work shirt that proclaimed KILLED ME A TREE TODAY. Over his shoulder, she could see his red truck, the rain sluicing off the cab and draining into the open bed.

He ran his hand across his damp freckled forehead and grinned. "Hope it's not too late to drop by."

She felt caught—obligated to him for the half cord of wood but still annoyed with him for his remarks about the arson. And she ached after her long day of swabbing dirty glass.

As if on cue, the mantel clock chimed eleven.

"I have to clean the Alpine Insurance office tomorrow morning—early." She rubbed her upper arms, hoping he would get the message she was tired.

The eager smile slipped from his face.

She sighed and opened the door wider, wishing she weren't such a chump when it came to other people's feelings. "Well, maybe for a few minutes."

He eased past her and strolled over to the bentwood rocker. Giving it a little push, he smiled boyishly as it creaked back and forth. "When you see what I've brought you, you're going to be glad I stopped by."

She couldn't imagine what he had, but she didn't like the notion of any further obligations. She was considering how she could politely convey to him their relationship had no future when he strode over to the mantel, wiped his hands on his jeans, and picked up a framed photo of Jonah and her. He studied it for a few moments, then set it down. Glancing around, he said, "You don't have much in the way of doodads in this house, do you? My ex is the worst. Give Darla a flat surface and she sticks something on it."

His gaze stopped on the sofa, a leopard-spotted velour aberrance her mother-in-law had given Patrick and her as a wedding gift. It didn't fit with the few antiques she'd managed to acquire, but it came with the divorce settlement. Although it was expensive, she doubted she'd ever find a buyer for it in Misp.

Pete shook his head in puzzlement. "I have to say your taste in furniture isn't a bit like Darla's either."

It seemed pointless to tell him she didn't make enough money to have much taste at all, and she had no intention of explaining how she came to have the sofa. "Pete," she said with as patient a smile as she could muster, "surely you didn't drop by to talk about Darla."

"Hell, no. She's one of those mistakes I'd like to forget." He turned back to the photo and fingered the frame. "Do you suppose this is the same kind of metal they make those miniature military figures out of?"

Jessica stiffened. "Military figures?"

He studied it closer. "Yeah, those little Confederate and Yankee soldiers your brother carries around."

"Pewter," she said.

"Huh?"

"The frame—it's pewter."

He dug something from his pocket and fingered it. Keeping it hidden, he grinned. "Don't you want to see what I've got here?"

She studied him for several seconds, then turned away. "Pete, I don't have time for games. I'm tired, and I still have work to do tonight."

Wearing the same maddening smile, he walked over and took her hand. She felt his warm fingers, thick with calluses, press a piece of metal against her palm. She didn't need to look at it to know he was delivering General Braxton Bragg. She rubbed the miniature between her fingers. It was gritty, not smooth the way it should be, and when she rolled it back onto her palm and examined it, she saw its paint was cracked and blackened. She closed her fingers tightly over the general.

Pete crossed to the sofa, dropped onto it, and slapped his hands together as though he'd just accomplished something important. "Well now, what say we have a beer and relax?" He looked around as if he expected one to materialize on the end table next to him.

"Why did you bring this to me?" she said coolly.

"Belongs to your brother, doesn't it?"

"I don't know."

"How many other guys in town play with those little fellas?"

"That's a question I've never thought about before."

Pete laced his hands behind his head, his elbows jutting straight out. "I picked Jonah up a few months ago when he was hiking along the road in the pouring rain. He had a whole pocketful of them. Sure does get to running off at the mouth about them, doesn't he?"

She didn't answer.

"Hell, I learned more about the Civil War in twenty minutes than I soaked up during a whole semester in old man Troxel's class, and—"

"So you found one of Jonah's miniature soldiers." She tucked General Bragg in her sweatshirt pocket. "Thanks. I'll give it to him the next time I see him."

He cocked his head. "Come on now. Don't you want to know where I found it?"

"Not really."

"I'll bet the sheriff would." The words slid out in a good-old-boy drawl.

"If you want to tell me something, Pete, do it."

He leaned forward. "Don't you get it?" he said softly. "I found it at the fire."

"And what were *you* doing there?"

He smiled amiably. "Bud Schultz and those state and federal arson fellows rounded up some of us to search the place—you know, sift through the ashes and junk."

She looked him over. "You're making too much of this. There's a good explanation why it might have turned up at the halfway house. Jonah doesn't drive. He walks everywhere—you know that. So, he was hiking from Lila's place to town. He cut across their property and accidentally dropped his soldier in the grass. Very simple."

"True," he said with such lack of concern that she wanted to throttle him, "except I found it in the corner of one of the bedrooms."

Deep breath. Her mind spun as she tried to think why General Bragg would be *inside* the house.

She felt his gaze on her, studying her.

"Hey, don't look so upset. The little fella's a gift."

"A gift or blackmail?"

His relaxed expression shifted to surprise. "Jesus Christ, what do you think I am?"

He rose, took three long strides, and clamped his arms around her before she had the time or the breath to protest. She felt his damp shirt and the large laminated button cool against her cheek. He smelled of sweat layered with English Leather.

With his index finger, he lifted her chin, and she realized he was going to kiss her. She dipped her face to avoid him.

"Hey, what's the deal?" He sounded genuinely shocked. "You used to be willing enough."

"Let go of me, Pete."

"Aw, come on, Jessica. I wouldn't really have turned that thing over to the sheriff even if Jonah was guilty," he said, his breath warm on her forehead. "You know that."

He relaxed his grip, and she squirmed away.

Pete's mouth flattened in irritation. "I can't figure you out. I thought you'd be grateful."

"Excuse me? You come here suggesting my brother is involved in arson and murder, and I'm supposed to be pleased that you've brought me evidence."

He looked indignant in a hurt puppy sort of way. "You're mixing it all up. I brought that here because—well, because I'm nuts about you and I don't want anything to happen to your brother. Why, last spring, when you came walking into Jelly's Diner, I almost fell over. You were so skinny in high school, no figure at all, and your hair always looked like it got caught in rotor blades. I turned to Lucile, who was taking my order, and said, 'Shit, if that's Jessica Moran how did she grow up to be so cute?' I decided right then I was going to ask you out. You turned me down the first two times, remember?"

She nodded. If she hadn't been so desperately lonely and her choice of men so limited, she might have continued turning him down. He had been charming and they'd had some good times with Mary Grace and Bob. But, every time she'd tried to end the relationship, he'd done something like bring her a half cord of wood or offer to level out the foundation on her house. She fingered General Bragg in her pocket.

He was watching her. "What if someone else had found that soldier and handed it over to . . . to those state know-it-alls who are in charge of this fire investigation?"

She noticed his unwillingness to mention Callum, although he must have known she was aware he was in town. "Look, Pete, finding that soldier in the halfway house doesn't make Jonah guilty of burning it down. One of the residents there probably ran across it outside and carried it into the house. He might not have even known where it came from." As she went through the explanation, it did seem reasonable.

Pete looked at her earnestly. "Don't you see *it doesn't make any difference*?"

"My God, Pete, how can you say that? Three men died in that fire."

He turned abruptly and strode to the sofa, his back muscles rigid under his shirt. He sank stiffly onto the cushions. "Too bad they all didn't."

"Oh, Pete."

"He went after my daughter," he said with chilling brevity.

Jessica blinked. "The survivor did?"

"Yeah, the flabby guy with the dirty blond hair halfway down his back."

"What do you mean 'went after'?"

"Followed her, tried to talk to her."

She thought of brown-haired Emily with her almond eyes and long, dark lashes—a prettier, sweeter, far more innocent version of Darla. "Oh, I see."

He glanced at her sharply, as if he didn't think she did. "If you had a daughter, you'd understand."

"I do understand, Pete. Really, I do," she said softly. She walked to the chair opposite him and eased into it, hesitating before she asked the question that surfaced in her mind. "Did he touch her?"

She looked at him in time to see his jaw muscles twitch, then set like cement.

"She had the good sense to run," he said crisply. "I'd warned her about them."

"What makes you so sure he was going to molest her?"

His face flared red. "Because that's what sexual predators do. I can't believe you're that naive."

"It's not a matter of naiveté. This guy served his sentence and probably has no desire to return to prison."

"They should never let those types out."

"Don't you think he deserves a chance to prove he's been rehabilitated?"

"Not at the risk of my daughter." He pushed himself up from the sofa, the tension still visible in his shoulders. "I'm not about to wait until *after* she's raped before I do something. If you had a nest of snakes under your front porch, would you wait until one of them slithered up the steps and bit you on the foot before you got rid of it?"

"We're not talking about snakes here, Pete. We're talking about men."

"The men in that halfway house were snakes, Jessica," he said coldly. He paced in front of the fireplace. "Look at what they did to this community. Before they moved here, we could go anywhere, night or day. Our kids could play outside, and nobody worried some pervert would grab them. We had problems—I'm not saying we didn't—but we took care of our own. Now, the state sends us the big city's problems too, and that isn't right." He turned and looked at her. "What if you find out Jonah did clean up that nest of snakes for us—for whatever reason—would you turn him in to the sheriff?"

She hesitated for several seconds, recalling the uneasy feeling she'd had that Jonah was concealing something. What if he had set the fire? Maybe out of fear of the men. Maybe he'd heard they were evil and got it in his head he should do something about them. Or maybe someone talked him into it, saying, "Come on, Jonah, just light this and toss it through the window. It won't hurt those bastards, but it sure will scare them."

She wondered if he could plead insanity or diminished capacity. But he *wasn't* retarded. She was no psychiatrist, so who was going to believe her layman's diagnosis of Asperger's syndrome? Even if they could find a psychiatrist who would testify he had it, it would be a weak, after-the-fact argument.

Homer could probably come up with five hundred witnesses who'd testify Jonah wasn't within that elusive range called "normal," but she didn't think an obsession with the Civil War constituted craziness. Every town had its share of oddballs, and there were plenty of people in Misp who could negate the entire concept of normality. If Pete was right, a jury here might release Jonah out of gratitude. Juries had done stranger things.

But a more objective panel of citizens in another town might see it differently. If by some remote chance Jonah had set the fire, could he be trusted not to do something like that again? She wasn't sure which was worse—her brother as victim or as assailant. But she couldn't allow Pete's question to spin into silence.

"Jonah is the most gentle person I know," she said. "I can't believe he would hurt anyone, but if I knew, truly knew for certain he set that fire, I'd have to turn him in."

He stared at her. "Jesus, what kind of sister are you? Where's your loyalty to your own flesh and blood?"

"I'd have to, Pete," she said in a low voice. "There are such things as right and wrong."

"It's more complicated than that."

"No more complicated now than it's ever been. Most people know the difference between right and wrong. They just don't want either one to cause them any grief."

He shook his head in disbelief. "You'd turn in your own brother."

She thought of the information the Meckler sisters had so kindly provided, the shoelace remnant coiled in the grass like a dried worm, and General Bragg in her pocket. Together, they troubled her. Individually, they could be explained away.

She fixed her gaze on Pete, and her voice took on strength. "I told you he didn't do it."

He looked down his nose at her. "Well, there are a lot of people in town who think he did. Bud Schultz says he wouldn't be surprised if it was Jonah."

"Damn it, Bud Schultz shouldn't be talking about any of this. That's completely unprofessional." Restlessly, she stood, brushed by him in annoyance, and walked into the kitchen.

He followed her. "Look, Jessica, I'm on your side. If it turns out Jonah did set that fire, there's nobody around here who'd blame him. Why, if you took a secret little poll right now, you'd find he's the most popular man in town."

She stopped in midmotion. She thought of all the schoolkids who had tormented Jonah through the years and all the adults who had belittled him. She conjured up an image of Pete, Bud, Wendell, Dewey Tyrrell, and some of the other men in town cheering him, lifting him to their shoulders, finally giving him the approval and acceptance he'd never had before—all because they believed he'd murdered three men, perhaps on their behalf. And she saw Jonah's face, his shy smile, his newfound pride mixed with wonder and pleasure. If that's what it took for them to accept him, she wanted nothing to do with them.

She spun around and stabbed a finger in the general direction of the front door. "Out!"

When Pete didn't move, she added, "Right now!"

He looked her over. "I thought I knew you, Jessica. Shit, what happened to you down there in California? You used to be so—"

"Out!"

He shook his head in disgust, then strode past her to the front door. She followed him, watching him stomp down the porch steps and thinking that she may have been lonely when she moved back to Misp but she didn't need to compound the problem by being foolish.

The rain had stopped. The sky was clearing. He turned to give her a final icy stare, the quarter moon hovering over his shoulder like a bright blinking eye. He climbed into his red truck, shifted it into gear with a grinding haste, and drove it into the gray night.

9

After Pete left, Jessica took the miniature of General Bragg from her pocket and stood it on the mantel, realizing she'd have to confront Jonah once again about the arson. He'd said he'd never gone inside the halfway house. He'd never talked to the residents. She felt disloyal even asking him about it, as if her questions implied his guilt.

The next morning, General Bragg stared at her from the mantel like a ghoulish reminder. She phoned Jonah at her mother's home and asked him to meet her in fifteen minutes at the highway turnoff to the mill. That way, she could avoid Lila. She then called Alpine Insurance and told the manager she would be an hour late.

Jonah, wearing a navy blue windbreaker, was standing at the turnoff under a big-leafed maple, his shoulders hunched against the steady mist. She opened the door, and he climbed in.

Backing the van into the private road, she turned the van toward town. "How about I buy you a coffee shake at the Express-O Hut?"

"Okay." He shifted in his seat, away from a spring poking through the fabric.

She drove into downtown Misp, pulled into the parking lot for Jack Everett's Boat and Hardware Center, and eased the van alongside the Express-O Hut. She lowered the window. "Hi, Kim. Coffee shake for Jonah, the usual for me."

Kim nodded agreeably and set to preparing the drinks.

Jonah glanced at the drugstore across the street. "Mr. Swain ordered a Civil War magazine for me. He said it should come in any day now."

"That was nice of him." She took the shake from Kim, passed it to Jonah, and turned back to the window. "Easy on the whipped cream for me."

"Are you kidding? That part's better than the cocoa," Kim said with a grin. She handed over a disposable cup with a red straw poking through the lid and took Jessica's money.

Jessica pulled the van into a parking space behind the hut, switched off the engine, and turned to Jonah, who was already noisily sucking on his straw. She reached into her sweatshirt pocket, withdrew the soldier, and held it on the flat of her hand.

When Jonah caught sight of it, his eyes brightened. "You found General Bragg."

He propped his drink between his knees and reached for the miniature. Jessica watched his expression closely as he turned it over. He looked up at her with what she would have sworn was genuine surprise. "He's all burnt."

He scraped at the charred flecks with his fingernail. "Well, I guess I can sand him down and repaint him."

Jessica sipped her cocoa. "Don't you want to know where he was?"

He chewed his lower lip for a few moments, then said, "Okay."

"Someone found him inside the halfway house and brought him to me."

"Oh." He turned away, but not before she saw the panic in his eyes.

"Jonah, how do you suppose General Bragg got in that house?"

"I don't know," he murmured.

She set her cup on a flat spot on the dash. "Look, Jonah, I'm scared. I know you said you never talked to those men and you never went inside that house, but I keep having this terrible feeling that you're involved with that fire somehow. Do you understand why I might think that?"

He shook his head.

She wondered how she could explain her concern to him. She couldn't tell him he was acting even stranger than usual because he didn't fully realize that he was strange to begin with. It wasn't as if he didn't have feelings. She knew he had plenty of those, but he didn't recognize that other people had them too. His brain was simply missing the translator necessary for interpreting them.

Her mission to clear that fog in his mind, to help him understand other people, suddenly seemed too daunting. She leaned her head against the back of her seat and closed her eyes.

"Jessie?" His voice sounded tentative. "I'm scared too."

She opened her eyes and looked at him. "Oh, sweetheart, I know you are." She thought of a possible reason for his fear. "You saw who set the fire. That's it, isn't it?"

Staring at the charred soldier in his hand, he shook his head, an emphatic, stubborn gesture. "No, I . . . I don't want to talk about it."

She rubbed the back of her neck, feeling the tension in her muscles. "Jonah, if you saw who did it or if you have some information the sheriff should know, you have to tell. You can't cover for other people. It's obvious they're not concerned about your welfare, and it wouldn't be right to let them get away with murder. Are you scared someone will come after you?"

He bent his head. "No." His voice was almost inaudible.

"There are ways of protecting witnesses," she said softly. "We wouldn't let anyone hurt you. Do you understand that?"

He nodded.

"This isn't something that will go away if you ignore it," she said. "It will just get worse."

When he didn't respond, she laid her hand against his cheek, feeling the almost invisible whiskers there, wishing she could erase his fears. She reached over and hugged him.

He didn't hug her back, but then he rarely expressed affection. When he did, he stepped outside the ordinary.

At the age of five, he picked a blackberry vine that was in full white bloom and brought it to her, his hands scratched raw. She could still see him standing in the entry of their house, smiling shyly, clutching the thorny runner—seemingly unaware of the blood springing from his puncture wounds and coursing down his bare arms.

She led him into the kitchen, stuck the bramble in a mason jar of water, and swabbed his hands and arms with witch hazel. The blackberry vine was his bouquet of flowers to her, and even though she knew dandelions would have been more appropriate, she tried to focus on the love behind his gift.

The cup in her hand was rapidly losing warmth. She looked at Jonah, who was absorbed in chipping blackened paint off General Bragg.

She didn't know how to find out what had scared him into silence. Callum or the sheriff weren't likely to divulge any information, and she didn't want to stir their interest by asking.

She couldn't simply wait to see how things turned out. The anxiety would be too great. And, if Callum or Milt Tarr should appear on Lila's doorstep to arrest Jonah, it would be a bit late to start helping him. While they frantically searched for evidence of his innocence, he would emotionally disintegrate in a jail cell.

She thought of the survivor who supposedly saw him throw rocks at the house. Either the man had been mistaken or he had deliberately targeted Jonah. Without talking to him, she could only guess.

"I'll have to find him," she murmured, knowing she was the only one in the van who was truly listening.

10

Jessica stopped by the *Misp Tribune* office the next day and flipped through the newspapers on file until she found the name of the survivor. The piece also mentioned New Life, the state-funded agency that operated the halfway house. Later, at home, when she called New Life and asked how she could locate Dennis Kretz, the woman who answered the phone said they didn't release that information.

Jessica tried to sound authoritative. "The law says you have to give me the address of a convicted sex offender."

The woman's tone was equally forceful. "Dennis Kretz was a target as well as a witness in a recent arson, so I'm not about to tell you where he is. If you don't like it, get a court order."

After Jessica hung up, she thought of Tim Morris, who ran Misp Family Services out of a dingy old building on Shade Street. Twice, she had donated her window-washing services to the center.

"Well," Tim wheezed across the phone line. He weighed more than three hundred pounds, and every breath was an effort. "I suspect they sent him back to Seattle. New Life has two supervised living facilities in Seattle. You aren't planning to talk to Kretz, are you?"

She hesitated. "I don't know if I can even find him."

There was a brief silence.

He cleared his throat. "Listen, Jessica, my advice is, don't try. I've heard enough rumors around town to have some idea why you're doing this, but, believe me, Kretz is someone to avoid."

"Why?"

"I have friends who run that program so I'd rather not be specific. But trust me on this one, okay?"

When she didn't reply, he added, "Why do I suspect you won't pay any attention to my advice?"

She laughed. "Now, I didn't say that, Tim."

He gave a labored sigh. "Well, if you're determined, talk to Howard Wall. He supervises the New Life halfway house in Seattle's Fremont district. Nice fellow. Maybe he'll arrange a meeting with Kretz—a chaperoned meeting, though. Got that?"

"Got it, Tim. Where in Fremont?"

"About a half mile from that statue of the people and the dog waiting for the trolley. Hold on a second. I've got the exact address somewhere in all this paper." After rustling through what sounded to Jessica like a foot-high stack of pages, he produced the information.

Postponing the window-cleaning job she'd scheduled in Big River for the next day, she planned a trip to Seattle instead.

The next morning, she bought gas for the van at Spud's Texaco in Misp. As she was driving from the station, Callum walked out of Jack Everett's Boat and Hardware Center across the street. Although there was a car behind her, she braked to a stop and watched him.

He wore a charcoal gray suit, and his carriage and stride held far more confidence than they had those many years ago when they were teenagers. He was so different at the age of sixteen. She remembered running into him once outside the Thrifty Food Market. It was late June—after he'd shown her the octopus in the tree but before she'd discovered his hideout.

He wore blue jeans that were too short and a plain white T-shirt. His sleek, black hair parted in the center so that it fell forward over his shoulders like wings. He seemed flustered. "How are you doing?" he murmured.

She shrugged. "I'd be better if I lived a thousand miles from here."

He glanced at her curiously, as though she'd spoken a foreign language. Jonah stood a few yards away, marching his soldiers along a rock ledge and imitating a fusillade of artillery.

She tried hard not to look directly at Callum. She was afraid that if she did, she would fix her gaze on the ragged scar notching his cheek.

He stared down at his feet. "I wanted to ask you something. A bunch of people from our tribe used to work at your family's mill." His voice was so quiet she had to lean forward to hear him.

"Your mother laid off all of them, and everybody's wondering why." He hesitated. "They asked me to ask you."

"Not enough work, I guess."

He looked everywhere but directly at her. "They said the mill just got a new contract to log some federal land. There's more work now than there's been in a long time, and she didn't lay off any of the others."

Jessica knew he meant the white workers. She tried to think of some reasonable answer, other than the obvious one. "Mom said something about reorganizing to make ends meet, and now everybody will have to work harder."

His gaze dropped to his worn running shoes. "Your dad once told my mom she could work circles around any secretary he knew, Indian or . . . or—" He stopped. "She was good at what she did. Everybody said so."

Jessica looked away. "Yeah, well . . ."

She knew his mother needed the job. The kids at school said his father rarely worked at all. Most people in town who didn't like Indians were subtle about it. Not her mother. Jessica thought she should apologize to Callum in some way, but she didn't know how.

She reached into her pocket, withdrew a pack of gum, and held it out to him. "Want some?"

He glanced at it, then shook his head in embarrassment.

Jessica looked at the five-pack of cinnamon Big Red and quickly stuffed it in her jacket pocket. *Stupid, stupid.* What was she thinking? Big Red, like she was making fun of his being an Indian. And as if a stick of chewing gum were some kind of consolation prize for his mother and the others losing their jobs. She wanted to duck her head and run.

Across the street, Wendell Schultz and two of his buddies came scuffing along the sidewalk, tripping and banging their elbows into each other. She saw Wendell look toward them, then say something to his friends. They nodded their heads and grinned. Wendell grabbed hold of the nearest lamppost and hopped around it, whooping loudly and chopping the air with an imaginary toma-hawk. The other two boys laughed like deranged hyenas.

Jessica felt her cheeks heat up, but she turned slowly and defiantly back to Callum. He was walking away, his ebony hair parted in back so that a triangle of skin showed above his T-shirt. His neck was blood red.

With Jonah trailing behind, she trudged directly to Thunder Lake Timber and barged into her mother's office without knock-ing. Mom sat behind the massive walnut desk Grandpa Jonah had built, studying a stapled, multipage document through her red-framed reading glasses. A sandy-haired, middle-aged man leaned across the desk, pointing a yellow pencil at something on the doc-ument. Jessica thought he looked familiar, that he might be the salesman who sold yarding machinery to her father.

She strode across the room, stopping two feet from the desk.

Mom frowned. "You can see I'm busy."

Jessica drew a steadying breath. "You fired all the Indians, didn't you? I want to know why."

The salesman bent his head, riffling through the papers in his briefcase as if he were missing a page critical to the conversation. A flush crept up his neck.

Mom's mouth tightened. "It's business," she said curtly.

"Dad wouldn't have done that."

"Business was something your father never understood."

"Bullshit, he was good at running things."

The salesman murmured something about returning later and stood to leave.

"No," Mom snapped. "Stay right there."

He dropped back onto the chair. She rose, placed her hands on the desk and leaned forward, the veins in her neck throbbing. "You will not have the pleasure of pitching a fit here, young lady. I'll deal with you later."

Jessica shot a parting glare. "People respected Dad. They liked him."

"Oh, yes, they certainly did. They all loved him," she murmured. "Big, handsome Michael Moran, everybody's friend. . . ."

The car behind Jessica honked, bringing her back to Spud's Texaco. She pulled onto Shade Street, away from the memory of her mother's bitter voice, and from any view of Callum.

The trip to Seattle took three hours, which included stopping at a fast-food restaurant in Olympia. The address Tim had given her belonged to a white World War II bungalow, flanked by overgrown lilac bushes, its front yard distinguishable from the others mainly by its lack of daffodils.

Cars jammed the narrow streets of Fremont, where parking was scarce. Jessica maneuvered the van into a space a half block from the house and walked back. Seventy-eight degrees was unseasonably warm for early April, bringing people from their homes and apartments to squint at the sun. Some were outdoors hosing off their cars, and anyone with a garden seemed to be working in it.

Two teenage girls in shorts and halter tops paraded past four bare-chested guys who reclined on aluminum lawn chairs, drank beer, and flirted with them. A boy somewhere around ten teetered near the curb on a skateboard, and a young man carrying a plastic Larry's Market bag with a box of lasagna noodles poking out the top strode along the sidewalk in the same direction Jessica was headed. She wondered how many of them realized they shared the neighborhood with a house full of ex-felons.

Falling into step a few paces behind the man with the grocery bag, she followed him to the white house with the address Tim had given her.

When he made a sharp left at the walkway, she hurried to catch up with him. "Is this the New Life house?"

He swung around, the grocery bag smacking against his leg. "Never heard of it." He was about twenty, lanky, with inch-short black hair and a bony Adam's apple that stuck out like a fist.

He'd answered much too quickly, she thought. She would have expected him to ask if she knew the address. His gaze slid over her. She wore jeans and a faded UCLA T-shirt so that she wouldn't appear intimidating. Obviously, the plan had worked too well.

When she tried to sidestep him, he moved into her path, blocking her with the grocery bag.

"I'm looking for Howard Wall," she said coolly.

He swallowed hard, his Adam's apple bouncing rhythmically. "He isn't here."

"I'd like to check for myself."

Finally, with a snort of disgust, he allowed her to pass.

As she walked up the steps, she smelled the fragrance of daphne that edged the porch. She poked her head through the open front door and saw a man lying stretched out on an overstuffed couch, his eyes closed, his high-top black Converse shoes propped on the sofa arm.

"Pardon me, I'm looking for Howard Wall," Jessica said in a voice that overrode the low din of a television.

The man shot up from the sofa and yelled, "Whoa!" as breathlessly as if he had jogged through the house. "Jesus," he said fuzzily, swiping his forearm across his eyes, "where'd you come from?"

"Misp, as a matter of fact."

He cocked his head, and she realized that, with the bright sun backlighting her, he probably couldn't see her face. She stepped a few paces into the room.

The caution came into his eyes. "Stop right there. Who are you?"

"Jessica Moran. I'm looking for Howard Wall."

"He's not here." He blinked, and in that moment she recognized Dennis Kretz from Edith Meyer's murky flyer.

She felt a little flash of accomplishment that she'd found him so easily.

Despite Tim's warning, he didn't look like much of a threat. His limp blond hair hung a hand's length down his back, and rolls of fat jiggled under his Chicago Bulls T-shirt. She wondered if he'd ever seen a day of exercise. She tried to imagine him crawling through his bedroom window onto the porch roof to escape the fire. It must have been a tight fit, but she couldn't see that he'd suffered any injuries.

She'd met truckloads of loggers who looked stronger and scarier than Kretz did. Of course, they'd earned their Frankenstein faces from trees crashing down on them or weighted cables kicking back at them, and underneath their burly chests beat marshmallow hearts.

She decided Tim was probably overreacting. He was a protective kind of guy. She'd seen that quality in the way he treated people who came into Family Services. If she turned around and walked out the door right now, she might be forfeiting her only opportunity to talk with Kretz. There was no guarantee Howard Wall would permit it.

The man carrying the Larry's Market bag walked in and brushed past her. "You're a fucking idiot, Kretz," he muttered, then bundled his groceries into the next room.

"Hey, Leo, where were you?" Kretz yelled after him. "I didn't invite her in."

She glanced around at the tired, circa 1970 furniture, none of it matching. On the television screen, two sweat-slick boxers were pummeling each other.

Kretz looked her over. "You a social worker?"

"No, I'm Jessica Moran, Jonah Moran's sister."

He sank onto the sofa and blinked a few times, as if trying to make the connection. "Oh, yeah, the Civil War guy with all the toy soldiers."

She shifted uncomfortably, surprised that he knew about Jonah's war.

He leaned back and clasped his hands behind his head. "So, what do you want?"

She stood behind a faded blue recliner, about eight feet from him and five feet from the door. She decided she was safe enough. "I heard you saw my brother throw rocks at the halfway house the night before the fire."

He hesitated, his gaze traveling over her again. Finally, he said, "Who told you that?"

"The sheriff, when he picked up my brother for questioning. How could you be sure it was Jonah? It was almost dark, wasn't it?"

"Not so dark that I couldn't see him."

She stepped around the side of the recliner. "But my brother isn't the kind of person who throws rocks at houses."

He barked a laugh. "Why? Because he's a retard?"

"He's not retarded. He has a neurological disorder."

He squinted at her. "A what?"

"He's just . . . a little different."

He reached over, grabbed a package of Oreos from the coffee table, and shook out a cookie. He pried it apart and gnawed off the frosting. "From what I could tell, Misp is packed full of people who are just a little different—like that church lady with the poofy blond hair, Edith Meyer."

"Edith has strong opinions."

His mouth thinned into a tight line. "Her and those other

women used to parade past our house clutching their white Bibles and waving their picket signs that read 'The Lord shall smite you down with the sword of the righteous.' " He popped the other half of the Oreo into his mouth. "And those were some of Misp's friendlier people."

She had trouble understanding him, not only because he was chewing the cookie but also because he barely moved his lips.

He propped his feet on the coffee table. "Surprised *me* when I saw your brother throwing those rocks. Maybe the church ladies converted him to their side. In the beginning he acted okay, although he yapped on and on about how the South should have won the war and how it would have if he'd been in charge."

"Jonah talked to you?"

He gave her a puzzled look. "Sure. Isn't that what he told you?"

She stepped closer to the coffee table and studied him with skepticism. "How did it happen?"

"What do you mean, 'How did it happen?' He was always cutting through our yard. It was no secret. The neighbors saw him."

"I know he did that, but did he just stop to talk or what?"

"Yeah, if one of us was out in the yard, he'd hang around. He seemed to have plenty of time to do whatever he wanted."

She tried to think why Jonah would deny they'd spoken. The only times she'd known him to lie was when he feared the truth would get him into trouble. Either that, or Dennis was lying.

He was watching her closely. "Misp," he said, shaking his head in disgust. "Jesus, I don't know how you can live in that swamp hole. It's the wettest, dullest town I've ever been in." He lifted his pale eyebrows. "How come I never saw you around?"

"I don't know."

"What part of town do you live in?"

A little alarm buzzed in her head. "The east side," she lied.

"Out by the high school?"

"Not far from there."

He ran his gaze over her, stopping on her T-shirt logo. Juvenile little creep, she thought, and crossed her arms over her breasts. She had the feeling he was trying to make her uncomfortable.

"So what kind of work do you do in exciting Misp?" he said.

"I'm not working right now." That was technically true, she thought. "Funny, but Jonah never mentioned he'd talked with you."

He shrugged. "He never mentioned you either."

She didn't like the way he kept shifting the conversation back to her. "Did my brother ever go *inside* your house?"

He didn't reply, but his eyes turned wary. He grabbed the TV remote and aimed it at the screen, punching up the sound so loud that when a bronze-skinned colossus in gold trunks landed a blow Jessica heard his opponent's jaw crunch.

She raised her voice above the noise. "It's an easy question."

He glanced at her. "Yeah, well, I don't have to answer it. You're not a cop."

"Look, my brother could be in a lot of trouble because of what you told the sheriff. Maybe you don't care about that, but I do. I don't believe he threw rocks at your house. He's never done anything like that before. I don't know why you accused him, but you're not exactly the most—"

He bounded off the sofa, dodged the coffee table, and grabbed her wrist so fast she didn't have time to jerk back. She wouldn't have believed he could move that quickly.

He closed his fingers over hers in a clammy, viselike grip. "You should be nice to me." His voice was low and tight. "I could call the sheriff, you know. I could tell him I saw your brother sitting on that covered oak barrel by our garage a few hours before the fire started. Clear as a picture. The sky turned orange that night, and I could see those yellow curls of his making him look like some angel." He paused meaningfully. "He's no angel, though, is he?"

She shivered. "What are you talking about?"

"People think he's just this crazy, dumb guy because he runs off at the mouth about toy soldiers and battles. But that isn't the only thing that's spooky about him. If I wanted to, I could tell the sheriff some other stuff. So don't get bitchy with me."

She found herself staring at his teeth, which were overlapped, crooked, and flecked with Oreos. He rapidly flattened his lips again as if he'd spent years training himself to conceal them.

He clamped tighter. "You're afraid of me, aren't you?"

"No." She hoped he couldn't feel her pulse pounding in her hand.

"Well, you should be. I could get your brother into a lot of trouble." Although he was close enough that she could smell the cookies on his breath, his voice seemed to come from a distance. "Don't barge in here asking questions and then call me a liar because you don't like the answers."

She opened her mouth to protest, then closed it.

"I know what you were thinking when you walked in. You were saying to yourself, 'He ain't much.' Weren't you?"

"No."

"I could see it in your face. You come in here wearing your college T-shirt and acting like some ball-buster. You figured I'd be too scared to do anything that would land me back in prison. You're thinking, sure, you can handle me, no problem—like I'm stupid or something."

She wondered if she opened her mouth wide and tried to scream, whether the sound would stick in her throat. The neighbors would think she was part of the television program.

Over the excited voice of the boxing announcer, she heard the *chop-chop-chop* of a knife striking a cutting board. Leo in the kitchen fixing a meal. There was audible hostility in that sound, contradicting the homey smells of tomato, garlic, and onion. She didn't think he would be much of an ally.

Dennis must have seen her look in the direction of the kitchen, because he said, "You can forget about Leo. When he was a kid and his old lady blew up at him, she'd pull up his shirt and grind out her cigarette on his back. It's covered with round scars . . . like pinworms crawling under his flesh."

He ran the flat of his hand up her bare arm. "Now, me, I actually *like* women." A single bead of sweat trickled down his temple.

"Dennis," she said softly.

"What?"

"I'm sorry I didn't believe you. It's nothing personal. I'm just upset and worried about Jonah."

He stared at her for an unusually long time without speaking. Then he wet his lips. "You want me to tell the sheriff I got it wrong? That it wasn't your brother after all?"

"Only if it's true."

He grinned. "Could be." His Oreo breath caught her full in the face.

She tried to keep her voice level. "Let go of me."

"You *are* scared, aren't you?"

She sucked in a breath. "Yes, I'm scared."

He laughed and relaxed his grip. She yanked her hand away and retreated several paces.

He still stood between her and the door, and for one long minute neither of them moved. She flexed her numb fingers, trying to work the blood back into them. Glancing toward the bright rectangle of light, she gauged her ability to outrun him.

He moved closer to the door, blocking her way. "I'll decide when you can leave."

She didn't answer.

He took a step forward, and she retreated a pace. He laughed.

Stepping aside, he waved his hand in dismissal. "Say hello to the good folks in Misp. I'll look you up sometime."

She eased past him out the door.

She made it back to the van, but as she unlocked the driver's door the strength abruptly drained from her legs. It was a struggle to climb onto the seat, pull the door closed, and punch down the lock. She felt violated. And she didn't even want to think about what he could have done.

She dug in her jeans for her van keys. As she yanked them out, she made the mistake of glancing in the side-view mirror. Dennis Kretz stood on the sidewalk behind the van, watching. Below him were the tiny, white letters OBJECTS IN MIRROR ARE CLOSER THAN THEY APPEAR.

She thrust the key into the ignition, jabbing it and forcing it until it caught on something and stuck halfway in. She tugged on it, then realizing it might break off, released it.

She looked out the window. He was gone.

It took her a full five minutes to work the jammed key out of the ignition.

SHE SPENT the first half of the return trip to Misp trying to forget his damp hand on hers.

She could report him to the New Life agency. He had threatened her, touched her, and he'd probably visit her in her nightmares for weeks to come. But she would have difficulty explaining why she'd gone there, and she felt somewhat responsible for what had happened. She couldn't deny that she'd been warned beforehand.

She spent the last seventy-five miles trying to make sense of what he had said about Jonah.

"He's no angel, though, is he?"

That taunt bothered her more than any of the others. Because she had never seen Jonah squash a bug, much less hurt a person, she did believe he deserved to occupy some celestial dimension for the sinless and life's chronic victims. By the time she crossed the two-lane, steel girder bridge over the Humptulips River, she'd come up with ten different interpretations, ranging from evil intent on Dennis's part to a well-concealed double life on Jonah's.

She arrived home exhausted. Checking her phone messages, she listened to Harold at the Cliffside Lodge in Moclips requesting her window-washing services and Pete Johnson asking her to call him.

Too tired to deal with Pete, she phoned Harold and left a reply on his answering machine. She showered and went directly to bed, but Dennis's remark about Jonah tormented her until midnight.

She no sooner fell asleep than the phone rang. Running barefoot into the kitchen, she caught it on the fourth ring, one beat before the recorder kicked in.

Automatically murmuring, "A Room with a View," she cradled the receiver on her shoulder and reached for the light switch. "Hello?"

At first, there was no answer, just the swish of phone air. Then his voice came across the line, soft and low. "You lied to me. You said you lived out by the high school."

She dropped the receiver into its cradle so quickly the ringer jangled.

What could she have been thinking, telling him her name? As if she'd left all her street smarts back in Los Angeles. But, of course, here she was in safe little Misp, where a single woman could feel comfortable listing her name and address in the telephone book. Dennis not only knew her phone number, he knew where she lived.

11

She took the phone off the hook and slept until six in the morning.

The sun was still a bright buttery smudge on the horizon as she toted a cardboard box of freshly washed rags to the van. The air smelled clean and salt-sweet—an ocean breeze coming in. She felt better already, knowing she would be working in Big River for the day, far away from her house. She didn't believe Dennis would return to Misp just to terrorize her, but he would probably call again.

Callum's Ford Explorer edged to the side of the street a few yards behind the van. She stiffened, thinking she didn't want to see him any more than she wanted to see Dennis.

He jumped out and strode toward her, straightening his shirt collar as if he'd dressed on the way. The suit was gone. He was wearing jeans, a sport shirt, and a brown leather jacket. "What the hell were you doing visiting Dennis Kretz?" he said.

She turned toward the van's open double doors and dropped the box onto the floor's rubber mat. "Who told you that?"

"That's not the question."

Damn that Tim Morris, she thought. She knew he meant well, but she didn't need Callum lecturing her.

She cocked her head. "I can talk with anyone I want."

He jammed his hands in his pockets and paced alongside the van. "It wasn't as though you were sitting on your front steps and he happened to wander by. You tracked him to Seattle."

No point telling him she was looking for Howard Wall. She kept her voice cool and level. "So?"

"So, if that's the case, I have some questions."

She raised her eyebrows in defiance. "Are you ordering me to answer them?"

"If you prefer, I can drive you to the sheriff's office and we can talk there."

"I didn't harass Dennis if that's what you're implying. We had a short conversation." She had no intention of telling him he had threatened her. She would not allow either one of them that satisfaction.

"*Dennis?* That's a bit friendly, isn't it?"

"Kretz or whatever you want to call him." The bright sun caught her full in the face, and she had to shade her eyes. "He's a liar, or haven't you figured that out yet?"

"Haven't you heard of obstruction of justice?"

"He accused my brother of a crime."

"He did not."

"Well, he implicated him, which is almost the same thing." She made a quick decision, knowing she was taking a risk. "When I asked him about Jonah, do you want to know what he said?"

"I can't imagine."

"He offered to tell the sheriff he was wrong about seeing Jonah throw the rocks. Now what does that suggest?"

"I don't know," he said through tight lips, "but I'm sure you have the answer to that one, too."

"He was either lying when he talked to the sheriff in the first place or he's lying now."

Callum raked his fingers through his hair in frustration. "You really are bullheaded, you know that? This is not *Nancy Drew and*

the Mystery of the Old Halfway House. You have no business inter-
fering. One, you don't know what you're doing. Two, you have
a vested interest in how it turns out. Three, and perhaps most important, it's illegal to interfere with an investigation. Do you have
any idea of how much you could screw things up?"

She knew he was right, but she hated having him state it quite
so convincingly.

"And worst of all, something could happen to you." His voice
had gone soft and, when she glanced at him, she saw his eyes were
dark with concern.

She lifted her chin. "I don't need you to protect me."

"I'm doing you a favor, Jess."

"Don't bother."

"Jonah admitted throwing those rocks."

"So? Under what kind of duress? He's so afraid of disapproval
he'd admit to almost anything. And then that idiot fire chief, Bud
Schultz, scared him by talking about rats in prison."

"Look, I realize it's not pleasant to be hauled in for questioning,
but no one's charged him with anything yet."

"They wouldn't even have bothered questioning him if he
weren't—well, unusual. Did you check into Kretz's background?
Maybe *he* likes to play with matches."

Callum jabbed his hands in the air in exasperation. "For God's
sake, do you think we're colossally stupid?" He stared at her.
"Maybe we should look at the arson in your background."

Her voice went frigid. "That's different, and you know it."

She swung around and started arranging the usual jumble of
supplies in her van: plastic buckets, the box of lint-free cleaning
cloths, her black rubber boots, the leather tool belt she used for
holding squeegees. She felt the sudden compulsion to put them in
order. Scooping up some soiled, damp rags, she tried to think what
to do with them. They smelled of pine-scented window-washing
detergent—the fragrance of an uncomplicated life.

"Tell me how it's different," he asked in a low voice.

She hurled the wad toward the back of the van. "No."

"Do you still have the urge to set fires?"

She gripped the van door. "Fuck you."

Closed it with a solid slam.

As she stepped onto the parking strip, her eyes caught movement at the Hinckels' window. Damned neighbors. Jessica turned toward her own house and marched up the front walk.

Callum was right behind her. When she reached her front steps, he touched her arm as though he meant to slow her. She stopped dead and stared at his hand.

He drew back, the blood rushing to his face. "Sorry," he mumbled. "I shouldn't have done that." He elbowed back his jacket and thrust his hands into his jeans pockets. "And I shouldn't have suggested you set that fire. I didn't come here to offend you."

They were silent for several moments. She glanced at his expression. Oh, shit, he was going to bring up the past. She could feel it coming.

"Can't we talk about what happened?" he asked in a low voice.

"We just did."

She looked over his shoulder. Up and down the street, window shades and curtains luffed like sails in the breeze. Reluctantly, she locked her gaze on him.

"I don't mean now," he said. "I mean before—before you left Misp."

"I'm not interested in some silly error in judgment I made years ago."

She saw the hurt leap to his eyes.

"Is that how you thought of it?" he said. "I loved you, Jess. I think I still do."

She stood unmoving, resisting him, because she hated pain more than she hated loneliness. He wasn't loyal or dependable. He wasn't even available, she told herself. He didn't deserve the attention she was giving him.

"Go away, Callum." She knew she sounded harsh and brittle and cold, and she hated that too.

"I was sixteen years old, Jess," he said. "I was thoughtless, stupid, and immature, but I didn't set out to hurt you. In fact, I cared more than you can—"

"If you're looking for forgiveness, you have it." But she couldn't seem to soften her words.

"I was hoping for more sincerity."

"All right, you have that too."

"And your trust."

She gave a sharp, ironic laugh. "Did you really expect that? If you weren't involved with the halfway house fire, your trustworthiness or lack of it would mean nothing to me now."

He didn't answer, but guilt and remorse registered in his expression.

"I'd like to get to know you again," he said quietly.

She laughed abruptly. "You can't be serious."

"We could at least be friends."

"No, Callum." Her eyes stung. She looked toward the cloudless sky to keep the tears from gathering and falling onto her cheeks. "There was a time, after my father died, when I thought I couldn't survive. I wasn't eating. I wasn't sleeping. I felt lonely and powerless and terribly sad. Then you came along and talked to me and held me and . . . and—" She shrugged. "And I was foolish enough to believe that you loved me, that I was more than just a trophy."

She glanced at him and saw him wince.

"Jess, I swear I never thought of you like that."

Her hand brushed the air dismissively. "Anyway, I discovered that I could survive without you—or anyone else. So, even if I could trust you again, and even if you weren't married, I don't know why I should—"

"I'm not married."

She stared at him, momentarily speechless. "But I heard . . ."

She stopped, then took a deep breath. "Well, that's not important. It's not as if you failed a lie detector test."

"My wife left me seven months ago." The color rose to his face, but his voice sounded emotionless, as if he'd trained himself to deliver the information stoically.

"Oh," she said, shrugging with what she hoped was nonchalance. "I'm sorry."

She told herself his marital status made no difference to her. She regretted even mentioning it. But what kind of town gossip was Mary Grace if she couldn't provide reliable information?

"What are you thinking, Jess?"

She gave him a wry smile. "I'm thinking if you're so perfect, why did she leave you?"

He didn't smile in return. He looked over her shoulder, studying the horizon intently as if a storm were rolling in. "Do you want the long, complicated version or the short one?"

"The short one will do."

"She ran off with my brother Andy."

"Oh, my God," Jessica said in a low voice, mentally scolding herself for being so flippant.

"I would appreciate it," he said with slow emphasis, "if you didn't look like that."

"Like what?"

"Like every pore in your body is oozing pity."

She straightened her shoulders. "Well, it wasn't. I'm just sorry things didn't work out for you." She hesitated. "Do you have children?"

He shook his head. "We intended to, once we got our careers established. But that never happened."

She'd been holding her breath. Of course, one child couldn't replace another, but she'd assumed he had a houseful of children. He would be a good father.

She wanted to tell him about their daughter, but the mere

thought set her hands shaking. She had to hide them in her jeans pockets so he wouldn't notice.

He lifted his gaze. "Why can't we be friends?"

What was he thinking? She couldn't imagine a platonic relationship with him. Just seeing him was painful enough.

"That's not possible, Callum, because of my brother."

"Are you worried he's guilty?"

"Of course not. But I know you still hold a grudge against my mother. How can I trust that you won't take your revenge through him?"

He looked at her in surprise. "I would never treat him differently than I would anyone else." His voice turned flat and cool. "The same goes for your mother."

"Really? Well, I'm sure you haven't forgotten that she fired all the Indians at the mill." She knew she was unfairly provoking him, but she couldn't think of any other way to maintain the rift between them. And she needed that distance. "I wonder what effect *that* will have on your objectivity."

The breath he released was long and audible.

Not waiting for any other reply, she strode into the house and shut the door behind her. As his car pulled away, she watched from the front window.

12

Jessica walked over to the sofa, sank onto its thick cushions, and pulled her knees up against her. She couldn't allow Callum into her life again. The next man she took her chances with would not be one who had hurt her before.

Besides, she had other things to concern her. She couldn't feel easy again until Jonah was safe. And, in six weeks, when her daughter turned eighteen, she would be able to locate her—if she had signed up with the adoption registries. A big "if," Jessica knew.

Getting over Callum the last time had been a long, slow easing of pain, a process that took years. It was one she would not want to repeat.

After she'd moved back to Misp in May, she'd purposefully avoided Thunder Lake, her father's grave site, and the woods where she and Callum used to meet. They held too many painful memories.

But then she found herself drawn to the lake. She visited it when she thought her mother wouldn't be around. She even walked out on the new dock. By August, she was able to swim in the lake and feel her father's soul nearby.

She couldn't bring herself to visit the historic little cemetery where his body rested. She either had to pass that on her way to town or take a longer route, and she took the longer route.

One rainless day, four months after she'd returned, she'd crossed onto the reservation while hiking. From there, she managed to talk herself into walking farther—until she reached the place where, years before, Callum had set up his hideout, an old tent that barely shed water.

As she stood in the middle of what had once been a clear-cut, she was reminded of the old joke of not being able to see the forest for the trees. The replanted conifers rose forty feet or more. In another few decades, they would be ready for harvesting.

The tent was gone, of course. Someone had either removed the carcass or it had rotted away. Its memory still held her, but she didn't cry.

It had been mid-June, eight weeks after her father died, when she and Jonah discovered Callum's hideout. Her job was to look after Jonah that summer. If their mother had known they were hiking on reservation land, she would have grounded both of them. But Lila was entrenched at the mill.

About a mile in, they strayed onto the pie-shaped clear-cut. Despite the name, there was nothing clear about it. Ugly, fractured stumps jutted from the ground. New foliage—mostly fireweed, tangled brush, and broadleaf alder—shot up around the debris, taking advantage of the burst of sunlight. Carpenter ants and bark beetles scuttled over rotting logs. Jessica heard a woodpecker, although she couldn't see it. It sounded like someone tapping a typewriter.

The tent was tucked against the side of a ravine and partly concealed with cedar branches. With its peaked shape, faded green canvas, and frayed tie-downs, it looked like a relic from the fifties. Glossy white patches dappled the places where someone had sealed water leaks with hot wax.

Jonah's eyes widened. "Can we go in, Jessie?"

She shook her head. "It's private property."

He was disappointed and, although she didn't tell him, so was she.

That night she lay in bed thinking about the tent, wondering who owned it. She wanted a hideout like that, and it occurred to her that Dad had owned a tent for hunting. If she could find it, if Mom hadn't tossed it out with most of his other belongings, she could pitch it in their woods.

She spent the next day searching the garage and the basement. Jonah followed her around, marching the toy soldiers Dad had given him across the shelves of the storage cabinets. He glanced up. "Whatcha looking for, Jessie?"

"Nothing, and don't tell Mom. Okay?"

"Okay."

She never did find the tent, but she came across Dad's sheathed hunting knife, which had been shoved between a coil of tire chains and a hand drill. She'd seen him use it to skin deer and elk, opening them with quick strokes, stripping their hides as if he were peeling the clothes off them. The blade was still keenly honed.

Deciding she would wear the knife when Mom wasn't around, she fastened the sheath on her belt and tucked the blade into it. "Don't tell Mom about the knife, Jonah. All right?"

He smiled agreeably. "All right."

She dreamed that night about the tent on the Quinault reservation. She woke around two A.M. When she couldn't fall back asleep, she dressed in jeans and a T-shirt and crept in stocking feet from her room down the long second-story hall, carrying her hiking boots and testing each worn board in case it should creak. With a flashlight borrowed from a kitchen drawer, she made her way along Reservation Road.

The night was warm, with a few thin clouds streaking the sky. The moon, round and silvery as a dime, hovered over the Olympic Mountains. Off the highway, Jessica arced the flashlight to keep from tangling her feet in the bracken and fallen tree branches. She thought the hideout would be easy to find again, but she made two false turns and had to double back.

About a mile onto the reservation, she saw the eerily dark tent. She waited and watched for several minutes to make sure it wasn't occupied, then flicked off the flashlight and approached as silently as she could. Moving the cedar branches aside, she found the entrance and lifted the canvas flap. Although she didn't like the idea of removing her boots, she tugged them off and left them outside.

The tent was about eight feet square. She stood in the center of it, sniffing its musty smell and staring at the full moon, hazy green through the canvas. She switched on the flashlight and panned the beam in a slow circle, stopping briefly on the deflated air mattress, the ragged patchwork quilt, the four white candle stubs stuck in a sand-filled coffee can, and the stack of comic books. She knelt down and thumbed through the magazines. Fire-breathing dragons and winged horses danced across their covers. At the bottom of the stack was a sketchbook with the name Callum Luke written in small, precise script on the first page. She flipped through it, stopping to glance at each of two dozen or so colored pencil drawings. They seemed as good as the ones in the comic books.

The memory of his shy presence came to her. His name turned up again on a history test tucked inside one of the comic books. She noticed he'd misspelled *revisionist,* but the teacher hadn't corrected it. She was careful to leave his belongings exactly as she found them.

The next night, she came at the same time, carrying a book of matches to light the candles in the coffee can.

She visited the tent two nights the following week and one night the week after that. She could tell when he had stopped by between her visits. Things were moved, added, changed. A scratched, dented Boy Scout canteen and a rusted cookie tin filled with baseball cards turned up near the comic books. He laid a pumpkin-orange shag carpet remnant just inside the tent door, and after that, Jessica no longer removed her shoes. She wiped them as she entered.

Whenever she heard a noise outside, she jumped, expecting Callum to walk in on her at any moment. She hadn't seen him since their talk in the woods, not since he'd shown her the octopus in the tree roots.

She fell in love with the tent. She was captivated by the way it closed out the world, its heady smell of mildew, greasy smoke, and candle wax, the moonlight filtered green through the worn canvas. It reminded her of the snug makeshift hideouts she and Dad built in the living room on Sunday mornings.

She returned to the tent every night during the first week in July. It was easy to get past Mom. She was showing the strain of rising at four A.M. to supervise the mill, returning home at four P.M., and working after dinner on company records. Most evenings, she fell into a doze at the dining room table, surrounded by paperwork. Jessica waited for her to stagger upstairs to bed, then left the house.

On Friday night, the sky was clear and windless, the stars so sharp they appeared within reach. She heard an owl hoot and a small animal crash away from her through the brush—night music so familiar it carried no threat.

She found the tent easily but, two yards from it, stepped in a clump of black excrement, the stench rising to her nose. "Shit," she swore under her breath.

Looking at it in the glow of her flashlight, she decided it was probably bear spoor. She scraped it off, removed her boots, and left them outside the tent. Inside, she lighted all four candle stubs and crawled onto Callum's shabby quilt. It had an odd briny smell, she thought, like the tidal pools at Ruby Beach.

She came close to dozing off when she heard a creak and a snap. A branch breaking under something's foot. She sat straight up, blew out the candles, and listened, her breath shallow.

She couldn't decide if it was the bear or Callum. Then again, Mom could have followed her. She wore thick-soled boots that could crack a branch the thickness of an arm, and she never walked softly. Of the three, Jessica thought she'd rather have it be the bear. She wished she hadn't left her boots outside the tent.

She sat motionless for several minutes but heard nothing. She came to the conclusion it was an animal, more afraid of her than she was of it. Easing her hand along the tent flap, she reached out and groped for her boots.

Just as her fingers found their padded leather edges, a strong hand clamped down on her wrist. She jerked her arm back but couldn't pull free. She gritted her teeth, strained, and pulled.

Abruptly, the shadowy hand released her wrist, and she toppled backward. The tent flap whipped open, and a flashlight snapped on, its bright glare almost blinding her. She made out a lanky figure behind the light.

"You have no right to be in my tent," he said.

She blinked. "I wasn't hurting anything."

He pointed the beam away from her eyes, and she saw his face, the scar stained blood red in the yellow light. "Makes no difference. If I walked into your bedroom at your house, I'll bet you wouldn't like it." He paused. "I'll bet your mother would have me arrested."

Jessica thought he was probably right. "So, is this your bedroom?"

He gave her a look of disgust. "No, I have a regular house just like you."

There was a long, awkward silence.

He stepped into the tent, then gave the interior a careful assessment. "What have you been doing in here?"

"I didn't mess it up, if that's what you mean."

"You burnt the candles all the way down one night."

"So? I replaced them."

"I could tell you did. That was really smart, wasn't it? You're not much of a spy."

"I wasn't spying."

He sniffed in contempt. "Well, if you had been, I would have caught you and shot you by now."

"That's stupid. People don't shoot spies anymore."

He gestured at the papers and books piled between the quilt and the sand-filled coffee can. "You been messing with any of those?"

"No."

He stood silently for several seconds before dropping onto the quilt and crossing his legs. "What makes you think you've got the right to be here?"

"I never said I did." She hesitated, debating how much she should tell him. "Sometimes I can't sleep at night."

"What's the problem? Not a single quiet spot in your thirty-room house?"

"My house doesn't have thirty rooms, and you know what? You're rude."

"I'm not the one who barged into someone else's hideout." He straightened the quilt. "Did you tell anybody about this place?"

She shook her head. "My brother was with me when we found it, but he hardly ever talks to other people. Besides, he probably couldn't find it again. It took me awhile the second time."

He pulled out a book of matches and lighted the candles, then switched off the flashlight. "I'm going to have to do a better job with the camouflage." He shifted the coffee can two inches to the left although she couldn't see anything wrong with the position it was in.

When he looked up, the candles seemed to flicker in his eyes. "I guess it's okay if you come here, but this is my tent so I'm the boss. You don't bring anyone else, and you keep out of my stuff. You got that?"

She nodded. To stay there with him for a few more hours, she would have agreed to almost anything.

13

Callum was still seething over her attack on his impartiality as he turned his Explorer off her street. He'd wanted to tell her he was investigating the arson and murder from every angle, that he was headed for the Hoh Rain Forest right now to track down information on the man who'd reported the fire from the Queets Community Center phone. He would be just as thorough and diligent in that search as he would in any other. And, if the arsonist turned out to be a Quinault, did she really believe he would treat him differently?

His ATF supervisor thought she was doing him a favor when she sent him to Misp.

"You know the area and the people. Besides, it'll be good for you to be around family and friends, especially after what you've been through," she'd said in her oblique reference to his divorce.

He didn't object because, at the time, any distraction seemed preferable to his pain.

In the past, when he and Tori visited, they stayed at the Quinault Lodge just outside the Olympic National Park. He knew his parents' feelings had been hurt, but Tori said she would never spend another night on any reservation.

This time, he couldn't insult them. He was sleeping in the room he'd once shared with his brother Andrew.

His mother had not only kept the desk he and Andy had covered with baseball team stickers; she'd stashed all his old comic books and high school artifacts in it. He went through the desk that first night and found a crumpled wallet-sized picture of Jessica tucked between a drawing of a 1980 blue Corvette and one of a futuristic, stainless steel, missile-shaped car. If he remembered correctly, this was the photo he'd accidentally dropped outside his bedroom.

His younger sister Bethany had taunted him with it. "Don't tell me you like *her*." She held the photo out of his reach. "She's so scrawny, her eyes are bigger than her face, and besides she's got that revolting hair."

He lunged for her, but she circled the coffee table and ran into the kitchen.

"Bet it's because she's white, isn't it?" she shrilled. "You think you're so hot because you've got a white girlfriend."

Callum felt the fury rise within him. "That's not true. You don't even know her."

Bethany stopped dead in the center of the kitchen and crushed the photo in her plump fist. "She's rich and ugly and white. Seems to me that's all I need to know."

He pinned her against the wall and wrenched the picture out of her hand, but it was too late to recover his secret.

By then, he was meeting Jessica at the tent as often as he could. She even turned up one July night in the middle of a rain shower wet from her hairline to her boots.

He heard her whisper, "Hey, the password is forty-eight days."

He lifted the flap. "What does that mean?"

"It's how long we have until school starts."

He groaned, then waved her in. "Take off your boots. I don't want you mucking the place up."

She gave a long, weary sigh. "When it's raining I always take them off and set them on that slab of carpet."

He nodded solemnly. "Yeah, that's what it's for."

She squatted down and untied her laces. "Sure is an awful color though. Couldn't you have found something other than pukey orange?"

"It's from the rug in my house."

"Oh." She quickly set her boots aside.

He ran his gaze over her. "Got soaked, didn't you?"

"Oh, I'm okay." Flopping onto the comforter, she unshouldered her backpack. "I brought food."

He dropped down beside her. "If we eat in here, we have to stay on the quilt so I can shake it out. We can't leave food because a bear or a raccoon will tear through. . . ."

"Where do you think I grew up? Downtown Seattle?"

"I'm just telling you the rules."

She reached in the pack and produced a box of saltine crackers. "You're worse than my brother, you know that?"

"Is that supposed to be an insult?"

"No-o, it's just that he's so particular about things. He's got tons of rules. If the lumps of food on his plate are touching, he won't eat them. He likes only one brand of toothpaste and one brand of orange juice, and he always wants his applesauce ground up fine in the blender. He lines his toy soldiers all in a row, and he's forever arranging and rearranging them. When he gets something in his mind, it's nearly impossible to change it."

"Well, I'm not that way. I'll eat anything, and at home I'm a slob."

She pulled out two Coke cans, handing him one. They popped them open at the same time. She took a drink, then set the container on the canvas floor.

He picked it up and stuck it in her boot.

She rolled her eyes. "I wasn't going to knock it over."

He ignored the remark.

When she offered the box of crackers, Callum noticed the sheathed knife strapped to her belt.

"Where'd you get that?"

"Belonged to my dad." She set the crackers aside and withdrew the knife. The blade, which had been so well used that it shone with a flat luster, measured about eight inches long.

Callum held out his hand. "Can I see it?"

"I guess so." She passed it over on her flattened palm, as if presenting a ceremonial sword.

He examined the leather-wrapped hilt that was dark brown with old sweat and the imprint of the large hand that had gripped it. "I guess you miss your dad a lot, huh?"

" 'Course. Wouldn't you if your father died?"

He didn't answer. He didn't want to tell her that he probably wouldn't, that his dad was mean when he drank—which was most of the time.

Carefully fingering the knife edge, he gave a low whistle. It was sharp enough to gut a bear. He looked up at her. "Bet you wonder how I got this scar on my cheek."

She shrugged. "Never really noticed it."

Callum raised the knife and angled it so that the candlelight sparked off the blade. "I jumped my little brother, but I didn't know he was holding an open pocket knife. His hand jerked up. Blade cut me right to the bone." He touched his fingertip to his cheek. "It was an accident though."

She was quiet for a moment. "Doesn't look like a knife wound."

"Well, it is."

She didn't say anything, and he wondered if some kids from the reservation had blabbed the truth at school. He studied the hunting knife for another few seconds, then handed it back.

She made a dismissive gesture. "You can borrow it if you want."

He looked at her in surprise. "You don't mind?"

"I don't want you to lose it or dull the blade."

"Don't you think I know how to use a knife?"

"I wouldn't let you borrow it if I didn't." She removed the

sheath and handed it over. The slits at the top puckered out as if the sheath had molded to the belt's thick leather.

He unfastened his own belt and looped it through the slits. "Have you ever talked to the kids at school about me?"

She shook her head. "I can't talk with any of them anymore."

Although he'd never been able to carry on a conversation with most of them either, he thought that was an odd answer. "Why not?"

She studied the bitten nails on her slender fingers, then chewed on a loose cuticle. "All they care about is stupid stuff, like how many beers they drank last weekend or what they watched on TV the night before." She turned away and made a big production of straightening the candles in the coffee can, nudging the sand against each one with the ragged nail of her index finger. "One of these days they're going to figure out there are more important things to think about."

"Like what?"

She hesitated only a second. "Like death. Then they'll wonder why they spent time on anything else out there." She nodded toward the tent flap as though it were a barrier that separated her from "out there."

He examined the knife for a few seconds, then slipped it into the sheath. It made him feel older, stronger, like a true warrior. "There are important things that don't have anything to do with death."

When she didn't answer, he looked up.

Her chin quivered, and her eyes brightened with tears. "Tell me what they are," she whispered.

He scooted closer to her, reached out, and took one of her hands in his. To his surprise, she didn't pull it back. It felt as cool and light as a page in a book. He leaned closer, pressed his mouth against her cheek, and tasted her salty teardrops. "I love you, Jessica," he said.

To his complete amazement, she burrowed against him. "I love you too," she murmured into his shirt.

After a few moments, she said, "Do you think a person can be trapped inside something like a lake?" She sounded in despair.

"Sure." He didn't quite grasp what she meant.

"I think my father is still in Thunder Lake."

That news surprised him. He'd heard some divers had brought up the body.

"But I thought they . . ." He stopped, unsure how to say the words without distressing her more.

She drew back and looked at him. "His soul's down there. I can feel it."

He nodded. "Yes, it could be."

That possibility didn't surprise him. He thought of all the people and animals he'd seen in trees, rocks, hillsides. Those were souls, he knew, but he didn't think whites usually saw them. When he had shown her the octopus in the stump, she seemed to accept it, but he didn't think she felt its spirit the way he did.

In the halo of candlelight, her eyes were so bright she looked feverish. "You believe me then?"

"Yeah, I believe you."

She didn't reply, but she folded her wrists one over the other and pressed her body against him as if she couldn't get close enough.

SHE DIDN'T COME to the tent for the following four nights, and he worried that he'd somehow angered her or that her mother had discovered she was meeting him.

The last week in July was usually warm and dry, but it rained again the night she returned. He heard the snap of twigs outside the tent.

"Forty-three days," she said, not bothering to whisper.

Callum jerked open the flap. "Don't touch the canvas walls or they'll leak."

She ducked and scrambled in. "I know that."

The four candles in the coffee can burned low, providing only a little illumination. She tugged off her boots, and he set them on the carpet square.

"I've been here since eleven o'clock," he said. "Once it started raining, I didn't think you'd come. I almost left."

"The rain's never stopped me from doing anything before." But her teeth were chattering so hard, she had to repeat her answer before he could understand her.

Her face looked soft in the light from the torch. The curves of her neck collected the shadows. "I'm glad I didn't," he said.

"Didn't what?"

"Didn't leave." He'd worn nice clothes—beige slacks and a new plaid shirt with a buttoned-down collar he'd borrowed from his brother—although Andy didn't know yet that it was missing.

She wiped her damp face with the back of her hand. "I had to stay away because my mom said she was sure she heard the back door creak two nights in a row."

"How do you know she didn't hear you this time?"

Jessica grinned. "Because I squirted gobs of oil on the hinges of every door in the house, except the one leading from her bed-room."

She was smart, he thought, and he liked that about her—that and her willfulness. It seemed to him she did exactly what she wanted. As often as he told himself that, at the tent, he was the boss, he still couldn't overcome his awe of her.

He lifted the quilt. "Wrap this around you."

She shook her head. "I'll get it wet."

"Well, if you don't warm up, you'll get hypothermia. I'd sure have a tough time explaining that. I'd have to say I found you passed out in the woods."

"That's stupid. It's at least sixty degrees outside. I'm not getting hypothermia, and I'm not passing out." She tugged off her sweat-shirt and dropped it in a corner of the tent. Just that one quick motion produced a fine, silvery tingle inside him. Her T-shirt was soaked around the edges.

He held the quilt so that it shielded her. "Take off your wet shirt and jeans. I won't look."

"Doesn't bother me if you do. I've gone skinny-dipping before." She stood and unbuttoned her jeans. They slid slowly down her hips. She tugged off her socks and T-shirt, then straightened.

She was wearing only white cotton panties that revealed everything they were meant to cover. He couldn't suppress his rapid inhalation of breath. Her breasts reminded him of winter apples.

He laid the quilt on the canvas floor, his heart thudding in his throat. She turned to him, her eyes wide and bright, but he felt paralyzed. He didn't know what she wanted him to do, what she would allow him to do. He thought he should turn away now, but then she reached down, skinned off her underpants, and dropped them into the drift of clothing at her feet.

She shivered slightly, but he didn't know if she was afraid or cold. He was scared. He worried he might do the wrong thing, and then she would—He realized he didn't know what she would do.

She slid to her knees on the quilt and reached toward him, her arm slender and cream-colored in the candlelight. He lowered himself onto the quilt, and she took his hand and pressed it to the valley between her small breasts. Her skin was cool and damp.

"I can feel your heart beating," he breathed.

"That's not where my heart is."

"Well, I can feel it anyway."

She nuzzled her head into the curve of his neck, her breath warming his throat, and he awkwardly wrapped his arms around her bare shoulders. The rain sounded like fir cones pelting the canvas.

He didn't have a condom. It hadn't occurred to him to buy one, just as it had never occurred to him that she would press her unclothed body against him. He tried to think how much trouble he could be in if people—especially her mother—knew they were here together. Being with her suddenly seemed dangerous, one of the most dangerous things he had ever done.

"Take off your clothes," she whispered.

He would have sworn his heart stopped. "Do you think this is okay?"

She unrolled the rest of the quilt and lay back on it. "No, but I want to do it anyway."

CALLUM LOVED HER. He loved her so much that he no longer cared that his sister teased him about her.

"Oh, God, look at him, Mother," Bethany groaned. "He's so disgustingly moony over her, he's pathetic."

They were standing in the kitchen, where he was finishing a half gallon of milk straight from the wax carton. Letting the milk dribble down his chin, he made a face at her.

She rolled her eyes. "Oh, God, get him out of here."

Their mother was scrambling eggs for dinner. She looked up. "Pour that milk into a glass, Callum." She turned and focused her tired eyes on Bethany. "Don't swear."

Bethany squinted from behind pink-framed glasses. "I didn't."

"You took the Lord's name in vain."

Callum grinned. "Yeah, Bethie, don't do that."

She spoke through clenched teeth. "If God really cared about me, he'd find me a better family."

It was only a day later that two of his Quinault friends, Steve Ross and Bill Stone, cornered him outside the community center in the Queets village.

Steve fell into step with Callum. "Hear you've got a girlfriend."

Callum kept on walking. "So? Don't you?"

That moron Bethany probably blabbed to Steve's sister Carolee, who, of course, owned the biggest mouth on the reservation.

Steve grinned. "Yeah, but she isn't Jessica Moran. Maybe you should marry her, Callum. Her family's got more money than you'll ever see."

"What he should do," Bill said, twirling a rabbit's-foot key ring on his finger, "is make her fall for him and then dump her. Her mom hates Indians." He had a slight lisp, which made anything he said sound childish.

Callum's temper rose. "It's not her fault what her mom does."

Steve laughed. "Hey, so it *is* true."

"Yeah, in his wet dreams," said Bill, who was walking ahead now. He accidentally dropped his key ring on the sidewalk. When he bent over to retrieve it, his T-shirt rode up in back, revealing some of the fifty pounds he needed to lose. "I've never seen them around town together. Or doesn't Miss Queen of the Universe speak to you in public?"

Later, Callum wished he had thought quickly enough to have laughed and claimed it was Steve's girlfriend he was secretly meeting. Instead, feeling humiliation heat up his neck, he said, "You think I'm going to hang out with her in town where you guys can point your grimy fingers at us and act like idiots. We've got a place we meet."

Steve grinned skeptically. "Where?"

Callum stared at him, trying to come up with an answer that would satisfy them. If he protested or denied anything now, they wouldn't believe him. "At my uncle Joe's house, where do you think?"

Bill blinked in surprise. "Aw, he wouldn't let you do that."

"That's right, Bill," Callum tossed over his shoulder as he sauntered away. "You think whatever you want."

He had sounded good. He'd answered with just the right amount of bluster, but, inside, he felt his muscles snap over his stomach like a clamp.

CALLUM ARRIVED at the tent around one o'clock in the morning, certain that Jessica would turn up. She'd said, once school started, they wouldn't be able to stay awake half the night and then go to classes, so they should take advantage of the last few weeks of summer vacation.

At eight o'clock the next morning, he walked the trail that ran along Thunder Lake from the reservation to Moran property. On the other side of the lake, the mill machinery clanked and hummed and sweetened the air with tree saps and resins. Crossing a grassy rise still shiny with dew, he saw Jessica leave her house, Jonah trailing her. She wore her customary hand-dyed black jeans, but her cotton shirt was crisply white and brand-new, not one left over from her dad. Her explosive curls looked tamer than usual.

He caught up with her, but she greeted him coolly, acting almost as if she didn't know him. Bill's words ". . . or doesn't Miss Queen of the Universe speak to you in public?" echoed in his head.

He edged closer to her, close enough to see the gauzy film of perspiration on her upper lip. "I thought you might come to the tent last night."

"I couldn't."

"Oh," he said, unsure if he was missing some message. When they were alone, she seemed so warm and sweet. He stared over her shoulder, at the smooth, grassy slope beyond her, gently curved like her body. "Let's go there now, Jess," he whispered.

She looked at him, shocked. "Not with Jonah."

"He could wait outside. He wouldn't know what we were doing."

"He's not stupid. And, besides, we agreed we wouldn't tell anyone we meet there."

"Right," he said. He couldn't bring himself to tell her their relationship was no longer a complete secret. "Will you come to the tent tonight?"

She glanced at Jonah, who was nudging a rock with the toe of his boot and humming to himself. "I'll try—if Mom isn't working on her papers at the dining room table. It's hard to sneak past her."

He wondered if her interest in him had spun down like a top or if she'd suddenly realized the social chasm between them was wider than the lake on the other side of the hill.

She studied him for a moment. "You think I don't want to, don't you?"

"No, I . . . I don't know."

She put her fingertips to her lips and touched them to his bare arm, surprising him. Her eyes held what seemed to Callum an almost unbearable tenderness, and he felt better than he'd thought possible. His doubts vanished. Her brand on his arm burned long after she withdrew her fingers.

She arrived earlier than usual at the tent that night. At eleven-thirty, Callum heard her whisper. "Thirteen days." He reached out his hand, grabbed her wrist, and pulled her into the tent. They tumbled onto the quilt, laughing and scuffling.

He nuzzled her neck and kissed the curve below her ear, realizing for the first time since they'd met that she had sprayed her skin with a flowery scent. In the past she'd often seemed like a tomboy but not anymore. Her coppery curls fell profusely across his face and tickled his nose. The shyness he felt with her that morning disappeared.

When he wasn't with her, his heart ached, and when he was with her, it was so filled with love for her that he thought it would push right out of his chest.

In health education class in high school, the teacher said that teenagers couldn't love each other the way adults did, that what they felt was only puppy love because the real thing came with time and experience. But Callum didn't believe that. He couldn't imagine his love for Jessica being any stronger than it was now. He wanted to marry her, and although he knew he couldn't speak to her of such a thing yet, it was a thrilling secret he held deep within him.

Callum had folded back one of the tent's window flaps to let in air. Even so, it smelled of dusty canvas and their body heat. It hadn't rained in any substantial amount for several weeks, and the trees and ferns and underbrush that soaked up the rain like sponges during the wet winters dried out quickly during the hot August days. A bird landing on a parched evergreen could send a cascade of withered needles falling to the earth, and the risk of forest fire shot up like a skyrocket.

Jessica struggled to her knees, more solemn now, and peeled off her sweat-damp T-shirt. "Come on."

She hadn't bothered to wear a bra, and in the candlelight her bathing suit strap lines crossed her shoulders like pale ribbons. Her skin below was coconut white, her breasts small with soft pink circles, and when he pressed his mouth between them, he tasted a warm saltiness and smelled that sweet flowery fragrance again. He wanted time to stop right where it was.

Her slender arms drew him tight against her. She tunneled below the waistband of his jeans and stroked the small of his back.

When her hand moved toward the front of his jeans and slid downward, his breath caught.

"I love you," she murmured, her eyes as bright and earnest as he'd ever seen them. "Come on. Take off your clothes."

He tugged off his jeans, careful not to bang his knees and elbows against her. Careful, easy movement was one thing he'd already learned from experience. He'd brought a condom. He knew he should use it, that he might make her pregnant if he didn't. But the thought of putting it on embarrassed him. He remembered the health education teacher saying sex without protection was like Russian roulette, only the odds might be worse. But Jess didn't seem worried. Next time, he would use the condom.

She yanked off her jeans and underpants and tossed them on top of her T-shirt. Dropping to her knees, she reached for him and nuzzled against his chest. They held and kissed each other for several minutes. Then she lay back on the quilt.

Just as he slid into her, he heard sounds outside—a rustle of underbrush, the crunch of dry fir cones and twigs. He glanced at Jessica. Her eyes were huge, the pupils black with panic.

She was staring at the window, where two shadowy faces grinned at them through the netting.

"Hey, he wasn't kidding," said a lisping voice. "He does have Jessica Moran in there."

As he pulled back from her, Callum saw her frozen look of horror and the larger vision of her milk-colored nakedness. He blew out the candles. The glow of her pale body hovered in the darkness like an afterimage.

Bill and Steve exploded into laughter and thumped on the side of the tent.

Callum fumbled for his clothes. "Get out of here, you assholes!"

His hand found denim, but when he tried to struggle into the jeans, they turned out to be Jessica's. He touched her hand and she jerked back as if he'd stung her. Outside, Steve and Bill were still thrashing around and hooting with laughter.

Callum located his pants and yanked them on. "I'll kill you guys. I swear to God I'll kill you."

He rummaged through his belongings until he found the flashlight. Switching it on, he aimed its bright beam at the entrance. The thought of looking at Jessica's face was unimaginable.

He pushed the door flap aside and scrambled out, feeling the scrub grass and fir cones and broken branches dig into his feet. Above him, a quarter moon in an expanse of gun-metal sky the width of the clear-cut, mocked him like a lopsided grin.

Beyond the clear-cut huddled the thick forest. He swept the light in a 180-degree arc.

It was already too late. He could hear their voices fading into the deep, absolute dark. They were still laughing.

Although he hadn't been aware of Jessica's leaving the tent, he sensed her presence behind him. He hesitated, then shone the light on her. She was dressed now except for her shoes, which she carried. Even under the yellow glare, her face had no color.

He felt so miserable he could barely think. "I . . . I don't know how they found us. They must have followed me."

"You told them about us. You knew they would come here." Her voice shook with pain and anger.

"No, I never thought they would do something like this, that they would—I never told them, Jess. It was an accident . . ." He couldn't utter a single coherent sentence, and besides she was walking away.

He fixed the flashlight beam on her proudly arched back and felt the struts that held up his life splinter and collapse.

THAT MEMORY still haunted Callum, although Jess had obviously gone on to build a life for herself, just as he had. She had tried to forget him, while he had held on to her. Even during the best days of his marriage, he kept her secreted in a small, private space inside him. Tori knew nothing about her. He meant no disrespect to his wife, but he didn't want to let go of Jess.

Ironically, he had married an Indian woman believing their common ancestry and purpose would bind them as tightly as it did those swans that mate for life. It didn't take long for him to discover that what Tori possessed was more important to her than what she did. She craved the upscale neighborhood, the expensive car, the designer wardrobe that two successful attorneys' incomes could provide.

But who was he kidding? In the beginning he'd wanted the same things she did. Like any boy coming out of poverty, he had longed for a few luxuries: a safe house where no one chased him with a broken beer bottle, decent food, suitable clothes, acceptance for his abilities. He fought hard to acquire these, and after he had them, it was easy to go for the finer things.

To his surprise, they didn't lead to a finer life. He and Tori began snapping and hissing and inflicting whatever pain they could on each other. They evolved into miserable, self-centered creatures who couldn't tolerate an afternoon together.

Feeling the sense of failure that had plagued him lately, he turned the Explorer off Highway 101 onto the narrow road that pierced the dense Hoh Rain Forest. It was March, before the tourist season began, but his uncle, Jim Luke, who managed the rain forest's visitor center at the end of the nineteen-mile road, would be there, preparing it for summer. If anyone could help him find the man who reported the fire, it would be his father's youngest brother. Having spent his life on the reservation, Jim could recite the names and personal histories of most of the eighteen hundred Quinaults who resided there.

And whatever reservation gossip he didn't know, Aunt Hannah would. She was serving her second term as secretary of the Quinault Indian Nation Tribal Council, and both were active members of the Indian Shaker Church.

Callum opened the driver's window and inhaled deeply, realizing he'd forgotten how the moist air here smelled and tasted of sweet decay. He hadn't traveled into this forest since he'd gone away to college and become a city Indian. Tori never liked backwater Misp, much less "those moldy tree swamps" as she called the brooding rain forests at the base of the Olympic Mountains. To Callum, they were reservoirs of pure calm.

With every mile that passed, the forest deepened. The conifers stretched toward the sky, their branches dragging beards of damp moss, their sinewy roots bulging under a layered carpet of lichen, vines, ferns, seedlings, and toppled logs. Vegetation here ambled through its cycle of sprouting, growing, reproducing, and dying. There was no technological advancement to short-circuit any of the stages. Nothing but nature ever interfered, and that was the beauty of it.

The mist hung low in the boughs like wood smoke, and the dampness tickled his skin. He had not yet encountered another vehicle on the rutted road.

Glancing at his hands on the steering wheel, he considered how he had changed in the years he'd been away from the reservation.

Recently, he'd obsessed on the thought that his skin had faded from the warm, dusky brown of his youth to a pasty beige. Well, of course, the color had lightened. It wasn't some bizarre psychosomatic reaction to divorce or his loss of identity. He just didn't get out in the sun enough these days.

However, he was experiencing a restlessness he'd felt once before. He clearly remembered standing at the window of his sixty-third-floor office in Columbia Tower, looking out over Puget Sound, watching the ferries crisscross the inlet between the mainland and the nearby islands. As the boats made pearl-white furrows in the deep blue water, he realized he couldn't face another day drafting corporate contracts. He wasn't naive enough to believe that comfort didn't come at a minimum price, but he'd been wrong to think that luxuries defined who he was. He took a pay cut and joined the ATF's arson and homicide unit because it seemed like public service, like some vague atonement for a half-dozen wasted years. Tori had hurled their Baccarat candy dish at him.

But he had married her for better or worse. Did anyone going into a marriage ever ask himself how bad the worst could be? It never occurred to him it could come in the form of his brother, although he couldn't have said which hurt more—his heart or his pride. Tori and Andy made a good pair. *He* wanted the upper-middle-class life she led, and she wanted someone who'd defer to her, who'd follow her like a panting puppy.

When the rustic, low-slung Forest Service visitor center came into view, Callum saw his uncle standing on the building's entrance ramp, lounging against the wooden railing, apparently ignoring the steady raindrops plopping from the canopy of trees.

Callum parked his car, stepped out, and waved a greeting. "You look like you've been expecting me, Uncle."

Jim grinned. "I heard you coming a long distance back." He touched his index finger to the device that looked like a lump of putty in his ear.

Callum recalled that he had suffered the hearing loss after a bout with mumps as a boy.

"That's the problem with this thing," Jim said. "Even in the middle of the forest, it gives me no peace and quiet."

Callum smiled. "You could turn it off."

"That would be worse. Then I'd have no one to listen to but myself." Jim strode down the ramp, the solid mound of his mid-section preceding the rest of him. "Should we walk a bit and work the kinks from our legs?"

"I'd like that."

Jim was forty-eight, ten years younger than Callum's father. They were half brothers, their Quinault father having remarried after his first wife died. Jim had the sandy brown hair of the Hoh River people, his mother's tribe.

Callum didn't recall ever having seen him in anything but a plaid flannel shirt and blue jeans. He had the healthy color and seamless skin texture of a man who'd spent decades living in perpetual moist air or, more likely, abstaining from cigarettes and alcohol.

While Callum was growing up, his father and Jim often quarreled, and during the years he'd been gone, their relationship hadn't improved.

When Callum asked his dad about Jim, he got a variation of the same irritable response. "He's still acting like the good Lord appointed him chief."

Walking side by side, Callum and his uncle headed toward a marked trail. The far-reaching network of fungi that clung to the earth, the forest duff, and the moss-wrapped trees that stood like cathedral columns muted all sound. Callum found himself hushing his voice because any loud noise here seemed irreverent.

He spoke first of family—not only because it was the bond they shared but also because it would have been rude to begin with the questions he'd come to ask. Before long, he found himself slipping into the familiar, relaxed speech cadence of the reservation.

Callum picked his way along the muddy trail. "I heard you talked with Dad about his drinking."

Jim turned to look at him. "I tried, but he thinks he doesn't have to listen because he's older than me. I said, 'Eddie, you know when you go to the tavern, you pick up bad spirits and bring them home.'" Jim splayed his fingers on his arm, demonstrating how they might cling to a man's clothing like sticky-footed spiders. "Once they catch hold, it's hard to shake them off. I told him to look at what he's doing to himself and the family. That's why your sister has that tumor on her neck."

Callum thought of Bethany, who was scheduled for surgery on her thyroid gland. The women from the Shaker Church had conducted a healing ceremony for her at his parents' house.

Jim stopped to pat the mossy trunk of an enormous cedar, like one old friend greeting another.

"Ed has poisoned Andrew with the evil spirits too. Now your brother is carrying them and hurting others." He averted his gaze, as though apologizing for any distress his words caused Callum. "It all comes from breaking too many of our beliefs."

Callum had grown up with the notion that spirits could be good or evil or sometimes just mischievous. The bad ones infected people the way viruses did, leading to other miseries—among them, illness and divorce. While he would have preferred that rationale for his own marital problems, he knew they had started long before his father took to boozing again.

He and Jim hiked for several minutes without speaking. The rustle of an animal scuttling through the thick foliage broke the intense silence. Because of the rain forest's distorted acoustics, Callum couldn't quite tell where the sound had come from. Glancing around, he spotted a flash of brown among the varying shades of green—the flank of a black-tailed deer. He and Jim talked for a time about the effects of human intrusion on the rain forest, one of his uncle's passionate concerns.

After they'd trekked another quarter mile, Callum brought up the subject of the arson fire. "Someone made a call from the Queets Community Center to report it. Have you heard anything about that, Uncle?"

He smiled. "I heard you've been asking folks on the reservation about it."

"Without any success," Callum admitted. "I thought you might be able to help me."

Jim didn't speak for such a long time that Callum thought he might not have heard him. "Uncle?"

"Those are other people's problems." Jim picked up a lichen-wrapped twig and tugged on the faded silver-green strands. "They don't have anything to do with us or the reservation."

Callum nodded slowly. "Sometimes we get caught up in their problems."

"And that's usually a mistake, isn't it?"

"It would be wrong to let someone get away with arson and murder."

His uncle's head snapped up, an uncharacteristic sudden movement. "When I see things that are not right, of course it hurts me inside, but no one from the reservation set that fire and killed those men."

"I'm not suggesting an Indian did, but someone saw the fire, drove to the reservation, and called the emergency number from the community center. We have the nine-one-one recording, but he didn't identify himself and his voice is muffled."

"So, he reported it as any good man would do, and now you want to cause problems for him and his family."

"I don't want to cause him problems, but maybe he saw something else that would help us."

Jim looked at him intently. "Why don't you talk with the people who live close to that halfway house?"

"We did, but none of them saw much. Answering a few questions isn't going to get the man into trouble, Uncle."

Jim stopped for a moment, staring at something in the distance that Callum couldn't see. "Doesn't it seem that every time we help them, we hurt ourselves a little more? It's always one-sided."

Callum didn't know how to respond. The question his uncle asked was larger than any answer he could give. He realized he was arguing his point from a white man's perspective. As an Indian, he couldn't promise that the man who reported the fire would be perfectly safe in stepping forward.

After Mike Moran's death, Jim had been one of the Quinaults Lila Moran laid off from Thunder Lake Timber. Callum knew Jim realized not all whites were like her. But it took only one bigot in a position of authority to twist suspicion around. Callum wouldn't insult his uncle by offering ironclad assurances.

As though reading his mind, Jim said, "People are saying Jonah Moran did it. Do you think his mother will stand for that?"

Callum knew Jim was familiar with his own complicated history with the Morans. He found it difficult to look at him. "I don't know. But, whether the arsonist turns out to be from the reservation or from the town, it won't change what I do."

"Not even if the arsonist is Jessica Moran's brother?" Jim's tone was low, free of accusation but uncommonly crisp and blunt.

"No," Callum said, "not even then." He owed too much to this bedrock of family and tribe, and he'd worked too hard building his professional reputation for integrity and impartiality. "But," he added, "I don't want to see the wrong person arrested either."

After they'd completed the two-mile loop that took them back to the visitor center, Jim removed his baseball cap, dampened by the steady drizzle, and rubbed his forehead. "Accusing the wrong person never seems to have bothered them before."

Callum nodded thoughtfully. "But that is not *your* way, Uncle. Would you become one of them?"

Jim gave him a penetrating stare. No wonder the tribe called him Stone Eyes, Callum thought. A hundred and fifty years ago, his uncle would have been leading battles against the land-hungry, bleached-skin invaders, scaring the life out of them.

Just when Callum had decided not to press his uncle any further, Jim shook his head firmly. "No, I would not become one of them. I will talk to the man who reported the fire and see if I can be as persuasive as you."

He left the rain forest on the same isolated road, feeling as though he'd exited a dimension where time and space were measured differently than they were in the bullet-paced world he'd become accustomed to.

Driving back, he thought about his uncle's implication that he might be treating the Morans differently. Meanwhile, Jess was accusing him of retaliation. He could easily dismiss her charge, but his uncle's stabbed him like a foot-long splinter on the ethical fence he felt he was trying to straddle.

Jim didn't know the half of it. His uncle hadn't seen him fighting the tidal pull Jess had on him. Not that his pathetic declaration of interest in her seemed to have much effect. She had looked a little flustered and shocked, especially about his divorce, but he was still clearly the enemy.

Just as his car tires crunched across the pitted intersection onto Highway 101, his car phone rang. It was Villalobos, the arson specialist from the state fire marshal's office, calling from the Misp fire station.

Callum pointed the Explorer back toward Misp. "What have you got, Rob?"

"Results from the lab."

Callum glanced at the clock on the dash. "I can be there in a half hour."

"I've got the sheriff coming. Bud Schultz isn't here right now, but I'll page him."

There was a short silence.

"Yes, he should be there," Callum said.

"Good old Bud. He's always got something insightful to add." Callum could hear the grin in Rob's voice.

"Right," Callum said, restraining himself from further comment.

Like Rob, he would have preferred to exclude the fire chief. It was bad enough that the man was a fool, but, despite his reminders on confidentiality, Callum worried Bud might be passing along information to others in the community.

That was just one of his concerns, he thought, as he punched the disconnect button on his cellular phone. Whatever the results from the crime lab, he hoped they wouldn't make him more of an enemy to the Moran family.

BY THE TIME Callum arrived at the fire station, Rob Villalobos, Milt Tarr, and Bud Schultz were already gathered around the rectangular, fold-up table used for meetings. A fax machine on an old metal typewriter stand and a bulky copier occupied one corner of the room. Firefighting gear lined a wall—thick, insulated tan coats with orange fluorescent stripes, visored helmets, black bunker boots—giving off the smells of smoke, rubber, and sweat.

Callum eased himself onto the chair across from Rob and flipped open his notebook. "What have we got?"

Peering over the top of his reading glasses, Rob pushed a sheet of paper across the table. "Well, first of all, we've got class three petroleum distillate."

Bud snorted, "Well, that's helpful . . ."

Callum looked at him. "The most common petroleum distillates are dry cleaning solvent, lighter fluid, and paint thinner."

Bud's eyes brightened. "Now, that makes more sense."

The sheriff rested his elbows on the table. "Don't combustible fluids have batch codes so you can trace them to the place of purchase—maybe even the owner if he kept any of the stuff?"

"Not anymore, unfortunately," Callum said. "Our job's a little harder now because we don't have those codes." He studied the fax from the crime lab, then shifted his attention back to Rob. "What else?"

Rob shoved over two other pieces of paper. "Here's the way it looks. The arsonist entered through the dining room window, which was broken before the fire started. We could tell that because of the way the window had fractured and because those glass fragments outside the house showed no sign of carbon soot on either side. He . . ." Rob paused. "It's more likely a *he* than a *they,* but I'll get to that later. He brought in three Kerr canning jars filled with a petroleum distillate. He placed one next to the living room sofa, one at the edge of the dining room, and one a few yards from the broken window. Then he ran a trailer of fuel-soaked newspaper strips between the jars and back to the window. He lit the fuse and crawled out the window. Oh, and he torched the dining room curtains for extra measure. This guy wanted to make sure the place would burn fast and the men in there would die of smoke inhalation without ever waking. The survivor was lucky he got out."

Callum underlined the words *petroleum distillate* and *newspaper trailer* in his notebook. "What about the footprint castings?"

Rob tapped his pencil on the remaining stack of papers. "Well, these guys didn't have a lot of visitors so we don't have as many different footprints as we usually get. We've managed to sort out the ones that belonged to the people who lived there, plus our own shoes. We've got bunker boots, of course—a stampede of them."

Callum grunted in affirmation. The firefighters themselves unintentionally contaminated more evidence at the scene than anyone else, no matter how many lectures they'd had on precautions.

Pinching his gray mustache between his thumb and forefinger, Rob studied his notes. "We found a couple of prints in the mud outside the house. One is a size seven Adidas athletic shoe, probably a woman's or a teenager's."

Callum nodded wearily. No sense pretending he didn't know whose prints those were. The neighbors probably saw her wandering around. He said, "Jessica Moran was walking outside the halfway house the morning after the fire." Noticing Bud's dark eyebrows shoot up, he added, "I'll check with her and see if we can get the shoes."

"There's another print we haven't matched to anybody yet. It's really peculiar," Rob said. "I have no idea how the lab guys tracked this one down, but it's a reproduction of a brogan worn by Confederate soldiers in the Civil War. It's a heavy, high-top work shoe, comes only in black with leather laces, available by mail order from a company called Grand Illusions Clothing for ninety-one dollars. This outfit specializes in period costumes, military uniforms, that sort of thing, and they go for real authenticity. Can't be that many people running around town in men's size-ten brogans with a Confederate insignia inside. Even if there were, this particular pair has its own pattern of nicks and cuts."

Callum drew a long breath. "And were those prints inside or outside?"

"Both," Rob said. "Some excellent impressions."

"Where inside?"

"Two partials, both in the kitchen—like the guy walked through it with muddy shoes."

The sheriff scratched the edge of his jaw. "Rained that entire day before the fire."

Rob smiled. "When doesn't it rain here in March?"

"And that's it?" Callum said. "No other prints?"

"None," Rob said in a tone that sounded regretful.

"And that broken leather boot lace?"

"The lab guys already matched it to a sample of the brogan lace they requested from Grand Illusions."

Bud, who had been leaning back in his chair, let the front legs fall to the floor with a thump. "Well, it doesn't take any fancy crime lab or arson genius to figure this one out. Fake Confederate shoes and paint thinner? That's easy."

Callum frowned. "What do you mean?"

"Jonah Moran," the sheriff said in a low voice. "He's got this crazy fascination with the Civil War."

Callum nodded. "I remember he used to collect toy soldiers."

"Well, now he's got a Civil War battlefield set up in his basement," Milt said, "and he paints these military miniatures he buys through the mail."

Bud rose to his feet. "Let's go. We can wrap this up today."

Callum shook his head. "Not yet. We have a lot of other things to check first."

Bud, who was still standing, rolled his eyes. "Shit, no wonder you city guys get paid so much. Takes you three times as long as anyone else to do the work."

Rob stiffened but didn't say anything.

"I told you who owns the shoes and the paint thinner."

Callum didn't look at Bud. "And I told you we need more than that."

Bud gave an exaggerated sigh. "Oh, I suppose you'll want a feasibility study and an environmental impact statement first. If we're lucky, we can stretch this investigation out a year or two."

When no one answered, he leveled his gaze on Callum. "The fact that we're dealing with the Morans doesn't make any difference, does it, Luke?"

Callum shifted his attention to the fire chief. "No, it doesn't."

Bud snorted. "Seems obvious to me, unless you think his sister did it. We've got one set of prints, both outside and inside, belonging to a guy who tromps around in phony Civil War shoes, who probably runs through a gallon of paint thinner a month and who was seen throwing rocks at the halfway house the night before the fire."

Callum raised his eyebrows. "And that's it? That's all you're basing it on?"

Bud's eyes narrowed. "No." His voice turned sarcastic. "The back door and the front door were locked. Doesn't make much sense that the survivor would have dragged that barrel over to the window, climbed into the dining room, set the fire, run upstairs, crawled out his bedroom window onto the porch roof, and jumped to the ground. That would have been pretty stupid."

"So that rules out Dennis Kretz and everybody else in town, right?" Callum said.

Bud frowned. "I didn't say that. I just said you're making this too hard, when we could haul in Jonah Moran right now."

"The person who owns the brogans may not be the arsonist. Supposing they are Jonah Moran's shoes, what's his motive for setting the fire?"

"Who cares? Maybe he thinks he's doing his civic duty by cleaning up the neighborhood."

"I doubt that would hold up in court." Callum stood and started gathering up the papers. "We don't have enough evidence. I'll let you know when we do."

Milt was already pulling a cigarette out of his pocket and heading outside to smoke it. Rob was jotting down a note.

Bud rocked on his heels. "Guess that means you'll at least visit Jonah and ask to see those shoes—unless you've got some reason for stalling."

Milt looked at Callum as if he thought the fire chief had a good point.

Callum turned away, too annoyed to deflect Bud's jab with humor. "In time," he said crisply.

Bud's lips twisted into a half-amused smile. "Is that Indian time, Luke, or regular time?"

Milt stared up at the ceiling. "Aw, shit, Bud."

Callum heard a long exhalation of breath from Rob, but he didn't pause to look at him. He strode out the door.

His shoes crunched on the gravel as he walked toward his car.

It was too soon to narrow his focus exclusively on Jonah, he told himself. He couldn't get a search warrant on what little evidence they had. He might find some local yokel judge who would issue one, but any evidence that came out of any search without probable cause wouldn't hold up in court.

Callum knew that he had handled the exchange with Bud poorly. It angered him that the fire chief's accusations contained just enough truth to make him doubt himself. Any good investigator would try to convince Jonah to cooperate without a warrant, but Callum had no intention of letting Bud Schultz dictate the pace of the investigation.

14

The next evening, Jessica opened her front door to Callum. He was wearing jeans, a blue shirt, and a brown jacket, and he brought in the smell of leather with the cool April breeze.

He gave her one of his slow-to-rise smiles. "I need to borrow your shoes."

She stared at him. "What shoes?"

He looked at the worn pink satin slippers on her feet. "Not those, obviously. The Adidas shoes you were wearing at the halfway house."

Her expression must have registered alarm because he quickly added, "It's just a formality. No one thinks you set the fire, but we want to account for all the footprints we found at the scene."

"All right. Come in then, and I'll get them." She opened the door wider, not meeting his gaze. He made her uneasy, but she couldn't leave him standing on the steps.

She turned and headed toward the kitchen. "They're muddy so I left them on the back porch."

He followed her. "Did you buy those slippers?"

She made a face. "My ex-husband gave them to me for Christmas one year."

"I would never have thought of you as the pink satin type."

"I'm not. That was the problem with our marriage. He thought I was." She gestured toward the dirty dishes on the drain board. "I was just cleaning up after dinner."

She opened the back door, picked up the shoes on the steps, and banged the soles together. Chunks of dried mud fell off. "How soon will I get these back?"

"Tomorrow morning, or if you need them before then, I can make a casting of them now and bring them back tonight."

"Tomorrow's fine." She set the shoes on the linoleum floor. "I'll get a bag for them."

As she turned toward the broom closet, the phone rang, first a clipped jangle, then a longer one. Intending to let the answering machine pick it up, she pulled out a paper grocery sack and shook it open.

After her invitation to leave a message, a man's low voice crooned, "Hello, Jessica Moran. Let's talk some more about—"

Oh, Lord, Dennis Kretz. She tossed the bag on the counter, lunged for the wall phone, and spoke a breathy hello into the receiver.

"Had the feeling you were there," he said.

She thought of his feral smile and his dead eyes and her own foolishness, and she could almost smell a whiff of Oreos. Her fear of him returned in a wave of nausea.

She'd had a message from him on the answering machine the evening before.

"About your brother," he'd said. "He likes to set fires. Did you know that? He says the North burnt its way across the South, and someday he's going to take revenge and—"

Without listening to the rest, she had erased the message.

Now he was calling, with Callum standing only a few feet away in front of the kitchen sink.

"So, how's your brother?" Dennis said.

"I can't talk right now," she murmured into the phone. She wondered if she hung up on him whether he'd just call back.

"You've got someone there with you, haven't you?"

He was mumbling, and it took Jessica a few rapid-paced heart-beats to figure out what he'd said.

"Actually I do," she said.

"A man, right?"

"No," she said almost too quickly.

"Yeah, I'll bet."

Callum was watching her, and she worried that her nervousness would give her away. Feeling tethered to the corded phone, she managed to smile at him.

"I really am busy," she said to Dennis. "Could I get your phone number and call you later?"

She realized she was afraid to hang up on him. If she pulled the shade on one dark window, he just might turn up behind another.

Callum sloshed liquid Joy on her plate and vigorously scrubbed it under a stream of steaming water. She didn't want him washing her dishes. She gestured in protest with her free hand, but he ignored her.

Dennis's voice increased in volume. "Did you come on to him like you did with me?"

The mere suggestion she might have invited Dennis's attention made her grimace. She turned away and pressed the receiver tight against her ear, hoping Callum wouldn't hear him. She wanted to ask Dennis to go back to mumbling.

"I'm sorry if you got that impression. I never intended it." She could feel the perspiration beading along her hairline.

Callum was rinsing the silverware.

"I could get a car and drive over to the peninsula." Dennis lowered his voice. "Would you like that?" There was a current of threat under the seductive murmur.

She tried to keep her voice level, but it came out sounding breathy and shallow. "No, I wouldn't."

Callum gave her a curious glance.

"Yeah, I just might do that," Dennis said.

She couldn't listen to him any longer. She pushed the disconnect lever but continued pressing the phone to her ear, aware that her hand was shaking so hard she might rattle the receiver returning it to its wall cradle. Finally, she managed to slip it back with a minimum of noise.

She felt Callum's gaze on her.

"Where do you keep your dish towels?" he asked.

Bending over, she tugged on the lowest drawer's porcelain knob. She handed him one of the clean, lint-free, blue surgical cloths she used for drying windows.

He buffed the crockery plate, studying her face all the while. "You're white."

"Well, of course I'm white," she snapped. "You're Indian. I'm white. We've been down that road before."

He gave her a disapproving look. "Come on, Jess."

She shook her head. "I'm sorry."

"Who was it? Your ex-husband?"

She wanted to say yes but couldn't bring herself to lie. "No."

When he raised his eyebrows skeptically, she added, "A guy I know, in Seattle. Is that okay with you, or do you think you've got some right to—"

"Since when do your boyfriends make you look like you're going to throw up?"

He handed her the dried plate, then walked over to the answering machine and punched the rewind button. Too late, she realized she hadn't turned off the tape recorder when she'd answered the phone. After the tape stopped, he pushed the play button and listened to the conversation.

Once it had finished, he looked at her. "That's Dennis Kretz, isn't it? Jesus, why did you tell him you'd call him back?"

She wrapped her hands around the plate, holding it against her midriff. "I wanted to get rid of him. You don't really think I'd call him, do you?"

"I'm not sure what you'd do. Why didn't you just hang up on him?"

When she shrugged, he shook his head. "Never mind. I know the answer to that. You thought you could handle him, just like you think you can handle everything else."

She looked down at the shiny white plate in her hands. She didn't want him to know that Dennis currently starred in her nightmares.

"For God's sake, Jess," Callum said in a husky rasp, "you have a convicted sex offender calling you on the phone and trying to arrange a date with you."

She lifted her chin in defiance. "Well, he's no more dangerous now than he was when he lived three miles from me."

"And what if he does drive here?"

"He won't. He hates this town."

Callum shook his head wearily. "Now that sounds like a good reason."

She swung abruptly toward one of the cabinets, opened the door, and shoved the plate inside. "You don't have to be sarcastic."

After a brief silence, he said softly, "How did he get your phone number?"

"Looked it up in the book, I guess. It's listed twice—under my name and under Room with a View." She hesitated. "He also saw my van. The phone number's painted on the side."

"Wonderful." He looked at her for several long moments, not saying anything but obviously weighing a decision in his mind.

The doorbell rang, and Jessica jumped as though someone had shot a gun behind her.

She laughed then, a false sound. "I normally lead a quiet life, so I can't imagine who's setting off all these bells."

She headed for the front door, praying that it would be her neighbor Ada Toobert standing on the porch, clutching a loaf of her freshly baked raisin bread—someone easy to deal with.

Passing the living room window, Jessica glanced outside. The sky was the dingy shade of wood smoke. As soon as she saw the bulky silhouette on the other side of the front door's curtained glass pane, she exhaled a low groan of disappointment. And, yet, she felt there was little choice but to open the door.

Pete Johnson, eyes slightly glazed, feet planted wide, boyish grin stretched cheek to cheek, teetered on the porch as if he were straddling a fallen log. "Bet you figured I'd given up on you."

She sighed. "No, Pete, somehow I knew you hadn't."

He staggered forward, grabbing the wrought iron railing for balance. She caught the drifting odor of beer.

"Hey, doll," he breathed, "thought we could ride up to Forks and catch a movie."

She turned her face away. "I've got company, Pete."

"Huh?"

"Another time, okay? I'll call you." She hated the way she sounded—overly cautious and appeasing.

He stifled a furry belch. "Why would you do that when you haven't answered my last three messages?"

"Pete, I'm busy this evening."

He nodded at a spot over her shoulder. "Yeah," he said, thick-tongued with resentment. "I can see that."

She looked over her shoulder. Callum stood in the kitchen doorway, his arms crossed, the yellow orb of the overhead fixture backlighting him. He had on his protective mask—his eyes dark and blank, his lips tight.

She swung back toward Pete. "I said *another time.*"

His expression went cold. "Shit, Jessica, I would have thought you would have had enough red meat in high school."

She stared at him, remembering what her mother had said when she confronted her about Callum that summer she was sixteen. *"Didn't you realize people would fall all over themselves to tell me an Indian buck was screwing my daughter in a squalid tent in the woods?"*

The anger rolled through her and rose in her throat. "Get off my porch, you son of a bitch."

She slammed the door, meeting resistance as it hit his heavy boot.

When he merely blinked at her in irritation, she pulled back and slammed it again, smashing it against his foot with all her strength. She felt the wooden door shudder and heard tiny splintering sounds. He yelped and jerked back, cursing under his breath. She realized—or at least hoped—she had caught part of his ankle.

Holding her hand firmly on the doorknob, she tracked his wavering shadow through the filmy curtain. There was a thrumming sound and she realized he'd kicked the railing.

Shoving the drape aside, she watched him stagger down the steps, cross the parking strip, and crawl into his truck. She wasn't sure, but she thought there might be another man inside it, Wendell Schultz maybe. So much for safety in numbers. Tires squealed on the pavement as the red pickup sped off.

When she swung around, Callum was standing in the same place, his expression unchanged. He gave a wry smile. "How did you get to be so popular?"

She rubbed her hand across her forehead. "I'm sorry."

"For what?" He strode to the front door and brushed the curtain aside.

"For what he said, for the way he acted."

"Since when are you responsible for Pete? He was a jerk in high school. He's still a jerk."

"Funny, I don't remember him that way, but I wanted to punch him when he made that remark." She paused. "Didn't you?"

"To tell the truth, Jess, I wanted to slam my knee directly between his legs, but if I did that to every guy who made a comment like that, I'd need a knee replacement."

As he walked back across the living room, a vehicle screeched around the corner and ground to a stop in front of her house.

"Ungrateful bitch!" Pete's voice boomed. "Injun lover. Slut!"

The engine roared, and the truck shot off again.

Callum exhaled a long, slow breath. "I'll phone the sheriff and have him picked up for drunk driving."

Jessica shook her head. "No, please, Callum. I have to live in this town."

He looked her over. "I can't figure out how you did it, but you managed to piss off two bastards in one evening."

"I'll be okay. I'll lock myself in tonight."

He strode back to the door. After fiddling with the lock for a half minute without success, he turned to her in disgust. "This lock is jammed or rusted shut. I'll bet it hasn't been used in decades. Do you even have the key?"

She smiled sheepishly.

He shook his head again, then walked over to the sofa and pressed his hand against its leopard-spotted cushion, as if testing for softness. "I'm sleeping here tonight."

She felt the heat spring to her cheeks. "You are not. Call the sheriff and have him send someone to patrol the house."

"Milt Tarr has some hardworking deputies, but he also has a few who would burrow into their cruisers and snore so loudly they wouldn't hear a bomb explode."

She straightened her spine and crossed her arms, hoping to convey the kind of authority Lila managed so easily. "You are overreacting. I admit Kretz is a little scary, but I've known Pete half my life. He's not going to do anything."

He laughed abruptly and sank onto the sofa as if her excuses tired him. "I work in a unit called Arson and Homicide Investigative Assistance Team. Let me just mention a couple of things I've run into the last few years. A spurned lover stalked and murdered the woman who had turned him down for a date. A sexual predator molested two teenage girls the week after he was released from prison. Then he tracked down the victim whose testimony had sent him to prison and burned down her house." He lifted his eyebrows. "Shall I go on?"

She shook her head.

"Then don't talk to me about what people will *do*." He fixed his eyes on her, as if checking to make sure she was listening. "Kretz did his best to scare you, and Pete, who doesn't seem to be in full control of what few faculties he has, hung out the window of his truck and called you several unpleasant names. Now, if you had any sense, you would be worried."

"I'll go stay at my mother's."

He gave a sharp laugh. "No, you won't. You'll make a big show of driving out there, and then once I've left you'll come back here. Your mother's the last person you'd stay with."

He was right. She would rather sleep on a park bench than spend a night in the same house with her mother. If Mary Grace didn't have a husband, four teenage kids, a son-in-law, a toddler grandchild, and too little room, she'd ask to visit there. But she had no desire to explain her reasons to Mary Grace or to anyone else.

Callum rose from the sofa. "I'll be back in a minute. I want to get something from my car."

He returned with a thick manila folder. "Dennis Kretz's criminal file, from 1986 to present day, the condensed edition." He sat on the sofa and patted the cushion beside him. "Sit down. Let's have a show-and-tell on what people sometimes do to each other, but first you might want to take something for your upset stomach."

"I don't have an upset stomach."

"You will."

Reluctantly, she eased onto the sofa, keeping a respectable distance from him.

He opened the folder and handed her a mug shot of a teenage boy. "Dennis at fourteen, about the time he began torturing the neighborhood cats and molesting little girls."

She recognized him immediately. Cold eyes, tightly drawn mouth pasted on skin that, even then, had the color and consistency of bread dough. He wore small wire-rimmed glasses that gave him a nerdy look. Jessica handed the picture back. "Angry back then too."

Callum slipped it into the file. "He had good reason to be." He handed her another photo.

This one showed a young man's bare back, his shoulders round and puffy as a boxer's gloves, his undershorts poking above the waistband of his jeans. Tiny circular scars the diameter of a cigarette dotted nearly every square inch of skin.

Jessica swallowed hard. "But he said this happened to—" She stopped, embarrassed.

Callum looked up and said in a low voice, "As you pointed out earlier, he's not particularly truthful, Jess."

"Maybe he did set the fire then."

"We're not ruling it out."

She couldn't resist adding, "Well, he's a more likely suspect than my brother. Maybe he didn't get along with the other guys in the house. Maybe they were going to report him for breaking the rules, something like that."

Callum didn't reply.

At least Dennis was honest about something, she thought. The scars did resemble worms, tiny white worms curled under his flesh. Her stomach rebelled. "They shouldn't have let him out of prison. They should have—done something." She handed the photo back.

Callum straightened the stack of papers. "Kretz is a level-three offender. That means that on a scale of one to three he's most likely to reoffend. But he was paroled, and we're always taking chances with released felons. Better to monitor them in halfway houses than to dump them back into the community without any supervision. Maybe three out of four of those men did want to change their lives, but I personally don't think Kretz was one of the three." He closed the folder. "Jess, he's a slimeball. I'm not trying to scare you, but I don't know how else to impress upon you—"

"I'm impressed, okay? You've done your job."

When he didn't reply, she grumbled, "Dammit, Callum, don't be such a Boy Scout."

His jaw tightened.

She immediately felt a surge of guilt, then a backwash of anger because he could so easily produce that emotional upheaval in her.

She couldn't imagine him stretched out half naked in her living room—or maybe she could, and that was the problem.

She looked away, unnerved by the possibility he might read her mind. "I don't want you sleeping on my sofa."

"Why? Do you think I'd do something to you?" He sounded annoyed. "I'm not going to touch you, Jess. I just don't want you here alone."

But he *had* already done something. "No," she whispered. "I can't have you in my house."

He stood, his stiff movements indicating she'd hurt his pride. "No problem. I'll watch from outside. I'll park my car out front."

"It's still cold at night."

"I have a jacket and a wool blanket in the car."

She waved her hand in exasperation. "All right, then, fine. Sleep out there if you want."

BEFORE HER HEAD touched the pillow, she knew she wouldn't get much sleep. She rose twice and stared out the living room window at the darkened Ford Explorer.

At twelve-thirty A.M., she tugged on her Eddie Bauer down jacket and padded out to his car with a pillow. He slouched sideways, his legs stretched out. A nearly full moon hovered over the trees. A light wind added to the chill. She exchanged a minimum of words with him and returned to the house.

At two A.M., she checked the thermometer on the back porch. It read thirty-nine degrees. She decided if it dipped any lower, she'd have to invite him in, and if it frosted, she'd have to treat him for hypothermia. Shivering, she wrapped her plaid flannel robe tight around her and crawled back in bed.

At three o'clock, she brewed two cups of tea and carried them to the car, wishing she'd thought of the hot drink earlier. He stayed in the driver's seat and she climbed in the back, neither one commenting on the odd arrangement. He told her about Bethany's upcoming surgery, their fear that the cancer might have spread, and the Shaker Church women's healing ceremony.

Jessica looked at him curiously. "They think they're shaking off evil spirits?"

He was leaning back against the driver's door, his legs arched over the console. "Why is that so strange?"

"Wel-ll . . ." she said uncomfortably.

From behind the leather headrest, he stared hard at her. "Is that really so different from counting little plastic beads, lighting candles for the dead, and drinking the blood of Christ?"

She hoped he couldn't see her flushed face in the moonlight that spilled through the side window. "No, I suppose not."

"It's a cultural thing," he said softly.

"Of course," she said, feeling chastised.

They were silent for a time.

Jessica shifted sideways so she could stretch out her legs. "I drove into Queets one afternoon a few months after I moved back here. I'd never been there before."

She had wanted to see where he lived as a boy, although she didn't mention that detail.

"Never?" he said.

She shook her head. "My mother would have grounded me for a year if she'd known I'd gone onto the reservation at all."

"Why?"

"I don't know, Callum. I can't explain why she's the way she is. I know my father occasionally drove into Queets. Sometimes, when I stopped by the mill to see him, Marie and Barbara in the office would tell me that's where he'd gone. Remember them?"

He nodded. "Yeah, I know them. They're my first cousins."

"Well, they would wink at each other and giggle like they were sharing a private joke. I was thirteen or fourteen and, like most kids that age, overly sensitive about my family. I remember I couldn't understand why they were laughing, but they hurt my feelings."

"They probably didn't mean anything by it," he murmured.

She thought he sounded less than truthful. A shadow shielded his face so she couldn't read his expression.

"So, what did you see when you drove through Queets?" he asked.

"An elderly man in a dinghy." She smiled at the memory.

The village was smaller than she had expected, consisting of a few squat wood frame buildings that might have been administrative offices and a string of modest homes that reminded her of the cookie-cutter houses on a military base. Some had peeling paint, mismatched siding, and satellite dishes the size of a dining table in their yards. Here and there, dogs sprawled on concrete front porch slabs, and although it was August, a plastic, three-foot-tall Santa Claus waved season's greetings from the roof of one house.

The speed limit on the main street that threaded through the community was fifteen miles per hour, but she kept the speedometer at twelve. Although it wasn't raining, somber clouds hung low in the sky that day.

She cruised past the Shaker Church and the community center where a heavyset woman with graying hair stood under the entrance canopy, sucking on a cigarette and blowing a ribbon of smoke heavenward. She stared at the van. As Jessica passed a playfield, three boys who looked to be seven or eight years old stopped their jumping and thrashing on a truck-sized inner tube to watch her. She considered asking them where the Luke family lived, but she'd already drawn more attention to herself than she wanted.

No sign said outsiders weren't welcome, but the reservation seemed to breathe that warning. Although the homes appeared mostly uninhabited, she saw the occasional moving shadow, the fluttering curtain. When the street reached a dead end, she backed up the van and turned down the only other paved road, one that curved into a section of newer two-story homes.

Conspicuous among them was an old, single-story light green bungalow with tarpaper poking between the vertical boards. In the front yard, about twenty feet from the street, rested a dinghy, its white paint cracked, its wood rotted in places. A man lay across the thwarts, his head propped against the prow and his arms arranged loosely over his chest. An orange baseball cap shielded his eyes against any slim possibility of sun. Jessica had to look twice to make sure he was real and not a bundle of old clothes stuffed with newspapers.

Thinking she heard strange sounds, she slowed the van and rolled down the window. "Ay-yah-yah-yah, ay-yah-yah-yah." He sat straight up, startling her, and she came to a stop.

Without so much as a break in his chant, he gave a toothy, conspiratorial smile, grabbed his hat, and flapped it in greeting. She grinned and waved back.

When she told Callum about the elder, he nodded. "That was Clement Brings Yellow. He's got such bad arthritis in his back he doesn't go out on the water anymore. He misses it, so he spends an hour or two in his boat every day."

"Brings Yellow? What kind of Quinault name is that?"

"I believe he's Sioux, but he married a Quinault. Did he bless you?"

"I think so." She told him how the elder had extended his left hand toward her, palm down, and slowly lowered it, then repeated the gesture.

"Well, then," Callum said, "you're doubly blessed. Clement has special powers."

She recalled the old man had leaned back in the boat and covered his eyes again. Thinking who was she to interrupt some elder's prayer or waterborne journey, she swung the van around and drove back toward Highway 101.

Through the years, she had met plenty of Native Americans—at school, at the mill, and in town. With six reservations dotting the Olympic Peninsula and five others nearby, she would have had to be a mole not to. She had once spent an hour chatting with the gregarious Queets overseer of the boat rental concession at Quinault Lodge. She collected her mail from the Chinook woman at the post office. Kim at the Express-O Hut was a mix of Quileute, Lummi, and Hawaiian.

Other Indians came into the stores, checked out books at the Misp library, ate breakfast at Jelly's Diner or at the Stormy Weather Pancake Corral, turned up singly or in small groups around town. But her encounter with the elder sitting in his beached dinghy had been an odd experience, a kind of wordless, cross-cultural connection.

During the time she and Callum sat in the cold car, the moon turned the sky a tarnished silver. She made another trip inside for hot tea.

After she scooted onto the backseat again, she said casually, "When did you get divorced?"

"The whole thing became final seven weeks ago."

"Seven weeks! That's no time at all."

"It still seems strange but—"

"That's because you're on the rebound. Believe me, I've been there. You're numb. Your emotions aren't trustworthy right now." She realized her own voice had gone a little shaky.

He looked at her curiously. "So what does that make me?"

"About as reliable as the shifting sands at Ocean Shores," she said, hoping she would remember that bit of wisdom herself if she felt tempted to resurrect any serious relationship with him.

He laughed, his scar crinkling like a twisted rubber band.

She sipped her tea. "Are your brother and your ex-wife . . . uh . . . married now?"

He shrugged. "I don't know. Probably not. Andy has a few character flaws that Tori will soon discover."

"Such as?"

"No honesty, no loyalty, no sense of responsibility—minor things. When he came to live with us, I knew what he was, but he can be charming and"—he shrugged again—"well, he's family."

Jessica cleared her throat. "I hate to point out the obvious, but your ex-wife—uh, what's her name—Tori?"

He nodded.

"Well, Tori must be a grown-up woman, who I assume makes her own choices, so you can't blame it totally on your brother."

"Now, that makes me feel a lot better."

"It was just a thought," she murmured.

"A lot of thoughts, including violence, have traveled through my mind in the last six months and twenty-one days."

They talked past four-thirty in the morning, until their warm breath and the steam from their drinks fogged up the windows.

"I'll take you with me to the reservation sometime," Callum said.

She nodded. "I would like that." She shifted her cramped legs. "This is crazy," she said finally.

"What's crazy?"

"Sitting out here nearly freezing to death."

"It's comfortable, like staying up half the night and talking in the tent the way we used to."

Too cozy in that respect, she thought.

"Time to leave," she said, opening the car door.

She tromped back into the house, dropped her coat on the sofa, and shuffled into the bedroom. As she flung back the covers and scrambled between the frigid sheets, the luminous digital numbers on her radio clicked to five o'clock. She turned to her other side, muttering, "It's not my fault he's doing this."

She lasted forty-two minutes.

With a groan of annoyance, she sat up, draped her legs over the side of the mattress and jammed her feet into her pink scuffs. In the hall, she flicked up the thermostat switch. In the kitchen, she dug out a saucepan, tossed a few handfuls of oatmeal into it, and added water. After setting it on the stove to simmer, she grabbed her jacket from the wooden peg and stomped out the front door.

The sun was struggling over the horizon. The moon had faded to a pale white wafer. Buster, up early, his jowls sagging almost to his chest, trotted into her yard and hoisted his rear leg over a baby azalea he'd already murdered. He shot a steaming jet at its furled brown leaves.

"Go home," she rasped.

Callum rolled down the driver's side window. His eyes were half closed, and his hair stuck out in black tufts like ruffled bird feathers. *She* hadn't had the intestinal fortitude to look in the mirror.

She strode over to the car. "I'll warn you, I'm cranky in the morning."

He lifted his eyebrows. "I wouldn't have guessed."

When she released a breath, it spiraled into a frosty cloud. "This was the stupidest exercise in futility I have participated in since . . . since I can't remember when. No one showed up, the neighbors probably wondered what the hell was going on. You made me feel so guilty about being in a bed, I couldn't sleep. I have a window-washing job at seven o'clock, and I'm beyond exhaustion. I could lie right down on this pavement."

He smiled. "But you're safe."

His words stopped her for a moment—but only a moment.

She took a deep breath. "Which I would have been even if you hadn't sat all night in a freezing car waiting for my nonexistent stalkers." She rolled her eyes. "And I can't believe I turned my toes into Popsicles just to keep you company."

"I'll be back after dinner this evening. Save my parking place."

She chose to ignore him. Instead, she watched Buster spray the corner of her porch step.

"You know," she said, "I used to love dogs. When I was eight years old, I saw *One Hundred and One Dalmatians* five times and wanted one of those little buggers more than anything else in the world, but Lila said they were too high-strung and they had hearing problems."

"They are high-strung, and they do have hearing problems."

She gave him a withering look. Clutching the edges of her jacket together with her left hand, she gestured toward the house with her right. "You might as well come in. I'm boiling oatmeal. You can forget bacon and eggs because I haven't got any."

She strode up the front walk, not waiting to see if he followed.

15

When Jessica opened the door that evening, Callum handed her the sack with the Adidas shoes.

She removed them from the bag and examined them. They looked cleaner than they had in months. "Does this mean I'm in the clear?"

He smiled. "Unless we find your fingerprints, your arson kit, and your written confession inside the house."

She thought of the possibility of another General Bragg hiding in the ashes and suddenly felt cold. "What about my brother?"

"What about him?"

"Well, is he still a suspect? Because, if he is, I think you should know he has a neurological disorder that influences how he behaves."

"My job is to find out who set the fire, not to judge Jonah or anyone else."

She looked over his shoulder at the darkness, annoyed at his inflexibility. "Well, I'm too tired to talk anyway. I washed windows all day."

His face changed. He was annoyed too. "Go to bed. I'm not stopping you. I've brought a thermos of black coffee, and I've got a biography of Harry S Truman in the car."

A gust of wind blew through the trees, producing a long, deep howl.

She stuck her head out the door. "It's going to storm. No one in his right mind will be out tonight."

"It rains here about five days and nights out of seven in early spring. Do you think Pete Johnson and Dennis Kretz aren't used to storms?" He was squinting from lack of sleep. "My car hasn't leaked yet."

She stared at him, wondering if she should tell him she was more afraid of him than she was of Pete or Dennis.

"Nothing's going to happen," she said. "Dennis didn't call today. Pete's probably embarrassed as hell, and the next time I see him he'll fall all over himself apologizing."

Callum turned around and started down the porch steps. "I'll be out in the car."

She closed the door and listened to the wind rattle the windows. She leaned against the door, recalling that the radio announcer on KEX out of Portland had predicted sixty-mile-per-hour gusts would hit the coast. In her imagination, she saw a shallow-rooted fir from the O'Briens' front yard topple onto the green Explorer. One of Callum's arms poked from the wreckage, his fingers still clutching the Harry S Truman biography.

She yanked open the door. "All right," she shouted into the darkness. "Come back."

She didn't hear his footsteps, but he suddenly appeared on the porch.

She stepped back from the doorway and pointed at the sofa. "All right! You can sleep there, but—"

"You won't even know I'm in the house."

HE WAS RIGHT. She fell into bed and slept soundly until four forty-five. The room was turning a lighter shade of gray. She sat up but didn't dare raise her bedroom window. The screeching, scraping noise would bring Callum in like a storm trooper poised to fend off her phantom attacker. She scooted to the side of the bed nearest the door, swung her legs over the edge, and poked around for her slippers. Not there. They were probably in the bathroom.

When she opened her bedroom door, it creaked, but no louder than the squeak of a mouse. She waited about thirty seconds, listening to the refrigerator hum in the kitchen. Apparently, no toppled evergreens had severed any electrical lines. If the storm was a genuine April tempest as predicted, the wind had howled and clattered branches against the windows, but she had not heard any of it.

She listened to the near-quiet for several seconds. Why didn't she hear Callum snoring? When her father had slept, he'd bellowed and snorted like a rutting bull. Patrick had snored in a genteel, almost effeminate way—small puffs emanating from his nostrils as though he believed that even in his sleep he must control his every breath. In their early days together, she admired that self-discipline, but she soon discovered that it was a thin veneer over a core of boot-shaking fear.

As she stood there in the doorway, it struck her that one of the more interesting aspects of Patrick was that no one in his family had died. Even his grandparents were still alive. Amazing, Jessica thought, not to know death. It hadn't occurred to her until now that such ignorance, especially in an adult, was a liability, not an asset.

It didn't take much to send Patrick into a teeth-grinding, thinly suppressed rage. A secretary handing him the wrong file once set him off. He couldn't seem to distinguish between the big concerns and the little ones.

Jessica took a few more steps, until she could see the clock on the fireplace mantel but not the sofa. She had switched off the chime so that it wouldn't wake Callum. Strange that he made no noise at all.

Perhaps, while she had slept so soundly, Pete and Wendell had broken into the house, seized him by the throat, and carried him off. They wouldn't murder him, but they might beat him up. She glanced at the time. A woman's imagination at four fifty-two in the morning could be a powerful thing.

It occurred to her he might have left, thinking she no longer needed him. If he had, she would feel disappointed—which meant he was nudging his way back into her life.

But for how long? What good was memory if she didn't learn from it?

She tiptoed across the cold, bare floor to the Persian rug and stood in front of him. He lay on his back, his arms curled above his head. How did men manage to sleep like they owned the world?

His mouth was slightly open. His eyelashes lay thick and black against skin that had softened to tan in the early morning light. A woman had no defenses against a slumbering man, she realized. He had that semblance of boyish vulnerability on his side, while she had only the reckless urge to slide her body next to his and hope he reflexively pulled her against him. She was already trembling.

Although she didn't move, his eyes blinked open. When he looked at her, he didn't seem the least bit startled.

"Hello." His throat sounded dry, slightly smoky.

"Good morning. Did the . . . uh, I mean, do you want . . ." Her own voice cracked.

For some crazy reason, tears welled up in her eyes. She wanted to ask if the lumpy sofa had bothered his back and if he'd like lumpy oatmeal again for breakfast, but she couldn't seem to organize the words in her head. She shuffled one tear-blinded step toward him, then stopped to sniffle and swab her nose against the sleeve of her nightshirt.

He pushed off the comforter and stood, but he didn't move toward her. Against his dusky skin, his white T-shirt and under-shorts seemed to glow in the dark. His face collected the shadows now, but his eyes looked bright and rested.

She swallowed hard and whispered, "I missed you."

Two steps and he had his arms around her, his face bent to hers. She felt the tenseness, the restraint in his limbs.

His voice came thick. "This is where you get to say, 'No, I don't want you to proceed any farther.' "

"And if I say, 'Proceed'?"

He pulled her closer so that her nipples grazed his chest and the thin layers of cloth between them seemed to burn away. "You give up your right to remain silent and your right to any other attorney." He slowly unbuttoned her nightshirt, slid it off her shoulder, and laid a trail of kisses from the teardrops on her right eyelid to her bare collarbone. "And anything you do say will definitely be held against you." He dragged her nightshirt over her head and tossed it onto the sofa.

As his mouth searched her body, her words came in one long shudder. "I plead guilty."

AT SEVEN A.M. she rolled onto her elbow and looked at Callum. He was sleeping. All her determination to avoid him, and she hadn't lasted two nights. She sighed. Now, here was a woman in control of her destiny, she thought.

She touched her lips to his warm cheek, damp from exertion. Feeling the ridged line there, she thought how much it resembled her cesarean scar, faded after all these years. Sometime, maybe the next time they made love, he'd ask her about it—and she would summon the courage to tell him.

16

Jessica looked up at the banner stretched across one inside wall of the community center in Queets: GREAT SPIRIT, WHOSE VOICE I HEAR IN THE WIND, I NEED YOUR STRENGTH, WISDOM, AND SE-RENITY.

Amen, she thought.

A small gathering, Callum had said. A preschool commence-ment. His niece would be one of the proud graduates.

Jessica's gaze swept the hundred or so people who'd drifted into conversational groups around the gymnasium. She thought the twelve preschoolers—bouncy little girls dressed in pink sateen caps and gowns, the boys in pale blue—looked like the candy mints hostesses served at baby showers. Callum had gone off to find his niece, leaving Jessica marooned on this island of Quinaults.

"Be back in a few minutes," he'd assured her.

Yeah, right. She'd worn her cream-colored fisherman's knit sweater, a plaid skirt, and green tights, thinking she'd make some connection with her own heritage. But she'd overdressed. With the exception of the tribal council, the adults wore sweat suits or jeans and T-shirts. Even Callum was casual in khakis and a blue denim shirt open at the neck.

The minigraduates carried their diplomas and their rewards—

Barbie dolls or Tonka trucks. The women bustled between the kitchen and two long portable banquet tables, lining up cans of Pepsi and single-serving cartons of milk. They set out platters of salmon and bowls of mashed potatoes, bread stuffing, potato salad, and fruit, until the room steamed with a holiday-style aroma. She hadn't seen this much food since the days her grandmother cooked Christmas dinner for the transient loggers.

She stood alone, feeling conspicuous. She noticed she was the only person with coiled hair the color of tarnished copper. The glaring minority, she thought. It was an odd feeling.

The three men near her talked about the need for more streetlights on the reservation and the drainage problems near the new medical clinic.

"What about the fire truck?" said a man wearing a T-shirt that read TAHOLAH ALL-STARS. "I think we should bring that up before the council. It's in such bad shape, you could light two matches and they'd be brighter than the headlights."

"What difference does it make?" asked a second man, whose black hair fell over his shoulders in two thick ropes. "No one's trained to use it anyway."

"Well, that's something else we should discuss," the third fellow said, rubbing his broad palms together.

Meanwhile, they eyed her with polite reserve.

Jessica knew the ancestral tribes of the Quinault Indian Nation were the Chehalis, Chinook, Cowlitz, Hoh, Quileute, Quinault, Queets, and Shoalwater. She'd learned that much in school.

The tribal council chief called for attention and invited an elder to say a blessing. Dressed in baggy black jeans, a blue windbreaker, and a new black baseball hat with the words NATIVE PRIDE stamped on it, a small, toothy, square-faced man walked stiffly to the front of the gymnasium.

She recognized him immediately as her seafaring friend, minus his dry-docked boat. He lifted his hands and his gaze heavenward and chanted words that sounded to Jessica like "Ay-yah-yah-yah, ay-yah-yah-yah."

His prayer, which began with the Indian chant and ended with "In the name of the Father, the Son, and the Holy Ghost," seemed to blend Native American spirituality and Christianity. He crossed himself, turned around three times, and then repeated the whole ritual.

After he'd finished, the knots of people unraveled into a single line along the edge of the auditorium where the buffet tables were set.

A middle-aged woman, a member of the tribal council, walked up, a pink carnation corsage bobbing on her navy blue dress. "You should get in line. The food will go fast."

"I'm not sure if we're staying. I'm here with . . ." Jessica stretched her neck to look for Callum.

The woman gave her a shrewd smile. "Oh, I know who you're with." She lifted her head slightly so her rose-framed eyeglasses reflected the bright overhead lights. "But it's one o'clock and you should eat. It's our custom to share food, and you would be insulting us if you didn't have some."

Jessica glanced at the feast spread across the tables, the mellow tang of alder-smoked salmon drifting over to her. She wondered if there was a single person in the cavernous auditorium who didn't know who she was. She returned the smile. "I will, thank you."

She felt a hand on her arm and turned to find Callum beside her, with a jet-haired, pink-gowned preschooler in tow. He lifted her onto his shoulder and introduced her as his niece Natalie. Clutching a Cinderella Barbie, she peered solemnly from her perch, and Jessica felt the same jab in the heart she always felt whenever she saw a tawny-skinned girl with brown velvet eyes.

"You lied," Jessica whispered to Callum. "This is no small gathering. It's a big event."

"When it comes to encouraging education, we like to start early."

With his niece aboard, Callum led Jessica across the auditorium to one of the portable picnic-style tables that were butted against each other in a long row. He introduced her to three gray-haired women—his mother and his two aunts. Next to his sparrow-sized aunts sat an elderly uncle, thin and stooped.

Callum's resemblance to his mother was clear. He had her broad cheekbones and finely sculpted nose and mouth, although her dark eyes were more wary than his. She nodded politely at Jessica but didn't say a word. The others also greeted her stiffly, avoiding her gaze. She felt as if a cool draft had blown through the room.

While Callum collected their food, Jessica waited at the table with his relatives. If his absence was a ploy to force conversation, it wasn't working, she thought. They already had their meals in front of them, and they pondered them intently, fiddling with their plastic forks but not eating.

Jessica tried to sound cheerful. "Please don't wait for us."

They looked at her.

"Really," she said, "your food will get cold."

They nodded. His mother flaked the salmon into small bites, carefully chewing each forkful as if it required her complete concentration. The others poked at the morsels on their plates, lifting their eyes occasionally to study the dust motes that danced in the air. Jessica felt as if she should apologize, as if she were responsible for people and events that weren't under her control. Even if she wanted to beg their forgiveness—and she wasn't sure she did—she would have had no idea where to begin.

She glanced at the banquet table, where a man in a fringed black leather vest had waylaid Callum. She could see Callum was trying to break away. He held their filled paper plates aloft and smiled in her direction.

By the classroom-style clock high on the wall, nine extraordinarily long minutes passed before he returned, and during that time, his family spoke a total of six words to her, mostly polite but cautious one-syllable answers to innocuous questions. Callum set a heaped plate in front of her and handed her some plastic utensils. The conversation picked up then, and they talked about the upcoming dedication of the new medical clinic. Despite Callum's attempts to include her, the tension hung as heavy in the air as the lingering smells of the food, and she drifted into defeated silence.

Later, riding home in his car, she realized her shoulders were just now relaxing. "You have a nice family."

She wondered which part they disliked most about her—that she was a white woman or that she was a Moran. She thought it more likely the latter.

Callum kept his eyes on the road. "They were quiet today. They'll talk more when they get to know you."

She wondered if they had any desire whatsoever to know her.

"That was just part of my family," he said, turning onto her street. He slowed the car so that Buster could stagger from the middle of the pavement to Jessica's yard. Buster flopped in a patch of sunshine on her walkway, his front legs splayed out, the underside of his muzzle flattened against the cement.

Callum parked the Explorer. "There are a few thousand other members of the Quinault Indian Nation who weren't there today."

She envied his lifetime membership in a far-reaching, identifiable family. "Don't you have to worry about marrying your first cousin or something like that?"

He nodded. "Any couple within the Quinault nation has to trace their lineage. Years ago, my aunt Pauline and a Hoh named Baldy George got down to the day before the wedding when they discovered he was her half brother. Must have been a lot of family confessing that went on during those final hours. Cussing too."

He switched off the key and turned to look at her. Reaching across, he stroked the curve of her neck with the back of his fingers.

She slumped against the seat. "I felt like an outsider, Callum, like I was trespassing on someone else's culture. I could dye my hair black and chant that prayer, but I couldn't ever be anything more than an Indian wanna-be."

He laughed. "Weekend warrior. That's what we call people like you."

"Yeah, well, I just realized I hate being a minority."

"Can't imagine why." He tugged on one of her curls. "Don't worry. No one's asking you to dye this black."

"There was a man at the community center whose hair was fair, almost blond. What tribe is he from?"

Callum laughed. "The Hoosier tribe. That's John Walker. He came to the reservation from Indiana about twenty years ago through a government program, and he never left." He paused. "Does that make you feel better?"

"A little." She leaned back against the seat and smiled. So there was hope for an outsider. What she didn't know was whether they would ever take in a Moran.

THEY SHOWERED TOGETHER that next sun-tinged morning, bumping hips and jockeying for position in her sloped, discolored, claw-footed tub. Callum made fun of her plastic shower curtain with the giant pink flamingos strutting through a brilliant tropical forest of coral, turquoise, and green bird-of-paradise plants. She said he had no taste. The water went ice-cold before they rinsed off.

Callum grabbed a towel and handed it to her. "Does this always happen with the water?"

Before she could answer, the telephone rang on the other side of the closed bathroom door. Clutching the towel around her, she climbed out of the tub and ran toward the kitchen, reaching the phone just before the message machine switched on.

"A Room with a View," she said.

Pete's contrite voice came shooting back at her. "Jessica, now don't hang up on me."

"All right, Pete, I won't."

He coughed twice, then cleared his throat. "I wanted to tell you—well, I didn't mean those things I said about you. You know I think the world of you."

"Apology accepted, Pete." She noticed he didn't mention the remarks he'd made about Callum. Cradling the receiver on her shoulder, she layered the towel over her breasts and tucked in the edges.

He cleared his throat again. "Uh, Misp's playing Timberline this Friday night, and Timberline's second in the state now and I've got a couple of tickets. . . ." He sounded distant, as though he'd turned away from the phone. She heard male voices in the background.

Terrific, she thought. She was going to turn him down with his friends standing nearby. "Pete, this won't work."

A more distant male voice came floating across the phone line. "What did she say?"

"Sorry, Jessica, I didn't catch that."

"I said, this won't work."

"Okay." His voice cooled slightly. "Well, maybe some other time."

She pressed her free hand to her forehead and closed her eyes. "Pete, I mean permanently. I don't want to date you anymore. We don't believe in the same things."

"That doesn't make sense, Jessica. I believe in the things other people around here do."

"I would hate to think that's true."

She felt an arm grip her around the waist, then a warm mouth nudge its way under her hair and kiss the back of her neck. Reaching around behind her, she ran her hand across the waist of Callum's jeans, meeting bare skin. Oh, God, she thought, could there be anything sexier than a bare-chested man in tight jeans?

"Hmm," she murmured, wishing Pete would just go away.

"What did you say?" Pete asked.

"I have to hang up."

"Can't you give me just two more minutes, Jessica?" His voice rose. "Jesus Christ, I'm apologizing, and this isn't easy for me."

"Pete, we are never going to agree."

"You're talking about the fire, aren't you?" He was practically shouting now. "Well, something had to be done, and if Wendell hadn't—" He stopped. "I mean, what are you going to do, wait until one of them rapes somebody's wife or kid?"

"No, but—"

"And another thing. I wasn't going to say anything against Luke, but you should stay away from him."

Aware that Callum was close enough to hear, she took a step toward the living room, stretching the cord. Callum held on to her.

"He's an Indian, for God's sake," Pete said. "He isn't one of us."

A chill ran through her, and she let the force of it travel into her voice. "Dammit, Pete, go peddle your prejudice somewhere else." She hung up the phone.

Callum gently turned her around, lifted her chin, and looked directly into her eyes. "It's okay, Jess. It's not like I haven't heard it before."

"Well, it's not okay with me."

Her wet hair dripped onto her face. Callum took a corner of her towel and wiped away the beads of water.

She managed a smile. "He's jealous of you, you know."

"He should be." He bent to kiss her.

But Pete's words wouldn't leave her. After she pulled back, she said, "Callum, I think Wendell Schultz set the fire."

17

Twice, Jessica went over her conversation with Pete. Callum sat next to her on the sofa and listened.

"That's it? You don't remember anything else?"

"Just the things he said about you."

Callum smiled wryly. "I don't need to hear those again."

"I think Pete started to say that if Wendell hadn't set the fire, he would have. You know what Wendell's like. He probably thought no one would dare arrest the fire chief's son for arson."

Callum leaned against the back of the sofa. "Listen, Jess, I know you want the arsonist to be anyone but Jonah. But Pete's not going to rat on his friend. He and Wendell are joined at the thumb."

"It was a slip. He didn't intend to say it."

"The problem is that I have no more reason to suspect Wendell than I do most other people in town. I know he fought the fire, but I have nothing that places him there before it started. I don't have a single fragment of evidence that implicates him."

She leaned toward him. "But you can look for it, can't you?"

"It doesn't work that way. We don't make a list of all the people in town we don't like and then try to find evidence to charge them with the crime." He paused. "We look at the evidence and see who it points to."

"Well, I'm sure you'll keep an open mind," she said, her tone sounding sharper than she'd intended.

When he didn't answer, she rose from the sofa. "I've got a job today at Seacoast Construction."

Callum stood. "I'll come back tonight."

He was still shirtless, and his hair, damp from their shower, fell against his neck like a black feather. She noticed he wore it longer than he had that first day at the halfway house.

"Yes," she said, "I'd like that."

As she walked from the house, the Tooberts' dog, Buster, waddled into her yard and peed on her new John F. Kennedy rosebush. The lower leaves were already brown. He was killing every plant in her yard, while ironically the Tooberts' grass and flowers looked like they were plucked from a Miracle-Gro advertisement. She decided she would have to do something about that dog.

As she crossed behind the van, she saw that someone had scrawled INJUN LOVER in the road dust on the rear window. She grabbed a rag and wiped off the slur. She wouldn't mention it to Callum.

The good mood she awoke with was slipping. It occurred to her that another phone call from Pete or Dennis could push it over the edge. Callum was right. She did want the arsonist to be anyone but Jonah. And what better revenge than to see his tormentor arrested.

On her way to Seacoast Construction, she decided how she would deal with Buster. She would encompass her most vulnerable plants and shrubs in chicken wire, until they were big enough to withstand Buster's lethal torrent. She didn't care how much wire it took. She would re-create the Berlin Wall if necessary.

A few hours later, she was teetering on a ladder, thinking that the people inside Seacoast must feel as if they worked underground. Dirt caked the windows, and when she added water, it trickled off in muddy rivulets. The air here smelled industrial, a mixture of wood, glue, paint, and diesel fuel.

Swabbing the glass, she thought about Callum. She needed to tell him about their daughter. Soon, she promised herself, perhaps tonight. But, in every scenario she ran through her head, she turned into a kamikaze pilot hurtling breakneck toward the ground.

She heard the crunch of boots on gravel behind her and looked over her shoulder.

Lila stood at the base of the ladder, her face drawn tight with anger. "What are you doing?"

"My job," Jessica said, not even bothering to keep the sarcasm from her tone.

"You know I'm talking about *him*. Come down here."

Jessica descended the ladder, then realized to her chagrin she had responded automatically, like the dutiful daughter. Setting her jaw, she swung around and faced her mother. "How did you know I was here?"

"Do you think I can't find you when I want to?" Her blue eyes blazed. "You're sleeping with him again, aren't you?"

"It's none of your business. What I do is private."

She gave an ironic laugh. "Private? It's all over town. Are you trying to humiliate me?"

Jessica felt her blood rise. "Really, Lila, could you stop thinking about yourself for once?"

"We have a family name to protect and—"

"Are you serious? Our family's screwed up, and everyone in Misp knows it."

"That is not true." Lila strung out the words, cold and clipped. "Callum Luke wants to arrest your brother, for God's sake."

"He's not going to arrest Jonah. He doesn't have enough evidence."

"How do you know he isn't trying to get the evidence through you?"

Jessica stared at her. Callum would never do anything that bad. That was betrayal beyond . . . she couldn't even think of it.

"He wouldn't," she said softly, wishing her voice held more conviction. "He's not like that."

"He *was* once," Lila said coolly. She looked off in the distance. "You're too much like your father, Jessica. You always have to learn the hard way."

Jessica straightened. "Telling me I'm like Dad is one of the few nice things you've ever said to me."

Lila smiled ironically. "You've told Callum Luke about the girl then, and he thinks that's just fine?"

Jessica bit her lip. "I will tonight."

"So you haven't." She looked disgusted. "His wife won't accept her. And neither will his own children."

"He's divorced, and he doesn't have children. Isn't the real point, Lila, that *you* won't accept her?"

"This town won't either. I can just about guarantee that."

"This town will follow your lead, and you know it."

"I think how all these years I've managed to keep that child a secret. And it wasn't easy." She fixed her gaze on Jessica. "If you had any decency, she would remain that way."

"Your method of *managing* the problem was to ship me off to California, with instructions never to return," Jessica said tersely.

Lila gave her a stunned look. "Do you think I wanted that? I was getting you away from *him* and from what people here would say. I made sure you were well taken care of. I paid for your college education. I protected you."

Jessica smiled wryly. "You protected me? What an odd way of putting it. You got rid of me."

Lila shook her head in disbelief. "You don't know how hard it was to let you go, especially after losing your father."

"As a matter of fact, I *do* know," Jessica shot back. "I gave up my daughter too, remember?"

She saw her mother flinch and knew she'd hit the target.

Lila turned away. "That was different. You were too young to take care of her, and she didn't have a decent father."

Jessica shook with fury, unsure which charge angered her more. "You might be able to dismiss my daughter that easily, but I can't. And I don't believe that business about protecting me and worrying what people would say. I think what really bothered you was that every time you looked at me you felt guilty. I was a giant conscience, walking around the house and reminding you that you'd caused my father's death."

Her words conveyed the arrow that rendered Lila barely able to speak.

"You don't know what you're talking about," she finally managed to choke out. "I put up with more than you can imagine. I . . . I will not allow you to—"

She stopped abruptly, obviously too injured to continue, and strode off.

After she'd rounded the corner of the building, Jessica leaned against the cold metal rungs of the ladder and allowed herself to cry for several minutes. She wiped her eyes with the blue cloth she used for drying windows.

Of course, Lila was wrong about Callum. She often saw duplicity where there was none. More than once she had accused Dad of lying to her.

And, yet, Jessica could still see the faces of Callum's friends pressed against the tent window, their features distorted by the black netting. She still burned with humiliation at the memory.

For several nights after his betrayal, she lay in bed, pressing the heels of her palms against her eyelids to stem the flow of tears.

As if adding to the insult, he still had her father's knife. She wanted it back. Its recovery became as important to her as the dock burning had been earlier in the summer. She could smell the knife's worn leather handle, seasoned with her father's sweat, and feel its cool blade against her hand.

She hoped Callum had left it in the tent. She didn't want to face him directly.

It rained that Saturday evening, a good, air-cleansing cloudburst that tamped down the dust. In the early hours of Sunday, she sneaked out of the house. She thought it was the least likely time he would be at the tent and the one day of the week her mother would sleep past daybreak.

Fog hugged the ground, limiting visibility to about ten feet, but she had no difficulty finding the clear-cut. She could have navigated the darkest woods strictly on the strength of her need.

When she reached the tent, she found it in a heap, rainwater pooled in the low pockets of canvas. Someone had yanked out the aluminum frame, bent the poles, and scattered them around like pickup sticks. Long slashes crisscrossed the collapsed walls. Jessica knew it had taken a strong, sharp blade to make those cuts.

She walked to the other side of the tent where the coffee can lay tipped over, its damp, sandy contents strewn across the ground, and searched until she found the knife imbedded in a fallen, half-rotted, cedar nurse log. She pried it loose and lowered herself onto the mossy log, barely aware of the dampness seeping through her jeans.

Through the slits in the tent canvas, she could see faded patches of the quilt, the fabric squares so thin in places that the yellowed cotton batting showed through. She drew the wet quilt from the tent and covered her head and shoulders with it, pressing her face to the fabric that smelled like the musty canvas, that smelled like *them*. Digging farther inside, she found the sheath for the knife and looped her belt through it.

The sun was edging above the Olympics by the time she reached home. She had stayed at the tent too long, but the house was dark and the chimney smokeless. She thought she should feel relieved to have the knife back, but she didn't. Still clutching the quilt, she opened the back door and slipped quietly into the dreary kitchen.

"No need to sneak in," her mother said in a low, flat voice. "You don't have to worry about waking me up."

Jessica could barely make her out at the walnut table in the shadowy corner, but she immediately smelled the coffee aroma drifting from the spatterware percolator. Her mother stood, tightened the sash of her blue velour robe, and moved into the gray morning light. Her eyes were red-rimmed with fatigue.

She wore feminine blue slippers that Jessica remembered buying her years ago as a Christmas gift. For a moment, Jessica thought her mother looked angelic, her loose white hair spinning a halo around her wan face, resembling the Madonna in St. Bavo's stained-glass window. Jessica realized she looked the way a mother was supposed to look. Not the usual blue jeans, plaid flannel shirt, rugged boots— not a man's clothes, but a mother's clothes, the kind a child could burrow into. Jessica wanted to nestle against her, but she couldn't take that first step.

Jessica dragged the end of the quilt across her face, wiping the perspiration from her upper lip.

"Where were you?" her mother asked softly.

"Out walking."

"Walking, huh?" Her voice turned deep with sarcasm. "Just out strolling the countryside at five in the morning. Sure, and your mother's the biggest fool in town."

Jessica took a step forward, intending to dart past her, but her mother's hand clamped down on her wrist. Twisting to the side, Jessica squirmed away. "Leave me alone, *Lila*."

Her mother stiffened, the skin around her mouth blanching. Backing up to block the doorway, she jerked her hand toward a chair. "Sit down."

Jessica sat, her chin high in the air.

Her mother walked to the stove, poured a mug of coffee, added milk and sugar, and set it purposefully in front of Jessica.

It had been Jessica's morning ritual to share coffee with her dad. From the time she could remember, she'd snuggled against him at breakfast, sipping the lukewarm dregs from his cup and screwing up her face at their bitterness. She hadn't tasted coffee since he'd died. Her stomach churned at the thought of drinking it.

Her mother studied her intently. "I never could drink coffee in the morning when I was pregnant. Are you pregnant yet?"

Jessica opened her mouth to protest—then shut it. She considered how to fight back, what she could say that would wound her mother the most. "I might be."

She didn't know if she was, but she realized she could be speaking the truth. She felt too numb to care.

The room was cold and silent. The big-bellied furnace in the basement below them hadn't switched on yet. Jessica gripped the quilt tight around her, then lifted the cup to her trembling lips and drained the coffee in four quick gulps. It bubbled back into her throat like bile, and she had to swallow several times to keep it down.

Her mother dragged a chair out from the table and sank onto it.

"Maybe," she muttered, kneading her forehead. "That's just what I need to hear. And, God help me, another *Indian*."

Jessica didn't say anything. She didn't need to ask how she knew. Callum's *friends* must have blabbed to half the town.

"Did you really think I wouldn't find out?" Her mother's eyes sparked with anger. "Didn't you realize people would fall all over themselves to tell me an Indian buck was screwing my daughter in a squalid tent in the woods?"

Jessica wanted to shout that the tent hadn't been squalid, that it glowed green in there, that the candlelight made their skin soft and dusky, and that for the span of six weeks she had never felt so beautiful or safe or loved as she had within those canvas walls. But she knew her mother would never understand.

Lila's voice cut into her thoughts. "You should have heard what they said." Her face twisted into a false mask of concern, and her tone became shrilly patronizing. " 'I knew you would want to know, Lila. If she were my daughter, I'd want someone to tell me.' "

Jessica still didn't say anything. Instead, she tried to drift off to another green world that smelled of damp cedar and salt wind and pungent, rain-heavy earth, to some hidden new place where no one—not Lila, not Callum, not the vicious gossips in town—could find her.

Her mother rested her elbows on the table and lowered her forehead onto her hands. She studied the tabletop as though its walnut grain contained some secret message. When she finally looked up, her eyes shone with tears.

Jessica stared at her. She thought she should feel some sympathy, but she felt only surprise. She didn't recall that she'd ever seen her mother cry.

"Or did you want me to find out?" Lila said wearily. "Is this my punishment, your carrying on with some no-account trash? You've got it in your head that I killed your father and you'll do whatever it takes to get back at me."

"This has nothing to do with you." She tried to recall where she'd heard that phrase before. Then she remembered her mother saying that same thing to Dad that morning on the dock, shaking her fist at him and yelling it. Jessica knew even then that tossing Jonah into that cold, murky water wasn't a random act, that it wasn't strictly some last-ditch attempt to teach him to swim, that, in fact, it had everything to do with Dad.

Jessica heard a shuffling sound, and Jonah appeared in the kitchen doorway, his eyelids heavy and gummy with sleep.

He blinked and yawned. "Why are you just sitting here, Mom?"

Lila pushed herself to her feet. "Your sister's going on a long trip today."

Jessica's first thought was that the answer had no connection to the question. It took a moment for its meaning to sink in. Her mother wiped her sleeve across her face and stood straighter.

Jonah looked puzzled. "Where you going, Jessie?"

"Nowhere. I'm not going anywhere." She felt stunned and frightened.

Her mother waved a hand in the general direction of the second floor. "Go on up and take a shower. You've got a busy day ahead of you." She started to turn away, then glanced back. "And get rid of that filthy blanket."

Jessica stumbled up the stairs, the sweet, thick coffee sloshing around in her stomach. She thought for a moment she might not make it to the bathroom. Pushing past the door, she skidded across the cold tile floor, dropped the quilt, and retched violently into the toilet.

When she tried to stand, her legs felt boneless. She sank onto the floor again and pressed her back against the tub, gagging spasmodically, feeling as though the blue-and-white tile were swelling and falling like an ocean wave. Even after the motion stopped, she sat there shaking, telling herself she would never get up. She couldn't think of a reason why she should. She decided she didn't have to worry about being pregnant. No one who felt as hollow as she did could grow something inside her.

After several minutes, she grabbed a damp white washcloth off the rim of the sink and swabbed her mouth with it. She wondered where Lila planned to send her and decided that it would not be any better or worse than Misp.

She thought of the suitcase filled with Dad's belongings that she'd stashed in the back of her closet. Not even Lila could stop her from taking that with her. It contained one of Dad's sweat-stained flannel shirts she'd excavated from the dirty laundry after he drowned, the cotton pillowcase from his side of the bed, his leather belt, the Harley-Davidson T-shirt she'd bought him for his last birthday (along with the card that promised she would deliver the motorcycle once she could afford it), his pocketknife, his spiral notebook filled with logger's poetry, and a cigar box of photographs she'd culled from the trunks in the attic.

Her father's soul would have to remain in the lake until she could figure out how to free it.

She would miss Jonah, who sometimes felt like a fifth limb. But he seemed caught up in his world of exploding cannon shells and marching soldiers, and she wondered if he even cared about her leaving. He didn't seem particularly upset by the news.

Grabbing the edge of the sink, she pulled herself up and gazed in the mirror at the grim, tear-streaked face with its nest of Medusa hair. She squirted an inch of toothpaste on her brush and scoured the taste of bile from her mouth, scrubbing so vigorously her gums bled. Through the register, she heard the snap and hum of their ancient oil furnace cranking up for the morning.

Suddenly, she couldn't wait to be away from Misp. Using the toe of her shoe, she nudged the dingy quilt into an untidy lump in the corner, then leaned over the tub and turned on the hot water faucet.

That same afternoon, Lila drove to Seattle and put her on a plane to Los Angeles. She went to live with Lila's great-aunt and her husband in Glendale, California. They were past seventy and childless. They treated her well, but Jessica knew they were unequipped to deal with a teenager, much less a pregnant one. Her aunt often seemed befuddled, as if she might be sliding into Alzheimer's. Jessica helped with the cooking and housework but otherwise kept to herself.

She went to a Glendale hospital on a sunny May morning, just a few weeks before the end of her junior year in high school and thirteen days after the first anniversary of her father's death. Her daughter was born at ten minutes before midnight. Two days later, she relinquished her for adoption.

After that, the Glendale high school she attended became her liberation, her salvation. It had a swim team, whereas Misp didn't even have a pool. She swam frequently and obsessively.

She started rising at five A.M. and training a total of five hours a day, working around her school schedule. After each half-mile warm-up, she swam as many 400-yard repeats as she could, resting no more than thirty seconds between sets. She then went on to swim a series of sprint repeats, employing various strokes. She cross-trained with weights, doing hundreds of repeats with pulleys to strengthen her upper arms and shoulders.

Her skin smelled constantly of chlorine. She had long thin muscles but no fat. She acquired a painful rash on her thighs from smacking the cement when she hoisted herself onto the ledge. Her hair developed a green-tinged brassiness and turned slimy when wet. Her eyes seemed to have permanent rings around them from the goggles.

She swam competitively during her senior year in high school and during college, usually placing within the top five, occasionally winning. She took no serious interest in ribbons and trophies, but she acquired a certain satisfaction in believing that, if necessary, she could rescue a 265-pound man from the lake floor.

JESSICA FINISHED the job at Seacoast Construction at five-thirty, allowing her time to stop at Everett's Boat and Hardware Center before it closed. Jack Everett peddled chicken wire in every size and configuration.

She pulled into the store's cratered parking lot and angled her van next to Bob Snow's dented blue Chevrolet pickup. It occurred to her she hadn't seen Bob in several weeks, and the last time she'd talked to Mary Grace was when she'd bought a tank of gas at the minimall.

Jessica hopped from the van and stepped over a chipped and pitted railroad tie that served as a barrier between the parking lot and the store entry. A sign in the window read STOCK BOY NEEDED. ASK JACK.

The building was old, dusty, and by far Jessica's favorite place in town.

As a youngster, she had trailed her father along the aisles, lugging his purchases for him, pawing through splintered wooden crates. Occasionally, she unearthed something of value—a brass fitting from a sunken vessel, a two-inch-long shark's tooth, a miniature lantern missing its glass globe. She carried her find to the front counter and set it in front of Jack. He haggled over it but then sold it to her for less than his original asking price.

Jack was one of the few store owners in town who still allowed customers to smoke and chew tobacco on the premises, although he did insist they toss their butts or spit their chaws in the lopped-off whiskey barrel near the front counter. The cigarette and cigar smoke, combined with fumes from fertilizer, turpentine, and a few other products, produced a noxious cloud and a ripe smell that, according to Jack, kept out finicky women and wusses.

Jessica walked inside and veered around a floor-to-ceiling pyramid of cans containing discontinued boat paint. She made a quick right and headed for the wire fencing at the back of the store.

She looked around for Bob Snow but saw no sign of him. Jack, who believed in self-service and the honor system, provided a tape measure and a pair of wire cutters on a shelf. Stretching out the wire, Jessica snipped off twenty feet. She rolled it into a tight cylinder and carried it toward the sales counter at the front of the store.

Three quarters of the way along the nuts-and-bolts aisle, she heard a familiar voice.

"You'd think they would have wrapped this up by now."

There he was—that bushy-haired old bear Bob Snow. She'd always been fond of him, even when he rubbed his knuckles against her head in grade school and called her Rustoleum. She slowed her pace and caught a glimpse of him between stacks of wooden bins filled with every conceivable fastener. He stood like a typical logger, his feet wide apart, his thumbs hooked at the base of his red suspenders, talking with Jack and two other men. One of them was Ralph Young, owner of a gill-netter called the *Mystic;* the other, Louie MacLeod, an engine mechanic who serviced the local fishing fleet. Louie was sharpening his pocketknife on a plate-sized whetstone on the counter.

Jack stood behind the long wooden counter cracking a roll of pennies into the cash register. "I hear the guy used paint thinner to set the fire."

Jessica stopped.

She saw Ralph flick his cigarette ashes into the whiskey barrel. "Who told you that?"

"Let's just say I heard it from someone who's working the investigation." Jack tucked a pencil over his right ear. "Right after the fire, I told people that if the guy used paint thinner I know who did it. Because I know who's in here all the time buying the stuff." He turned to Louie. "Didn't I say that?"

Louie nodded. "Yeah, you did."

Jessica gripped the chicken wire harder, feeling the strands cut into her fingers.

"Shit," Bob said, "if you're talking about Jonah Moran, that don't make him a murderer. There isn't a man in this town who doesn't have paint thinner in his garage or shop."

"Or a woman either," Ralph said in his raspy smoker's voice. "Hell, I'll bet Lila's got a dozen gallons stashed somewhere."

Louie's wide grin exposed a trench between his two front teeth. "Sure, and I can just see Lila building a bonfire alongside that halfway house. Can't imagine why though. As far as I know, there weren't any Indians living in it."

They all laughed.

Jack plucked the pencil from behind his ear and scratched his bald pate with the eraser. "Like I said from the beginning, it's either an outsider or someone daft in the head. Jonah Moran's a nice enough kid, but he's definitely a few bubbles off plumb. If it was an outsider, someone would have noticed him, and if it was one of our young hotheads, he'd be bragging about it all over town."

Louie hunched over the whetstone and ran his knife blade across it with a light feathering motion, producing an unnerving, high-pitched whine. "Lila's never going to let anyone arrest Jonah, even it means she has to look the other way while her daughter screws that Indian again." He glanced up. "At least maybe this time Jessica will get something out of it."

"Makes you wonder who's getting what," Jack put in. "Don't they call that sleeping with the enemy?"

Ralph took a drag on his cigarette and released the smoke slowly. "I'd say they call it history repeating itself."

"That's right," Jack said reflectively. "I'd almost forgotten about Big Mike. Couldn't keep his hands off them either, could he now? Must run in the family."

There were murmurs of agreement.

The contemptible sons of bitches, Jessica thought. Bob was her best friend's husband. The others were supposed to be friends too, good folks her family had known and done business with for years. They'd played poker with her father, drank his beer, and pretended to respect him. They came to his funeral and shed tears over him. And, yet, here they were, snickering and spewing lies and rumors about him and everyone else in her family. For a moment, she wished the pain of their gossip and suspicion on them, although she knew that curses had a way of turning back on themselves.

She had to get out of the store. Upending the roll of chicken wire, she set it on the sagging planks. She took a few steps toward the front door, then stopped. They might be such cowards that they couldn't express their opinions to someone's face, but she didn't have to act that way. She went back for the wire, grabbed it, and headed around the corner to the front counter.

When she stepped into their view, all four men stopped short. The most transparent expression of guilt she'd ever seen settled on Bob's face. Ralph reared up suddenly, and Louie nailed his gaze directly on the whetstone.

Jack stared at her. "Lord, Jessica, where did you come from?"

She hoisted the roll onto the counter. "How much is it, Jack?"

He looked long and hard at it. "Why, there's not much there." His tone was low, repentant. "I can't say as I should charge you anything for that little bit of wire."

She heard the door open and shut with a clatter. She couldn't see who was on the other side of the paint can tower, but a male voice boomed, "Hey, fellows!" Heavy boots clunked noisily down one of the aisles.

Jack gazed at the paint pyramid and murmured, "Gotta move those damned things."

Ralph stubbed his cigarette against the inside of the barrel as though it could be the most important thing he would do that day.

Feeling a surge of satisfaction, Jessica pulled a rumpled twenty from her pocket and smoothed it out on the counter. "That should cover it."

She started to walk away.

"Wait a second, Jessica." The cash register binged. "That's way too much."

"Don't worry about it, Jack. Without my family's business, you may need the money." She looked at each of them. "Gentlemen," she said, and strode out the door.

18

She drove directly home and spent the next hour constructing cone-shaped, chicken-wire barricades around her plants, feeling an almost frenzied need to control something.

Her mind rocketed back to the conversation at the store. *"Couldn't keep his hands off them either, could he now?"* Those bastards.

They had made her father's simple affection for others seem sordid. He was a man who touched people, often flinging his arm around a drinking buddy's neck or hoisting a neighbor child to his shoulder. He didn't mean anything by it.

Plenty of women flirted with him—from the coy Meckler sisters to seductive Darla Johnson. She recalled his easy banter with them, but he never paid any special attention to the Indian women.

She stood back and surveyed her work. Her front yard looked like a scene from *The Beverly Hillbillies*. All she needed was a wrecked car filled with petunias. But at least her plants were safe now.

In the bathroom, she peeled off her grimy clothes and climbed into the tub. Yanking the flamingo-studded shower curtain across the rod, she stood there shivering until the water turned hot. Then she stepped under it and cranked the faucet so far to the left that the steaming droplets stung.

She wondered what event could have triggered the rumors about her father. There was one time—something she'd forgotten until now. She and Jonah walked into the mill office while Dad was standing over one of the Quinault clerks, reading some papers. His hand rested on her neck. The clerk squirmed away and made a big production of walking over to a file cabinet to search for another document. Then Dad turned and saw them in the doorway. He grinned and made a joke about a tree falling in the woods and one owl wing flapping. Jonah didn't get it, but the uncomfortable moment had passed.

It could have begun that easily. A single isolated incident, probably misinterpreted by the clerk, who later passed on a distorted version of it.

She flung the pink flamingos aside, stepped from the tub, and grabbed the green towel that hung on a hook above the register. It was the one Callum had used that morning. She buried her face in it.

An hour later, she was pacing the kitchen, waiting for his two quick raps on the back door.

When he did arrive, he took her into his arms, his cool fingertips insinuating themselves under her sweater and stroking her bare back just above the waistline of her jeans.

He burrowed into the hollow of her neck. Her shoulders were stiff, too tense to welcome him.

He pulled back. "What's wrong?"

"Nothing. Rough day at the office."

She glanced past him and saw Ada Toobert staring at her from the bright yellow square of her kitchen window. Ada seemed to glow with the thrill of possessing visible proof of Misp's hottest new rumor. Jessica gritted her teeth and, reaching behind Callum, flipped off the light switch.

IT SEEMED to Jessica the most incongruous of moments. She wanted to tell him about their daughter, but her timing could not have been worse.

She lay motionless on the bed, the top sheet and the comforter thrown back, three wavering candle flames illuminating the room. Callum knelt beside her on the bed and dragged a blue marker across her bare skin. The pen strokes felt like caresses, slow and lazy. Tomorrow, she would tell him. Just one more night couldn't hurt.

He capped the blue pen and chose a cranberry-colored one from the assortment that lay on the pillow next to her. "What do you think of the famous Callum Luke relaxation technique?"

She propped herself on her elbows and stared at the faint lines he'd just sketched. They looked like the delicate rivers of her veins.

"So, you've drawn on other women, then?"

He smiled. "I didn't say that."

"Do we know where else these Magic Markers have been?"

He made a dramatic brush stroke. "Oh, they're not mine. They belong to my niece. She asked me to carry them in my coat pocket, but I forgot to give them back. I'll tell her they were put to good use."

He leaned back and surveyed his work.

She was hesitant to question the drawing's symbolism. A lithe, copper-haired mermaid glided up her left leg, swimming through undulating blue reeds and golden bubbles, and a muddy brown sea monster slithered up her right leg, its snout and head partly concealed by a coastal Indian salmon mask. "This reminds me of one of the pictures from your sketchbook in the tent."

"You weren't supposed to look at those."

She smiled wryly. "There were a lot of things I wasn't supposed to do back then."

He gently pushed her back against the pillow. He leaned closer, intent on his work. His knee pressed against her hip as he colored in the spaces. "You realize this is a Callum Luke fantasy original and could be worth millions on the open market, especially since it was drawn under stressful conditions." He deliberately strayed from the lines. "Oops. See how difficult it is to keep focused in these circumstances?"

"Oh, I think your focus is entirely clear. If I have the misfortune to be in a car accident, how will I explain this at the hospital?"

He studied her from different angles, the way an artist would. "Tell them you're a traveling work of art."

She fixed her gaze on the ceiling. "Callum, how long will this last?"

"I don't know. Forever, I guess—if you don't bathe."

Maybe now was the time after all, she thought. "That's not what I meant. I meant us."

He smiled. "The same, if that's what you want."

She opened her mouth to answer, then closed it. She shouldn't have waited this long. How was she going to say it now? *I need to know, Callum, because we have a daughter.* The words lodged in her throat.

He was watching her. "That is what you want, isn't it?"

She couldn't answer. Several seconds passed, and by then she realized he'd misread her hesitation.

"Guess not," he said, swinging his legs over the edge of the bed. He stood and started methodically gathering up the pens, his eyes no longer on her. "My mother always said, 'Don't ask the question unless you're willing to accept the answer.' I was foolish to ask the question."

"No, Callum, it's not what you're thinking. It's just that the answer is more complicated than the question."

He turned to her, his eyes dark and guarded. "Well, of course, it's complicated. The whole damn thing has been, from the beginning. I know people are talking, but I don't care." He inserted the pens in the box with a detached deliberateness, arranging them in a spectrum. He stopped and looked at her. "You do though, don't you?"

She shook her head.

He sat on the edge of the bed, looking at her for several long moments. "Who was it? Your mother or someone else?" His voice

was softer. He laid his hand over hers, rubbing his fingertips between her knuckles.

She shook her head. "It makes no difference."

"I'm sorry. I should have realized it would be worse for you."

"No, that isn't it. I can deal with them." She dragged the sheet
over her breasts and hugged herself.

He reached for her, pulling her to him.

"Callum," she whispered, pressing her face against his shoulder,
"we have a daughter."

There was a moment of pure silence. Then his head snapped up.
"What?"

"A . . . a daughter."

He drew back and stared at her. "That's impossible. How could
you know that already?"

"She's almost eighteen. I'm not asking you to do anything about
it. I mean, it's up to you." The words spilled out now. "I couldn't
hide it from you any longer. I had to tell you because I hope . . . I
hope. . . ."

Even in the dim light, she could see the dark color rise up his
neck. His face turned splotchy, as if she'd slapped him. "You raised
her yourself?"

"My mother sent me to live with my great-aunt. I couldn't take
care of a baby. I was barely seventeen. I was still in high school
when she was born."

He gripped her by the shoulders, his fingertips digging into her
muscles. *"You gave her away?"*

She had to force herself to look at him. He didn't understand.
She could see that in his expression of horror.

He didn't realize how terrible it had been. The hard, unrelenting
labor before the doctor resorted to the cesarean, the awful fear that
she was going to die before she saw the baby. Only a nurse to hold
her hand.

She pressed her fist to her mouth. "I had no choice. My mother
wouldn't help me raise her."

Callum stood and walked to the chair where his shirt and jeans lay.

She looked at him, the tears flowing now. "I wanted what was best for her. What would you have had me do?"

"We would have taken her. The tribe would have raised her." His words were measured and harsh, his eyes as dark and shiny as black ice. "We don't give our children away."

She rubbed her eyes with the edge of the sheet. "Lila didn't want anyone else to know."

He made a brusque, dismissive gesture. "That's not good enough. You don't give up your own flesh and blood because you're worried about what people will say."

He didn't realize how worthless she'd felt. He couldn't know what it was like. The anger spiraled through her. "*You* did not have to go through it!"

He stared at her for the longest time without speaking, as if he hadn't even heard. "I can't believe you went along with your mother. In high school, you were a rebel. You burned down your mom's dock. You screwed around with me, for Christ's sake. Why, then, when you *needed* to, couldn't you fight back?"

"Because . . . because I was tired!"

His mouth twisted in disbelief. "What kind of answer is that?"

"I was worn out, sick of fighting, beaten down. I wasn't as strong as you think I was. I was nothing by then."

"You don't even know who raised her, do you?" His face resembled a hard mask.

She shook her head. She was trembling with cold sweat. The sheet was a tangled mess. "A Catholic social services agency arranged the adoption."

"Did you tell them she was half Native American? We have laws that protect our children from adoption by outsiders."

Jessica looked at him from under wet lashes. "Lila persuaded me to say she was part Mexican."

He stared at her fiercely, struggling to speak. "I don't know if . . ." His voice cracked. "I don't know if I can forgive you. I don't know if I can love you."

"That's certainly a long way from an hour ago."

He grabbed his jeans from the chair and yanked them on. "Where is she now?" His tone was tight and clipped.

"I'm trying to find her. If she wants to contact me, the agency will release my name. I've also sent information to every adoption registry in the country. The only other thing I can do is hire an independent searcher, but—"

"How long is all this supposed to take?"

"I don't know. She might contact the registries when she turns eighteen next month. She might wait years. If she doesn't want to know me, it could be never. Maybe she . . ." She tried to say, *Maybe she hates me for what I did,* but she choked on the words.

Dropping to his hands and knees, he searched under her bed, finally emerging with two athletic shoes in the grip of dust balls. He stood, clutching one in each hand, his eyes blazing. "When you find her, tell her how to reach me. Tell her I would never have given her away." He let the shoes fall to the floor, then jammed his bare feet into them.

She swallowed hard, wondering just how much pain they would inflict on each other. "You know I actually did feel sorry for you— all that business about your wife running off with your brother."

He took his watch from her dresser and clasped it on his wrist with a click that sounded as definitive as a door locking. "I don't know what made me think our relationship was worth resurrecting." He reached for his jacket, which hung on the back of the chair. "Obviously, I made a mistake."

AFTER CALLUM LEFT, she sat on the edge of the bed, her head in her hands—remembering.

The second day in the hospital came back to her. She was cradling the dark-haired baby in her arms, demanding that privilege before she would sign any papers. She watched her daughter's thick-lashed eyes open, then squeeze shut. Her mouth puckered urgently, hungrily.

Jessica laid the baby in her lap and unwrapped the light flannel blanket. She peeled off the tiny cotton shirt and diaper, and touched her fingertips to the baby's chest. Felt the flutter of her heart just below the skin. Tugged on the little legs clasped as tight as wings against the round tummy with its black button. And her foot—oh, the baby's foot with the mother-of-pearl toenails, so miniature, so perfect.

Her skin had faint red lines as though it had been recently unfolded. Jessica pressed her nose to her downy cheek and inhaled its warm, milky scent. She was certain she'd never before held anything so extraordinary. When she gave her unnamed daughter to the nurse, she felt as if she were handing over her own heart.

But Callum didn't know any of that. He wasn't there. She could understand his shock, even some of his outrage, but not his lack of forgiveness. He hadn't been forced to struggle with a decision that had no possibility of a happy ending.

She shuffled into the bathroom. Her temples pounded rhythmically—a headache in full throb. Avoiding her reflection in the mirror above the sink, she splashed water on her face, then patted it dry with a hand towel.

She forgot about the full-length mirror on the back of the door. Swinging around, she confronted her image in its grim entirety. She had seen the puffy red eyes and nose before, but she stared for several moments at Callum's candy-colored artwork, looking ironically sensuous and playful.

The love behind it hadn't lasted long.

She tossed the towel into the tub, grabbed her plaid robe from a hook, and slipped it on. With a flat learning curve like hers, she deserved everything she got, she told herself. She didn't have any respect for women who kept taking back the men who hurt them.

She wandered into the living room. Outside, the night would be quiet, the misty air as refreshing as a cool hand on her forehead.

She opened the front door and stepped onto the dark porch. Callum's car sat directly across the street, the yellow porch light from the opposite house backlighting his silhouette.

He hadn't left. He had simply moved his car over from the next block. She wondered if he was thinking about his daughter, regretting what he'd missed for eighteen years.

She retreated into the house and closed the door. More likely, he was still guarding her against Pete Johnson and Dennis Kretz—not because of any lingering affection or respect but because of his self-righteous sense of obligation. Merely performing his duty so he could say at least *he* knew how to do the right thing.

She dug out a spare blanket from the hall closet and, curling up on the sofa, dozed with her arms cradled under her head. Several times during the night, she awoke—stiff, dry-mouthed, and disoriented. Each time, she stumbled to the front window, stared first at her own wild-haired, ghostly reflection in the glass pane, then through the silvery drizzle at Callum, sitting in his car. She wondered if he'd slept at all.

At five A.M., she fixed herself a cup of tea, thinking it would calm her beleaguered body. With mug in hand, she walked to the front window, parted the curtain and looked out at a sky patched with flimsy clouds.

Between the trees, the sun was rising like soft music. A rectangle of dry pavement marked the place where Callum's car had been.

WRAPPING HER ROBE tight around her, Jessica stepped onto the porch. Her temples beat with pain. The ache deep inside her felt sharp and familiar. How well she had come to know the physical symptoms of loss.

She wondered if she chose men who she knew would leave her emotionally, if not bodily. Of course, Patrick would say, and had said, that all her failed relationships—meaning primarily theirs—could be traced to her father's death. In the bitter aftermath of their divorce, he'd said she was looking for a man to take her father's place, and no husband could do that. She'd told him that was psychological bullshit.

Patrick had shrugged. "People repeat their mistakes until they learn from them." If she could rewind the conversation, she would have shot back, "And just what does that say about your choosing me as your wife?"

She hated the notion that she was a victim of her past, but mostly she hated the thought that Patrick could be right about anything.

The *Misp Tribune* rested in a puddle of rainwater near her bare feet. She bent to retrieve it, and when she lifted her gaze, she saw a wobbling, slobbery Buster amble into her yard. Let him come, she thought, with a little jolt of satisfaction.

Buster circled her John F. Kennedy rosebush, poked his wet, black nose through one of the octagonal holes in the wire and pawed at the base of the cage. The dog retreated, as if to study this new challenge, then sidled up to the cage, lifted his leg, and fired a yellow stream farther than Jessica thought possible. It hit the rosebush's tender green leaves like a bullet. They seemed to curl and die right in front of her.

Under normal circumstances, she would have yelled at him or widened the diameter of the cage, but she wasn't feeling the least bit normal, or charitable.

Reacting without reflection, she raised the soggy, rolled-up *Tribune* and hurled it at the broad cedar to the right of Buster. She missed by exactly two feet and nailed the dog square on the side of his grizzled, slack-jowled head. She could not have been more accurate if she had intended him as her target. He toppled to the ground like a cardboard cutout.

"Oh, Lord," she whispered, "I've killed him."

She sprinted barefoot across the slippery grass, dropped to her knees beside him, and pressed her fingers to what she hoped was his carotid artery. She felt no pulse.

No more than five seconds later, Ada rushed from her home, pink duster flapping against her white legs, flip-flops smacking the wet sidewalk. Her sleep-flattened, steel-gray hair was caught up in a blue net, giving it the appearance of a Brillo pad. Her face looked polished with cream. "What have you done to him?" Her voice was low, ominous, almost threatening.

Jessica stared at her, feeling dazed. "I didn't mean to. I was aiming for the tree."

Ada squatted next to Buster and tried to scoop him up—no easy matter with an overweight dog shaped like a cigar butt. She looked at Jessica. "What kind of person hurts a helpless old dog?"

Jessica felt the tears pool in her eyes. "I swear I only meant to scare him."

Ada smacked Buster's chest, obviously hoping to restore a beat in his heart. Jessica took his head in her lap and stroked his muzzle, thinking for one gruesome moment she might have to resort to mouth-to-mouth resuscitation. She'd once seen a fireman on television revive a kitten that way. She bent closer, then caught a whiff of Buster's breath (an overpowering stench that reminded her of a dead whale washed up on the beach) and jerked her head back.

"Come on, Buster, come on, baby," Ada crooned, rubbing his paws.

Jessica knelt there, wondering what meanness, subconscious or otherwise, had gripped her when she pitched the newspaper. What she had done, she realized, was a canine version of "kicking the cat."

"I like dogs, really I do," she said to Ada, "but I had a bad night, and my plants are dying."

Ada looked at her as if she'd gone crazy. "Sometimes I wonder about people like you. Did you ever consider what Buster means to Morrie and me?"

Jessica stared down at the dog. "I'm sorry."

His eyes fluttered.

"He's alive," Ada breathed. "Oh, thank goodness." She jumped to her feet. "I have to get him to Dr. Musgrove."

"I'll drive you. We can put him in the van." Hopping up, Jessica dug reflexively in the pocket of her robe for her keys, then realized they were in the house.

Ada drew back from her in revulsion. "Absolutely not. I wouldn't let you drive us to the end of the block. Morrie will take us."

Jessica watched her hurry away.

Halfway to her house, Ada paused to look at her. "You're paying the vet bill, and I'm reporting you to the animal cruelty people."

Jessica dropped to her heels alongside Buster, hoping he didn't know what had hit him or who had thrown it. His limbs twitched. He opened his eyes—gentle, damp, trusting eyes, not quite focused yet.

She knelt on the cold, wet grass and stroked his ears, suddenly feeling maternal toward him. "Oh, Buster, you're soft as a baby. I never realized that."

Her shoulders began to shake uncontrollably.

19

Jessica arrived an hour late at the two-story, brick-and-clapboard home she had scheduled for window-cleaning. It was turning out to be a day of warm, shifting breezes and popcorn clouds.

Pamela Fields opened the door and frowned from behind blue, plastic-framed lenses that magnified her most striking feature, her violet eyes. "I've been waiting for you. I've got the civic garden club coming here tomorrow and I have errands to run. I was beginning to wonder if you were going to show up."

Jessica managed a smile. "Sorry, there was a small accident with the Tooberts' dog. I had to help."

Pamela's interest perked up. "Did Buster get hit by a car?"

"No, a flying object." Ada would probably tell everyone she'd tried to murder him.

"Is he going to be all right?"

"I think so."

Pamela ran her tongue across her immaculate white teeth. "Are you going to have time to do all the windows?"

"I'll be finished by late afternoon." Jessica leaned against the doorframe and kicked off her sneakers.

Pamela stepped aside to let her in. "What happened to your eyes? You look like someone punched you."

"Didn't sleep well last night."

"Bet it's allergies. Worst month of the year for pollen. I get it so bad sometimes my eyes swell shut. You want a couple of my pills?"

Jessica shook her head.

"All right," Pamela said, "but you should do something about it because you look awful."

"Thanks, Pamela, I will."

Jessica carried her plastic bucket filled with squeegees, lint-free surgical cloths, and a bottle of janitorial detergent inside.

Pamela decorated her home with dried flowers, vine wreaths, scented votive candles, and porcelain angels. The bathrooms reeked of rose potpourri, more than enough to trigger a sneezing fit in anyone mildly allergic, Jessica thought.

Pamela murmured she would return in a few hours and left Jessica to the peaceful sounds of birds and distant traffic—and a stretch of unclocked solitude that gave her more time to think about Callum than she wanted.

She realized that, despite all the caution signals, she had been conjuring up white-picket-fence fantasies of a life with him. She would have to give those up now and focus only on Jonah and her daughter. For the next two hours, she thought about them, and about Lila, Pete, Wendell, and Dennis. But each connection led back to Callum. She wondered how hard he would search now for evidence against Wendell or anyone else.

She saw him sitting in his cold, dark car in front of her house, protecting her. She hoped she could rely on that Boy Scout integrity when it came to her brother.

She was rinsing sponges in the kitchen sink when Pamela arrived home, jostling bags of groceries on her bony hips like twin toddlers. She dropped the sacks on the counter and huffed, "You aren't going to believe what I found out."

Jessica turned off the water with a firm twist. "If you don't mind, I'm a bit overdosed on gossip these days."

"You'll want to hear this." Her violet eyes glowed.

Jessica realized these were the moments this woman lived for, and she almost felt sorry for her.

Pamela flung open the sliding glass door. "How do you stand these detergent fumes?" She thrust her face close to the screen and breathed deeply, watching Jessica from the corner of her eye.

Jessica tossed the sponge into the bucket. "Okay, tell me."

"The sheriff's going to your mother's house to arrest Jonah."

"Who told you that?"

"I can't say."

"Oh, come on, Pam, this isn't a White House investigation."

"Well, I *can* tell you it came from a reliable source who sits right outside Milt Tarr's office and who happened to be at the Thrifty Market buying cigarettes while I was there."

Jessica grabbed the bucket and headed for the front door.

"Hey," Pamela yelled after her, "did you finish all the windows?"

Jessica stopped, her stocking feet skidding on the waxed floor. "I still have the upstairs. I'll come back later."

"Well—"

Jessica's shoulders slumped. "How about I call you and tell you what happens at my mother's house?"

A smug smile crept across Pamela's face. "Okay. Sure."

JESSICA CAREENED DOWN the pitted highway, hoping that if the sheriff were about to arrest Jonah, all the deputies would be at her mother's house. She was doing eighty in a fifty-mile-an-hour zone.

She glanced at the van clock. Twelve-thirty. Maybe Jonah wouldn't be there. The weatherman was predicting a storm, but she saw no sign of it yet. With the weather as nice as it was now, Jonah might be out roaming the hillsides.

Jessica wondered what part Callum was playing in this arrest. Perhaps he had instigated it. She floored the accelerator. The van skimmed over potholes and shot through the long, straight tunnel between trees that bordered the highway. When she came to the Y in the road near her mother's house, she nearly collided with an empty logging truck. She swerved to the left and headed into the driveway, bringing the van to a sharp, gravel-spitting halt in front of Lila's home.

There was no sheriff's car, no sign of any commotion at all. When she saw Jonah grinning at her from his upstairs bedroom window, she wrapped her arms around the steering wheel and laughed in relief. Misp's rumor web had obviously snapped in some vital places.

She would go inside and say hello to him, perhaps suggest he return with her to Pamela's home just to be safe. Pamela might not be all that happy to see him under the circumstances, but he could stay in the van if necessary. She would feel a lot more comfortable with him nearby.

She opened the van door and stepped out, reflexively inhaling the wood smell drifting from the mill. In the distance, saws gave off their high-pitched whine, and she heard the steady, solid clunks of the stacker dropping raw logs at the sort yard. She'd grown up with these sounds, and they were as reassuring as a lullaby.

Shading her eyes, Jessica looked up at the house again.

Her brother was leaning out of the screenless upstairs window, exuberantly waving a rolled-up magazine, like a boy in his own private treehouse. "Hey, Jessie, I have something to show you."

She smiled and waved back, feeling a swell in her throat and a sudden gratitude for having him. "Be there in a minute."

She strode across the grass into the warm, stuffy house and immediately smelled boiled coffee, another aromatic memory from her childhood.

Leaving the door open to air out the house, she met Jonah on the stairs. He gripped the wooden banister as if he had just slid down it.

"I'm going to Gettysburg." His voice jangled with excitement.

"What?" She thought she must have misunderstood. He had never wanted to go anywhere before.

"To Gettysburg in July." He unfolded the magazine and held it out. The cover read *Civil War Times*.

She took the rumpled magazine. It opened readily to a food-stained page rimmed with photos of Union and Confederate soldiers, marching in formation, kneeling in firing positions and aiming muskets at each other. But the photos appeared recent. The participants looked modern, like contemporary Americans in period dress.

Jessica scanned the text. Thousands of people were expected to descend on Gettysburg for the one hundred and thirty-fifth anniversary of the pivotal Civil War battle, planning to reenact it. She flipped to the next page, which showed photos of similar battle reenactments. In one picture, a surgeon treated a wounded soldier in a mock Union Army field hospital. In another, a company of men toting reproduction bayonets and muskets that shot blanks gathered around a drummer boy.

"Can you imagine, Jessie, the Civil War like it's real?" His words spilled out in a rush. "I can buy an authentic Confederate cavalry uniform by mail from Grand Illusions. I've been saving the money Mom gives me. I already have the shoes."

She stared down at his black brogans. To her dismay, they had no laces at all. "Oh, God," she sighed. She could just imagine what Callum would think if he saw them.

Jonah's eyes darted in agitation. She knew nothing frightened him more than uncertainty. He realized he had screwed up, but he didn't grasp the problem.

She managed a comforting smile. "You need new laces."

He looked down at his shoes. "I don't have any. I have to order them."

"Jonah, do they have to be authentic? Couldn't you put in some others temporarily?"

He chewed on his lower lip, and she knew he wouldn't.

She felt a flash of frustration. He seemed completely oblivious that he could be arrested at any time. Pamela may have misunderstood some of what Milt Tarr's deputy said, but that didn't mean she had it all wrong. "Put away the shoes, Jonah, will you? Just don't wear them until you get new laces."

He nodded slowly. "Yeah, I guess I could do that."

When she turned to look at the magazine again, his face lighted with excitement.

He pointed at an authentic-looking Confederate uniform on the page. "One of these costs eight hundred dollars, and a musket costs five hundred. I need to earn a lot of money before July. Jack Everett is hiring someone at his store, and I was thinking maybe I could work there."

She closed the *Civil War Times* and handed it to him, trying to think what she should say. For the first time that she was aware of, he wanted something enough to work for it.

But what irony that he thought Jack might hire him. Even if he were not about to be arrested, his fantasy of Gettysburg in July seemed about as realistic as Paris in April.

She could see the attraction for him. He would meet people who shared his interests. He could participate in a battle reenactment that surpassed any he could assemble on the four-by-eight-foot board in the basement. He was trembling with the thrill of it. He'd never wanted to leave Misp before, and she would have to explain to him why he couldn't now.

She brushed a smudge of powdered sugar from his chin, probably the residue of a breakfast doughnut. It bothered her because it made him look defenseless. "I need to tell you something, Jonah."

He scrubbed his jaw with the back of his hand. "What?"

"About Gettysburg . . ." She stopped.

She thought of Clement Brings Yellow stretched out in his beached rowboat, launching a journey that advanced only in his imagination. Maybe the boat never moved an inch, but that wasn't the point. She had no more right to destroy Jonah's dream than she had to tell the old Indian he was crazy for sailing on land.

She smiled at Jonah. "I just want to tell you how much I love you."

He nodded shyly.

A breeze blew through the open door, carrying a drift of dust from the mill. She reluctantly closed it.

"Come with me to the Fieldses' house. We can talk while I'm washing windows. It'll be just a few hours, and then I'll drive you back here."

She turned in time to see him grimace. "What?" she said. "What's the problem?"

"I don't like her."

"Why not?"

"She has scary eyes."

Jessica made a face. "To tell the truth, Jonah, I think she wears purple contacts."

He nodded as if he believed her.

She grinned and poked him in the ribs. "It was a joke."

He looked confused, and she realized he didn't see the humor in it. She patted his arm. "Come back with me, okay?"

He shook his head.

"Jonah, please." She took a deep breath. "There are rumors around town that the sheriff might be coming to . . . well, to see you. I didn't want to scare you, but I don't want to leave you here to deal with him alone."

Jonah looked stunned. "The sheriff?"

The phone rang, giving her a little jolt.

"I'll get that." She headed toward the kitchen. "You grab some more Civil War magazines or your soldiers to take along."

She picked up the receiver, and Lila's voice boomed across the line. "What's going on over there?"

Jessica bristled. "Nothing. I just stopped by to see Jonah."

"Hell, I don't mean that. One of the fellows came running in and said he saw the county sheriff's car barreling toward my house."

Jessica felt the air rush from her chest. "I don't know."

The doorbell rang twice in quick succession.

"Oh, Jesus," she whispered into the phone. "Someone's outside."

"Don't let them in my house! Where's Jonah?"

Jessica looked at the open cellar door. She hadn't even seen him slip by. "In the basement, I think."

"Don't let them in my house," Lila repeated. "Jessica, do you hear me?"

Jessica stepped around the corner into the hall, stretching the phone cord with her. She could make out the silhouettes of two men, possibly more, through the opaque windows that flanked the front door. "I don't know if I can stop them."

"I'm coming right over."

Jessica heard the receiver on the other end of the line slam down. She returned to the kitchen and hung up the phone, trying to think how she could keep them out, especially if they had a warrant.

She heard a loud knock on the door. She waited a few more seconds, then walked with measured steps toward the entry.

20

Callum stood a few feet away from Milt Tarr and Bud Schultz on the Moran front porch. He looked again at Jessica's van. He hadn't expected her to be here, and he didn't want to interrogate her brother with her nearby. Of course, she would see any action involving Jonah as one more sign of betrayal.

He had so little evidence in this case. The survivor's charge that Jonah threw rocks at the house. A few shoe prints, but only one set that stood out in the crowd. A broken shoelace from a reproduction of a Civil War brogan. The remains of three canning jars that had contained a petroleum distillate.

It had rained the night of the fire. It had rained most of the previous six months. The ground was saturated. Only a spirit could have tramped around the perimeter of that house without leaving footprints. And yet, after dark, someone had dragged the oak cask from the rear of the house to the dining room window. The neighbor, Larry Parks, said it wasn't there earlier in the evening. It appeared as if that same someone had climbed through the window, started the fire, and then left the way he came. And yet the only prints they had leading from the property came from the brogans and the firemen.

Dennis Kretz was barefoot and dressed for bed when he crawled from his window onto the porch roof. Parks and a few other neighbors verified that. And the investigation turned up Kretz's shoes in his room. They were dry and free of mud. Callum found nothing to implicate him, no fire-setting materials in his room, no history of playing with matches, no apparent motive. Kretz might be a pervert, but there was no evidence he was an arsonist.

As for Wendell, Callum had only Jess's phone conversation with Pete as a reason to suspect him. Wendell may have wished misfortune on the halfway house residents, but so did most of the other folks in town. He glanced at Bud, thinking he had no more evidence against Wendell than he had against the fire chief himself. Now, there was a potential suspect if he were playing guessing games. Bud might be a fool, but he probably knew how to set a fire without leaving a trail.

Callum had hoped by now to have the name of the Quinault who'd reported the fire.

"He doesn't want to talk to you," his uncle Jim said on the phone that morning. "He says people won't believe him, so why bother?"

"*I'll* believe him. Tell him that, will you, Uncle?"

"It's not you he's worried about." Jim's voice was firm. "He means white people."

Once again, Callum felt caught between his tribe and the townspeople, and he was beginning to wonder if he could even locate a bridge between them.

"Does he know who set the fire, Uncle? Because if he does, it would be morally wrong to withhold that information." It would also be illegal, but no sense threatening him.

"He said he doesn't know," Jim answered.

The fax Rob Villalobos had handed Callum that morning contained information they'd requested from Grand Illusions. The company had only one client in Misp, in fact only one on the entire Olympic Peninsula, and that was Jonah Moran. He bought size ten Confederate brogans last December. Every fragment of evidence they had kept pointing back to Jonah.

Callum knew he didn't have enough to arrest him. He didn't even have enough for a search warrant. Unless something turned up, all he could do was talk to Jonah, try to persuade him to turn over the shoes, answer questions, and cooperate. Callum felt sure he would have more success with Jonah than Milt and Bud had—if he could keep Jess and her mother out of the way.

He couldn't think about last night's events. He couldn't think about his daughter or his anger toward Jess. If he did, he might not be able to maintain his objectivity. He could—and would—keep his feelings for her separate.

He watched the sheriff pop an Altoid in his mouth. He'd asked Milt to deal with Lila if, by chance, she turned up. Normally, he wouldn't have delegated that authority, but the sheriff had known her for years, and he would be more likely to get her cooperation than Callum would.

Bud Schultz stared smugly down his bulbous nose. If the circumstances hadn't been so serious, Callum would have laughed at the fire chief's comical display of power. Callum didn't want him along, but he'd insisted—and, in the long run, it seemed better to have him with them than back in town spreading rumors of what might be happening. Callum remembered all the times in high school that he saw Wendell act like an asshole. The pathetic little guy could not have had a better role model for that behavior than his father.

Jessica opened the door. Her face was all red smudges and shadows. Callum realized she must have spent the night crying. And yet, she still looked pretty with that hair the color of cedar heartwood and those pinpoint brown freckles splashed across her cheekbones and nose.

He gripped the porch railing, fingering the rough wood, fighting the urge to feel sorry for her. She had already proved that under that soft exterior was a resolve so strong she could endure anything. If she could give away their daughter, she could certainly survive the loss of him, he thought bitterly.

Schultz nodded at her, and the sheriff removed his hat in what seemed to Callum an old-fashioned, almost gallant swoop of respect. With them, she managed a strained smile. When she nodded at him, he could tell she wanted to add, *You bastard*. She didn't need to. Her coldness conveyed the unspoken words. She probably thought he had planned this invasion, that it was his own personal revenge.

"Hello, Jess," Callum said evenly. "Is your brother here?"

Flecks of perspiration dotted her upper lip. A slight flush colored her face. "I don't know. I just arrived myself." She avoided his gaze.

He realized she was an awful liar.

"Mind if we step inside and wait for him?"

"I can't allow that." Her voice was low, slightly shaky. "The house doesn't belong to me."

When the beads of perspiration threatened to topple off, she pulled a blue window-washing rag from her back pocket, bent her head, and coughed into it, wiping her mouth. "Excuse me," she murmured.

Callum heard the deep growl of a truck engine behind him and saw the look of relief on Jessica's face. He turned to see a blue Chevy pickup charging toward them, kicking up dust and grit. It stopped just short of the sheriff's cruiser. Lila jumped from the cab and strode across the parking area, the gravel cracking under her heavy boots like a succession of gunshots. She was wearing a long-sleeved plaid flannel shirt and khaki slacks.

She stopped on the grass a few feet from the porch and squinted up at them. "Just what the hell are you men doing here?"

Milt took a pace forward, looking down at her from the top step. "Why, Lila, we've just come over to talk to Jonah." His voice was steady, calm.

"What for?"

Milt pinched the crown of his hat with his nicotine-stained fingers. "Wel-l-l, it's about that fire. Now why else would we be here?"

It occurred to Callum that when folks in Misp confronted each other, they sounded like the worst kind of rednecks, as if a drawl took the sting from their words.

Milt hooked a thumb in the direction of the fire chief and Callum. "You know Bud here, and this is Callum Luke. I suspect you remember him from way back when."

If she didn't, she would have to have experienced a dramatic memory lapse, Callum thought. He had plenty of experience with Misp's standard game of polite pretense.

She gave the fire chief a curt nod. She barely looked at him. "You've already asked Jonah enough questions," she said to Milt.

"Well, we've got some new ones."

Lila strode up the stairs, crossed directly between Milt and Bud, and swung around, planting herself in the doorway like a stone monolith.

Milt sighed. "Come on now, Lila, we're not going to scare the boy. Swear to God."

"He's a twenty-eight-year-old man," Jessica said, "not a boy."

The sheriff rubbed the tip of his nose. "Yes, well, I know that."

Wonderful, Callum thought, two mule-headed women who couldn't even recognize that if Jonah were really a man, if they just allowed him to be, he wouldn't need their skirts to hide behind. When it occurred to him that neither of them was wearing a skirt, he suppressed a smile.

Jessica, who stood just outside the threshold, glanced at him, her mouth tightening into a rigid line. She probably thought he was enjoying all this. He let his face go impassive and walked to the edge of the porch, surveying the expanse of grass and trees, distancing himself. He would give the sheriff a chance to handle things first. He knew Lila and Jess would resist any efforts on his part. And they had the leverage. They could refuse to cooperate.

He turned and leaned against the railing, drawn to look at her again. Her eyes fixed on some distant point and briefly glazed over. She was listening to Milt argue that it was in Jonah's best interests to talk with them, to get this matter behind him. He and the sheriff had discussed these points beforehand. If Milt could persuade Lila to allow them inside, if she gave them permission to search without a warrant, they could inspect the cellar and the other common areas. They would need Jonah's consent to enter his room.

He listened to Milt's easy drawl, but he kept his gaze on Jess. Her weary vulnerability reminded him of the way she had looked shortly after her father's death—the time he had come upon her in the clear-cut swath of forest. She'd seemed so fragile, as painful to watch as a wounded bird, and he had held her, when he knew he shouldn't.

He suddenly wanted to hold her again. And there was nothing he could do about it.

She glanced anxiously over her shoulder, and he knew without question that Jonah was in the house.

He turned around and stared at the old-growth cedars that rimmed the yard. A breeze caught their branches, and they wavered like silver-green flags. He saw another motion—someone running from the rear of the house, a slight young man in a dark blue wind-breaker and jeans with a day pack over his shoulder.

It took Jonah less than a minute to reach the path to Thunder Lake, and during those passing seconds, Callum argued with himself. He told himself he should call out, that he couldn't let him escape. By running, Jonah was practically admitting guilt. He disappeared among the trees.

Across the front porch, Tarr was sweet-talking Lila.

She blocked the doorway, her arms folded like crossbars. "I don't want you men tramping through here."

Milt adjusted his black specs. "Well, Lila, we could get a warrant, you know. We could get Judge Densmore to sign it this afternoon."

Callum wished Milt hadn't said that. It sounded too much like coercion.

"I don't give a shit about that flathead Densmore," Lila sniffed. "This isn't Seattle or New York City, Milt. We don't operate the way those places do. When I say my son didn't set that fire, I expect you to believe me."

Bud rolled on the balls of his feet. "We don't need a warrant. Let's just go in there."

"That's enough, Bud," Callum said sharply, not even looking at the fire chief.

"Damned right it is," Lila snapped.

Callum stepped between the other men and faced her. "Mrs. Moran, we believe your son was in that halfway house at some point. We don't want to accuse him of anything, but we would like to ask him some questions." He wondered if she knew Jonah had left the house.

She looked him over, not saying anything, and Callum considered what might be going through her mind. He decided her thoughts weren't likely to favor him.

Finally, Jessica cleared her throat. "Let them in, Lila." Her voice was quiet but firm.

Lila frowned. "You're a big help."

Jessica proudly drew herself up. "Jonah's innocent, and we've got nothing to hide."

Callum felt certain she knew her brother had gone out the back door.

A flush spread across Bud Schultz's face, and his eyes took on an eager brightness. God in Heaven, Callum thought, the son of a bitch couldn't wait to corner Jonah.

Lila's hard gaze fell on Callum. She jerked her thumb at him. "He stays out here."

Callum saw the fury leap into Jessica's eyes and the sheriff's face tighten in disgust.

Before they could object, he said, "No problem. I'll wait out here, but I want to talk to Milt and Bud first."

When Lila didn't object, he took them aside. "Check the basement. Look for the shoes and for anything that might have been used to set a fire. If he's got papers down there—war game diagrams, that sort of thing—go through them and see if any relate to the halfway house. Be careful how you handle things, and, remember, don't go into his bedroom."

"If he's in there," Milt said, "do you want us to bring him out."

Callum nodded. "Yeah, do that."

The fire chief turned toward the door, but Callum grabbed his sleeve. "There's no rush, Bud. This isn't a television cop show."

Bud answered with a smirk, then followed Milt inside.

JESSICA WATCHED Lila's gaze sweep over Callum again as if he were soiled clothes. No one said a word, but after a few uncomfortable seconds, he crossed in front of them and strode down the steps toward the sheriff's cruiser. When he reached it, he leaned against the passenger door, drew a pair of mirrored sunglasses from his pocket, and slid them on, all without any haste.

Her mother set her hands on her hips, tracking his movements, both of them stonily watching each other. This is great, Jessica thought, her mother and her ex-lover. At the moment, she couldn't decide whom she disliked more.

"Bad taste," Lila said.

"What?"

"You have bad taste in men," she said, raising her voice.

"Terrific. Why don't you say it louder?"

"Thought I just did."

Jessica heard Schultz yell from the kitchen. "Back door's wide open."

Jessica rubbed the tender spots above her eyebrows with her fingertips. "They'll go after him."

"So will we," her mother murmured, "once they've left."

21

Lila's Chevy truck bounced along a narrow, rutted logging road that snaked up the slope. Jessica could sense her mother's exasperation. She was driving too fast.

Cold coffee sloshed over Lila's cup on the dash. Jessica rolled down the window and dumped it out. The bottom half inch was thick as grease. Not that it would have mattered much if the whole thing had tipped over. The hard-used truck already had the musty odor of a persistent water leak and tracked-in dirt and sawdust.

"Admit it," Jessica said, setting the empty, brown-stained cup inside a coiled rope on the floor, "you're just guessing he headed this way."

"You can't give me credit for anything, can you?" Lila chewed on her thumbnail, gripping the steering wheel with one hand. "I'll bet he took off behind the house, skirted the lake, hiked a mile, crossed 101, and picked up this road."

"That's ridiculous. He couldn't have made it to the cutoff in less than an hour."

"He could have hitched a ride partway. He's hiking toward Stubble Falls."

Jessica shook her head in disbelief. "Stubble Falls is at least ten miles from the cutoff."

Her mother zigzagged the truck around a fallen tree branch. "More like seven. He knows that area, and it's one of the few places that's not crawling with backpackers."

"Oh, no problem then. What's a few hundred acres to cover in the rain?" She ducked her head and peered through the windshield at the sky. "Does he know this storm's going to be a big one? They're predicting seventy-mile-an-hour winds."

"I don't know," Lila said in a subdued voice.

Jessica studied the thunderclouds boiling on the horizon, blowing in from the ocean. "Maybe he'll head back to the house."

"Not if he sees a deputy sheriff's car parked anywhere near it. And I'm not letting him spend a night out here."

As she spoke, the clouds briefly parted, and the late-afternoon sun gilded a single green hill on the other side of the ravine. Jessica's eye caught sight of a long silver ribbon, a tinseled waterfall splitting a swell of trees. Compared with the giant jail rats Bud Schultz had threatened, the forest probably looked benevolent to Jonah, as familiar as an old blanket he could burrow into.

"I'll bet he would rather be out here tonight than in the county jail," Jessica said.

Lila gave her a sharp glance. "What the hell are you talking about? I'm not hauling him back so they can arrest him."

"You may not have a choice. They took his Civil War shoes from the basement, so they must think they've got some evidence now." It was her mistake in telling him to remove them. Otherwise, they would probably be on his feet, she thought.

Lila jerked the truck to a brakes-squealing halt, then looked at her with winter in her eyes. "If you're not going to stand by me on this one, get out."

Jessica shook her head. "No. We haven't seen a vehicle since we turned onto this road. I am not walking back."

They sat there for several long moments, eyes locked in a standoff. Lila shifted into first gear, and the truck lurched forward. "You do it my way then."

Jessica didn't reply.

Lila drove on, hugging the narrow dirt road, following switchback after switchback up the increasingly steep slope. The wind picked up. Twigs and conifer needles pelted the truck like rain.

Finally, Jessica said, "He couldn't have hiked this far even if he did get a ride to the cutoff. You are so bullheaded you'd rather wander all over this mountainside than admit you're wrong."

Her mother careened around the next curve. "Shut up or I'll throw you out of this truck myself."

Jessica gripped the armrest. "Oh, you're really good at force, aren't you? Whether it's pitching people off a dock or out of your life." She knew she was headed for trouble, but the words seemed caught in their own current. "And you've always acted like it's for our own good, for our own protection. Well, I don't know which was worse—being protected by you or ignored by you. You wanted a strong son and a submissive daughter, but somehow we got reversed and you've never been able to accept either of us."

Lila floored the accelerator without responding. They jolted along the precarious road, hitting every rut, skidding over rocks and wood debris. More than once Jessica came close to thumping her head on the cab roof.

She started to say *Slow down* when she saw the shadow ahead, an ominous fissure that stretched from one side of the road to the other. She managed a breathless "Watch out!"

Lila rammed the brakes. The big tires ground into the dirt and shot up grit and dust.

The truck clung to the road for a few seconds, then teetered and dropped over the lip of the washout. The steel frame hit the earth with a crashing boom, and Jessica thought for a flash that the cab and the bed were going to slide right off. The pickup rattled and reverberated, its frame settling onto the edge of the cleft with a slow, rolling shudder.

Jessica was tipped forward, anchored only by her seat belt, feeling it dig into her hips and chest. She looked at Lila, who was in a similar position. "You okay?"

"Yeah," Lila said huskily.

It would be too easy to yell at her, Jessica thought. But she knew if *she* had been driving, Lila would be furious.

She shifted her weight a little to the right and cautiously unsnapped her seat belt, expecting the truck to plummet downward at any second. When it didn't, she opened her door until its lower edge hung over solid ground, leaving her a foot-wide space to step onto. She moved slowly, taking a long, anxious minute to work her way out. The truck creaked at one point but remained in place.

She stood alongside the truck, examining the fissure. It was the width of the one-lane road and four feet deep. The rear two thirds of the truck rested on flat ground, but its front wheels hung suspended in air, several feet above anything the tires could get a purchase on.

Jessica walked stiffly to the back of the pickup, knelt, and inspected the underside. Although she could taste stirred-up road dust, it held no smell of gasoline. And she saw no sign of a punctured tank. As she rose to her feet and brushed off her hands, the driver's door swung open with a creak, and Lila crawled out.

On one side of the road, a sheer cliff striated by dozens of rivulet waterfalls shot straight up a hundred feet. Boulders and rock chips, the result of slides, edged the base of the wall.

Lila walked to the other side, where Jessica stood surveying the concrete drainpipe that lay scattered in broken sections across the steep slope.

"Must have had so much water rushing over it that it pushed the pipe right out of the culvert, and the road collapsed," Jessica said.

Her mother nodded. "Probably happened last weekend when we had that gully-swamper."

A bank of clouds, brutally purple with rain, hovered on the southwestern horizon. Long gray threads slanted toward a distant slope; it was pouring several miles away. Jessica released an audible breath. "I want off this hillside."

"While you're at it, wish for a tow truck."

"Well, you got us into—" She stopped. Blood was oozing through a tear in her mother's khaki slacks, just above the right knee. "What happened to your leg?"

Lila stared down at it without much concern. "Must have hit the underside of the dash. I didn't even feel it."

"Well, you will soon. You got a first-aid kit in there?"

Lila nodded.

Jessica opened the driver's door, crawled into the truck, and retrieved the plastic box from behind the seat. When she emerged, she saw her mother had removed the red scarf from her braid and was pressing it against her leg, turning the cloth a deeper crimson. Jessica squatted down and opened the medical kit.

Lila took it from her. "I'm not some little kid."

"You need stitches."

"It's nothing. You should have seen Chip Parrish the other day. Sawed the tip of his middle finger right off, and he was just going to stick a Band-Aid on it."

"Well, just because Chip Parrish is an idiot—"

As if to satisfy her, Lila made a production of ripping away the fabric, wiping the wound with an antiseptic towelette, and taping a gauze pad to her leg.

Jessica studied the position of the tires. "Okay, well, it's a four-wheel drive so maybe we can back it out."

Her mother grunted in agreement.

Jessica gingerly climbed into the driver's seat, switched on the ignition, and shifted the truck into four-wheel drive. She eased the transmission into reverse and gunned the engine, feeling the front tires spin and the rear ones dig into the road.

She rolled down the window and stuck her head out. "Can you wedge a couple of rocks under those rear tires so I can get some traction?"

Lila hefted a craggy fragment from the nearby rockslide and carried it over. She positioned it, then went back for another one. Once the rocks were in place, Jessica depressed the accelerator and released the brake. Again, the front tires spun and the back ones dug into the earth.

Jessica hopped out, strode to the rear of the pickup, and lifted the frayed tarp in the bed. "What have you got in here?"

"Nothing worth anything."

There was the spare tire, a hydraulic jack, a half-full red gasoline can, a Styrofoam six-pack cooler without its lid, a broken ax handle, and enough wood chips and conifer needles to fill a five-gallon bucket. She dropped the tarp with a little huff of exasperation. "Where's your chain saw?"

Her mother glanced away. "You don't want to know."

"What kind of logger doesn't carry a saw?"

"What good would it do? You gonna fell a tree, poke it under the truck, and lever the son of a bitch out?"

"I've heard worse ideas." She walked to the edge of the road, then scanned the wooded hillside below them. "Anybody logging up here now?"

Lila, who was standing a few yards away, took several seconds to answer. "No. It's good timber. If anyone were, we'd be doing it."

Sitka spruce and cedar dotted the ridge on the cliffside. The wind gusted, and Jessica watched the trees sway in unison like the fans at a football game. She eyed the truck. "Well, we don't have a come-along, so we can't hook on to anything and pull it out. With this wind, we can't build a fire to attract attention. What do you suggest?"

"We put some weight in the truck bed."

"All right." She jerked her thumb toward the rocks. "Think you can help me haul some of those?"

Lila nodded.

Jessica skinned off her sweatshirt and tossed it through the open driver's window into the cab. "Okay, let's do it."

Wordlessly, they loaded a dozen boulder fragments into the pickup. Lila stumbled more than once, and Jessica could see she was trying to pretend her leg didn't hurt. The wind blew in bursts, showering the road with fir cones and broken branches.

When the truck bed sagged with the weight of rocks, Lila scrambled onto the tailgate. Jessica climbed into the cab. Murmuring a little prayer under her breath, she shifted into reverse and accelerated. She could feel the rear tires bite into the dirt, but the truck itself snaked back only a few inches.

"Stop!" Lila shouted. "You're just digging deeper holes back here."

Jessica opened the driver's door and stepped out. She looked at the depressions under the rear tires. "Well, this is just terrific."

Lila eased off the tailgate but didn't say anything. A gust of wind whipped her loose white hair around her face. Brushing it away from her eyes, she walked over to the ditch and lowered herself in. She knelt, poked her head under the truck frame, and examined the suspension. She pulled back and rose to her feet. "We're not going anywhere. We could load this bed with five tons of boulders, and it wouldn't help."

The wind suddenly felt colder. Jessica raised her voice so she could be heard over it. "Why not?"

"Can't get the wheels up. They've dropped down from the suspension, and without anything opposing the springs, they're going to stay there." She hoisted herself out of the hole and brushed off her hands. "And the frame's caught on the edge of the ditch."

Jessica knelt on the edge of the washout and looked under the truck. Her mother was right. They were fighting the whole weight of the front wheels and frame. She stood and wiped the sweat from her forehead with the back of her hand. "What now?"

"We walk."

Jessica thought of the seemingly endless switchbacks behind them. "That's crazy. You won't make it with that leg."

"Yes, I will."

"No, you wait here. I'll hike it alone."

Lila glanced up at the black clouds prowling the sky. "I'm going with you."

"You said yourself the truck is stuck solid. You'll be safer in it than you would be on the road."

Lila swung around. "I'm not thinking about the truck or me. This storm's coming in so strong, I can smell the stink of salt and fish in it. Can't you? We're going to have thunder and lightning and more water than these hills can handle. There'll be trees crashing every which direction. I don't want you out in it by yourself."

Jessica gave a little snort of surprise. "Protecting me again, huh? After all these years, I wouldn't have guessed my welfare was high on your list."

"There are a lot of things you've never guessed. But then you wouldn't have wanted to hear them."

Jessica lifted her eyebrows. "If you're talking about Dad, I was there, remember? I know what happened."

"Everything?"

"Enough."

"Then you knew about the other women."

Jessica barely heard her words above the wind, but she realized she had not misunderstood them. Once again, the laughter of the men in the hardware store and Jack Everett's words stung her ears. *"Big Mike Moran couldn't keep his hands off them either."*

"There were no other women," she said fiercely. "He wouldn't have done that."

Lila gave a sharp, mirthless laugh. "Oh, that's right. I forgot you canonized him after he died. While he was alive though, I had it thrown in my face every third day of the week. The snide remarks. 'Oh, Lila, Mike must be buying a lot of insurance these days.' " She raised her voice in shrill imitation of what could have been any one of a dozen women in town. " 'He's been running in and out of that State Farm office all week. Goodness, that Indian girl in there sure is a young thing to be managing a business by herself, isn't she?' "

Jessica thought at that moment she could have lifted the truck out of the ditch entirely on her own. She clenched her hands, feeling her nails bite into her palms. "How could you believe them? Misp has always had more than its share of people spreading vicious rumors. You shouldn't have believed them."

Lila shrugged.

Jessica felt the tears spring to her eyes. The noise of the storm created a low roar in her head.

"We might as well start walking," her mother said wearily.

"No!" She wiped her eyes with the back of her hand.

"Well, fine. Do it your way then." Lila rested her hand on the tailgate. "You do have a way, don't you?"

Jessica didn't answer. She tried to focus on the truck. There had to be one, and if she could just think clearly, she might come up with it. They had an ax handle and a rope, but she didn't know how they could use them. Fashion some kind of winch or pulley maybe. Even if they had the brute strength to work it, the rope wasn't strong enough to hoist a pickup out of a four-foot ditch. It would snap and the truck would smash down.

She hadn't done any physical work yet, and she felt exhausted. The hole seemed like one more abyss in her life, not all that different from a lake that swallowed souls. And she couldn't do anything about that crater either. She leaned against the cold metal of the truck fender.

Her mother strode closer to the washout. She picked up a small stone and hurled it at the front wheel. It hit the hubcap with a ping, then fell in the ditch directly below the tire. She lobbed another pebble with the same effect.

Jessica joined her and stared at the trench for several seconds, realizing what she had just seen. "That's it."

Lila blinked. "What's it?"

"We'll build a rock platform under the front tires. We'll fill the hole."

Lila waved her hand brusquely. "That won't work. The truck'll slide right off it."

"Well, let's not have any positive thinking here."

"You can be as positive as you want. It still won't work."

Jessica reached into the truck bed and chose the largest, flattest rock from the pile of boulder chips. "I'll do it alone." She stopped then, looked at her mother, and added softly, "But wouldn't it be nice if we could cooperate on something?"

Lila didn't answer, but Jessica saw a shadow of regret pass across her face.

She carried the rock to the edge of the ditch and dropped it in. When she turned around, her mother stood behind her, holding one the size of a basketball. Wondering when the temperature in hell had dropped below freezing, she took the rock from Lila. "Don't overdo it with that leg. I'll handle the bigger ones."

They spent the next hour transferring the boulder fragments from the truck bed to the washout. The wind caught Jessica's hair, and she looked up. The sky was an odd silver-gray, more beautiful now than menacing, but there wasn't a single seabird overhead. Anything with any sense had taken refuge.

The rocks formed a three-foot-high pyramid in the hole. By the time there were enough to build the platform, sweat drenched her T-shirt and she was huffing from exertion. She wished she hadn't thrown out the cold dregs of Lila's coffee.

Lila sat on the edge of the ditch, looking pale. A rush of air billowed her flannel shirt and pressed her collar flat against her tanned neck. The bandage on her leg was caked with blood, but she hadn't complained.

Jessica studied the suspension again and realized she couldn't simply pile rocks under the front tires. She would have to build a mound just inside each of the wheels and use the jack to compress the suspension, lifting the frame off the ground.

She constructed the secondary platforms, then cautiously scooted under the truck, scraping her back on the coarse dirt and rock chips. Away from the howling storm, she felt sheltered but no safer from danger. She stared up at the truck's massive underbelly, knowing the whole business could pitch forward at any second and crush her.

Her mother's voice rose above the wail of the wind. "Get out from under there! You're going to kill yourself."

Jessica eased herself out and sat up. "I have to jack up the suspension."

Her mother's mouth twisted. "Don't do this to me—please."

Jessica rose to her feet and felt the sudden rush of chill air. "What are you talking about? I'm just trying to get us off this hillside."

"I know what you're doing." Two red splotches colored her cheeks. "You want to scare me, putting yourself under a half-ton chunk of metal like that. Well, you've succeeded. I'll stay here, and you walk."

A few raindrops smacked Jessica's bare arms. "This will work. I know it will." At least it would if the platform didn't collapse.

She crawled under the truck again. After trying several positions, all of them awkward, she rolled onto her shoulder and placed the jack on the rock pile next to the right wheel.

She saw a blur of movement and then her mother's sturdy legs and feet directly in front of the truck. "What are you doing?"

Two broad hands gripped the underside of the bumper. "I'll hold it up if I have to."

A laugh bubbled up Jessica's throat. "You'll what?" Her voice sounded tinny, like she was shouting inside a garbage can.

"If you're so set on doing this," Lila growled, "then get on with it."

Jessica started cranking again, shoving more rocks in the spaces she'd created. At one point, when the truck shifted precariously,

Lila's hands clamped tighter. Jessica had no doubt her mother could hold it if she had to.

She watched Lila plant her feet farther apart. The bandage above her knee bloomed a brighter shade of red.

Repositioning herself, Jessica accidentally tapped her head on the suspension bar, dislodging particles of grit. A flake landed in her eye, feeling as big as a thumb. Tears welled up. She cranked the jack handle with a vengeance.

When she wriggled out to collect more rocks, she sat up and found herself staring straight up at her mother. Lila's eyes were wide with dread, and it occurred to Jessica that she had not seen the look of pure fear on her face since the morning Dad drowned.

Wordlessly, Lila backed off, reached for a slab of wood, then handed it over. Jessica packed the split log under the left front tire, then rose to her feet.

A jagged white streak split the vast gray sky and illuminated the bony skeletons of the trees on the ridge above them with an eerie, chalky glow. A deafening boom closely followed—much too close, Jessica thought. The air took on a metallic taste.

They gathered more debris, working together in silence. They could do no more than yell now anyway. The wind was coming in on a low moan, gathering momentum and tilting the trees into question marks. The raindrops were splashing faster, hitting the truck metal with a steady *ping-ping-ping*.

Jessica increased her pace on the makeshift platform, raising each tire a few inches at a time, shifting from one side to the other to keep the wheels reasonably even. After wedging one last rain-slick rock under the left tire, she scrambled out, struggled to her feet, and leaned against the edge of the crevasse. Dirt coated her hair, skin, and clothes. Her arms and legs throbbed. Her bruised palms stung from working the jack handle.

Lila stood on the edge of the washout, listing like the mast on a ship, struggling against a gust that almost knocked her off her feet. She eased herself into the hole and examined the platform as if she were gauging the sturdiness of a tree. "Just might do it," she yelled, but Jessica saw the skepticism in her eyes and wasn't fooled.

The wind howled above them now like wolves. Jessica felt the only thing that saved them from being scraped off the road was the tree-studded butte between them and the Pacific Ocean. She knew that when the sky opened, there would be no shelter from the deluge. The late afternoon was turning dark as evening.

As Lila was climbing out of the ditch, a prolonged, ominous creak sounded on the bluff above them. A series of pops and bangs, like a string of firecrackers going off, rose above the roar of wind. Jessica looked at her mother, whose eyes widened in instant recognition of danger.

Jessica grabbed Lila's wrist, yanked her out of the hole, and pulled her toward the cliff wall. They flattened themselves against the wet slab, waiting for the final chilling snap. It came in seconds, followed by a noise that could have been the *whoosh* of a passing missile. The tree swept over the bluff and slammed down to the road with an earth-jarring explosion of bullet-shaped cones, moss, bark chips, and severed branches. They watched the centuries-old cedar shift and settle twenty feet in front of the truck.

"Considering our luck," Lila shouted, "I'm surprised it didn't land directly on—" The wind snatched away the rest of her words.

Dust and debris swirled in the updraft around them.

Jessica tugged on her mother's shirt and motioned toward the pickup. "Let's go!"

While Jessica climbed in, Lila shoved the tarp from the truck bed under the wheels for traction. She stood aside and signaled with a wave of her hand.

Jessica started the engine and shoved the gearshift in reverse, coaxing, rocking the pickup. The wheels spun and ground. A wrenching, splintering sound came from the platform, rising above the whistling white noise of the storm. Rocks shot from under the front wheels, and the truck dropped a good ten inches. The platform hadn't held.

She turned off the engine and lowered her forehead onto the steering wheel.

When she looked up again, Lila was crawling into the passenger's seat. To her surprise, she looked calm. Her eyes glinted with resolve. "We'll rebuild it. It almost worked."

Jessica's shoulders slumped. "I can't. I'm too tired."

"Yes, you can."

"We don't have enough time." As if to emphasize her words, a branch the size of an arm thudded against the hood and bounced off.

"Most of the platform is still there. Rebuilding it will go faster." Lila's voice was equally firm, as if the sheer strength of her own conviction would pry Jessica out of the pickup. "I shouldn't have given you those logs. They splintered under the weight. We'll use only rocks."

"It's too dangerous out there now. We're safer in here."

Lila pointed toward the cliff. "Think about the water rushing off that with enough force to shove a concrete pipe over the hill. What do you suppose a flash flood like that could do to a truck—and us?"

Jessica frowned. "How come you were willing to stay here earlier?"

"Because you were going to hike down the hillside, remember? *You* wouldn't be here with me."

Jessica stared at her, as the implication of her mother's words seeped through her exhaustion.

The tears trickled down her cheeks. "I can't." But, even as she said it, she knew she would try again.

Lila raised her eyebrows. "Of course you can." She drew a deep breath. "You're acting like a little kid."

Slowly, Jessica opened the door and stepped out. A blast of air chilled the sweat on her skin.

They inspected the fallen platform. The front tires had torn through the tarp, polishing the rocks to a black shine in places. The swirling air, more subdued in the depths of the trench, held the odor of burnt rubber.

Once she was back under the truck, Jessica gripped the jack handle and found a reservoir of strength. Her mother scoured the area for larger rocks and dropped them down. She removed the splintered logs and wedged the new rocks under the wheels, listening all the while to the rapid ping of raindrops hitting metal. Lila stood at the front of the truck, ready to hold it up if necessary. By the time Jessica had brought the truck level with the road again, her hands were cut and bleeding and her arms felt numb.

Lila stood in the rain, refolding the tarp and cramming it behind the front tires. She tossed the jack into the truck bed.

They climbed out of the ditch, and Jessica crawled back into the truck. In the rearview mirror, she could see Lila standing to the side. A gust strong enough to rattle teeth ripped through the gorge, caught her white hair, and fanned it out so that she looked like a whirling dervish.

Jessica started the engine, slipped the gearshift into reverse, and eased the truck back. It swayed precariously, but she realized the wind might have rocked it. She accelerated again and felt the rubble shift. The pickup dropped a few inches. Slow and easy wasn't going to work.

She gunned the engine. The front tires spun in place for several seconds. She felt them catch the tarp and the lip of the washout. The truck shot backward, bumped over the rim and landed on solid ground with a crashing thud.

Jessica leaned her head on the steering wheel and closed her eyes in relief and gratitude.

A few seconds later, Lila climbed into the cab. She grinned, pushing her hair back from her dirt-streaked face. "I honestly didn't think you could do it."

Jessica groaned. "*Now* you tell me."

She took a long breath and sat up straighter, feeling triumphant.

She realized that if Lila had been Mary Grace they would have grabbed each other in a bear hug.

Lila flexed her injured leg.

Jessica glanced at it. "You should apply some pressure to that."

"I'll stick on another bandage. Drive, will you?"

It took her five minutes to turn the truck around on the narrow road. As they began the downward ride, the sky split open. The rain hammered the windshield, nearly blinding her.

Staring out the side window, Lila shifted restlessly in her seat. "We can't leave him out here."

Jessica glanced at her in surprise. "We don't have a choice. He knows enough to find shelter. We're in more danger than he is, driving around in this storm."

Lila tightened her lips but didn't argue anymore.

Jessica hugged the switchback's right edge, inching at ten miles an hour into the creeping gray night, as rain and debris thrashed the truck.

THE CLOCK ON the truck dash read seven-fifteen by the time they reached Misp.

The rain still came in long threads, a thick, silver curtain veiling the headlights. Jessica drove through standing water on First Street. Fir needles and fallen leaves had collected in the gutters and clogged the storm drains.

She stopped at the pay phone outside the Thrifty Market and called Dr. Shipley at his home. He agreed to meet them at his office on Fourth and Front streets.

Ten minutes later, Jessica sat in his small surgery, watching him clean and stitch Lila's wound. He didn't seem interested in how she'd acquired it. She ran a sawmill, and he spent most of his time patching up loggers. Her injury was minor compared with the one J. T. Frey suffered earlier that week. He'd somehow managed to sever his left hand with his own chain saw.

They walked out with a half-dozen sample packets of antibiotics, and Jessica drove her mother home.

A sheriff's cruiser waited in the driveway, its headlights blazing. As the rain sloshed over the truck, the deputy checked the cab thoroughly before he allowed them to go inside. Neither of them had the energy to argue with him.

He returned to his cruiser, and they shuffled into the house like zombies. Lila switched on the brass lamp in the entry and sagged onto the rough-hewn bench there. She looked sickly yellow under the pyramid of light.

Jessica leaned against the wall. She thought back to their conversation on the hillside. "What you said earlier about those rumors," she began hesitantly. "If you had asked Dad, he would have told you they weren't true."

Lila sighed. "Oh, I did."

"And?"

"He denied them."

Jessica felt a measure of satisfaction. "See what I mean."

"I found him in the mill office one evening in the arms of his little insurance agent. Or vice versa." Her voice was flat. "They were so tangled up I couldn't tell whose legs and arms were whose. Just a bunch of bare brown and white skin all stuck together with sweat. Now that was a pretty sight."

"No," Jessica whispered.

Her mother looked at her but didn't answer.

"But he loved you," Jessica said. "I know he did. So, he made one mistake. You could have forgiven him."

Lila smiled faintly. "Oh, I did, that time and the next and the next. I forgave him right up to a few days before he died. And then he went too far."

Jessica searched her mind for the events that led up to the drowning. "I knew you two were fighting, but I didn't know why."

The shadows in the house still hummed with their angry exchanges.

"Earlier that week, a woman came to the door," Lila said. "Not the insurance girl. *She* was long gone, but a younger one—a Makah, no more than eighteen or nineteen. She worked as a waitress at Sharkey's Cafe." The muscles around Lila's mouth tightened like a purse string. "She wasn't even pretty, but that made no difference to him. She was standing on my porch, four months pregnant—by my husband, or so she claimed."

Jessica shook her head. "That can't be true."

Lila shrugged. "Why don't you ask Callum Luke? He probably knows. I'm sure all those people do."

Jessica hated the thought that Callum knew. What if everyone else in town knew—except her?

The blood vessels in her temples felt like the tributaries of a swollen river. She massaged them with her fingertips. "What did Dad say?"

"He didn't deny it, if that's what you mean. We had a real screaming match that evening."

Jessica tried to remember where she had been. Then, she recalled going to a high school concert a few nights before the drowning. She wondered if Jonah had heard their fight, if he understood the reasons behind it.

"So that's why you threw Jonah in the water."

Lila raised her hands, covering her eyes with her palms. "No, no, I just wanted him to swim." But her words sounded weak, without conviction.

Jessica thought back to her father's drowning. "Everything—all of it—happened because you pushed him off the dock."

When Lila lifted her eyes, they had a wet sheen. "Don't you think I know that?"

"You killed Dad." Her voice trembled.

Lila fixed an impassive gaze on her for several seconds, then shook her head. "Oh, I admit I wanted him to suffer. But not to die."

"Either way, that's what happened."

Her mother slumped against the bench. "Don't you think that haunts me? I've lived with it every waking and sleeping moment since then." She blinked. "I hardly know how to sleep anymore." Pushing back her wind-tangled hair, she studied Jessica intently. "Haven't you ever made a mistake, one so terrible that it changes everything? A mistake that turns your world upside down, and you can't figure out how to put it right again?" Her voice dropped to a whisper. "I know you have."

Jessica glared at her mother, her throat so tight she could barely answer. "She wasn't a mistake."

"No, you're right. She wasn't. I suspect she was one of the most intentional things you've ever done."

Jessica took a deep breath, feeling it tremble in her lungs. No sense denying that accusation any longer. Her body had seemed one of the few things she could control then, always had been. Nothing else—certainly, no other person, as it had turned out—was reliable. But her love for Callum those many years ago, and for the child who resulted, had been sweeter and more authentic than any rebellion she might have planned. Her father would have recognized the difference.

She looked at Lila. "When Dad died, our family died too. How could you have let that happen?"

Lila sighed. "He left behind a hole the size of the Grand Canyon. How do you fill it?"

Jessica closed her eyes. "You could have tried."

"I knew you blamed me," Lila said softly. "I knew you were hurting—Jonah too, but I couldn't think what to do. I couldn't help myself, much less you kids."

"You ignored us. You worked all the time."

"I was trying to save the business. We almost lost it." She made a gesture, as if to ward off Jessica's expected reply. "Oh, I'm not saying it was all Mike's fault, what with the logging restrictions the government imposed on us. But, even in the best of times, he didn't have what you would call good business sense." She looked at her raw hands, then exhaled slowly. "I knew you wanted a different mother, one who wore housedresses and baked cookies and smiled all the time, but I couldn't be that person."

"I hated your meanness."

"What you saw as meanness, I saw as strength and determination. I was doing everything I could to save what we had left."

"You could have told us. Then we wouldn't have thought it was us."

She looked up in surprise. "What?"

"Then Jonah and I wouldn't have believed something was wrong with us."

Her brow furrowed. "What are you talking about? Even now, when I say a word against your father, you blow up. I can't imagine what you'd have done then. Would you really have wanted to hear about all those Indian women? What if one of them happened to be Callum Luke's mother?"

Jessica felt the room slide out of focus. She grabbed the edge of the library table. "Don't even say that!"

"See what I mean," her mother said calmly.

She opened her mouth to shout something back, then shut it. She had to wait for her anger to subside so she could control her voice. "Was she one of them?"

Lila didn't respond.

"Tell me. *Was one of them Callum's mother?*"

She shrugged wearily. "Probably not. There were rumors, but he tended to like the younger ones."

Jessica slumped against the cedar wall, wondering if she could ever *know* the truth of anything.

They were silent for a time. Lila sagged on the bench, her hands folded in her lap, her eyes lightly closed. Her face had a thin glaze of perspiration, and she looked beyond exhaustion. Jessica felt warm tears push their way to the surface. She wanted to cry for all of them: her father, Jonah, Callum, the daughter they didn't know, even for Lila.

She wiped her sleeve across her nose, then dug her van keys out of her pocket. "If we can ditch the sheriff and his deputies tomorrow, we can go out and look for Jonah again."

Lila's eyes blinked open. "You're willing to do that?"

Jessica nodded. "Yeah, I'm willing."

22

During the ten-minute drive to her own home, Jessica worried she might fall asleep and veer off the slippery, debris-strewn road. She felt incapable of thinking about everything that had happened. She'd once had the stamina to swim from morning until night. Now, she just hoped she would have the strength to climb in and out of the bathtub for a shower before she fell into bed.

She pulled the van into her driveway and sat there with her hands on the steering wheel, staring at the house, dark and forlorn in the rain. She wondered why she could never remember to leave a light on inside.

Despite the torrential rain, she didn't run from the van to the front door. She was too tired. Besides, what was a little more water, she thought. Kicking off her muddy shoes in the entry, she groped her way toward the kitchen and switched on the light above the sink. The message machine indicated three messages. Hoping Jonah might have phoned, she pressed the play button.

"You said you would call," Pamela's accusing voice snapped. "And what am I supposed to do with this ladder and your cleaning stuff? If I even touch these soapy rags, I'll get hives. I hope you don't expect me to pay you for—"

Jessica fast-forwarded the tape. Next came a wordless stretch, the normal noise of a telephone line followed by someone humming a few bars of a song in a low, off-key tone. The tune sounded familiar, but she couldn't place it. It had a sinister quality, like something from a horror movie.

Her eyes swept the kitchen, looking for anything out of place, and landed on a streak of wet dirt near the back door. A rubber sole with ridges and a sawtooth edge had left its muddy print on the imitation redbrick linoleum. It was larger than any shoe she owned, and she hadn't come in that way.

A woman alone on a dark night, the rain pounding the roof so hard no one in the neighborhood would hear. That would be Dennis's style.

She remembered the tune now. It was the theme song from the movie *Halloween*.

Her van keys lay on the counter near the phone. She wouldn't be stupid this time. Her mother's home, Mary Grace's store, anyplace else would feel safer than this house right now. As her hand closed over the keys, she caught a glimpse of a shadowy figure lurking in the darkened living room.

She was backing up when he appeared in the doorway.

"I thought you were never going to come home," he said in a low voice.

She grabbed the counter edge for support. "Shit, Jonah, I could have had a heart attack."

His shoulders were hunched under his windbreaker. His thin ankles poked out of his jeans, and the tied ends of extra-long, frayed laces dangled over his hiking shoes. He looked as if he'd rolled in the dirt.

But, relieved, she reached out to hug him. "I really am glad to see you, but for God's sake, why did you sneak up on me?"

He blinked in the bright kitchen light. "I wasn't sure it was you. I thought you might be the sheriff looking for me."

She set the van keys on the counter. "Where have you been?"

"I hid in the bushes until dark. Then I came in and crawled under your bed."

"You mean you walked here directly from Lila's?"

He nodded. "I could see the storm coming. I didn't want to spend the night outside in the rain."

Jessica dragged a chair from the table and dropped onto it. Resting her forehead in her hands, she shook with laughter.

"Jessie?" His voice turned nervous.

"Yeah?" She wiped her eyes with her sleeve.

"What's wrong?"

She shook her head. "Nothing. It's just that sometimes you're smarter than Lila and me put together."

His grateful smile hurt, and she had to look away.

She glanced at the window over the sink, then ran over and yanked down the shade. Luckily, the Tooberts' house was dark. She tried to recall if she had seen any unfamiliar cars in the neighborhood when she drove home. She'd been so exhausted that a sheriff's cruiser could have parked on her front lawn and she wouldn't have noticed.

"I'm not thinking clearly," she murmured.

Something else nagged at her. The humming on the phone had to have come from Kretz. She walked over and pulled down the other kitchen shades.

Leaning back against the counter, she covered her eyes, rubbing the heels of her palms against them. "I don't know what I'm going to do with you, Jonah. I know the right thing to do, but—"

"Maybe I could just live in your bedroom."

Feeling the laughter almost convulse her again, she grinned a little wildly. She caught sight of herself in her old chrome Sears toaster and immediately sobered up. Her red hair looked as if it had caught fire and exploded. Dirt streaked her face. "I need a bath and something to eat. Have you eaten since this morning?"

He shook his head.

She gestured for him to follow her. "You can wait in my bedroom. I can't have you wandering around the house, because the neighbors might see you, and I can't pull all the shades because that would look even more suspicious. Shut up tighter than a cracker tin, just like Pearl Hobbs's house. Might as well spray-paint HE'S RIGHT HERE, FOLKS on my front window."

He scratched the side of his face. "You and Mom went looking for me, huh?"

Jessica flipped on the bedroom light. "She got this idea that you were heading toward Stubble Falls."

He looked puzzled. "Why would I have gone there?"

She laughed. "That's what I said. I'll tell you what happened after I take a shower." She opened the closet door. "I almost forgot. We have to call Lila."

He looked down at his feet. "She'll be mad at me."

"I can promise you she won't."

She was lifting her robe off its hanger when the doorbell rang. She held the robe in midair, while one reassuring thought spun through her mind. It was unlikely Kretz would bother with the bell.

She looked at Jonah. He was trembling. "I don't want to go to jail."

Flinging the robe over her shoulder, she opened the closet door wider. "In here."

"I don't want them to put me in jail."

"Shhh. I'm going to turn off the light. I'll leave the door cracked, but don't move and don't say anything. Don't even breathe." She was halfway across the living room when she realized he might take her literally. She went back and poked her head in. "Forget what I said about breathing. You can do that but don't do it loudly."

He sat on his heels in a dark corner, hugging himself.

There was no question about answering the door. She needed to buy some dead bolts, though. Forget small-town conventions.

She pushed aside the filmy white curtain and stared straight into Callum's eyes. He was wearing a lightweight jacket that was soaking wet. She let the curtain drop, took several deep breaths, and opened the door.

The rain slanted toward the south now, whipped by the wind, and water poured over the house gutters onto the porch steps. They looked at each other for several seconds without speaking.

"Traitor," she said at last.

He regarded her impassively. "Everything was reasonable and legal. Your brother only raised more suspicion by running away."

"He didn't *run*. He had the right to walk out of his own home."

"Interesting distinction."

Jessica chewed on her chapped lower lip and tried to pretend she wasn't going to topple over if a gust of wind caught her. "What do you want, Callum?"

He tilted his head so that the light from the porch fixture cut directly across his scar. "I'd like to come in and talk with you."

"It's late, I'm tired, and I have absolutely nothing to say to you."

"Where did you and your mother go?"

"Drove up the road to Stubble Falls looking for Jonah."

"You look like you fell in the mud."

"I did."

"Did you find him?"

She hoped to God the answer wasn't written across her face. "Do you think I'd be standing here if I did?"

When he didn't respond, she said, "Go to hell, Callum."

He shifted his gaze to a spot over her shoulder. "I'm sorry," he said.

She wasn't sure if he meant he was sorry about Jonah, the arson fire, their own collapsed, short-lived relationship, or their daughter. She shook her head. "It's too soon for simple apologies. I hurt all over, and if this is the punishment you wished for me, you have it."

Pinpoints of water clung to his dark lashes. One fell like a tear on his cheek. He brushed his sleeve across his face, then without another word turned and walked down the steps to his car.

She sagged against the doorframe, pushing down the thickness in her throat.

She walked back into the bedroom and opened the closet door. Jonah's eyes looked shiny black in the dark.

"It's okay," she said. "You can come out."

He uncoiled himself and warily stepped from the closet.

Jessica switched on a small lamp on the nightstand. "It was Callum, but he's gone."

Just as she eased herself onto the edge of the bed, the phone rang. She sighed. "It might be Lila. Stay here. I'll be back in a minute."

She picked up the phone in her office and heard the low, tuneless humming of the theme song from *Halloween*.

She gritted her teeth. "I realize, Dennis, that you get a lot of perverted satisfaction out of these moments, but I'm getting real tired of them."

"I could tell you things about your brother that would make your hair curl." He laughed then, as if amused by his own cleverness. "I figured out how he set the fire. I'm thinking I should tell the sheriff. What do you think?"

She hesitated, realizing he knew exactly how to manipulate her. She couldn't ask him what he was talking about, because she couldn't give him that control.

"Dennis," she said in a flat tone, "if you ever try to contact me again in any way, I'll call the sheriff, your supervisor, the New Life officials, and anyone else I can think of."

"He's got that funny belly button, like the doctor didn't chop enough of it—"

She hung up the phone, her hand trembling.

She walked directly into her bedroom. Jonah stood where she had left him, examining one of his miniatures under the light. She dropped onto the bed and patted the space beside her. "Sit here. We need to talk."

He showed her the soldier. "I got some new Confederate cavalrymen through the mail. I painted them last night."

She took hold of his wrist. "No soldiers, no Civil War, Jonah. Look at me. No, don't stare at the light, look at me!"

He turned his head just enough so that his eyes met hers. "I want to go to Gettysburg."

"We'll discuss that later. First, tell me absolutely everything you know about the halfway house and the men in it."

He chewed on his lower lip, not answering.

She softened her voice. "I know something happened—something more than just those men teasing you." When he didn't respond, she added, "It's me asking, Jonah. Not the sheriff, not Lila, just me. And you know I'll always do whatever I can to keep you safe."

"You saved me from the water, didn't you?" He sounded distant, as if remembering.

"Yes," she whispered, "I did."

They were quiet for a moment.

"Did someone else put you up to it? Wendell Schultz maybe?"

He shook his head.

"One of the other guys?"

"No."

"Why did you throw the rocks then?"

"I didn't like that place."

She looked at him searchingly. "Why?"

He shrugged, averting his gaze.

"What did the men in that house do to you?" As soon as the words left her mouth, she realized how harsh they sounded, even to her.

He pressed his lips together. The scalloped edge of the lampshade cast a wavy shadow, creating an odd little mask on his face. He hunched on the edge of the bed and stared at his slender hands, which lay like broken wings in his lap.

"Jonah? I won't tell. . . ."

No, she couldn't say that. She couldn't make that promise.

He lifted his head, tears pooling in his eyes.

"Oh, God." She leaned her shoulder against the cherrywood headboard. "Oh, my God, Jonah, they molested you, didn't they?"

He went dead still. Outside, branches buffeted by the wind scratched persistently at the window.

She wrapped an arm around him and pulled him against her, feeling a tremor run through him. "Jonah, is that what happened?"

After a time, he nodded, his curls brushing her cheek.

She sat motionless. "All the men or just one?"

"One."

"His name was Dennis, wasn't it?"

He nodded.

She thought of Kretz, leaning against her, gripping her hand. Her mistake had been to think he assaulted only women.

She fought for control of her voice. "What did he do?"

Jonah mumbled something.

She gripped him tighter. "What?"

"He rubbed my . . . my . . ." His mouth contorted as he wrestled with the word. Finally, he pressed his hand against his crotch.

"Did he . . . did he do anything else?"

Jonah shook his head. "He laughed at me." His voice fell to a near-whisper. "He said it was my fault, that I wanted him to do it. But I didn't. I swear I didn't, Jessie, but he said I'd better not tell or people would know I was a . . . a . . ."

She looked at Jonah through her tears. His face appeared distorted, larger than usual, as if she were peering at him underwater.

She sucked in a breath. "Where did this happen?"

"In his bedroom," he said thickly. "At first, we were outside talking. He said he had a Civil War book to show me, but when we got up there, he didn't." He choked and swallowed several times, then forced the words out on a sob. "He pushed me down and . . . and unzipped my pants and . . . and . . ."

"And that's when General Bragg fell out of your pocket?"

"I guess so," he whispered.

"Did you yell or try to hit Dennis?"

"He said he had a knife, and he'd cut my throat."

"Did you see the knife?"

His head sank lower.

She fiercely massaged his shaking back. "Makes no difference, Jonah, makes no difference at all."

She realized Kretz had been taunting her with his distortion of the truth, telling her Jonah was no angel and hinting he'd seen him without clothes. She thought that if Kretz walked in right now, she would kill him. No arrest, no trial. Just immediate retribution.

She reached out and took her brother's chin in her hand. "What that man did to you was *not* your fault."

He tried to duck his head.

"Look at me, Jonah."

When he lifted his red-rimmed eyes, tears shone bright on his cheeks.

"Do you understand he was the bad one, not you?"

He nodded, the smallest tilt of his head.

"I shoved him," he murmured.

"Good for you."

"He was taking his pants off. I shoved him and he fell on the floor. That's when I pulled up my pants and ran out. He couldn't chase me because he got all tangled up in his jeans."

"Was anyone else in the house?"

"Two men were coming up the stairs. They yelled at the one who . . . who touched me. A guy with an ugly voice straightened my clothes and took me to the back door."

"Did he say anything to you?"

"He said not to worry, they'd take care of Dennis."

Lila couldn't have known about the assault. If she had, she would have sawed Kretz into pieces and burned down the halfway house herself.

Jonah wiped his sleeve across his nose, then pulled another miniature soldier from his pocket. "General Bragg tried to take away Lieutenant General Forrest's command after Shiloh, but Forrest fought back." His jaw tightened. "That's what I did. I fought back." He squeezed the soldier in his fist until his knuckles turned white.

Jessica studied his face, recognizing something she'd never seen in him before—cold rage fused with determination. It came to her that he'd had little experience with such extreme anger.

Maybe the litany Lila had hurled at him through the years— "Don't be so weak-kneed!" "Be a man!" "For God's sake, defend yourself!"—had finally lodged in his brain like a fishhook, festering there, working toward eruption.

Like Lila, she had urged him to fight back. But what if he had no concept of limits? It had never occurred to her he might go too far in the other direction.

She couldn't ask him if he'd set the fire, because she no longer wanted to know the answer. A wife couldn't be compelled to testify against her husband in court, but a sister didn't have that option.

Besides, what had she said to Pete? If she knew, absolutely knew, that Jonah committed arson, she would have to turn him in. It made no difference that the targets of the arson were criminals themselves, she'd said. That was no excuse for murder. But she had made those passionate declarations weeks ago, before she knew the sexual predator in that halfway house had violated her brother.

Jonah sat quietly now, leaning against her shoulder, fingering his soldiers. His blue eyes were guileless. "What are we going to do, Jessie?"

She shook her head wearily. "I have no idea."

JESSICA TELEPHONED LILA. "He's safe," she said. She heard her mother's sigh of relief.

"Where?"

"I don't want to say." She realized someone could be monitoring her phone.

"But you're sure."

"I'm sure. I'll see you first thing tomorrow."

After she hung up, she fixed tuna sandwiches and arranged them with sliced fresh melon and pickles on two plates, careful that Jonah's portions didn't touch. She carried them to the bedroom on a tray with two cups of hot tea, and they settled on a throw rug on the floor as if they were on a family picnic.

His fork and knife clinked against his plate. He was meticulous, carefully cutting the melon. She knew he would eat each portion in clockwise order beginning with the twelve o'clock position. The easiest way to drive him wild was to arrange his food haphazardly.

Once, when she was about fourteen and forced to baby-sit him on a day she'd had other plans, she slopped his lunch on the plate so that red Jell-O puddled under his sandwich. He was seven years old at the time. Paralyzed with frustration, he cried for two straight hours. Years later, when she learned about his mental disorder, she realized how cruel she had been.

Jessica watched him munch his pickle, his jaw muscles bouncing rhythmically to a count of ten with each bite. After they'd finished their meal, she hauled out the extra blanket and directed him toward the sofa, warning him to stay away from the windows. Then she climbed into the hottest bath she could stand and soaked for a half hour. She watched Callum's vivid drawing fade completely from her skin. It hadn't lasted long at all.

She stepped out of the tub, toweled herself off, and pulled on her robe. As she passed through the hall, she heard Jonah's steady, even breathing. He hadn't said a word about his usual inability to sleep without the orange stain above his head.

In her own bed, Jessica listened to the hard smack of rain on the roof. The familiar noise didn't bother her. What kept her awake half the night was the expectation the sheriff and Callum would come pounding at her door. She wondered what a person did when her only lessons for dealing with crime came from television or movies. It didn't seem smart to model her plans after a TV cop show.

Perhaps she should consult with Homer Nichol. There was such a thing as lawyer/client confidentiality, but of course he would advise her to turn Jonah in. Until she knew what might happen to him, that option was unthinkable. First-degree murder was a capital offense in Washington State.

Although she couldn't imagine any jury choosing the death penalty under these circumstances, she couldn't take the chance. She could never sentence her brother to death.

23

The next morning, her eyes abruptly blinked open. Still befogged by apprehension and sleep deprivation, she struggled to her feet and walked into the living room. Jonah was stretched out on the sofa, his long limbs jutting from under the quilt, his bony feet propped on the armrest. He looked the image of innocence.

Outside, the sky was a leaden gray, but the rain had stopped. She called Pamela Fields, apologized for her delay, and promised to pick up the ladder and cleaning supplies before the garden club meeting. Pamela said Jessica didn't have to bother telling her what had happened at Lila's because she already knew and, besides that, Jessica didn't need to finish the windows. Pamela would find someone else.

After Jessica hung up, Jonah came wandering into the kitchen.

She gestured toward the cupboards. "Cereal's in there. Fix yourself some breakfast."

He glanced at the drawn shade over the sink. "Should I eat in your bedroom?"

She nodded. "I normally keep the shades lowered in there and in the bathroom, so you can stay in those two rooms today. I have to open up the kitchen or the Tooberts will think something's going on."

He followed her into her bedroom. She turned on the television and handed him the remote. "I'm going to Lila's. I'll come back once we figure out where we can hide you."

He looked forlorn. "Bet you wish you didn't have me, huh, Jessie?"

She stopped in the doorway. He'd never before asked how she felt about anything.

"No, Jonah, in all your life, I have never once thought that."

She had been teaching him that other people had feelings too. He didn't get them right this time, she thought, but he was trying.

THE STREETS LOOKED as if they'd been hit with forest shrapnel. Tree branches, leaves, fir cones, along with garbage can lids and roof shingles, littered the neighborhood.

At Pamela's house, Jessica felt as though she were stealing her own equipment, but she managed to avoid any further conversation. From there, she drove directly to Lila's.

A sheriff's cruiser was still parked in her mother's driveway. Toadie Tyler, the deputy on duty, leaned against the car, smoke curling from a cigarette pinched between his fingers.

When she pulled in, he stuck his head through her open window. "Gotta inspect your van, Jessica. Milt says so."

She leaned back and sighed. "Toadie, don't you think I would have to be stupid to hide my brother in here?"

He scratched his chin. "Can't say as I'd know what you'd do."

"Jesus, Toadie, get a brain."

Close up, he reeked of smoke. When she thrust open the van door, he backed away and she drew a fresh breath.

She climbed down from the driver's seat. "Paw through that junk all you want. Just don't rile the python. It hasn't eaten in a week."

She left him looking startled and uncertain.

As she walked into the house, she realized she'd said exactly the sort of thing her mother would have said.

Garth Brooks was singing in the kitchen.

She found Lila at the table, her face waxen with fatigue, slugging down coffee and listening to a cheating-woman song on the radio. She had on a clean plaid shirt and jeans, but her white hair straggled to her shoulders. Her eyes looked as if they were streaked with red tire tracks.

Jessica dragged out a chair and sank onto it. "Anyone else in the house?"

Lila shook her head.

Jessica told her about Jonah hiding in her home.

Her mother rubbed the heels of her hands against her eyes. "I didn't give him enough credit."

"Neither did I." She paused, summoning her courage. "One of the men in that halfway house molested him."

Lila lifted her gaze. "What?"

Her voice was so eerily controlled that Jessica hesitated repeating the words. She felt as if she were walking into the strange green calm that precedes a tornado.

"One of the men in that halfway house lured Jonah inside, took off his clothes, and . . ." She caught her breath and held it a moment. "Well, he touched him. I don't know exactly how far it went. Jonah could hardly get the words out. I guess the guy threatened him with a knife and—"

"Did Jonah see the knife?"

Jessica felt her exasperation rise. "No, but he managed to push him away. Then he ran out and—"

"Which one did it?"

"I don't know. What difference does it make? He's probably dead now."

Her mother's eyes turned shrewd. "Is he?"

Jessica glanced away. "I don't know."

"He'd better be, because if he isn't, I'll kill him."

"If I thought it would make things better, I'd do it myself."

"Then he's alive."

"Look, we have enough to deal with right now. At least it means Jonah had a good reason to do what he did."

"To do what he did? Dammit, don't talk like that. He didn't set that fire. He wouldn't have had the guts."

Jessica leaned forward and spoke with quiet firmness. "I honestly don't know whether he did or not. And I don't want to know. What are we going to do with him?"

"No fancy lawyers."

"Agreed—at least not yet."

"We sneak him out of town."

"But where do we take him?"

Lila thought for a moment. "Canada maybe."

Jessica shook her head. "Oh, no. I am not driving him to Canada. Even if we made it to the border, I don't lie well. You know that part where the guard says, 'What's the purpose of your visit, folks?' If Jonah didn't blurt out that he was trying to escape arrest, I probably would." She looked at her mother. "Want to know what he said last night?"

"What?"

"He still thinks he's going to Gettysburg to reenact the Civil War."

"He's been talking nonstop about that trip lately."

"I don't think he understands the kind of trouble he's in."

"Oh, he understands. He just doesn't know what to do about it."

Jessica thought about her conversation with him that morning. "Maybe you're right. Just before I left, he asked me how I felt about something."

Lila pushed herself up from the table and walked over to the stove. "Guess those people with Asperger's syndrome have trouble figuring that out."

Jessica stared at her in surprise. "You've been reading about it."

"A little." She gestured toward a blue speckled pot. "Want some?"

"That stuff doesn't even resemble coffee."

Lila shrugged. She poured herself another cup and returned to the table. "Where are we going to hide him?"

Jessica chewed on her thumbnail. "How about that little store-room at the mill?"

"Too many people coming and going."

"An old logger's shack then. There are still some of those around."

"Backpackers have taken to sleeping in them. And don't suggest one of those caves up there. They flood this time of year."

Jessica slumped against the back of her chair. "I can't believe I'm doing this. I can't believe I'm sitting here trying to figure out how to help my brother escape arrest. I've never done anything this insane."

"Yes, you did. You torched the dock." Lila's voice remained level, the way she might have mentioned a picnic in the park that took place years ago.

Jessica wasn't fooled. "That wasn't the same. Besides, I was a kid then. It wouldn't have landed me in prison. This could."

They were both quiet for several moments. Lila thoughtfully sipped her coffee. Jessica took a paper napkin from a wicker basket on the table and folded it into a cootie-catcher that she felt sure the Meckler sisters would have been proud of. She poked her fingers between the pleats and flexed it.

She sat up straighter. "How about a tent? We'll hide him so far out in the woods no one could find him. This time of year it's warm enough that he won't freeze to death."

"He's more likely to float away."

Jessica spun out of her chair and paced the length of the kitchen. "You figure it out then. You've shot down every idea I've had." She covered her face with her hands. "You want me to rescue him, but I don't know how. I can't always be expected to save him."

She heard an abrupt scrape of a chair, and the next thing she knew Lila was wrapping her arms around her, pulling her so tight she felt the air forced from her lungs. She knew Lila must have hugged her sometime in the distant past, but that memory eluded her.

She smelled of wood, as if the saps and oils from the trees had permeated her skin and tanned it like the hide of an animal. She had a grip as strong as a man's, but Jessica felt her trembling deep inside.

"I'm sorry," Lila said simply. "The tent will work. I've got a good one at the mill. We can use it."

Jessica nodded.

Lila suddenly released her and, muttering "Damn him," stomped over to the kitchen door. She flung it open. "Toadie, what the hell you doing sneaking around my house?"

The deputy straightened and hitched up his pants, his gaze swiveling from Lila to Jessica and back again. "It's my job to walk around every once in a while and make sure no one is—"

Lila slammed the door.

Jessica could see him through the window, apparently trying to decide what to do now. He stood on the porch a minute or so, then wandered off.

Lila walked back to the table, picked up her coffee cup, and drained it. "I'll tell Toadie I can't hang around here all day entertaining him. I've got to get back to work. We're logging the fourth quad up on Moss Creek slope so I'll go to the mill like I normally would, load the tent in the back of my truck, and on my way to the quad drop it off behind that big fir where Moss Creek crosses Bogachiel Road. You sneak Jonah out and pick up the tent on your way to Preacher's Point."

"Preacher's Point? Why, that's the last place I would—"

"And the last place they'd look."

Jessica nodded. "All right. I'll take him there after dark."

24

Callum watched Jessica make two trips between her house and her van in the alley, carrying cardboard boxes.

He'd heard from the sheriff that she'd been visiting her mother earlier in the day. In a beater Ford truck he'd borrowed from his cousin, he followed her for part of the afternoon. It didn't require much skill. She seemed preoccupied.

She stopped at a bookstore, Mary Grace's minimart and gas station, and a recreational equipment store. After she left the last place, he went in and spoke with the clerk. She had bought flashlight batteries, fuel for a backpack stove, and enough packets of freeze-dried food to last one person two weeks. On the way out, he shook his head in amazement. As a criminal, she had no finesse whatsoever.

He waited in the truck at the end of the alley, keeping his head down so she wouldn't notice him. It was well into twilight, and tiny brown bats swooped low, feasting on moths and mosquitoes. The interior of the truck smelled of cigarettes. His cousin was killing himself with two packs a day.

Leaning against the cracked steering wheel, Callum thought of Tori's tearful call the night before. Andrew had blown a thousand dollars of her money at the Emerald Queen Casino, and she had kicked him out. After she'd spent fifteen minutes weeping and systematically ticking off his brother's flaws, she whispered in a plaintive voice, "I miss you."

The words didn't sound at all the same as when Jess had said them, but they affected him anyway. He could see why a separated couple might return to each other before they solved their problems. There was something appealing about familiarity. It was like eating at McDonald's. The food wasn't that great, but you always knew what you were going to get.

Callum saw two shadowed figures emerge from Jessica's house and walk toward the van.

The streetlights flashed on, illuminating the corner with a hazy glow. He could see them better now. Jonah, dressed in a watch cap, a navy rain jacket, jeans, and hiking boots, shuffled along, his sister close behind. Well, look at that, Callum thought. She'd probably had Jonah in the house when he stopped by last night.

Her hair was coiled tight as damp wool. Without a hat to conceal it, she acted as if she were not even trying to hide. She was handling this problem the way she did any other—with straightforward purpose and determination. He saw it in her self-possessed stride.

He thought about how hard she had tried to fit in at the tribal assembly, how she had uncharacteristically pelted his relatives with questions—never realizing all that chatter was unnecessary. He had appreciated her attempt, but she had stood out like a red flare.

He watched Jessica back up the van, its taillights flashing white, and turn it in the direction away from him. A simple call to the sheriff, and Tarr would pick them up before they reached the edge of town. A good investigator would handle it that way, he thought.

Just as he reached into his jacket pocket for his cell phone, it rang.

He punched the talk button. "Callum Luke."

"This is your uncle Jim."

Callum sat straighter in the seat. "Yes, Uncle."

"The man you're looking for is sitting across from me at my

kitchen table. If you can come to the reservation now, he'll talk to you."

Callum hesitated as he watched Jessica drive off. "I'll be right there," he said to his uncle.

JESSICA INTENDED to take Jonah only as far as Jimmycomelately Creek in the Olympic National Forest, thinking he could pack in the rest of the way, but she was so sure they weren't being followed that she zigzagged up a rough, little-used forest service road toward Preacher's Point.

The sky was brilliantly clear, revealing every star and planet. The air smelled rain-washed. It seemed to Jessica that Nature had temporarily used up its store of spring storms, smacking the coast with them like a mother doling out discipline, reminding everyone who was in charge. There was still a little wind but nothing threatening.

They unloaded the equipment and by the light of a battery lantern set up an old logging tent between some moss-wrapped conifers backed by a stone wall. More a deep bowl than a cave, it offered some protection. They could hear the creak of swaying trees on the other side of the ridge. After only a few minutes among the promontory's centuries-old giants, Jessica lost the urgency of time.

She had brought along her father's hunting knife. When they discovered a pole was missing, Jonah hacked off a low-growing alder branch to brace the tent.

After it was properly hoisted and anchored, she stepped inside and breathed its dusty ripeness. Despite what was happening off this mountain, this place felt right.

Sitting cross-legged on the tent floor, she ticked off the supplies they'd brought: sleeping bag, backpacker's camp stove, mess kit, clothes, matches, flashlight, packaged food, bottled water, and a cigar box filled with military miniatures. He'd wanted more soldiers, but she'd been able to sneak only a few handfuls from her mother's basement.

From a green paper bag with the logo MISP RAINY DAY READS,

she took out a history book she'd bought him. She handed him *Gettysburg 1863, High Tide of the Confederacy*.

He opened it and shone the flashlight on its illustrated pages. "Thanks, Jessie."

She folded the bag. "Jonah, why do you suppose you're so fascinated with the Civil War?"

He closed the book. "I don't know. I guess because if I'd been leading the Confederacy, we could have won."

"The North had more men, money, and materials."

He nodded. "Yes, but the South was defending its land and its way of life."

"Its way of life had one big moral dilemma. Doesn't it bother you that you're defending something you know is morally wrong?"

A look of regret crossed his face. "I try not to think about that."

She rested her elbows on her knees. "Yeah, me neither."

He began to talk about the upcoming Gettysburg battle reenactment, as if Misp, the arson fire, and the investigation occupied some other dimension. For him, they did, she thought with envy.

He unrolled his sleeping bag and arranged it in place. "They're going to have tents and equipment just like they used in the eighteen sixties. I read where they try to make it as real as possible. You're not allowed to wear wristwatches or clothes with zippers." His eyes shone in the flashlight's glow. "We'll sit around the campfires in the evening and talk about strategy, and in the morning someone will play the fife to wake us up. I probably won't sleep anyway. Can you imagine hearing that sound and knowing you're going into battle in a few hours?"

No, she couldn't. Nor could she imagine telling him it was unlikely he would make it to Gettysburg in July. Maybe, reality wasn't so hot after all, she thought.

"Jonah, how much do you remember about Dad?"

He set down the bottle of water he was holding. "He was tall and big and he laughed a lot. That's about it."

Jessica wrapped her arms around her knees and pulled them

close. "After he died, I hated every day that passed. I was scared I would forget how he looked and how his voice sounded." She looked up at Jonah. "And the worst thing is that I have forgotten."

He dug around in the breast pocket of his plaid shirt and produced a photo so deeply creased and faded that the man and the boy in it were barely recognizable. "I look at this every once in a while, but it doesn't always help because I can't remember him in my head."

"He would like that, though, knowing you carried his picture with you. When we get back to Misp, I'll find you a new one."

Jonah pocketed the crumpled photo, then bent his head so low his chin grazed his chest. "Guess he wouldn't be very proud of me, huh?"

Jessica rose to her feet. "Sure, he would. He wasn't always the best person himself, but he . . ." Her voice faltered. "But he loved us." She touched her fingers to Jonah's arm. "He would think you're just fine."

He made a face that indicated he wasn't sure. Outside the tent, a coyote howled.

"I'll take off now. You going to be okay?"

He nodded.

She hugged him, promising that either she or Lila would bring him more supplies before he ran out. She crawled out of the tent and reluctantly climbed into the van, knowing she wouldn't find the same peace of mind back in Misp.

The trip home was slower than the upward journey had been. Ground fog settled over the dark roads, so thick in places she felt as if she were wrapped in a cocoon.

She drove through downtown Misp. The shops and businesses were closed, their display signs a neon blur through the fog. She glanced at the van clock. One A.M. She threaded the van along the streets to her house and, bone-weary, went directly to bed.

• • •

SHE AWOKE ABRUPTLY the next morning, first incorporating the banging noise into her dream, then realizing someone was pounding on her front door. The digital clock on the nightstand glowed six A.M.

She hesitated, sorting through the possibilities, finally deciding Callum and the sheriff had found Jonah and now they were coming to arrest her for helping him escape. In a way, it would be a relief, she thought. At least it would be done with. She pulled on her plaid robe and headed for the living room.

Pushing aside the nylon curtain, she saw Ada Toobert on the front porch, her generous gray eyebrows joined in a frown.

Ada hadn't spoken to her since she'd paid the vet bill. Jessica hoped she wasn't here to tell her Buster had died. She reluctantly opened the door. When the dog emerged from behind a fog-shrouded rhododendron and whizzed on her limp geraniums, she felt almost grateful.

Ada ignored the dog. "Something's wrong with your phone. Your mom called me because she couldn't get hold of you. She kept getting that stupid answering machine."

"Thanks, Ada, I'll check it." She sighed, remembering she'd turned off the ringer so Jonah wouldn't be tempted to answer it. "Did Lila say there was some problem?"

Ada's flabby chin tightened. "Well, I told her I'd walk over here because I didn't know if anybody else had told you. I figured you'd want to know, you being good friends with Mary Grace and all."

Jessica felt cold. "Know what?"

Ada's eyebrows rose. "Guess you haven't heard about Bob Snow and Caroline Johnson then, huh?"

Jessica shook her head to clear the fuzziness. Maybe if she could think straight, she wouldn't have this sense of impending disaster. Caroline, Pete Johnson's cousin, was twenty-one years old and a recent nursing graduate of Peninsula Community College. As far as Jessica knew, she was still living in Forks.

"Ada," she said slowly and distinctly, "what do Bob Snow and Caroline Johnson have to do with each other?"

"Why, they were together in his truck barreling along Willow Creek Road when he hit the elk and killed all three of them right there on the spot."

Jessica's heart careened. "All three? Mary Grace too?"

She frowned. "Of course not. Bob, Caroline, and the elk."

"Where were they going?"

"Bob was *supposed* to be on his way to work, because it was around four o'clock this morning. But he must have had something other than chopping trees in mind." She lifted one eyebrow meaningfully, then gestured toward the fog behind her. "Milo Puterman was driving to Allied when he saw the smashed-up truck and the dead elk. Said there wasn't anything he could do by then except call the sheriff. Said it was so soupy out he almost hit the truck himself." She shook her head. "Terrible thing, Bob dying with Caroline right beside him. Practically laying in his lap, they said. Anyway, I wouldn't have come here to tell you, because I'm not talking to you, except I figure Mary Grace is going to need all the sympathy she can get."

Jessica rubbed her forehead. "There could have been a good reason why Caroline was with him."

Ada harrumphed. "Well, if you can come up with one, tell it to Mary Grace." She turned and lowered a flip-flop onto the next step. "I've got to go fix a casserole for her and those poor kids."

25

Jessica pulled into the crowded parking lot of the Misp Mall. Through the cottony fog, the bleak pink neon PEN glowed from the store window.

She parked between Homer Nichol's Buick and Louie Mac-Leod's old Dodge rustbucket. Stepping out of the van, she drew in several deep breaths of cool air. She should have exactly the right words to say to Mary Grace, but at the moment she couldn't think of a single comforting phrase.

She crossed the paved parking lot to the store. Nearly everyone in town would pass through its doors today. She knew the grieving ritual well. They would bring flowers and inspirational books and enough food to fill a deep-freeze. They would hug Mary Grace and murmur words she wouldn't remember, and they would look at her with pained eyes that said, *There but for the grace of God go I.* Yes, Jessica thought, it was a familiar ritual and one that helped.

And, if the sun ever did shine again, Mary Grace would wonder how the rest of the world could spin forward as if nothing had happened.

Jessica walked into the minimart alongside Lanita Snapp, who was carrying a foil-wrapped platter. Jessica thought some of the women in town must stockpile homemade offerings for such occasions.

Tear tracks streaked Lanita's cheeks. "Such a tragedy," she said. Jessica nodded.

Inside, Edith Meyer operated the cash register, where people lined up to buy coffee and pastries.

"Might as well make some money for her," Edith intoned. "She's going to need it now."

The men, wearing their work clothes, hunched in solemn clusters. Lanita eyed them as though they were collectively responsible for Bob's indiscretion.

"Good for nothings," she muttered under her breath.

Mary Grace's son Daniel stood with Pete and Wendell. He suddenly seemed taller, his back as straight as a post. Jessica realized that at sixteen he was taking on the role of eldest male in the family. She walked over and hugged him, and he encircled her shoulders awkwardly. He seemed unsure about what to do with the extra length in his skinny arms. A red flush crept up his neck.

"Hello, Jessica," Pete said, sipping from a Styrofoam coffee cup. "Terrible reason for a community to come together, isn't it?"

She nodded, then turned and said hello to Wendell. He returned the greeting, minus his usual smirk.

Edith was making change for Milt Tarr. The sheriff gave a friendly nod to Jessica, making it clear the arson fire and the town's prime suspect wouldn't be mentioned today. She didn't see Callum.

Edith caught sight of her and waved a hand toward the rear of the store. "The other women are in the house with Mary Grace."

Jessica thanked her and headed toward the passage that connected the store to the house. She stumbled for the hundredth time on a raised strip of wood in the doorway. Bob kept saying he was going to fix it someday—that and the burned-out O in OPEN. Nothing would be done about them now. Jessica decided she would stop by in a few weeks and remove the strip, or paint it a bright fluorescent color.

The women's voices and the mingled aromas of apples, cinnamon, tomatoes, pickles, and cooked meats drifted through the hall. Jessica stopped at the kitchen doorway and surveyed the counters and table cluttered with casseroles, desserts, breads, and trays of fresh fruits and vegetables. Pamela Fields and the Meckler sisters were packaging the freezable food in white butcher wrap and labeling it.

"You know what surprises me?" one of the Meckler sisters was saying. "Pearl Hobbs isn't here. She used to be the first one at the house at a time like this, what with her husband being a logger and dying that gruesome way he did."

Pamela slapped a strip of masking tape on a bowl-shaped bundle. "No one's seen her lately. Edith says the fire scared her so bad she's still holed up in her house." Pamela scrawled TUNA & TATERTOT CASSEROLE FROM LOTTIE VANDERWALL in black marker on the butcher wrap. She lifted the lid on an amber-colored Pyrex dish and stared at the contents for several seconds. "Does anybody know what this is?"

Glancing up, she fixed her violet eyes on Jessica. A gleam of barely concealed excitement came into them. "Are you as shocked as I am?" she said to Jessica. "Who would have guessed Bob would do *that*?"

"It's a little early to pass judgment."

Pamela touched her fingers to her throat. "Well, it certainly looks bad."

"Where's Mary Grace?" Jessica said, a little too sharply.

The Meckler sisters both pointed toward the living room.

Jessica found her standing in front of the fireplace, looking like a stunned bird. She didn't think it was possible for someone so pale to be breathing. Anna McHale from St. Bavo's Church gripped her hand, and a dozen or so other women hovered around her.

Her eighteen-year-old daughter Monica sat in a cracked Naugahyde chair. Sue Beth, who was fourteen, perched next to her sister on the duct-taped arm. They dabbed at their eyes.

The room was filled with softly chattering women. Jessica said hello to the Quinault postal clerk who stopped by the Snow store every morning for coffee and doughnuts and to Kim from the Express-O Hut. She heard a little squeal and realized Monica's toddler son Brent was crawling up the stairs with a teenage relative in pursuit.

Mary Grace glanced in Jessica's direction, and a slow awareness came into her eyes. She wordlessly crossed the room and took Jessica into her arms. She clasped her so tightly that Jessica wasn't sure who was comforting whom. Mary Grace's cheek against her own felt as cool as marble.

"Bob told me what happened at the hardware store," she said in a low voice. "He felt awful about it."

The tears rose to Jessica's eyes at the thought that Mary Grace could be concerned about her at the moment.

"It's not important," she said. "How are *you* doing?"

"All right, I guess." Her voice was soft but strong. "This whole Caroline business hurts, but other people don't know Bob the way I do. There's a good explanation for it."

Jessica squeezed her hand. "I'm sure of it."

"Lila was here about ten minutes ago. She had some big lumber powwow to go to, but she said she'd be back. She tried to call you but couldn't get through."

"I had the ringer on my phone turned off. Ada came over and told me."

Mary Grace looked steadily into Jessica's eyes. "You know, I used to be scared to death a tree would fall on him. His dad died that way—in the woods. I can't believe Bob hit a damned elk. It isn't right."

"No, it isn't."

She remembered her father's friend Jake saying the same thing about him. Felling trees was one of the most dangerous jobs in the world. Every year, Misp lost two or three loggers. Any misstep, any rot in the tree, and it could go thundering to the ground in the wrong direction. A lake shouldn't have taken her father, and a truck accident was not a noble death for Bob.

Mary Grace was looking over Jessica's shoulder and, as impossible as it seemed, growing paler. Jessica swung around and saw Callum standing in the doorway. He was looking collegiate in jeans and a beige pullover sweater. Every woman in the room was staring at him.

He strode over to Mary Grace and took both her hands in his. "Toadie Tyler and I found Caroline Johnson's Honda Civic on the road to Moclips." His voice was low and gentle. "Don't know what she was doing headed that direction, but the car's fuel gauge was on empty. Bob must have picked her up on his way to his job, planning to drop her off at the nearest gas station."

Jessica realized Callum had gone out looking for the car. Without asking, he had known the one thing that would console her.

Mary Grace listed slightly, then slid onto the arm of the swaybacked couch, still clutching his hand. "Thank you."

Jessica experienced a similar relief. But she had no desire to talk with him. She felt his gaze on her as she eased out of the room.

HE CAUGHT UP with her in the parking lot. The sun was just beginning to burn through the fog.

He gestured toward his Explorer, which sat two cars away from the van. "I would like you to go somewhere with me."

She avoided looking at him. "No."

"Please, Jess, it's important."

"If you told me I would never have to see you again, *that* would be important."

He swung his head heavenward, raking his fingers through his hair. Finally, he turned back to her. "Listen, Jess, I have a witness to the fire."

She fixed her gaze on him. "Where?"

He walked over to the Explorer and opened the passenger door. "Are you getting in or not?"

She hesitated. She didn't want to be anywhere near him.

He smiled faintly. "I'll have you back within the hour."

She scooted onto the leather seat and, conveying what she hoped was a no-nonsense position, folded her arms across the UCLA logo on her sweater.

He closed her door, walked to the driver's side, and climbed in.

"All right," she said, "who is this witness?"

He started the engine. "Someone on the reservation."

"A him or a her?"

"Him."

"Someone I know?"

He shrugged. "I have no idea."

"But this 'him' said Jonah didn't do it."

"Yes, although you'll have to judge his story for yourself." He drove the Explorer across the parking lot, waited for traffic to clear, then pulled onto the highway.

"Dammit, Callum, what does that mean?"

He drove over the railroad tracks. "Wait until you talk with him, will you? I don't want to bias you ahead of time."

"Does he have a criminal record or something like that?"

"Nothing more than a speeding ticket."

She made a face. "That doesn't count. I have a few of those myself. All he has to do is swear it wasn't Jonah. Can he do that?"

"Yes, he could do that."

She felt the strain of the past month recede like a tide. "I already believe the guy."

The man's story had to be true, she thought. Why would he lie? She studied Callum's solemn profile. "How did you find him?"

"I managed to track him down with the help of my uncle."

"Why did you do that?"

He gave her a half-amused smile. "Because it's my job."

She settled against the leather seat with a measure of satisfaction. He didn't need to know about the incriminating evidence she had concealed, her moments of doubt about Jonah's innocence, and her discovery that he had been molested.

At the turnoff to Queets, they drove out of the fog. The sun spilled through the recently cleaned windshield, warming her.

She looked at Callum. "That was a nice thing you did for Mary Grace."

He kept his eyes on the road. "I have my moments."

He drove slowly along the main street of Queets and wound onto the side road. He parked the Explorer in front of a mint-green house, its ragged tarpaper underlay jutting between the siding and flapping in the breeze.

Jessica stared at the dilapidated dinghy in the front yard. "This is Clement Brings Yellow's house."

Callum set the emergency brake with a sharp snap and opened his door. "We're going to talk with his son Russell."

"Russell Brings Yellow actually saw the fire?" Jessica asked as they walked up the graveled front path.

Callum nodded. "He was driving home from his job with the railroad." He knocked on the scarred door.

She lowered her voice. "Why didn't he report it?"

"He did, although he didn't identify himself. He waited until he got back to the reservation and made the call from the community center's pay phone. By the time the fire trucks got there, the house was filled with smoke and flames."

"My God, he should have run up to the halfway house or banged on a neighbor's door. He should have done *something*. Isn't it illegal not to report a fire like that immediately?"

Callum turned his dark eyes on her. "More illegal than helping a suspect in an arson and murder investigation escape?"

She looked away.

"Jess, he is a forty-five-year-old male who appears, shall we say, very Native American. Now, if you were Russell, who would you think might be the first person they would suspect?"

"I see your point," she said quietly.

He studied her face. "Does that surprise you?"

She dropped her gaze to her scuffed white tennis shoes and shook her head.

Clement Brings Yellow opened the door.

He smiled at Jessica, his black eyes bright above the ridges of his ocher cheekbones. "I remember you."

"Been boating lately?"

His grin broadened. "Hit a deadhead yesterday and nearly sank." He waved her and Callum into the house.

"How are your family?" he asked Callum.

Callum smiled. "They're fine, thank you."

Clement directed them to a sofa covered with an orange-and-green crocheted throw. "I'll tell Russell you're here."

Worn but comfortable furniture packed the small living room. A large-screen TV occupied almost half the space along one wall. Callum eased himself onto the sofa, but Jessica walked to the other side of the room, to a stack of unpainted shelves propped on cement blocks. The top shelf held eight finely woven baskets ranging in size from a few inches to two feet in diameter. The bottom two shelves held rows of well-thumbed paperbacks.

She scanned the authors' names on the worn spines: Terry Brooks, Stephen Donaldson, Irene Radford, William Gibson, Karen MacLeod, Greg Bear. Someone in the house was a fantasy reader.

Clement knocked on a door down the hall and summoned Russell. She was examining the baskets when the older man returned to the living room.

"He'll be here in a minute," Clement said. "He works late so he doesn't usually get up until noon."

Jessica lightly touched the smallest basket, feeling the nub of the woven grasses. The design incorporated tiny spread-winged black eagles and salmon. "Who made this, Mr. Brings Yellow?"

"My wife, Sarah." Pride crept into his face, and somehow she knew without asking that his wife had passed away. "I used to strip the bark from the red cedar trees. Our daughter Eva collected the bear grass for her." His voice took on the slow, measured cadence that Jessica associated with people who had learned life is not a race.

He lifted a basket and handed it to Jessica to inspect. Stylized black figures of men paddling canoes edged the rim.

"Sarah was good at weaving," he said, "and fast too. She made this one in a single day while our daughter Helen drove Eva and us to Seattle and all over that city. Helen got it in her head that we should visit the museum at the University of Washington to see what she called Indian artifacts. So, we traveled up and down those steep hills and waited in traffic for hours. I thought no wonder the eagles and the other animals don't want to live there anymore—all that concrete and those car fumes. I wouldn't either. Anyway, we finally found the museum."

He paused, lost in the memory, and Jessica waited patiently. "As it turned out," he said with a grin, "it wasn't worth the fuss, because their baskets weren't any better than the ones Sarah made."

Jessica turned over the one he'd handed her. On the underside was a tiny strip of white paper with the neatly inked words MADE IN SEATTLE. She smiled and set it back on the shelf.

Russell strode in, running his fingers through shoulder-length hair that looked as if it had been lacquered black. He was broad-shouldered and slightly paunchy. Callum was right. Although Russell Brings Yellow dressed in the universal American uniform of jeans, T-shirt, and running shoes, he had the nut-brown skin and the broad cheekbones of a full-blooded coastal Indian. He wore steel-rimmed glasses with tinted bronze lenses and a silver cross around his neck, but the object that caught Jessica's attention was his wristwatch, its wide, hammered-silver band inset with turquoise stones the size of robin's eggs. Even from several feet away, she could see the workmanship was extraordinary.

Callum introduced her, then eased himself onto the spavined sofa. Avoiding her gaze, Russell folded himself into a chair opposite them. Clement hovered nearby, and she had the impression he hoped his presence would go unnoticed.

Leaning his elbows on his knees, Callum steepled his fingers and nodded toward Russell. "Could you please tell Jessica what you saw at the halfway house."

Behind the lightly tinted lenses, Russell's eyes looked wary. "I called in the fire as soon as I got to a phone."

"She knows that," Callum said. "I'm talking about the man crawling out the window."

He shifted uncomfortably in the overstuffed chair, tension working the corners of his mouth.

Jessica leaned forward. "Do you know my brother, Jonah Moran?"

He nodded, still not looking directly at her. "I've seen him walking down the highway and around town."

"Was he the man you saw?"

He shook his head. "This fellow was heavier and taller than your brother. And his hair was straight. No curls."

She sat back, limp with relief. Then, a question entered her mind and without much thought traveled past her lips. "But if he was crawling out the window, how could you see how tall he was?"

Russell's expression hardened. He stood and turned to Callum. "I told you this was going to get me into trouble. They're not going to believe me, and before you know it, they'll be saying I did it."

She felt panic set in. "No, please, I didn't mean to sound as if I didn't believe you. I'm just trying to figure this out."

He glanced at Callum, who gave him a reassuring nod.

"What did the man's face look like?" Jessica asked.

Russell hesitated, then sat down again. "I didn't see his face, only the upper part of his body and the back of his head. He was turned away from me. There was a keg—like a covered whiskey barrel—below the window, and he acted like he was checking to see if anyone was outside before he crawled out."

Jessica thought of Dennis Kretz—big, pinkish, dough-belly

Dennis, who claimed he went out the upstairs window onto the porch roof. His hair was dirty blond and straight.

"Could the man have been—" She stopped. Pointing her finger at someone other than Jonah was too easy. She saw how suspicion could grow with very little tending.

"I don't know who he was." Russell's voice rose in irritation. "But I'm telling you it wasn't your brother. Isn't that good enough for you?"

Clement turned and slouched toward the kitchen, obviously embarrassed by his son's abruptness. "I made some tea," he murmured. "I'll get it."

Russell rolled his eyes at Callum. "He boils the bark of crab apple trees. It tastes like old socks." He rose and strode after his father. "They don't want any tea, Dad."

Jessica leaned toward Callum and whispered, "All he has to do is say it wasn't Jonah. He doesn't have to know who it was."

"When he comes back in here, talk to him about that," Callum suggested.

From the kitchen, Clement said, "It's good for arthritis and for the stomach. It's very calming."

Russell returned to the living room, walked over to Callum, and said in a low voice, "You'd better tell him you don't want it."

With an understanding grin, Callum raised himself from the sunken sofa and strode into the kitchen. She heard him say, "Thanks, Uncle, but we can't stay much longer. Jessica has to get to her job."

She turned to Russell. "Will you be willing to tell other people—the sheriff, for instance—that it wasn't Jonah you saw leaving the halfway house?" She would plead if she had to. She would do whatever it took to convince him.

He looked at her for several long moments. "I could tell the sheriff—but he won't believe me."

She glanced in triumph at Callum, who was standing in the kitchen doorway.

Seeing the exchange, Russell said sharply, "Didn't you hear what I said? He won't believe me."

Jessica smiled reassuringly. "Of course he will. Why wouldn't he?"

"Last November, he stopped me for speeding."

She waved her hand in dismissal. "That's nothing. Milt Tarr has stopped me three times for speeding. If that were a big crime out here, we'd all be rotting in prison."

The corner of Russell's mouth twitched in annoyance. "I was driving too fast because of the Sasquatch."

She sat back against the sofa and stared at him. "The Sasquatch?"

"Bigfoot. Same thing."

She wondered if this was some kind of joke. Callum still stood in the kitchen doorway, wearing a perfectly straight face.

She turned back to Russell with a sarcastic laugh. "And what were you smoking that night?"

To her surprise, his expression didn't flicker. "I don't smoke, and I don't drink."

She thought of driving through the woods at night, how tree stumps could metamorphose into monsters, how an animal crossing the highway could take on the form of a moving boulder. She tried to make her tone more conciliatory. "I'll bet it was a bear."

He shook his head. "Don't you think I know what a bear looks like? I saw the Sasquatch square in the middle of my headlights, as clear as you sitting here. It was about one-thirty in the morning. He was crouched on the shoulder of Reservation Road with his elbows on his knees and his head propped in his hands. I stopped the truck. He raised his head and looked directly at me. I could see he didn't like me bothering him. He bared his teeth, got up, and walked off. This thing wasn't even built like a bear, and he didn't walk like one."

He was so earnest and matter-of-fact that she found herself half believing him—but only half. "What did you do then?"

He shrugged. "Got the hell out of there."

"He could have been a man." She wanted it to be anything but a Sasquatch, which 99 percent of Americans, if they'd even heard of it, probably ranked alongside Santa Claus on the plausibility scale.

Russell regarded her with a serious expression. "How many eight-foot-tall men with broad shoulders, skinny hips, long swinging arms, and thick hair all over their bodies have you ever seen?"

It occurred to her to say she'd once run into one on a Hollywood movie lot, but she suspected Russell didn't have a sense of humor about the subject.

"And you told the sheriff about the . . . the encounter?" she asked.

He nodded.

She searched his face. There was no hint of cunning or madness, just that weariness of knowing he wouldn't be believed. It was that absolute sincerity that swayed her. *He* was certain he saw the Sasquatch. She felt truth, fact, plausibility, slip like mercury between her fingertips.

Jessica stood. There seemed little point in asking Russell Brings Yellow anything more. She thanked him and his father.

Once she and Callum were in the car, she snapped on her seat belt with more force than necessary. "So, what was that? Put one over on the white woman?"

He didn't seem surprised. "No, as a matter of fact, it was a peace offering—from me to you."

She stared at him for several seconds, then turned to look out the window at the reservation houses and buildings. "So you're sure he's telling the truth."

"Which part? The man crawling out the halfway house or Bigfoot sitting alongside the road."

"You can't have one without the other, can you? Imagine him testifying in a courtroom. The prosecutor would tear him apart." She cleared her throat. " 'So, Mr. Brings Yellow, please tell the jury about the Sasquatch you saw. Was he crouching by the highway or was he sneaking out of the halfway house? Is it possible *he* could have set the fire? And, if he did, why didn't he leave very large footprints?' "

"Actually, the footprint issue has been bothering me. We seem to have a short supply of them, or at least of the right ones."

He was silent for a few seconds, as if pondering the problem. He braked at the stop sign and pulled onto Highway 101. "Anyway, I believe Russell."

"Why?"

"I've known him a number of years, and he's a good man."

"And when is the last time *you* saw a Sasquatch?"

He looked at her. "I've never seen one, but I believe we don't see some things until we need to. When I was younger, I saw people and creatures in trees and rocks and hillsides, but that wasn't the sort of experience that got an Indian extra points in law school. So, I denied the gift myself, and after a while, I lost it. I was the little kid who grew up and stopped seeing any wonder in the world." He smiled faintly. "I became an adult."

She bit back a cynical reply. Two spandex-clad bicyclists rode the edge of the highway, and she watched them pedal furiously, as if they were in some race. "I'm beginning to think Pete was right."

Callum gave her a quizzical look. "What does he have to do with it?"

"He said the truth doesn't matter. He makes sweeping pronouncements like that."

"Funny, I've never thought of Pete as a philosopher."

"Me neither—until recently."

Callum didn't say anything. He seemed lost in thought.

As much as she wanted Jonah to be innocent, as much as she wanted to trust Russell, she couldn't accept the mythical, furry man-creature that lumbered along with him.

She looked out the window, away from Callum's gaze. "I don't know what to believe, but I can't give Jonah up."

"I know that."

"Callum, there's something else." She hesitated. "Dennis Kretz molested him."

She heard Callum's quick intake of breath.

"Kretz can be sent back to prison, of course." He glanced at her. "But you realize sexual assault is not an excuse for murder."

"Not unless you're an advocate of vigilante justice."

"If I were, I wouldn't be in this job."

Callum pulled his car into the Misp Mall parking lot. It was still crowded with the vehicles of people making condolence calls. He stopped next to her van, and she opened the passenger door.

"All the evidence against Jonah is circumstantial," she said.

"That's all we usually have in arson fires. Motive and circumstantial evidence."

"But Russell said Jonah wasn't the man he saw crawling out the window."

"Ah, yes, we're back to Russell."

She was silent for several moments. Finally, she said, "Maybe someone else saw something."

"We interviewed the neighbors."

"Pearl Hobbs too?"

He nodded. "Claimed she didn't see a thing."

She thought of the cheerful, bright-eyed woman who had stood on her front steps and passed out fresh lemonade to a thirsty newspaper carrier. "Then why has she cooped herself up in that house?"

"Still scared probably."

"But all that's left of the halfway house is a burned-out ruin. The men are gone. There's no danger now." Jessica fingered the chrome door handle. "Pearl wasn't at Mary Grace's this morning. People commented on how odd that was. Pearl's husband died in the woods when we were just kids, remember?"

"Yeah, but that was years ago. Maybe she doesn't like to be reminded of it."

Jessica firmly shook her head. "You don't forget what the community does for you at a time like that. When that stacker crushed

Earl Schuler's spine last fall, Pearl was the first one at his house comforting Joan and the kids."

"She's getting older, Jess. I talked to her myself. She could barely focus her eyes on me, and half her answers made no sense at all. I don't think she could have remembered what she had for breakfast that morning."

Jessica thought about the last time she'd seen Pearl. She was standing on her front porch with Pete's mother, clutching that little poodle of hers and waving exuberantly. When had that been? Just a day or two before the fire.

"Callum, that is *not* the Pearl Hobbs I know." She pulled the door shut with a slam. "Let's go talk to her."

He gave her a long look, and she knew he was debating whether to indulge her. "All right." He released the parking brake and shifted the car into gear.

26

Jessica stood with Callum on the sidewalk leading to Pearl's home. All the window shades were drawn, but the flower beds had been weeded and the grass recently trimmed. On the scrubbed porch, a pot of paper-white jonquils with orange centers swayed in the breeze. An ancient, tiger-striped tomcat swaggered lazily across the front lawn.

Callum studied the house. "Well, she must go out sometime. Someone's taking care of the place."

Jessica noted the drawn drapes on every window. "When I was fourteen, this house was on my newspaper route. During the nice weather, Pearl flung open all the windows and doors. She loved the fresh air. She used to say the only way to survive in a dreary climate like this was to run outside on every nice day and shout 'Glory be to God!' "

"You're not going to be happy until you talk to her yourself."

"That's right."

The front door was solid wood, painted white, with no window. She tapped the weathered brass knocker that was shaped like an anchor. When no one answered, she banged on the door.

Callum waited on the bottom porch step. "Doesn't she have a daughter somewhere?"

"Boise. She has a grandchild too."

"She's probably gone to visit them."

Jessica used the side of her fist, giving the door three solid thumps.

"Forget it, Jess. She's not here."

She leaned over the porch railing, trying to look through the crack between the window frame and the drapes, nearly tumbling into the forsythia shrubs. She couldn't see anything inside the dark house. Pressing her ear to the door, she banged on it again, then stopped.

She beckoned Callum to join her. "Listen to this."

He walked up the steps and bent close to the door. She hammered hard on the wood and waited. She heard the sound again—a sharp yip, faint and short-circuited as if someone had stifled it.

Callum turned and looked at her. "It's that dog Pearl owns— the little beige puffball on legs."

She nodded with satisfaction. "Apricot. It's an apricot teacup poodle, and you know Pearl is not going to shut that surrogate child in a dark cellar and leave town."

"You might as well quit your banging," a male voice behind them said.

Pearl's neighbor, Larry Parks, stood in the front yard leaning on a steel-pronged rake. He was short and stoop-shouldered, a retired logger with hands crippled by white finger, the result of years of operating chain saws. "She's not going to answer the door," he said.

"How do you know that, Mr. Parks?" Callum said.

"She hasn't come out since the fire."

"I spoke to her the following day."

"Didn't come out though, did she?" He shifted something from one side of his mouth to the other, and Jessica realized he was chewing tobacco.

"No," Callum said reflectively. "No, she didn't." He nodded toward the yard. "But somebody's been keeping things up."

"Oh, that's Leona and me. I mowed the grass this morning. Leona's been weeding." He gestured toward the halfway house. "It's bad enough having that burnt-out wreck still standing here without the rest of the neighborhood turning into a slum. We got three grocery sacks full of Pearl's newspapers. She left them laying outside, and that Gerson boy didn't have enough sense to stop delivering them." He eyed Jessica. "Newspaper carriers aren't what they used to be."

"Maybe something happened to Pearl," Jessica said. "She could have fallen or had a stroke."

Larry shook his head. "Me and the wife see her walking around at night. She carries a candle, and it flickers behind the shades like a lightning bug. Ever see one of them little things?"

Jessica nodded. "A few times—in the Midwest."

He shook his head thoughtfully. "Wonder how they glow like that."

Callum cleared his throat. "Doesn't it seem odd, Mrs. Hobbs shutting herself up this way?"

"Well, sure, but what are you going to do?" He rubbed the side of his nose with his knobby index finger. "We tried to call her on the telephone to see if she's okay, but she doesn't answer."

"What about her daughter?" Callum said.

"Oh, the one in Boise? We'd have phoned her, but we couldn't remember her married name." He thought a moment, then frowned. "You know this isn't like some big city where people are always butting in and telling other folks how they should live. It really isn't any of our business if she wants to stay in there."

Jessica saw a wry smile curve Callum's lips. She wondered if he was thinking what she was—that people in Misp took an interest when it suited their purposes.

The old man was glancing around, and she could tell that with the tobacco juice pooling in his mouth he was looking for a discreet way to dispose of it.

"Thanks," she said, "we'll just check around back. If she still doesn't answer the door, we'll try to track down her daughter."

He waved his hand in acknowledgment and shuffled toward his home, leaning on the rake as if it were a walking stick.

Jessica followed Callum along the south side of the house, stopping to knock on the kitchen door. When no one answered, she stepped off the porch, lingering on a decorative concrete paver between two pink-flowering rhododendrons to study the halfway house, realizing that Pearl had a clear view of its dining room window.

In the backyard, spiny green horsetails were shooting through the decaying leaves in last year's vegetable garden. She heard the *plink-plink* of water dripping from the rain spout onto a concrete trough.

Callum glanced at the roof. "Her gutters are plugged with fir needles and leaves."

They walked around the shuttered house but had no luck seeing into it. On the north side, Jessica stepped over an ankle-high concrete wall into a basement window well, her shoes crunching on the pea gravel that drained the rainwater. Moss clung to the chipped wall, thriving in the deep shadows of salal and Oregon grape.

She stared at the casement window. Someone had tacked two strips of board across the glass from the inside. The tips of carpenter's nails poked through the wooden frame like a dozen tiny spikes, as if sheer quantity could guarantee security. From somewhere in the depths of the house came the manic yip of the poodle.

Jessica gauged the size of the small-paned window. "I could wriggle through this if we could get it open."

Callum took a few paces back from the concrete rim. "I'd rather call Tarr."

"If she's scared, she's more likely to talk to me than to him."

"And what if she thinks you're a burglar? She's probably got a rifle in there. Frank must have kept guns."

"I'll let her know who I am." Jessica tested the frame with the toe of her shoe. It didn't budge. "She's not going to shoot me."

"Why not?"

"Because I was her newspaper girl."

He gave a little snort. "Well, now, that's a logical train of thought."

"In Misp, you can shoot outsiders, swindlers, and adulterous spouses, but you don't shoot your newspaper carrier. You ought to know that."

"Wouldn't want to disrupt service." He waved her aside. "Move out then, and I'll kick it open. But don't go in there until we know she doesn't have a gun."

She couldn't help grinning. "What happened to the law-abiding Boy Scout?"

"I don't want to minimize your influence, Jess, but I can rationalize this one all on my own."

Jessica stepped out of the shallow well, and Callum took her place.

"Not much room here," he said, studying the casement window. It was hinged at the top and swung outward. "You know, this isn't going to work unless I break the window."

"Try it anyway. At least it might get her attention."

Standing at a diagonal, he pulled back and gave the frame a good solid kick at the bottom edge. The glass pane clattered and vibrated but didn't crack. "Well, that ought to bring on the artillery."

A shrill, trembling voice came from deep inside the basement. "You get away from there, you hear? I've got a gun, and I'm not afraid to use it!"

Giving Jessica a told-you-so look, Callum stepped out of the window well.

She leaned over, close to the glass but out of direct view of the basement's interior. "Pearl, it's Jessica Moran."

"Who?" Over the dog's piercing bark, she sounded like an owl hooting.

"Jessica Moran." When Pearl didn't answer, she added, "Lila's daughter."

"What are you doing out there?" Pearl shouted.

"I'd like to talk with you."

There was a long pause, punctuated by hysterical barks. Finally, her high, thin voice pierced the racket. "Can't right now. Some other time."

"It's very important, Pearl. Could you come to the kitchen door for a few minutes?"

There was another long pause.

"Pearl?"

"I'm busy." The voice had moved closer but was more querulous now.

Jessica looked at Callum. He shrugged. She turned back to the window, hunching lower so she could see between the wooden slats.

Callum was beside her in an instant, yanking her away. "Dammit, Jess."

She squirmed out of his grip. "Oh, for God's sake, she's got a baseball bat, not a gun. We haven't had too many baseball-bat deaths recently." She hopped back into the well. "Pearl, you still owe me money for delivering the newspaper." She hated to deceive her, but she couldn't think of how else to lure her outside.

"What?"

"The *Misp Tribune*. I was your paper girl, remember?"

"I always pay my bills."

"I know you do. That's why I was sure you'd want to settle this one. Remember when I was sixteen, and I suddenly left town?"

"Now, I never was one of those people who spread gossip about you."

"I'm sure you weren't, but I didn't get the chance to collect before I left."

"Oh." There was a brief silence. "That was a long time ago. I don't even remember how much it was." She sounded befuddled.

"Three dollars."

"I always gave you a tip. Does that include the tip?"

Jessica looked at Callum and rolled her eyes. "After all these years, I don't deserve anything extra."

"Well . . ." She hesitated for several seconds. "All right, I'll bring the money to the kitchen door."

Jessica glanced at Callum, and he nodded. He followed her to the side of the house and stood a few yards away in the filtered shade of the pink rhododendrons.

She waited on the back steps for several minutes before she heard any sound inside. The blue gingham curtain fluttered. Then came the long creak and groan of a board being pried off the doorframe. The dead bolt clicked. The door cracked slightly, and a faded blue eye underscored by a dark purple smudge appeared in the shadowed trench.

Jessica heard coins rattle in a change purse.

"All I have are quarters, no dollar bills."

Jessica smiled. "That's fine. Whatever you have is fine." She took a deep breath. "By the way, you do know that all the men in the halfway house are gone, don't you?"

"I don't talk about what happened there." Her throat sounded dry, scratchy. "You shouldn't either." She counted the quarters. "One, two, three, four . . ." The dog was nowhere in sight, but Jessica could still hear it.

"I've only got two-seventy-five."

"That's plenty." Jessica managed an easy laugh. "I don't charge interest."

"Well, here then." The door opened a little wider, and a liver-spotted hand shot out. The coins lay in her cupped palm.

Jessica inhaled a quick breath. Loose skin hung from arm bones that were creepily definable. She wondered how anyone could lose that much weight that fast. She plucked the coins one by one to delay the transaction and tucked them in her jeans pocket.

Hesitating on the last quarter, she said softly, "Pearl, what's wrong?"

Several seconds passed before she heard a cautious "Nothing."

She removed the last coin from the outstretched palm, but before Pearl could withdraw her hand, she reached for it and held on. The wrinkled skin felt cool and loose and rubbery. The bones trembled.

Jessica lowered her voice. "I'm worried about you. Have you been ill?"

"A little." Her breath wavered.

"I'm sorry to hear that. What have you had?"

"This and that."

They were both silent for a moment.

Then Jessica clasped the frondlike hand to her own warm cheek. She felt the knuckles twisted by arthritis, the fingertips work-worn to emery-board scratchiness, the soft folds in aged skin.

From behind the door came barely suppressed hiccups of despair.

"Please tell me what's wrong," Jessica said softly.

The door swung in, until she could see all of the older woman's face. Her lilac print cotton dress bagged over her limbs like walrus skin. She seemed to have shrunk to half her usual size. Her hair, usually tinted blue-gray, had roots the color of old teeth. Tears slid from her dark-rimmed eyes onto hollowed cheeks.

Jessica gently wrapped her arms around her. "It's that halfway house fire, isn't it?"

Pearl, giving off the odor of sour bubble gum, nodded against her shoulder in affirmation, spilling tears onto Jessica's sweater. "I'm going to die and go to hell."

Jessica gripped tighter. "I can't imagine that. Are you scared that the man who survived the fire will come back and hurt you? Is that what it is?"

Pearl shook her head.

Jessica thought she must have misinterpreted the gesture. "You aren't?"

"No," she sobbed quietly. "It's not that. I just wish I'd never seen any of it. I wish I'd never taken Dixie out to piddle that night. I wish I'd never seen *him* crawl out that window."

Jessica felt the air leave her lungs.

Pearl drew back, her eyes bright with tears. "Many's the time, I looked after him and changed his diaper when he was a baby. I taught him the Scripture in Sunday school. I worked in the church league and the firemen's auxiliary alongside his mother. But there he was sitting on that windowsill." She stared unblinking across the stretch of yard and shrubs at the boarded-up halfway house. "I thought, Oh, my goodness, it's Pete Johnson. He didn't see me, but I saw him and the red flames of hell were shooting up behind him."

Jessica couldn't move.

Pearl took a great, gulping breath. "I've always thought of myself as a good Christian woman, but I didn't even try to save those men. I didn't call the fire department, and when that young investigator asked me if I saw anything I said I was asleep. I didn't want to talk to anybody in case I might accidentally tell. Frank always said I never could keep a secret." Her voice quavered with anguish. "Don't you see? I couldn't turn Pete in. He was one of *us*."

She hunched over and lowered her head into her hands, her breath coming in shallow gasps. "I was as much to blame as he was. What kind of person lets other people die?"

Jessica patted her bony back. "You'll feel better after you talk to the investigator again," she said softly. "Could you do that?"

After several long moments, the blue, gray, and ivory hair bobbed. "All right," came the muffled words. Some of the tenseness seemed to seep from her frame.

"I'll stay with you just as long as you need me," Jessica said. She glanced at Callum.

He was walking toward his car. She knew he would call the sheriff.

27

The eulogy for Bob's funeral at St. Bavo's Church struck Jessica as ironic. Whereas, a few days earlier, he'd been regarded as a philanderer, he was now praised as a hero and a Good Samaritan for stopping to help Caroline Johnson.

Everyone in town knew Pete had been arrested. That news almost overshadowed the accident. Combined with Caroline's death, it created a double tragedy for the Johnson family.

It also made for some conspicuous absences at the funeral, Jessica thought. She didn't see Pete's mother, Charlotte Johnson, or the Schultz family. Pete was supposed to be a pallbearer, but at the last minute Bob's cousin from Portland took his place. Callum wasn't at the funeral either, but Jessica knew he was tied up with the investigation.

Lanita Snapp brought Pearl, who had apparently insisted on attending. Leaning on Lanita's arm, she walked slowly up the church steps. She stayed only long enough to trigger speculation that she was near death herself.

A neon sun hovered directly above the church spire. Funerals seemed to produce intensely blue skies on this perpetually rainy peninsula, Jessica thought. After the mass, folks gathered in clusters outside the church. She could hear some of them debating what should be done with Pete. He'd already confessed, so they couldn't argue about whether he was guilty. She knew they would have disputed that point, if they'd been given the chance.

Pete insisted Wendell wasn't directly involved, and Callum said he had no reason to doubt him. Wendell came up with an idea for setting the fire without getting caught, but he claimed he was just shooting off his mouth and never expected Pete to use it. According to Callum, Wendell figured that a volunteer fireman wearing bunker boots could set the fire. Later, he would return to fight it, knowing that any boot prints he left on either occasion wouldn't attract attention. Pete said it never occurred to him that Jonah would become a suspect, and he felt genuinely bad about that.

"Not bad enough," Jessica had said under her breath.

She wandered across the church plaza, listening to some of the remarks people were making.

Jane Carlson, a broad-shouldered woman who created wooden sculptures and other chain saw art, said she and Pete were born on exactly the same day and she practically grew up with him. "It's not like he's some creep. He's the best-looking guy in town. It's hard to believe he did it."

"Not for me," said Jenny Flint, Darla Johnson's cousin. She tightened her lips. "No one knows a man better than his ex-wife. I've heard enough from Darla to convince me."

When they noticed Jessica, they stopped talking.

She walked on, slowing as she passed a group of businessmen.

Jack Everett was saying he didn't think Pete should be prosecuted. "If he did it, if he killed three people, I say he's already paid a high price. Everybody pays a price for what he does."

Jessica sighed.

Hearing high heels click on the church steps behind her, she turned around and stared directly into Pamela's violet eyes.

Pamela laid the tips of her mauve nails on Jessica's sleeve. "I just want you to know," she said in a low voice, "that I never did believe a word they said about your brother."

Jessica wondered why it had taken her so long then to express her support. "Thank you," she said politely.

Pamela adjusted the pink flowered scarf around her neck. "Well, it was lucky that I overheard that the sheriff was going to arrest Jonah. Gave him a chance to escape. Otherwise, things might not have worked out as well as they did."

Jessica pointedly didn't answer, glancing around instead. "Have you seen my mother and Jonah?"

"A minute ago, they were talking to Mary Grace's oldest sister in the church parking lot."

"Thanks." She turned and hurried toward the parked cars, happy to be out of the grip of Pamela's mauve nails.

"Wait," Pamela shouted after her. "I wanted to ask you a few questions. You were dating Pete, weren't you?"

Jessica smiled over her shoulder. "Later, Pamela. I have to catch them before they leave."

She found her mother and brother walking toward Lila's truck.

Her mother stopped when she caught sight of her. "Want a ride to the cemetery?"

Jessica shook her head. "Thanks, but no sense your driving me back here to get my van." She took Jonah's hand in hers. "How does it feel to be back to sea level?"

"It wasn't so bad up there."

She studied the pattern of light and shadows that stained the pavement. "There's something we have to talk about. Callum said that if you want to report what Dennis Kretz did to you, he'll help you."

Jonah chewed on his lower lip. "Do I have to?"

"No, but you might prevent him from hurting other people."

Jonah shifted uncomfortably. "I want to go to Gettysburg."

"Well, you might have to testify, but I'm sure that wouldn't interfere with your trip."

"I don't want to see that man again. I just want to go to Gettysburg."

Jessica looked at her mother for support.

"I'm taking him there in July," Lila said.

"You are?"

"Yeah, well, I can't even remember the last vacation I had." She lifted her eyebrows. "You're not going to make him do what he doesn't want to do. I've been trying for years, and it hasn't worked yet. I don't know where you kids got your stubbornness."

Jessica stared at her, still surprised. "You really are taking him to this reenactment?"

Lila set her lips sternly. "Well, I told him he'd have to earn half the money, either working at the mill or somewhere. People don't appreciate things they don't have to work for."

"My goodness," Jessica said under her breath.

Lila shook her head as if she couldn't believe she was agreeing to the trip either. "When I told him he needed to make something of himself, I never thought it would be a phony general in a war that happened more than a century ago."

JESSICA RODE by herself to Pleasant Ridge Cemetery. Her van was the final vehicle in the procession.

At the grave site, Mary Grace was surrounded by family: her children, her mother, and her sister; Bob's aunts, uncles, and cousins. Jessica stood next to Lila and Jonah as Bob's casket was lowered into the ground. Hundreds of gnats dipped and spiraled around the heads of the mourners, and Jessica thought she saw one fly into Father Adrian's mouth as he intoned a prayer.

She looked over the priest's head at a brilliant spot in a gnarled big-leafed maple. It was an odd sight—a child's yellow balloon caught in the high branches, tethered like a second sun. They'd had high winds again the night before, and she wondered how a fragile balloon could have survived up there when sturdy trees had toppled.

The crowd broke up, and people strolled almost reluctantly to their cars, as if it had all happened too quickly, as if laying a man to his final rest should take longer.

"Going to the VFW hall for the meal?" Lila asked.

"In a bit."

There would be food at the gathering, long, burgeoning tables of it, and stories about Bob told and retold. The fellows from Everett's Boat and Hardware would recall the eight-point Roosevelt elk bull that Bob shot near Jimmycomelately Creek in the fall of '97. Nobody in Misp had seen one like it since and probably never would.

Jessica waved good-bye, then walked along the narrow road that wound through the cemetery. She glanced at the tombstones, ticking off the familiar surnames in her head. *Ruth Adah Fritsch, Beloved Wife and Mother. Michael Dutoi, in Loving Memory. Alfred Dutoi, Infant Son of . . .* Markers so weathered that some of the letters were almost gone. Fresh-cut flowers here and there and handkerchief-sized American flags on the veterans' graves.

Suddenly veering in a direction away from her van, Jessica stepped carefully between the coffin-sized plots until she came to one surrounded by a waist-high iron fence with an opening where a gate might once have been. In the center rested a white memorial stone, the sun glinting off the mica embedded in it. Jessica walked over the newly shorn grass and touched her fingertips to the family name inscribed on it: *Moran*.

There, alongside the graves of her paternal grandmother, Kathleen, and grandfather, James, was the one burial site she'd avoided since the day she'd seen his casket lowered into the damp earth. The gray headstone etched along the top with towering evergreens read *Michael Moran, Beloved Husband and Father,* along with the dates of his birth and death. Her eyes blurred. When she could focus again, she saw the name to the left of her father's: *Lila Moran, 1942–*

Strange how matters settled themselves in death.

His grave site, delineated by a shallow indentation in the earth, was well tended, the headstone straight, the grass around the marker neatly clipped. A bouquet of red and yellow tulips in front of the stone fluttered in the light breeze. She wondered how often her mother brought flowers here.

Jessica didn't like to think of his body under the mound of dirt. She would have preferred cremation, with his ashes scattered in the forest. But cremation was against his religion.

She wondered about his soul? His body was here, but where was his soul? It seemed strange that after all these years she still felt his presence only at the lake. It seemed to rise to the surface and surround her with a calming warmth. She knew it was an illusion, but it seemed as though he were comforting her.

She bent and placed her hand on his headstone, trying to summon him here. The heat from the granite slab pulsed through her palm, but otherwise she felt nothing.

"What are the chances you're going to find this daughter of yours?" asked a quiet voice behind her.

Jessica swung around to see Lila standing just outside the iron fence, her fingers gripping one of its decorative spear-tipped posts. "I thought you were heading toward the VFW hall."

"Oh, I'll get there. I usually like to say hello to your father when I'm close-by." Lila gazed at the gravestone. "He always was partial to girls. When you were little, you'd wind him around your finger so tight, he wouldn't move unless you did. He called you Sunshine. Do you remember that?"

Jessica nodded, feeling her eyes sting.

Lila thrust her hands in the skirt pockets of her loose navy dress, the one she described as her going-to-funerals outfit. She had a new belt for it, but otherwise it looked the same as it had at her husband's burial.

Lila laughed quietly. "I'm almost fifty-six years old. Can you believe that? When we got married, I was just a little snot, eighteen and right out of high school. Your dad was twenty-one. Met him at a dance up in Forks." She was silent for a moment. "My Lord, he was the most handsome devil I'd ever seen. And he *was* a devil. Drank too much, drove too fast, raised hell. Three weeks later, he asked me to marry him, and I couldn't say yes quick enough." She laughed lightly. "My pa said it'd never last. If I hadn't been his only child, he'd have cut me out of the will right then and there." She stared off at the row of trees that bordered the southern edge of the cemetery.

A breeze blew through, and they watched the white blossoms from a cherry tree fall slowly to the ground like tears.

Lila squinted against the light. "Anyway, I was thinking that if this daughter of yours did turn up, it might not be so bad having her visit here—that is, if she wants to. She might not, you know." Her voice toughened slightly. "Shouldn't get your hopes up."

"I haven't," Jessica said.

Lila sighed. "I suppose you'll marry Callum Luke now."

Jessica raised her eyebrows. "I'm not planning on it."

Lila waved her hand in resignation. "Oh, you probably will. And I think about how I did everything I could to save you from him."

Jessica couldn't help but smile. She pushed the toe of her shoe into the cemetery plot's intensely green grass.

Murmuring "damned panty hose," Lila hitched up her waist-band. "Well, Jonah's waiting in the truck."

Jessica felt something inside her release, spin free.

"Mom?" she said. She hadn't used the word in so long it almost stuck in her throat.

Lila slowly turned back, her blue eyes glazed with moisture. "Yes?"

"Would you tell Mary Grace I'll be along in a few minutes?"

"Sure, I'll do that."

28

Callum heard the snap and rustle of a small animal, a squirrel perhaps, charging through the thick underbrush that flanked the overgrown path to Thunder Lake.

It was early May, a week after Pete's arrest, and it was turning out to be the warmest spring day so far. The trees and the loamy earth smelled rich and darkly sweet. New blackberry shoots and sword ferns were springing from mother plants everywhere. Horsetails erupted with a survival instinct strong enough to pierce blacktop. Trilliums, the white orchids of the forest, patched the hillside like clumps of melting snow.

The path cut through a stand of western red cedar that had to be seven or eight hundred years old, their forms so majestic that Callum, who had grown up with these towering conifers, still marveled at their size. It was ironic, he thought, that a family who had leveled miles of timber through the decades retained the old-growth trees on their own property. Lila Moran probably attached great sentimental value to them, but he didn't doubt for a minute that she would harvest them if she needed to.

Although it was Sunday and the mill wasn't operating, the air was thick with the fragrance of wood. Only the heart-swelling scream of an eagle disturbed the silence.

Underneath the quiet, though, echoed the sounds of the past. Callum thought he could hear the pounding steps of long-dead animals, the thundering crashes of too many falling trees to count, and the strong, rhythmic voices of his grandparents and their grandparents. The salmon bones the Quinaults tossed back into the river each year to ensure their future catches reminded him of that cyclic continuity.

He was glad to be home.

He reached the Morans' dock. A small aluminum rowboat bobbed against two old tires nailed to the wood. He knew this lake well, but as a boy he had learned its secrets from the other side, the reservation side.

He saw Jessica swimming toward a wooden float some thirty yards away. The water had to be cold, but she gave no sign of it. She stretched her arms in the most graceful crawl he thought he'd ever seen and executed the smooth turns of a competitive swimmer. He had learned to swim at about the same time he'd started to walk, but he had never excelled at it. After she touched the float, she dipped briefly from view. He leaned against a tree, waiting for the next glimpse of her sleek arms rising from the water.

Another ten minutes passed, and she kept a steady pace back and forth. Finally, she hoisted herself onto the dock, and with her chest softly rising and falling from her exertion, she studied the numbers on her sports watch. He could tell by her expression she wasn't pleased. She grabbed an oversized towel and clutched it around her shoulders, then took one end of it and used it to twist the water from her hair. He remembered touching that hair, not as he had a few days ago, but with the innocence and desire of a teenage boy.

She hadn't seen him yet. She reclined on the dock, pressing her body flat against the weathered boards, as if soaking in what warmth she could find in them. It was a sensual pose, all the more so for her unawareness of it.

He believed she would forgive him a second time, not because he deserved forgiveness (he had already decided he didn't), but because she didn't give up easily on people.

He walked onto the dock. She must have heard his footsteps on the planks, because she immediately sat up.

He tapped his watch. "How bad was it?"

She grimaced. "I'm five seconds slower than I was a year ago. I'm getting old."

He squatted on his heels and looked her over. "Not so that anyone would notice."

She tugged on the outer corners of her eyes. "I have these little lines."

"It's that paleface skin. What do you expect?"

"How did you know I was here?"

"I picked up Jonah walking along the road. He was carrying a package from the post office—a full-sized reproduction of a Civil War musket. Said he was going to Gettysburg to take part in a reenactment of the battle there. Is that true?"

She nodded. "Mother's taking him."

He noticed she said Mother, not Lila, but he didn't remark on it.

She stared down at her fingers tightly gripping the towel. "I talked to him about Kretz. Jonah won't even discuss what happened." She looked up. "I keep thinking of those scars on Dennis's back. The other night I dreamed of little white worms crawling all over me and burrowing under my skin. I know I should feel sorry for him, but I don't."

She turned toward the lake. There were still those massive trees down there. Without the weeds to shroud them, they reposed like blackened skeletons on the lake floor.

After a time, she said, "I used to think my dad's soul was trapped in this lake."

"Maybe it was."

The light caught the shine in her tears. She brushed them away, but they kept falling. "I couldn't figure out how to free him. I was so angry," she whispered. "I burned the dock."

She was silent for several seconds. Then she looked up with a wry smile. "My mother built this one with wood that's treated with a fire retardant. Isn't that just like her?"

He studied the way the damp curls fell across the nape of her neck—tight, feathery tendrils that had always made her look vulnerable to him. "I'm sorry about the things I said to you."

She hesitated—too long, he worried—but then she nodded. "Yes, me too."

He inhaled deeply, realizing he'd been holding his breath. "I mean, about all of it—including the parts about our daughter."

"That's what I meant." Tears started in her eyes again, and she bent her head as if to hide them. "I'm scared she won't call. I'm a terrible coward."

"Jess, you have *never* been a coward."

"If she's as angry toward me as I was toward my mother, I won't hear from her."

"Daughters seem to be built with a gene for forgiveness." He stood and held out his hand.

She gripped it, and he pulled her to her feet.

His eyes caught a movement behind her, and he stopped. He watched it in awe.

Some people would have said it was a shadow, nothing more than an elaborate design one of the nearby trees had cast on the lake's surface. Others would have claimed it was only wisps of fog rising off the water. But Callum would have disagreed, arguing that it had more form, more substance than either fog or shadows. It was clearly the image of a large man.

He knew the naysayers would have insisted that a person staring up at the clouds could always find whatever he wanted in those swirling shapes. But he also knew what he saw, and the same sense of wonder he had experienced as a boy came over him. Whether anyone else believed him made no difference.

The image was gone in an instant. He would not tell Jess about it. She would discover what she needed to know in time.

MARJORIE REYNOLDS is the author of *The Starlite Drive-in*. A former newspaper reporter and movie advertising executive, she lives with her husband and son on Mercer Island, Washington.